Harber & Brothers

Harper's Graded Arithmetics

Second Book in Arithmetic - Vol. 2

Harber & Brothers

Harper's Graded Arithmetics
Second Book in Arithmetic - Vol. 2

ISBN/EAN: 9783337780364

Printed in Europe, USA, Canada, Australia, Japan

Cover: Foto ©Andreas Hilbeck / pixelio.de

More available books at **www.hansebooks.com**

HARPERS' GRADED ARITHMETICS

SECOND BOOK IN ARITHMETIC

COMPRISING

FOUR·YEARS OF ORAL AND WRITTEN WORK

IN THE ELEMENTS OF NUMBERS

NEW YORK

HARPER & BROTHERS, FRANKLIN SQUARE

1888

PREFACE.

This is the second of a series of two books embracing a complete course in arithmetic both oral and written, for schools below the high-school grade.

The first 276 pages comprise a *brief course* in the rudiments of arithmetic, including, in their order, integers, decimals, properties of numbers, fractions, compound numbers, measurements, and percentage; and closing with outlines for reviews and examinations.

The subjects of this brief course are those essential to preparation for business, or for advanced study; and they are as fully treated as the average age and advancement of pupils in such a course will justify.

Oral and written work are combined throughout the brief course. Every method of computation is introduced by simple problems that contain only small numbers, and can be solved orally. These are followed by similar problems that contain larger numbers, and require written solutions.

The arrangement of the matter conforms to the synthetic or inductive method of instruction; every principle and process of computation, and every essential fact or principle being developed by inductive questions.

The definitions, principles, and rules are simple, clear, concise, and comprehensive. All rules for computations are based upon principles previously deduced by inductive questioning; and the number of definitions, principles, and rules is reduced to the minimum.

Incomplete forms of the elementary combinations are given in tables, which the pupil is required to copy, complete, and memorize.

The oral exercises in adding, subtracting, multiplying, and dividing *in series*, and the written exercises in forming combinations at sight, secure accuracy and rapidity in the use of numbers.

The problems in written work are ample for all needed drill and practice. They furnish copious illustrations of methods and processes, and abundant exercise in the application of these methods and processes to business computations in the various occupations, trades, and professions.

Pages 277–364 comprise matter strictly *supplementary* to the subjects in the brief course. They contain articles on methods of proof, general principles of division and fractions, short methods of computations, converse reductions; price, quantity, and cost; longitude and time; compound numbers, the metric system, percentage, proportion, involution, and evolution; measurements, and forms of business paper.

The arrangement of this *supplement* is such, that the study of the several subjects may immediately follow the study of the same subjects in the body of the book; or the supplement may be taken up in course, after the study of the body of the book is completed.

The book contains as much work in the theory and practice of numbers as can profitably be done in four school years of eight to ten months each, — the *brief course* occupying three years, and the *supplement* one year.

Two editions of this book are published—one with answers to the problems, and the other without answers.

The work is submitted to the public, with the confident belief that it contains all the essentials of a model text-book.

CONTENTS.

SECOND BOOK IN ARITHMETIC.

CHAPTER I.
INTEGERS.

SECTION I.
NOTATION AND NUMERATION.

1. *Arithmetic* is the science of numbers and the art of using them.

2. A *unit* is a *single thing* or *one*.

One apple, one dollar, one dozen, one hundred, are units.

3. A *number* is a unit, or two or more units.

One, fifteen, forty-six apples, two hundred pounds, are numbers.

4. The *unit of a number* is a single thing or *one*, of the kind expressed by the number.

The unit of fifteen is one; of forty apples, one apple; of two hundred twenty-five pounds, one pound.

5. An *integer* is a number that expresses whole or undivided things.

Integers are also called *whole numbers*.

6. Ten figures are used in writing numbers. They are

0　　1　　2　　3　　4　　5　　6　　7　　8　　9

a. The naught is often called *cipher* or *zero*.
b. The other figures are called *digits*.

7. To express an integer not greater than nine, only one figure is used.

8. To express an integer greater than nine, two or more figures are used.

Ten ones   are   one ten.

9. *Ten ones* taken together are *a ten.*

Ten is written 10

Two tens are written 20		Six tens are written	60
Three tens " " 30		Seven tens are "	70
Four tens " " 40		Eight tens " "	80
Five tens " " 50		Nine tens " "	90

10. When an integer is expressed by two figures, the left-hand figure expresses the *tens,* and the right-hand figure the *ones.*

1 ten and 6 ones are written 16

3 tens and 5 ones, written 35	7 tens and 0 ones, written 70
5 tens " 8 " " 58	9 tens " 1 one, " 91

Ten tens   are   one hundred.

11. *Ten tens* taken together are *a hundred.*

One hundred is written 100

Two hundred is written 200		Six hundred is written	600
Three hundred " " 300		Seven hundred " "	700
Four hundred " " 400		Eight hundred " "	800
Five hundred " " 500		Nine hundred " "	900

12. When an integer is expressed by three figures, the left-hand figure expresses *hundreds;* the middle figure, *tens;* and the right-hand figure, *ones.*

2 hundreds, 4 tens, 3 ones are two hundred forty-three, written 243
4 hundreds, 6 tens, 2 ones are four hundred sixty-two,   "   462
6 hundreds, 7 tens, 0 ones are six hundred seventy,   "   670
8 hundreds, 0 tens, 4 ones are eight hundred four,   "   804
9 hundreds, 1 ten, 2 ones are nine hundred twelve,   "   912

EXERCISES.

A. Write and read the numbers expressed by

1 hundred 2 tens and 4 ones.	6 hundreds 5 tens and 1 one.
2 hundreds 2 " " 4 "	7 " 4 " " 0 ones.
3 " 3 " " 4 "	9 " 0 " " 8 "
4 " 4 " " 4 "	2 " 9 " " 3 "
5 " 2 " " 7 "	8 " 6 " " 5 "

B. Read

12	64	130	427
51	99	216	745
80	76	952	810
28	17	305	685

C. Write in words

13	88	611	821
71	65	193	450
20	94	308	734
59	47	572	206

D. Express by figures

1. Eighty-two.	*4.* Forty.	*7.* Seventy-nine.
2. Twenty-seven.	*5.* Sixty-nine.	*8.* Fourteen.
3. Ninety-three.	*6.* Fifty-five.	*9.* Thirty-seven.

10. One hundred seventeen.
11. Two hundred ninety-one.
12. Four hundred sixty-three.
13. Six hundred seventy-six.
14. Three hundred thirty-eight.
15. Seven hundred fifty-two.
16. Eight hundred twenty-four.
17. Nine hundred forty-five.
18. Five hundred eighty-nine.

19. Nine hundred.
20. Five hundred sixty.
21. Three hundred ten.
22. Six hundred ninety.
23. Eight hundred forty.
24. Six hundred six.
25. Seven hundred two.
26. Five hundred seven.
27. Four hundred nine.

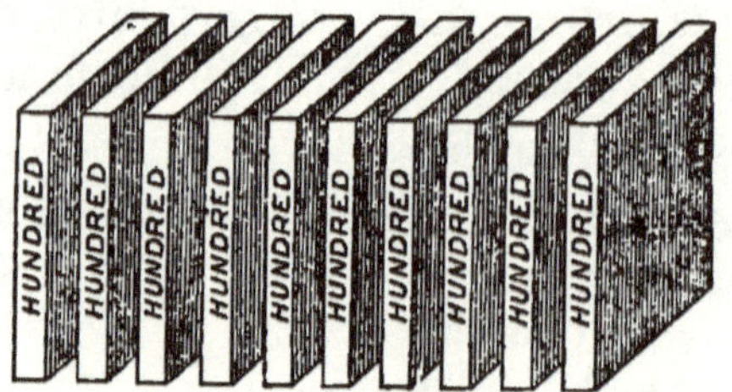

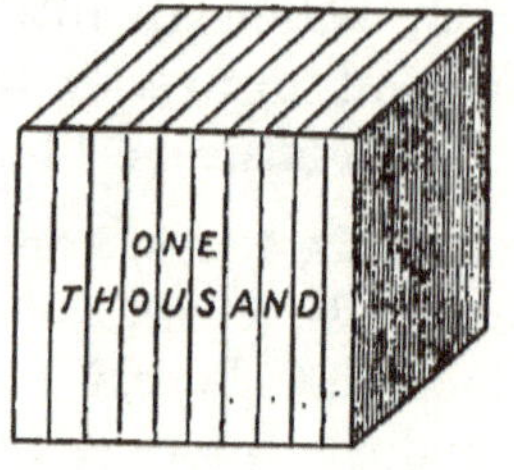

Ten hundreds   are   **one thousand.**

13. *Ten hundreds* taken together are *a thousand.*

One thousand is written 1,000

Two thousand,	2,000	Six thousand,	6,000
Three thousand,	3,000	Seven thousand,	7,000
Four thousand,	4,000	Eight thousand,	8,000
Five thousand,	5,000	Nine thousand,	9,000

14. *Ten thousands* taken together are *a ten-thousand.* *Ten ten-thousands* taken together are *a hundred-thousand.*

One ten-thousand is written   10,000
Two ten-thousands are twenty thousand, written 20,000
Eight ten-thousands are eighty thousand,   "   80,000
One hundred-thousand is written   100,000
Five hundred-thousands are written   500,000

15. When an integer is expressed by more than three figures, the figure at the left of hundreds expresses *thousands;* the figure at the left of thousands expresses *ten-thousands;* and the figure at the left of ten-thousands expresses *hundred-thousands.*

16. Every three figures in an integer, counting from the right, are a ***period.*** Periods of figures are separated by commas.

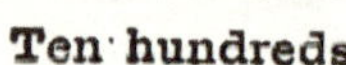

The first or right-hand period consists of *ones, tens, and*

hundreds; and the second period of *ones* of thousands, *tens* of thousands, and *hundreds* of thousands.

Eighteen thousand five hundred thirty-six is written	18,536
Thirty-two thousand eight	" "	32,008
Forty-seven thousand two hundred	" "	47,200
Sixty thousand four hundred twenty	" "	60,420
Two hundred forty thousand	" "	240,000
Four hundred eight thousand five hundred	" "	408,500
Five hundred thousand three hundred two	" "	500,302
Six hundred fifty-two thousand ten	" "	652,010
Eight hundred fifty thousand sixty-one	" "	850,061

EXERCISES.

A. Read

8,000	26,506	574,000	809,051	100,905
5,400	37,081	629,005	40,269	50,041
2,560	93,274	700,044	660,020	482,070

B. Express by words

6,014	33,000	19,040	530,240	404,040
3,405	80,900	855,480	902,105	40,040
4,009	90,209	300,070	20,007	876,543

C. Express by figures

1. Five thousand; sixty thousand; two hundred thousand; seven hundred sixty-five thousand.

2. Nine thousand eight hundred; two thousand six; seventy-two thousand four hundred; seven hundred forty-seven thousand two hundred.

3. Fifty thousand twenty; seven hundred ten thousand; eight thousand fifty.

4. Eight hundred one thousand four; two hundred thousand six hundred forty; four thousand fifty-six.

5. Sixty-three thousand four; six thousand eight hundred nineteen; three hundred thirty thousand seventy.

6. One hundred five thousand four hundred seventy; seven thousand two hundred forty; nineteen thousand three hundred one; fifty-six thousand eleven.

7. Five hundred forty thousand seventy-two; one thousand nine hundred three; nine hundred fifty-seven thousand five hundred three.

8. Nine hundred thousand six hundred; six hundred eighty thousand five; three hundred sixty-five thousand two hundred ninety-four.

9. One thousand ten; fifty thousand three hundred sixty-seven; four hundred sixty thousand twenty; eight hundred three thousand.

10. Five hundred thousand three hundred eighty-four; twelve thousand nineteen; nine hundred nine thousand nine hundred nine.

17. The third period of figures expresses *ones* of millions, *tens* of millions, and *hundreds* of millions; and the fourth period expresses *ones* of billions, *tens* of billions, and *hundreds* of billions.

Two million five thousand eighty	is written	2,005,080
Thirty-four billion three hundred twenty-four thousand five hundred eighty-six	" "	34,000,324,586
Forty million forty-four thousand twelve	" "	40,044,012
One hundred twenty-nine million three hundred seventeen thousand five hundred	" "	129,317,500
Seven hundred fifty million two hundred thousand seventy	" "	750,200,070
Nine hundred three billion fifty million five hundred ninety-four thousand	" "	903,050,594,000
Four billion six hundred million seven hundred eighty-six	" "	4,600,000,786

18. In any period the right-hand figure expresses ones, the second figure expresses tens, and the third figure expresses hundreds.

19. The *order of a unit* takes its name from the place it occupies.

A digit written in the first place, expresses *units of the first order;* in the second place, it expresses *units of the second order;* in the third place, *units of the third order;* in the fourth place, *units of the fourth order;* and so on.

20. A digit, in any place except the first, expresses two values—*simple* and *local.*

21. The *simple value* of a digit is the value expressed by its name.

22. The *local value* of a digit is the value given to it by the place it occupies.

12th. Hundred-billions.	11th. Ten-billions.	10th. *Billions.*	9th. Hundred-millions.	8th. Ten-millions.	7th. *Millions.*	6th. Hundred-thousands.	5th. Ten-thousands.	4th. *Thousands.*	3d. Hundreds.	2d. Tens.	1st. Ones.	
												} *Names of Units.*
12th.	11th.	10th.	9th.	8th.	7th.	6th.	5th.	4th.	3d.	2d.	1st.	{ *Places, and Orders of Units.*
1	6	0,	3	7	4,	5	0	8,	2	9	4,	*Figures.*

Fourth. Billions.	Third. Millions.	Second. Thousands.	First. Ones.	Numbers. Names.	} *Periods.*

23. *Notation* is the writing of numbers.

24. *Numeration* is the reading of numbers.

25. Principles of Notation.

I. *Ten units of any order are one unit of the next higher order.*

II. *One unit of any order is ten units of the next lower order.*

EXERCISES.

A. Copy and read

4,650,738	232,107,008	800,014,000,200	8,080,800,880
93,066,840	3,050,300,125	58,700,025,090	70,707,070
450,502,000	13,006,010,050	242,424,242,424	999,999,999,999

B. Write in figures

1. Eight million five thousand three hundred four.

2. Eighteen million nineteen ; fifty-six thousand.

3. Eight hundred million seven hundred seven thousand five hundred six.

4. Two hundred four million ninety thousand two hundred seventeen ; fifty million thirty thousand three.

5. Six hundred fifty-nine million twenty-five.

6. Four billion two hundred fifty-nine thousand thirty.

7. Eighty billion seven million four hundred thousand.

8. Seventy-four billion seven hundred four million nine thousand ninety-nine.

9. Seven hundred sixty billion eighty thousand two hundred ninety-one.

10. Three hundred billion seven hundred million two hundred thousand.

C. Write in words

9,708	72,059,209,000	200,007,000	12,065,587
400,009	30,030	80,025,780,240	3,031,050,004
40,080,276	1,702,050	220,202	135,700,009,015

26. The *sign of dollars* is **$.** It is called the *dollar mark*.

A *period* (.) is placed before any number expressing cents. This period is called the *decimal point.*

$38 is 38 dollars.	$5.10 is 5 dollars 10 cents.
$.69 is 69 cents.	$41.08 is 41 dollars 8 cents.
$.07 is 7 cents.	$9,013.44 is 9,013 dollars 44 cents.

Copy and read these numbers:

$759	$.27	$95.72
$23,401	$.19	$9,450.11
$107,970	$.04	$762,308.05
$60,060,660	$.09	$300.91
$5,328,153	$.45	$8,026,540.00

27. In expressing cents, or dollars and cents, by figures,

1. *Place the dollar mark before the number.*

2. *Place the decimal point before the cents.*

3. *Place a cipher between the decimal point and any number of cents less than 10.*

Express these numbers by figures:

Twenty cents.	Eighty dollars seventy-one cents.
Sixty-five cents.	Two hundred dollars sixty cents.
Eight cents.	Nine thousand five dollars one cent.
Three cents.	Four billion fifty dollars eleven cents.
Ten cents.	Three dollars seventeen cents.
Fifty-six cents.	Ten thousand ten dollars nine cents.

28. RULE FOR NOTATION.

Beginning at the left, write the hundreds, tens, and ones of each period in order; write ciphers in all vacant places; and separate the periods by commas.

29. RULE FOR NUMERATION.

Begin at the left and read each period, omitting the name of the last period and the names of all places filled with ciphers.

EXERCISES IN NOTATION AND NUMERATION.

A. Copy and read

25,025,025	600,000,000,000	15,015,155	18,018
3,003	55,055,000,000	200,386	901,020,002,950
40,425	8,208	1,000,890	25,025
2,002,002,002	66,606,066	260,010,003	791,056,809

B. Write and read the numbers expressed by

1. 6 millions, 3 tens; 7 ten-thousands, 4 tens, 5 ones.

2. 1 ten-million, 6 millions, 4 hundred-thousands, 8 thousands, 5 tens, 2 ones.

3. 7 hundred-thousands, 3 ten-thousands, 3 hundreds, 7 tens, 8 ones.

4. 4 billions, 8 ten-thousands, 3 hundreds, 6 ones.

5. 3 ten-billions, 9 billions, 7 hundred-thousands, 9 thousands.

6. 4 hundred-billions, 2 ten-billions, 9 ten-millions, 5 millions, 7 tens.

C. Express by figures

1. Thirty-seven million ninety-eight thousand four hundred twenty.

2. Eight million fifty thousand; ninety million six hundred thousand nine; eighty-one thousand twelve.

3. Six hundred one million three hundred six.

4. Nine billion two hundred seventy thousand.

5. Ninety dollars ten cents; twelve cents.

6. Twenty thousand six hundred seven dollars eight cents; forty-nine dollars.

7. Fifteen billion four million nine thousand eight hundred twenty.

8. Six thousand one hundred one dollars five cents.

9. One hundred million twenty-five thousand four hundred; four hundred billion seven hundred thousand.

10. Nine hundred seventeen billion three million sixteen; ninety thousand five.

Note 1.—For *outlines of notation and numeration* for review, see page 269.

Note 2.—Teachers who prefer that decimals should be studied in connection with integers, will now require their pupils to study notation and numeration of decimals, pages 111–120.

SECTION II.

ADDITION.

Oral Work.—**30.** *1.* Richard has 3 doves, and Thomas has 6. How many doves have the two boys?

The two boys have 3 doves and 6 doves, which are 9 doves.

2. If you pay 4 cents for figs, and 7 cents for raisins, how many cents do you pay out?

3. James has 9 marbles, and his brother George has 4 more than he has. How many marbles has George?

4. Sarah has 9 plums, and Emma has 4. How many plums have the two girls?

5. A grocer sold 5 pounds of Japan tea, and 8 pounds of black tea. How many pounds of tea did he sell?

6. Six boys and seven girls are in the same class. How many pupils are in the class?

7. If you go 8 miles east, and I go 9 miles west from this school-house, how far apart shall we be?

8. A hunter shot 8 pigeons and 8 quails. How many birds did he shoot?

9. A man paid 9 dollars for flour, and 9 dollars for coal. How much did he pay for both?

31. *A.* To every tenth number, from 11 to 91 inclusive,

1. Add 1.	*3.* Add 3.	*5.* Add 5.	*7.* Add 7.	*9.* Add 9.
2. Add 2.	*4.* Add 4.	*6.* Add 6.	*8.* Add 8.	*10.* Add 10.

B. To every tenth number, from 12 to 92 inclusive,

1. Add 1.	*3.* Add 3.	*5.* Add 5.	*7.* Add 7.	*9.* Add 9.
2. Add 2.	*4.* Add 4.	*6.* Add 6.	*8.* Add 8.	*10.* Add 10.

C. To every tenth number, from 13 to 93 inclusive,

1. Add 1.	*3.* Add 3.	*5.* Add 5.	*7.* Add 7.	*9.* Add 9.
2. Add 2.	*4.* Add 4.	*6.* Add 6.	*8.* Add 8.	*10.* Add 10.

32. *Like numbers* are numbers that have the same unit.

33. *Unlike numbers* are numbers that have different units.

    a. The numbers 5 trees, 19 trees, 237 trees are *like numbers*, because they have the same unit—1 tree.

    b. The numbers 5 trees, 19 men, 237 dollars are *unlike numbers*, because they have different units—1 tree, 1 man, 1 dollar.

34. *Addition* is the process of finding the sum of two or more like numbers.

    a. The numbers added are the **parts.**

    b. The number obtained by adding is the **sum** or **amount.**

EXERCISES.

1. Which of the numbers 5 rods, 16 days, 7 gallons, 3 days, 9 rods, 12 days, 4 gallons, 13, 6, 87 yards, are like numbers? Why?

2. Add 8, 5, and 3. Add 6 books, 4 books, and 7 books.

3. What is the sum of 9 miles, and 4 miles, and 8 miles?

4. The parts are 4, 11, and 7. What is the amount?

5. The parts are 13 bushels, 5 bushels, and 6 bushels. What is the sum?

6. A lady bought a bracelet for 8 dollars, and a locket for 15 dollars. How much did her purchases amount to?

7. A cabinet-maker paid 12 dollars for oak lumber, and 9 dollars for cherry. What sum did he pay for lumber?

35. *A.* To every tenth number, from 14 to 94 inclusive,

1. Add 1.	*3.* Add 3.	*5.* Add 5.	*7.* Add 7.	*9.* Add 9.
2. Add 2.	*4.* Add 4.	*6.* Add 6.	*8.* Add 8.	*10.* Add 10.

B. To every tenth number, from 15 to 95 inclusive,

1. Add 1.	*3.* Add 3.	*5.* Add 5.	*7.* Add 7.	*9.* Add 9.
2. Add 2.	*4.* Add 4.	*6.* Add 6.	*8.* Add 8.	*10.* Add 10.

36. The *sign of addition* is an upright cross, $+$. It is read *and* or *plus*; *plus* means *more*.

37. The *sign of equality* is two short, parallel, horizontal lines of equal length, $=$.

$4 + 7 + 16 = 27$ may be read "4 plus 7 plus 16 equal 27;" or "4 and 7 and 16 are 27;" or "the sum of 4, 7, and 16 is 27."

A. Read—*1.* $8 + 7 + 9 + 23 = 47$. | *2.* $\$145 + \$37 = \$182$.

3. 3 men $+ 4$ men $+ 17$ men $= 24$ men.

4. 21 pounds $+ 13$ pounds $= 34$ pounds.

5. 8 ounces $+ 11$ ounces $+ 6$ ounces $= 25$ ounces.

Written Work.—B. Use the proper signs, and write

1. 9, 13, and 38 are 60.

2. 7 dollars plus 16 dollars equal 23 dollars.

3. The sum of 7 quarts plus 15 quarts plus 9 quarts is 31 quarts.

4. 14 miles, and 27 miles, and 7 miles are 48 miles.

5. 145 rods added to 572 rods equal 717 rods.

C. Copy and complete each of the following exercises:

1. $6 + 8 + 2 =$	*3.* $5 + 8 + 7 + 4 =$	*5.* $16 + 3 + 2 + 4 =$
2. $9 + 4 + 12 =$	*4.* $17 + 10 + 3 + 8 =$	*6.* $29 + 5 + 3 + 10 =$

Oral Work.—38. A. To every tenth number, from 16 to 96 inclusive,

1. Add 1.	*3.* Add 3.	*5.* Add 5.	*7.* Add 7.	*9.* Add 9.
2. Add 2.	*4.* Add 4.	*6.* Add 6.	*8.* Add 8.	*10.* Add 10.

B. To every tenth number, from 17 to 97 inclusive,

1. Add 1.	*3.* Add 3.	*5.* Add 5.	*7.* Add 7.	*9.* Add 9.
2. Add 2.	*4.* Add 4.	*6.* Add 6.	*8.* Add 8.	*10.* Add 10.

Written Work.*—39.** Copy the exercises in ***A, B, and ***C,*** and add each exercise twice, in the order numbered, adding each column first upward and then downward, and each line first from the left and then from the right.

A

	1	2	3	4	5		10	11	12	13	14
6	2	8	5	3	1	15	3	7	1	6	4
7	6	3	9	6	2	16	8	2	6	1	2
8	9	7	4	1	4	17	5	7	3	9	8
9	2	1	8	5	7	18	3	4	9	5	4

B

	1	2	3	4	5		12	13	14	15	16	17
6	8	4	6	5	7	18	5	3	9	0	4	2
7	3	9	0	2	8	19	8	2	8	3	5	3
8	6	5	3	7	4	20	7	1	7	8	5	4
9	7	2	5	8	9	21	6	0	6	7	0	5
10	9	0	7	4	7	22	9	8	5	7	8	6
11	9	6	8	7	6	23	5	7	4	9	8	0

C

	1	2	3	4	5	6	7	8	9	10	11	12
13	7	6	0	4	3	8	2	5	6	2	4	8
14	4	8	3	9	9	6	5	7	2	8	8	3
15	9	5	8	9	5	8	4	6	5	9	9	5
16	8	4	7	9	8	8	9	3	7	9	8	0
17	7	0	9	9	6	8	3	2	3	9	7	4
18	6	5	7	8	2	8	2	9	7	9	6	9
19	5	3	6	8	4	8	0	7	6	5	5	3
20	4	9	7	8	4	8	7	6	7	9	4	6
21	7	5	6	7	3	8	6	8	4	9	3	0
22	8	2	7	7	9	8	9	2	7	9	2	5
23	9	0	4	7	9	8	8	8	2	5	9	8
24	7	9	7	6	7	8	7	4	7	9	0	2
25	7	7	5	6	8	8	2	9	-9	9	8	3
26	8	8	7	6	8	8	2	3	7	9	9	9
27	6	5	2	0	7	3	8	9	7	8	7	3

40. Copy, complete, learn, and recite the

TABLE OF PRIMARY COMBINATIONS IN ADDITION.

$1+1=$	$2+1=$	$3+1=$	$4+1=$
		$2+2=$	$3+2=$
$8+1=$	$7+1=$		
$7+2=$	$6+2=$	$6+1=$	$5+1=$
$6+3=$	$5+3=$	$5+2=$	$4+2=$
$5+4=$	$4+4=$	$4+3=$	$3+3=$
$9+1=$	$9+2=$	$9+3=$	$9+4=$
$8+2=$	$8+3=$	$8+4=$	$8+5=$
$7+3=$	$7+4=$	$7+5=$	$7+6=$
$6+4=$	$6+5=$	$6+6=$	
$5+5=$			$9+5=$
	$9+7=$	$9+6=$	$8+6=$
$9+8=$	$8+8=$	$8+7=$	$7+7=$

$$9+9=$$

NOTE.—This table contains all the combinations that can be formed by adding any two of the first nine integers.

41. EXERCISES IN ADDITION AT SIGHT.

	1	2	3	4	5	6	7	8	9
1	5 / 1	1 / 1	9 / 1	4 / 1	8 / 1	3 / 1	7 / 1	2 / 1	6 / 1
2	8 / 2	2 / 2	5 / 2	3 / 2	9 / 2	6 / 2	4 / 2	7 / 2	3 / 3
3	6 / 3	9 / 3	5 / 3	8 / 3	4 / 3	7 / 3	5 / 4	9 / 4	6 / 4
4	8 / 4	4 / 4	7 / 4	5 / 5	7 / 5	8 / 5	6 / 5	9 / 5	7 / 6
5	9 / 6	6 / 6	8 / 6	9 / 7	7 / 7	8 / 7	9 / 8	8 / 8	9 / 9

NOTE.—The preceding exercises are to be written upon the board, and used in class drill daily, until every pupil can give, at sight, the sum of the numbers expressed by any two digits.

***Oral Work.*—42. *A.* To every tenth number, from 18 to 98 inclusive,

1. Add 1.	*3.* Add 3.	*5.* Add 5.	*7.* Add 7.	*9.* Add 9.
2. Add 2.	*4.* Add 4.	*6.* Add 6.	*8.* Add 8.	*10.* Add 10.

B. To every tenth number, from 19 to 99 inclusive,

1. Add 1.	*3.* Add 3.	*5.* Add 5.	*7.* Add 7.	*9.* Add 9.
2. Add 2.	*4.* Add 4.	*6.* Add 6.	*8.* Add 8.	*10.* Add 10.

C. To every tenth number, from 10 to 100 inclusive,

1. Add 1.	*3.* Add 3.	*5.* Add 5.	*7.* Add 7.	*9.* Add 9.
2. Add 2.	*4.* Add 4.	*6.* Add 6.	*8.* Add 8.	*10.* Add 10.

43. *A.* (*a*) 15 days, 230 days, 9 rods, 70 pounds, 16 bushels, 50 days, 37 rods.

(*b*) 194 pears, \$3,115, 280, \$16, 75 pears, \$36, 283 pears.

(*c*) 68 boys, 13 horses, 291 sheep, 8 houses, 1,751 pigeons.

1. Which numbers in (*a*) can be added? Why?

2. Which numbers in (*b*) can be added? Why?

3. Which numbers in (*b*) can not be added? Why?

4. Which numbers in (*c*) can be added? Why?

5. What numbers can be added?

6. What numbers can not be added?

B. 1. Ones must be added to what?

2. Tens must be added to what? Hundreds, to what?

3. To what can a unit or units of any order be added?

4. To what can not a unit or units of any order be added?

5. Add 300, 200, 700, 500, and 100.

6. Add \$.10, \$.90, \$.30, \$.50, \$.80, and \$.60.

7. Add 7,000, 1,000, 4,000, 2,000, and 5,000.

C. How many ones and how many tens are there

1. In the sum of 7, 5, 8, and 3?

2. In the sum of 4, 9, 6, 2, and 1?

3. In the sum of 10, 30, 20, and 40?

44. PRINCIPLES OF ADDITION.

I. *A whole equals the sum of all its parts.*

II. *Only units of like orders can be added.*

Written Work. — 45. Ex. The parts are 720, 4,813, 1,327, 504, and 6,732.   What is their sum?

PROCESS.

$$\left.\begin{array}{r} 720 \\ 4,813 \\ 1,327 \\ 504 \\ 6,732 \end{array}\right\} \text{Parts.}$$

$$\overline{14,096} \text{ Sum.}$$

EXPLANATION.—I write the parts—ones under ones, tens under tens, and so on—and draw a horizontal line below the last number.

Adding the ones, I have 16 (= 6 ones and 1 ten), and I write the 6 ones below the line, for the ones of the required sum.   Adding the 1 ten with the tens of the given numbers, I have 9 tens, which I write for the tens of the sum.   Adding the hundreds, I have 30 (= 3 thousands), and I write 0 in the place of hundreds in the sum.   Adding the 3 thousands with the given thousands, I have 14 thousands (= 4 thousands and 1 ten-thousand), which I write for the thousands and ten-thousand of the sum.

The result, 14,096, is the required sum.

PROBLEMS.

A	1	2	3	4	5
	657	$3,140	36	$52.41	4,213
	360	1,205	725	.78	145
	208	4,332	1,413	48.36	32
	845	2,011	9,879	9.29	5,276
		$		$	

6	7	8	9
$100,872	125,600	$ 132.79	5,267
63,494	85,638	31.48	221,532
926,735	7,257	238.40	99,835
19,622	735,528	9,478.43	892,763
5,368	863,264	68.57	81,676
824,463	856,470	2.56	725,052

B. Copy these exercises and add each one twice, in the order numbered, adding each column first upward and then downward, and each line first from the left and then from the right.

	1	2	3	4		10	11	12	13
5	$20	$15	$30	$12	14	100	333	350	116
6	$19	$10	$17	$44	15	321	240	175	210
7	$55	$27	$13	$36	16	105	500	920	800
8	$32	$16	$11	$23	17	621	127	155	513
9	$40	$21	$34	$18	18	584	321	230	109

	19	20	21	22	23	24
25	$25.30	$ 9.37	$60	$88.94	$75.30	$ .08
26	$18.05	$28.25	$ 3.55	$73	$ .04	$15.15
27	$50.15	$ .09	$ .90	$16.91	$59.50	$11.11
28	$ .75	$10.06	$35.16	$ .07	$65.95	$ 8
29	$36	$49.29	$70	$66.10	$ 4	$17.40
30	$40.10	$ 5.03	$12.22	$ 4	$97.10	$ 9.09

***Oral Work.*—C. *1*.** Albert has 19 apples, Frank has 5, Edgar has 7, and Charles has 10. How many apples have the four boys?

The four boys have the sum of 19 apples, 5 apples, 7 apples, and 10 apples, which is 41 apples.

2. One winter a farmer fed 14 tons of hay to his cows, 5 tons to his horses, and 9 tons to his sheep. How much hay did it take to winter his live stock?

3. A farmer sowed 20 acres of land to oats, 30 acres to wheat, and 10 acres to corn. How many acres did he sow?

4. A boy gave 60 cents for an arithmetic and 20 cents for a slate. How much did he give for both?

5. What is the sum of 66, 5, 6, and 9?

6. How many are $48 + 3 + 6 + 9 + 4$?

7. What is the amount of $32, $9, $6, $4, and $7?

8. I paid 30 cents for a pound of coffee, and 14 cents for a quart of molasses. How much did I pay for both?

I paid the sum of 30 cents and 14 cents; 14 cents are 10 cents + 4 cents; 30 cents and 10 cents are 40 cents, and 4 cents are 44 cents. Hence, I paid 44 cents for both.

9. A grazier has 70 head of cattle in one pasture, and 41 head in another. How many cattle has he?

10. A shoe dealer sold 40 pairs of kip boots, and 38 pairs of calf boots. How many pairs of boots did he sell?

11. A hatter bought 70 cases of silk hats, and 56 cases of felt hats. How many cases of hats did he buy?

12. A clothier sold 30 sack coats, 40 dress coats, and 18 overcoats. How many coats did he sell?

13. How many books are 40 books + 20 books + 56 books?

14. What is the amount of $.80, $.30, $.40, and $.25?

15. What is the sum of 200, 700, 300, and 250?

Written Work.

D. 1	2	3	4	7
7,887	600,054	$ 4,718.85	$5,109.32	$ 9,300.25
7,538	432,708	28,569.09	84.69	16,000.10
5,852	759,890	1,296.52	730	44,999.87
3,929	635,428	54,903.28	8.05	65,874.08
4,387	970,325	4,925	6,043.17	3.75
25		$	$	7,444.15
8,110				68,974
478				13.64
9				98,525.23
808				.09
2,491				400.45
6				22,776
374				18,106.30
9,466				78,003.14
				$

5	6
1,325,086	1,368,122,097
764,572	4,513,265,928
3,426,515	9,157,934,684
1,812,328	1,369,668,624
25,680,087	7,117,944,958
7,548,766	461,371,480
6,754,645	804,875,333

B

Oral Work.—E. *1.* Alva paid 21 cents for a knife, and 18 cents for a ball. How much did both cost him?

Both cost him the sum of 21 cents and 18 cents; 21 cents and 10 cents are 31 cents, and 8 cents are 39 cents. Hence, both cost him 39 cents.

2. Helen paid 63 cents for butter, and 31 cents for cheese. How much did her purchases amount to?

3. A lady paid 48 dollars for a book-case, and 12 dollars for a table. How much did she pay for both?

4. Enos gave $.45 for a sled, and $.18 to have it painted. How much did the sled cost him?

5. A merchant sold one cloak for $28, and another for $27. How much did he receive for both?

6. Lucy paid $.38 for a pair of gloves, and $.25 for a comb. How much did she pay for all?

7. A coal dealer bought 90 tons, 73 tons, and 85 tons of coal. How many tons did he buy?

8. Upon a steamboat are 85 men, 64 women, and 13 children. How many persons are on the boat?

9. How many horses are 41 horses, 98 horses, and 11 horses?

10. $34 + $27 + $45 = how many dollars?

11. 56 sheep + 18 sheep + 47 sheep = how many sheep?

12. What is the sum of 44, 37, 16, and 7?

13. The parts are 59, 34, 83, and 12. Find the amount.

Written Work.—F: *1.* What is the sum of 123 pounds, 103 pounds, and 3,140 pounds?

2. What is the amount of $96.12, $132.07, $98.76, $72.38, and $115.25?

3. Add $7.28, $241.09, $.42, $.96, and $44.52.

4. A miller bought 1,284 bushels of wheat, and 859 bushels of corn. How many bushels of grain did he buy?

5. The four quarters of an ox weighed 142 pounds, 137 pounds, 181 pounds, and 184 pounds. What was their total weight?

6. In five days a dairyman made 37 pounds, 42 pounds, 34 pounds, 55 pounds, and 43 pounds of butter. How many pounds of butter did he make in the five days?

7. I sold a wash-stand for $6.50, a bureau for $11.63, and an easy-chair for $8.25. How much did I receive for them?

8. One week a railroad company bought 154 cords, 115 cords, 180 cords, 145 cords, 94 cords, and 269 cords of wood. How many cords were bought that week?

9. A merchant gained $218 on a lot of goods that cost him $463. For how much did he sell the goods?

10. Three men, A, B, and C, buy a machine-shop, A furnishing $2,163 of the purchase money, B $3,085, and C $1,236. How much does the shop cost?

11. A lumberman drove seven rafts of logs down Penobscot River to Bangor. In the first raft were 1,276 logs, in the second 859, in the third 1,009, in the fourth 793, in the fifth 1,318, in the sixth 925, and in the seventh 1,158. How many logs were in all the rafts?

12. I bought a village lot for $325, and paid $22.63 for taxes. For how much must I sell it, to gain $72.37?

46. RULE FOR ADDITION OF INTEGERS.

I. *Write the numbers so that units of the same order may be in the same column.*

II. *Add the units of the lowest order, write the ones of the sum in the result, and add the tens of the sum with the units of the next order.*

III. *So proceed with the units of each order, and write the entire sum of the units of the highest order.*

PROBLEMS.

A. 1. Add 346, 5,279, and 8,165.

2. What is the sum of 376, 128, 593, and 842?

3. $2,317, $954, $1,683, $75, and $381 amount to how many dollars?

4. Find the sum of 56, 1,642, 485, 691, 3,482, and 22,849.

5. What is the amount of $.93, $.25, $.81, $.19, $.44, $.75, and $.50?

6. Add 720, 4,813, 1,327, 504, and 6,732.

WRITTEN PROCESS.	MAKING THE COMPUTATION.
720	6, 13, 16; write 6 (add 1).
4,813	4, 6, 7, 9; write 9.
1,327	12, 15, 23, 30; write 0 (add 3).
504	9, 10, 14; write 14.
6,732	Result, 14,096.
14,096	

7. A lady paid $25 for a bureau, $42 for 6 chairs, $65 for a sofa, $57 for three tables, and $35 for a bedstead. How much did her purchases amount to?

8. One forenoon a street car made 5 trips, carrying 54 passengers the first trip, 48 the second, 63 the third, 62 the fourth, and 49 the fifth. How many passengers did the car carry that forenoon?

9. A fruit grower sold 74 barrels of russet apples, 56 barrels of greenings, and 152 barrels of pippins. How many barrels of apples did he sell?

10. How many rods of fence will it take to inclose a field that is 43 rods long and 24 rods wide?

11. In nine days I travel 60 miles, 110 miles, 35 miles, 69 miles, 86 miles, 94 miles, 115 miles, 25 miles, and 100 miles. How many miles do I travel?

12. A store on the first floor of a building rents for $1,365 a year, the offices on the second floor rent for $762, and a photograph room on the third floor rents for $278. How much is the whole rent of the building?

13. A produce dealer bought 720 bushels, 145 bushels, and 1,124 bushels of oats. How many bushels of oats did he buy?

Oral Work.—B. *1.* In an orchard are 20 pear-trees, 10 more apple-trees than pear-trees, 15 plum-trees, and 6 more cherry-trees than plum-trees. How many trees are in the orchard?

2. A Swede came to America when he was 11 years old; 14 years afterward he married; 6 years later his wife died, and she has been dead 13 years. What is his age?

3. In a park are an elm 40 feet high, an oak 50 feet higher than the elm, and a pine 60 feet higher than the oak. What is the height of each tree?

4. A nurseryman sold 60 pear-trees to one farmer, 30 to another, and 17 to another. How many pear-trees did he sell?

5. A farmer has 14 cattle, 11 horses, and 23 sheep. How many head of live stock has he?

6. In building a bridge it took 64 days to do the mason work, 46 days the wood work, and 18 days the grading. How many days did it take to build the bridge?

7. I paid 84 cents for fruit, and 66 cents for candies. How much did I pay for all?

8. James paid 25 cents for a slate, and 37 cents for a reader. How many cents did he pay for both?

9. A lady taught a summer term of 65 days, and a winter term of 76 days. How many days did she teach in the year?

10. My cows give 49 quarts of milk in the morning, and 67 quarts in the evening. How many quarts do they give in a day?

11. Orson found 28 plums under one tree, and 94 plums under another. How many plums did he find?

12. A steamship landed in New York with 45 first-class, 16 second-class, and 72 steerage passengers. How many passengers did she bring?

13. Louise is 15 years old, her mother is 27 years older than she, and her grandmother is 35 years older than her mother. How old is her grandmother?

14. A farmer has 28 acres of woodland, 40 acres of pasture, 30 acres of meadow, 16 acres in wheat, 3 acres in potatoes, 4 acres in corn, 20 acres in oats, 2 acres in root crops, and 1 acre in yard and garden. How many acres are there in his farm?

Written Work.—C. 1. A real-estate agent sold two houses for $1,830 each, a city lot for $2,210, and a farm for $12,125. How much did the sales amount to?

2. C has $4,258, B has $328 more than C, A has $529 more than B, and D has as much as B, C, and A. How much money have the four men?

3. What is the sum of thirty-five million eight hundred seventy-six thousand one hundred twenty, three hundred ninety-six thousand four hundred ninety-one, and five hundred forty-three thousand six hundred seven?

4. A man bought three houses, paying for them $1,804, $1,602, and $2,355. He sold them for $2,395 above cost. How much did he receive for them?

5. A fruit dealer paid $15.45 for oranges, $20.34 for lemons, $27.59 for pine-apples, and $16.72 for cocoa-nuts. How much did the fruit cost him?

6. A man paid \$3,256 for a farm, \$1,217 for the live stock, \$557 for farming implements, \$373 for the crops on the ground, and \$439 for repairs. How much was his total outlay?

7. A contractor received \$14,100 for building a hotel, \$885 for building a livery stable, \$2,637 for building a house, and \$3,233 for building a warehouse. How much did he receive for the four jobs?

8. Monday I deposited \$52.18 in the bank, Tuesday \$68.47, Wednesday \$45.52, Thursday \$78.77, Friday \$80.16, and Saturday \$119.82. What was the amount of my deposits for the week?

9. One month a grocer received \$486.69 for sugars, \$390.25 for teas, \$166.50 for fruits, and \$1,767 for other goods. What was the amount of his sales for the month?

10. Find the sum of 15 million 9 thousand 17, 9 million 508, 675 thousand 899, and 245 million 326 thousand 8.

11. North America contains 8,593,000 square miles, South America 7,362,000 square miles, Europe 3,825,000 square miles, Asia 17,300,000 square miles, and Africa 11,557,000 square miles. How many square miles are there in these five continents?

12. In seven piles of wood, measuring 364 cords, 729 cords, 95 cords, 832 cords, 723 cords, 407 cords, and 634 cords, are how many cords?

13. A butcher bought five oxen, which weighed 1,120 pounds, 1,312 pounds, 1,250 pounds, 1,547 pounds, and 1,420 pounds. What was the total weight?

14. What is the sum of \$1,328,654, \$6,863, \$11,496, \$2,000,342, \$658, \$9,891, \$78,620, \$1,060,909, \$5,683, \$22,408, \$23,684,901, \$846, \$29, and \$4,803?

15. A merchant tailor paid \$315.78 for broadcloths, \$282.25 for cassimeres, \$106.45 for vestings, \$24.90 for linings, and \$14.04 for thread, silk, and buttons. How much did he pay out for stock?

16. What is the amount of \$58.48, \$368, \$37.28, \$9.99, \$48.06, \$768.04, \$362.22, and \$8.37?

17. A druggist pays \$1,335 a year for rent, \$2,447 for clerk hire, \$292.25 for fuel, \$259.19 for gas, \$875 for freight and cartage, and \$1,936 for other expenses. How much are his yearly expenses?

18. A merchant's cash sales Monday were \$98.19, Tuesday \$132, Wednesday \$198.07, Thursday \$272.63, Friday \$115.01, and Saturday \$295. What was the amount of his cash sales for the week?

19. A farmer raised 1,286 bushels of wheat, 229 bushels of corn, 144 bushels of buckwheat, 683 bushels of oats, 257 bushels of rye, and 599 bushels of barley. How many bushels of grain did he raise?

20. A owes B \$901.32, C \$321.09, D \$288.58, E \$124.15, F \$150.75, and G \$50.90. How much does he owe?

21. What is the sum of ninety-nine thousand ninety-nine, twenty-seven million five hundred, forty-two million two thousand five, four hundred eight thousand ninety-six, and five thousand four hundred thirty-seven?

22. Find the amount of nine hundred seven million eight hundred five thousand seventy-four, one thousand nine hundred fifty, twenty-four million twenty-four, seven million eight hundred nineteen thousand, six hundred twelve, and one hundred fifty-seven.

Note 1.—For *outlines of addition* for review, see page 269.

Note 2.—Teachers who prefer that decimals should be studied in connection with integers, will now require their pupils to study addition of decimals, pages 121, 122.

SECTION III.

SUBTRACTION.

Oral Work.—**47.** *1.* On a tree were 8 peaches, but Laura picked 5 of them. How many peaches were left on the tree?

There were left on the tree 8 peaches less 5 peaches, which are 3 peaches.

2. James has 7 rabbits; 4 of them are gray, and the others are white. How many white rabbits has he?

3. A man bought 9 pounds of butter, and in a week his family used all but 3 pounds of it. How many pounds of butter were used?

4. If a factory girl earns $12 in a week, and pays $3 for board, how much money has she left?

5. I paid $13 for a silver cake basket, and $4 less for a set of tea-spoons. How much did the spoons cost me?

6. A boy bought a water-melon for 15 cents, and a bunch of grapes for 6 cents. How much more did he pay for the melon than for the grapes?

7. A farmer having 16 cows, sold 7 of them. How many did he keep?

8. Nelson is 17 years old; how old was he 9 years ago?

9. There are 6 passengers in a street car which has seats for 18 passengers. How many seats are vacant?

48. *A.* From every tenth number, from 11 to 91 inclusive,

1. Subtract 1.	*3.* Subtract 3.	*6.* Subtract 6.	*9.* Subtract 9.
2. Subtract 2.	*4.* Subtract 4.	*7.* Subtract 7.	*10.* Subtract 10.
	5. Subtract 5.	*8.* Subtract 8.	

B 2

B. From every tenth number, from 12 to 92 inclusive,

1. Subtract 1.	*3.* Subtract 3.	*6.* Subtract 6.	*9.* Subtract 9.
2. Subtract 2.	*4.* Subtract 4.	*7.* Subtract 7.	*10.* Subtract 16.
	5. Subtract 5.	*8.* Subtract 8.	

C. From every tenth number, from 13 to 93 inclusive,

1. Subtract 1.	*3.* Subtract 3.	*6.* Subtract 6.	*9.* Subtract 9.
2. Subtract 2.	*4.* Subtract 4.	*7.* Subtract 7.	*10.* Subtract 10.
	5. Subtract 5.	*8.* Subtract 8.	

49. *Subtraction* is the process of taking one of two like numbers from the other.

> *a.* That one of the two numbers from which the other is to be taken is the *minuend.*
>
> *b.* The number to be taken from the minuend is the *subtrahend.*
>
> *c.* The number obtained by subtracting is the *difference* or *remainder.*

Exercises.

1. Subtract 7 books from 11 books.

2. Subtract 9 pins from 15 pins.

3. What is the difference between 13 horses and 4 horses?

4. Take 8 leaves from 17 leaves. What is the remainder?

5. If you subtract 6 cents from 15 cents, what is the remainder?

6. The minuend is 14, and the subtrahend is 5. What is the difference?

7. A cook having 16 eggs, used 9. How many had she left?

8. In question 7, which number is the minuend? Which is the subtrahend? Which is the remainder?

9. In a garden is one vase worth $19, and another worth $14. What is the difference in their values?

10. In going 12 miles, I walked 5 miles, and rode the remainder of the distance.   How many miles did I ride?

11. The minuend is $.25, and the subtrahend is $.15. What is the difference?

50. *A.* From every tenth number, from 14 to 94 inclusive,

1. Subtract 1.	*3.* Subtract 3.	*6.* Subtract 6.	*9.* Subtract 9.
2. Subtract 2.	*4.* Subtract 4.	*7.* Subtract 7.	*10.* Subtract 10.
	5. Subtract 5.	*8.* Subtract 8.	

B. From every tenth number, from 15 to 95 inclusive,

1. Subtract 1.	*3.* Subtract 3.	*6.* Subtract 6.	*9.* Subtract 9.
2. Subtract 2.	*4.* Subtract 4.	*7.* Subtract 7.	*10.* Subtract 10.
	5. Subtract 5.	*8.* Subtract 8.	

51. The *sign of subtraction* is a short, horizontal line, —. It is read *minus* or *less; minus* means *less.*

25 − 16 may be read "25 minus 16," or "25 less 16."

A. Read these exercises:

1. $23 - 9 = 14$

2. $\$182 - \$37 = \$145$

3. $\$.87 - \$.31 = \$.56$

4. $\$31.10 - \$9.75 = \$21.35$

5. 32 men − 25 men = 7 men.

6. 50 pounds − 32 pounds = 18 pounds.

Written Work.—B. Write each of these exercises, using the proper signs:

1. 14 from 21 leaves 7.

2. 15 guns less 9 guns equal 6 guns.

3. 23 men minus 16 men equal 7 men.

4. $525 less $500 are $25.

5. 48 miles from 60 miles equal 12 miles.

6. 15 rods taken from 145 rods leave 130 rods.

C. Copy and complete these exercises:

1. $10 - 4 =$

2. $41 - 21 =$

3. $17 - 9 =$

4. $\$19 - \$4 =$

5. 41 lemons − 21 lemons =

6. 17 books − 9 books =

7. 36 yards − 5 yards =

8. 25 fishes − 17 fishes =

9. 40 cars − 31 cars =

10. 32 bricks − 8 bricks =   bricks.

11. 51 steps − 40 steps =   steps.

12. 100 cents − 90 cents =   cents.

13. 43 dollars − 30 dollars =   dollars.

Oral Work.*—52. *A. From every tenth number, from 16 to 96 inclusive,

1. Subtract 1.	*3.* Subtract 3.	*6.* Subtract 6.	*9.* Subtract 9.
2. Subtract 2.	*4.* Subtract 4.	*7.* Subtract 7.	*10.* Subtract 10.
	5. Subtract 5.	*8.* Subtract 8.	

B. From every tenth number, from 17 to 97 inclusive,

1. Subtract 1.	*3.* Subtract 3.	*6.* Subtract 6.	*9.* Subtract 9.
2. Subtract 2	*4.* Subtract 4.	*7.* Subtract 7.	*10.* Subtract 10.
	5. Subtract 5.	*8.* Subtract 8.	

***Written Work.*—53.** Copy, complete, learn, and recite the

TABLE OF PRIMARY COMBINATIONS IN SUBTRACTION.

$2-1=$	$3-1=$	$4-1=$	$5-1=$
$6-1=$	$3-2=$	$4-3=$	$5-4=$
$6-5=$	$7-1=$	$4-2=$	$5-2=$
$6-2=$	$7-6=$	$8-1=$	$5-3=$
$6-4=$	$7-2=$	$8-7=$	$9-1=$
$6-3=$	$7-5=$	$8-2=$	$9-8=$
$10-1=$	$7-3=$	$8-6=$	$9-2=$
$10-9=$	$7-4=$	$8-3=$	$9-7=$
$10-2=$	$11-2=$	$8-5=$	$9-3=$
$10-8=$	$11-9=$	$8-4=$	$9-6=$
$10-3=$	$11-3=$	$12-3=$	$9-4=$
$10-7=$	$11-8=$	$12-9=$	$9-5=$
$10-4=$	$11-4=$	$12-4=$	$13-4=$
$10-6=$	$11-7=$	$12-8=$	$13-9=$
$10-5=$	$11-5=$	$12-5=$	$13-5=$
$14-5=$	$11-6=$	$12-7=$	$13-8=$
$14-9=$	$15-6=$	$12-6=$	$13-6=$
$14-6=$	$15-9=$	$16-7=$	$13-7=$
$14-8=$	$15-7=$	$16-9=$	$17-8=$
$14-7=$	$15-8=$	$16-8=$	$17-9=$

$$18-9=$$

54. Exercises in Subtraction at Sight.

1 { 1	4	7	10	2	5	8	3	6	9
1	1	1	1	1	1	1	1	1	1
2 { 2	7	3	8	4	9	5	10	6	11
2	2	2	2	2	2	2	2	2	2
3 { 5	10	6	11	7	12	4	9	3	8
3	3	3	3	3	3	3	3	3	3
4 { 6	9	12	5	8	11	4	7	10	13
4	4	4	4	4	4	4	4	4	4
5 { 8	12	6	10	14	7	11	5	9	13
5	5	5	5	5	5	5	5	5	5
6 { 15	10	14	9	13	8	12	7	11	6
6	6	6	6	6	6	6	6	6	6
7 { 13	16	9	12	15	8	11	14	7	10
7	7	7	7	7	7	7	7	7	7
8 { 12	16	10	14	8	11	15	13	9	17
8	8	8	8	8	8	8	8	8	8
9 { 11	14	17	10	13	16	12	9	18	15
9	9	9	9	9	9	9	9	9	9

NOTE.—The preceding exercises are to be written upon the board, and used in class drill daily, until every pupil can give, at sight, the difference of any two of the numbers.

***Oral Work.*—55. A.** From every tenth number, from 18 to 98 inclusive,

1. Subtract 1.	*3.* Subtract 3.	*6.* Subtract 6.	*9.* Subtract 9.
2. Subtract 2.	*4.* Subtract 4.	*7.* Subtract 7.	*10.* Subtract 10.
	5. Subtract 5.	*8.* Subtract 8.	

B. From every tenth number, from 19 to 99 inclusive,

1. Subtract 1.	*3.* Subtract 3.	*6.* Subtract 6.	*9.* Subtract 9.
2. Subtract 2.	*4.* Subtract 4.	*7.* Subtract 7.	*10.* Subtract 10.
	5. Subtract 5.	*8.* Subtract 8.	

C. From every tenth number, from 10 to 100 inclusive,

1. Subtract 1.	*3.* Subtract 3.	*6.* Subtract 6.	*9.* Subtract 9.
2. Subtract 2.	*4.* Subtract 4.	*7.* Subtract 7.	*10.* Subtract 10.
	5. Subtract 5.	*8.* Subtract 8.	

56. *1.* From 9 take 7; take 5; take 2.

2. From 14 take 6; take 10; take 5.

3. From 18 take 10; take 8; take 0.

4. From 11 take 3; take 7; take 11.

5. From 16 take 7; take 9; take 6.

6. Take 6 from 11; from 15; from 12.

7. Take 3 from 12; from 7; from 10.

8. Take 8 from 15; from 17; from 13.

9. Take 9 from 19; from 15; from 13.

10. Take 7 from 15; from 7; from 14.

How many are

11. 32—25?   20—13?   47—6?   21—9?   30—23?

12. 17 minus 9?   25 minus 18?   34—7?   15—6?

13. 28 less 18?   45 less 8?   16 less 11?   43 less 35?
50 less 41?

Find the value of each of these expressions:

14. Apples: 21—7; 18—10; 26—8; 32—20.

15. Oranges: 38 less 29; 62 less 55; 48 less 7; 24 less 10.

16. Lemons: 52 minus 40; 31 minus 27; 23 minus 9;
16 minus 7.

17. Figs: 14 from 23; 9 from 30; 12 from 18; 48 from 56.

18. Peaches: 15 from 31; 12 from 29; 20 from 45.

57. *A.* (*a*) 75 pears, 36 dollars, 115, 283 dollars, 491 pears.

1. What number in line (*a*) can be subtracted from 283 dollars? Why?

2. What number from 491 pears? Why? What number from 115? Why?

3. Ones can be subtracted from what only?

4. Tens must be subtracted from what? Hundreds, from what?

5. Subtract 10 from 50; 100 from 500; 1,000 from 5,000; 10,000 from 50,000.

6. Take $.04 from $.09; $.40 from $.90; $40 from $90; $400 from $900; $4,000 from $9,000.

7. From 10 subtract 7; from 100 subtract 70; from 1,000 subtract 700; from 10,000 subtract 7,000.

8. From $.20 subtract $.04; from $2 subtract $.40.

9. From $20 subtract $4; from $200 subtract $40.

B. 1. 30 is 2 tens and how many ones?

2. 37 is 2 tens and how many ones?

3. 54 is 40 and how many?

4. 300 is 2 hundreds and how many tens?

5. 370 is 2 hundreds and how many tens?

6. 268 is 25 tens and how many ones?

7. 1,000 is 9 hundreds, 9 tens, and how many ones?

8. 10,000 is 0 ones, 10 tens, and how many hundreds and thousands?

9. 420 is 300 and how many?

10. 423 is 410 and how many?

11. 900 is 800 and how many tens?

12. 905 is 890 and how many?

58. Principle of Subtraction.

Units of any order can be subtracted from units of the same order only.

***Written Work.*—59.** Ex. What is the difference between 40,375 and 2,869?

Explanation.—I write the subtrahend under the minuend—ones under ones, tens under tens, and so on—and draw a horizontal line below the subtrahend.

PROCESS.

$$40,375 \text{ Minuend.}$$
$$2,869 \text{ Subtrahend.}$$
$$37,506 \text{ Difference.}$$

Since 9 ones can not be taken from 5 ones, I take from the 7 tens 1 ten (= 10 ones), and unite it with the 5 ones, making 15 ones; then, 9 ones from 15 ones leave 6 ones, which I write in the result.

6 tens from the remaining 6 tens of the minuend leave 0, which I write in tens' place in the result.

Since 8 hundreds can not be taken from 3 hundreds, and there are 0 thousands in the minuend, I take from the 4 ten-thousands 1 ten-thousand (= 10 thousands); from these 10 thousands I take 1 thousand (= 10 hundreds), and unite it with the 3 hundreds, making 13 hundreds; then, 8 hundreds from 13 hundreds leave 5 hundreds, which I write in the result.

2 thousands from the remaining 9 thousands leave 7 thousands, which I write in the result.

Since there are 0 ten-thousands in the subtrahend, I write the remaining 3 ten-thousands of the minuend in the result.

The entire result, 37,506, is the required difference.

Problems.

A	1	2	3	4	5	6
	584	725	680	805	943	1,308
	152	314	244	431	576	1,245

7	8	9	10
635 pins	3,544 soldiers	7,953 shingles	59,700 pounds
412 pins	2,836 soldiers	5,468 shingles	43,708 pounds

11	12	13	14
$57,698	$6,750.02	$42,301.00	$16,065.00
43,257	2,945.04	5,174.56	10,438.25

Oral Work.—Exercises to be solved at sight.

B	From	Take		From	Take
	1.	*2.*		*13.*	*14.*
3. From 87		50	*15.* From 25 cents		15 cents
4. Take 60		20	*16.* Take 13 cents		6 cents
	5.	*6.*		*17.*	*18.*
7. From 99		73	*19.* From 65 cents		50 cents
8. Take 62		41	*20.* Take 37 cents		25 cents
	9.	*10.*		*21.*	*22.*
11. From 78		48	*23.* From 100 cents		75 cents
12. Take 57		43	*24.* Take 87 cents		31 cents

C	Minuends.	Subtrahends.		Minuends.	Subtrahends.
	1.	*2.*		*5.*	*6.*
3. Minuends	44 hats	34 hats	*7.*	57 coats	43 coats
4. Subtrahends	16 hats	9 hats	*8.*	36 coats	19 coats
	9.	*10.*		*13.*	*14.*
11. Minuends	84 tons	69 tons	*15.*	64 pens	55 pens
12. Subtrahends	78 tons	45 tons	*16.*	39 pens	24 pens
	17.	*18.*		*21.*	*22.*
19. Minuends	$2.00	$.50	*23.*	$10.00	$5.00
20. Subtrahends	$ .75	$.37	*24.*	$ 2.50	$ .50

D. 1. A man bought a cow for $30, and paid all but $10. How much did he pay?

He paid the difference between $30 and $10, which is $20.

2. Julia had 100 cents, but she paid 20 cents for some paper. How many cents had she left?

3. 60 gallons of syrup have been drawn from a hogshead that contained 80 gallons. How many gallons are left?

4. A fisherman caught 110 pounds of fish, and sold 76 pounds. How many pounds had he left?

5. A man having $63 paid $20 for a harness. How many dollars had he left?

6. Of the 75 pupils in a school 40 are girls. How many pupils are boys?

7. A girl having 79 chickens, sold 30 of them. How many chickens had she left?

8. A gentleman paid $87 for a sleigh, and $60 less for a robe. How much did the robe cost him?

9. A paper-box maker having 72 sheets of straw-board, used 60 of them. How many sheets had he left?

10. I buy potatoes at 90 cents a bushel, and sell them at 108 cents. How much do I gain on a bushel?

Written Work.

E

1	2	3	4
348,794	2,174,943	84,125,800	167,065,149
127,586	480,765	9,632,486	39,999

5	6	7	8	9
104,021	$9,004	50,096	$123.45	1,000,000
99,034	2,876	13,188	109.86	31,276

10	11	12	13
7,408,215	300,300,333	$18,123.05	$386.00
59,326	47,008,296	3,109.86	.21
		$	$

Oral Work.—F. 1. A merchant tailor used 15 yards of broadcloth from a piece containing 39 yards. How many yards were left in the piece?

There was left the difference between 39 yards and 15 yards. 10 yards from 39 yards leave 29 yards, and 5 yards from 29 yards leave 24 yards.

2. A shoe dealer having 48 pairs of ladies' shoes, sold 25 pairs. How many pairs had he left?

3. I own a farm of 69 acres, and 58 acres of it are cleared land. How many acres are woodland?

4. A cooper made 53 apple barrels in a week, and sold 44 of them. How many barrels had he left?

5. A fruit dealer bought 72 crates of peaches. After selling 56 crates, how many crates had he yet to sell?

6. A wood dealer sold 83 cords of oak wood, and 57 cords of pine. How many more cords of oak than pine wood did he sell?

7. A butcher killed one calf that weighed 91 pounds, and another that weighed 26 pounds less. How much did the lighter calf weigh?

8. A man owing $75, gave his note for $47, and paid the balance in cash. How much cash did he pay?

9. I exchanged a horse worth $84, for a gold watch and $19 in money. How much did the watch cost me?

10. 111 swallows are how many more than 28 swallows?

11. 108 robins — 99 robins are how many robins?

12. 56 cents are how many less than 100 cents?

Written Work.—*G.* *1.* How many tons are 52,719 tons — 24,112 tons?

2. A fruit dealer, having 1,247 baskets of peaches, sold 965 baskets. How many baskets had he left?

3. A man whose income is $2,250 a year, expends $1,473. How much does he save?

4. A dealer bought horses for $4,960, and sold them for $6,424. How much did he gain?

5. In a certain city are 16,447 children, of whom 11,096 attend school. How many do not attend school?

6. A man having $17,974 in the bank, drew out $8,598. How much money had he left on deposit?

7. In November a merchant's sales amounted to $2,928.93, and in December to $3,743.69. How much less were the November sales than those of December?

8. A gentleman's income last year was fifteen thousand four hundred thirty-one dollars, and his expenses were nine thousand three hundred fifty dollars nineteen cents. How much did he save?

9. One year the value of my farm products was $4,307, and my farm expenses were $2,427. How much were my profits?

10. A ship builder received $19,000 for a brig that cost him $16,728. How much was his gain?

11. A miller in St. Louis has 36,500 barrels of flour. How many barrels will he have in store, after shipping 21,987 barrels to New Orleans?

12. A broker sold Government bonds for $328,700 that cost him $281,908. How much did he gain?

13. How many acres are 1,367 acres − 1,108 acres?

14. How many cords are 22,197 cords − 20,174 cords?

15. 103,035 feet − 83,616 feet = how many feet?

16. A load of hay and the wagon weighed 2,481 pounds, and the wagon weighed 812 pounds. What was the weight of the hay?

17. At a city election one candidate for mayor received 52,918 votes, and the other candidate 28,434 votes. What was the majority of the successful candidate?

18. The Island of Cuba contains 43,220 square miles, and the State of Ohio 41,060 square miles. How much larger is Cuba than Ohio?

19. The live weight of ten beeves was 9,742 pounds, and the dressed weight was 6,495 pounds. How much was the shrinkage?

60. RULE FOR SUBTRACTION OF INTEGERS.

I. *Write the subtrahend under the minuend—ones under ones, tens under tens, and so on.*

II. *Beginning at the right, subtract the units of each order in the subtrahend from the units of the same order in the minuend, and write the difference in the result.*

III. *When there are more units of any order in the subtrahend than of the same order in the minuend, add 10 to the units of the minuend before subtracting; then, consider the units of the next higher order in the minuend 1 less.*

PROBLEMS.

A.	From	Take		From	Take
1.	9,426	8,563.	*4.*	9,111,525,202	527,029.
2.	$400,385	$27,690.	*5.*	$6,000.07	$375.68.
3.	69,504,300	609,572.	*6.*	$22,025.15	$19,936.93.

B. Ex. Subtract 2,869 from 40,375.

PROCESS.

$$40,375$$
$$2,869$$
$$\overline{37,506}$$

MAKING THE COMPUTATION.

9 from 15, 6; write 6.
6 from 6, 0; write 0.
8 from 13, 5; write 5.
2 from 9, 7; write 7.
Write 3.
Result, 37,506.

Subtract each number in column I from the numbers on the same line in columns II, III, IV; the numbers in column II from those in columns III and IV; the numbers in column III from those in column IV.

	I.	II.	III.	IV.
1– 6.	77	463	645	48,100
7–12.	160	1,098	2,150	10,360
13–18.	80	515	9,100	100,125
19–24.	$ .75	$954	$4,759	$98,467
25–30.	$ .05	$8.91	$64.07	$180.63

31. What is the difference between nine thousand nineteen and seven thousand twenty-one?

32. From fifteen million two thousand four take eighteen.

33. From 100 thousand 82 take 1 thousand 9.

34. The greater of two numbers is 11,419, and the less is 7,255. What is the difference?

Oral Work.—C. *1.* A merchant pays one clerk $35 a month, and another $9 less. How much are the monthly wages of the second clerk?

2. From a board fifteen feet long, a carpenter cut off a piece nine feet long. What was the length of the part left?

3. A gentleman paid $22 for a lawn mower, and after using it one season, sold it for $9 less than cost. How much did he receive for it?

4. If you start from New York and travel north 90 miles, and then south 50 miles, how far will you be from New York?

5. An ice harvester housed 97 tons of ice one week, and 27 tons less the following week. How many tons did he house the second week?

6. Mark had 60 cents, and Thomas had 46. Mark spent as many cents as Thomas earned, and he then had 51 cents. How many cents did Thomas then have?

7. Peter husked 35 bushels of corn Monday, and 62 bushels Monday and Tuesday. How many more bushels did he husk Monday than Tuesday?

Written Work.—D. *1.* Oliver Goldsmith died in the year 1774, at the age of 46. In what year was he born?

2. A man died in the year 1799, aged 67 years. In what year was he born?

How many years elapsed

3. From the settlement of St. Augustine in 1565, to the settlement of New York in 1613?

4. Between the settlement of St. Augustine, and the settlement of Plymouth in 1620?

5. From the settlement of St. Augustine to the Declaration of Independence in 1776?

6. From the settlement of Plymouth until the discovery of gold in California in 1848?

7. From the discovery of America to the present year?

8. The taxes on a town are \$11,000; of this amount \$5,680 are county and state tax. What is the town tax?

9. The receipts of a machine-shop for a year are \$33,296, and the running expenses are \$22,535. What are the net earnings for the year?

10. Mount Sorata, a peak of the Andes, is 21,286 feet high, and 5,506 feet higher than Mont Blanc, the highest peak of the Alps. How high is Mont Blanc?

11. A contractor delivered 50,000 rifles for the army, but only 41,715 of them were accepted. How many of them were condemned as imperfect?

12. The minuend is one hundred twenty-five million three hundred sixty-five thousand nine hundred forty-eight, and the subtrahend is eight million seven hundred thousand nine hundred sixty-six. What is the remainder?

13. 26,957,229 bushels of salt, less 14,094,227 bushels are how many bushels?

14. A is worth \$25,864; B is worth \$1,350 less than A; C \$965 less than B; and D \$7,393 less than C. How much is D worth?

Note.—For *outlines of subtraction* for review, see page 269.

Review Problems.

Oral Work.—*1.* From $40 + 8 + 16 + 9 + 7 + 8 + 11$ take $20 + 10 + 25 + 7$.

2. From $13 + 10 + 5 + 12 + 7 + 9$ take $6 + 6 + 6 + 6$.

3. From 250 take $75 + 10 + 25 + 50$.

4. From $175 - 45$ take $25 + 25 + 9 + 9$.

5. A boy who had 45 doves, sold 20, and afterward bought 17 more. How many doves had he then?

6. A bell maker melted together 25 pounds of tin and 6 pounds of copper. He used 4 pounds of the bell-metal for call-bells, 8 pounds for hand-bells, and the remainder for sleigh-bells. How many pounds did he use for sleigh-bells?

7. A man owing $120, paid $49 one day, and $28 the next day. How much did he then owe?

8. Luther had $ .23, and earned $ .44. He then spent $ .27, and lost $ .05. How many cents had he left?

9. Jasper has 15 peaches in a basket, 4 in his pockets, and 3 in his hand. If he gives 5 peaches to Ann, and 7 to Jane, how many peaches will he then have?

10. A boy gave a dollar bill to pay for a slate that cost $ .36, a writing-book that cost $ .20, and some ink that cost $ .15. How much change should he receive?

Written Work.—*1.* A father and his two sons earned $2,395 in a year, the elder son earning $709, and the younger son $531. How much did the father earn?

2. On a certain day 93,825 persons entered the city of New York. Of this number 26,759 came by railroads, 60,048 by steamboats, and the others by steamships and sailing vessels from foreign countries. How many arrived from foreign countries?

3. A dealer paid $25,267 for horses, his expenses in taking them to market were $6,485, and he sold them for $37,496. How much were his profits?

4. From the sum of thirty-six million five, one hundred five thousand seven hundred one, and nine million nine thousand ninety, subtract the sum of ninety-six thousand three hundred, and forty-two thousand nine.

5. A woman received $439 for early vegetables, and $218 for poultry. The expense of raising the vegetables was $124, and of the poultry $84. What were her profits?

6. A speculator at one time gained $6,760, and then lost $3,400; at another time he gained $3,650, and then lost $3,954. How much did he gain in all?

7. January 1, A had property worth $10,350.75, but he owed $1,050.31. During the year he earned $1,156, and expended $975.25, and his property increased $550. How much was he worth at the end of the year?

8. A grocer purchased 370 hogsheads of sugar weighing 372,960 pounds, and sold 195 hogsheads weighing 196,725 pounds. How many hogsheads had he left, and what was their weight?

9. In five weeks 415,678 tons of coal were carried to Philadelphia by the Reading Railroad, 234,509 tons of which were carried in the first four weeks. How many tons were carried the fifth week?

10. On the first of January an edition of 11,000 copies of a book was published. In January 996 copies were sold, in February 1,025, in March 2,363, in April 1,808, in May 845, and in June 2,471. How many copies remained unsold, July 1?

Note.—Teachers who prefer that decimals should be studied in connection with integers, will now require their pupils to study subtraction of decimals, pages 123-125.

C

SECTION IV.

MULTIPLICATION.

Oral Work.*—61. *A.* *1. A wagon has 4 wheels. How many wheels have 3 wagons?

Three wagons have the sum of 4 wheels, and 4 wheels, and 4 wheels, which is 12 wheels. Or,

Three wagons have 3 times 4 wheels, which are 12 wheels.

2. How many wheels have 4 wagons?

3. How many feet have 5 horses?

4. How many hands have 2 men?   3 men?   4 men?

5. How many cherries are there in 2 clusters of 3 cherries each?   In 3 clusters?   In 4 clusters?

6. How many cents are 3 5-cent pieces?   Are 5 5-cent pieces?

How many are

7. 3 cherries and 3 cherries, or 2 times 3 cherries?

8. 4 boxes and 4 boxes, or 2 times 4 boxes?

9. 3 hats, and 3 hats, and 3 hats, and 3 hats, or 4 times 3 hats?

10. 4 mats, and 4 mats, and 4 mats, or 3 times 4 mats?

11. \$.02, and \$.02, and \$.02, and \$.02, and \$.02, or 5 times 2 cents?

12. 5 dimes and 5 dimes, or 2 times 5 dimes?

13. 5 times \$3, or 3 times \$5?   5 times 4 men, or 4 times 5 men?

B. *1.* How many are $2+2$? $2+2+2$? $2+2+2+2$?

2. How many are two 2's?   Three 2's?   Four 2's?

3. How many are 2 times 2?   3 times 2?   4 times 2?

Add	Subtract
4. By 2's, from 0 to 20.	*5.* By 2's, from 20 to 0.
6. By 3's, from 0 to 30.	*7.* By 3's, from 30 to 0.

62. *Multiplication* is the process of finding the sum of one of two numbers taken as many times as there are ones in the other.

   a. The number to be taken is the *multiplicand.*

   b. The number that shows how many times the multiplicand is to be taken is the *multiplier.*

   c. The multiplicand and multiplier are *factors.*

   d. The number obtained by multiplying is the *product.*

Multiplication may also be defined—a short process of adding equal numbers.

EXERCISES.

A. 7 times 8 are 56.

   1. Which of these numbers is the multiplicand?

   2. Which is the multiplier? Which is the product?

   3. Which are the factors?

   4. What is the product of the factors 10 and 7?

   5. What is the product of 6 times 8 loaves of bread?

   6. The factors are 5, 4, and 7. What is the product?

   7. The multiplicand is 8, and the multiplier is 5. What is the product?

B. In a garden are 5 rows of fruit-trees, and in each row are 7 trees. How many trees are in the garden?

First Solution.—In the garden are 7 trees + 7 trees + 7 trees + 7 trees, + 7 trees, which are 35 trees. Or,

Second Solution.—In the garden are 5 times 7 trees, which are 35 trees.

   7 trees, the *multiplicand* in the second solution, is *one of the equal parts* in the first solution.

   5, the *multiplier* in the second solution, is *the number of equal parts* in the first solution.

   35 trees, the *product* in the second solution, is *the sum* in the first solution.

63. Add   Subtract

1. By 4's, from 0 to 40.   *2.* By 4's, from 40 to 0.
3. By 5's, from 0 to 50.   *4.* By 5's, from 50 to 0.
5. By 6's, from 0 to 60.   *6.* By 6's, from 60 to 0.

64. The *sign* of *multiplication* is an oblique cross, $\times$. It is read *times*, or *multiplied by*.

5×8 may be read "5 times 8," or "5 multiplied by 8."

A. Read these exercises :

1. $7 \times 12 = 84$ *3.* $9 \times 63 = 567$ *5.* $3 \times 8 = 4 \times 6$
2. $4 \times 25 = 100$ *4.* $144 \times 25 = 3,600$ *6.* $3 \times 4 \times 5 = 60$
7. $3 \times 5 \times 6 = 10 \times 9$ *9.* $16 \times 14 = 4 \times 7 \times 8$
8. $2 \times 6 \times 12 = 3 \times 8 \times 6$ *10.* $6 \times 9 \times 4 = 2 \times 3 \times 6 \times 6$

Written Work.

B. Write each of these exercises, using the proper signs·

1. 5 times 25 are 125.   *4.* \$2.25 multiplied by 5 are \$11.25.
2. 15 times 4 quarts are 60 quarts.   *5.* The product of 2, 3, 4, and 5 is 120.
3. 3 times 7 equal 21.   *6.* 4 times \$ .63 are \$2.52.

C. Copy and complete

1. $4 \times 9 =$ *7.* 4 apples $\times 10 =$ apples.
2. $9 \times 4 =$ *8.* $3 \times 2 \times 5$ balls $=$ balls.
3. $8 \times 7 =$ *9.* $4 \times \$20 = \$$
4. $5 \times 10 \times 2 =$ *10.* $8 \times \$.05 = \$$
5. 6×7 melons $=$ melons.   *11.* $\$1.50 \times 2 = \$$
6. 10×4 apples $=$ apples.   *12.* $\$5.10 \times 3 = \$$

Oral Work.

D. Add   Subtract

1. By 7's, from 0 to 70.   *2.* By 7's, from 70 to 0.
3. By 8's, from 0 to 80.   *4.* By 8's, from 80 to 0.
5. By 9's, from 0 to 90.   *6.* By 9's, from 90 to 0.

Written Work.--**65.** Copy, complete, learn, and recite the

TABLE OF PRIMARY COMBINATIONS IN MULTIPLICATION.

$1 \times 1 =$	$2 \times 2 =$	$3 \times 3 =$	$4 \times 4 =$
$2 \times 1 =$	$3 \times 2 =$	$4 \times 3 =$	$5 \times 4 =$
$3 \times 1 =$	$4 \times 2 =$	$5 \times 3 =$	$6 \times 4 =$
$4 \times 1 =$	$5 \times 2 =$	$6 \times 3 =$	$7 \times 4 =$
$5 \times 1 =$	$6 \times 2 =$	$7 \times 3 =$	$8 \times 4 =$
$6 \times 1 =$	$7 \times 2 =$	$8 \times 3 =$	$9 \times 4 =$
$7 \times 1 =$	$8 \times 2 =$	$9 \times 3 =$	
$8 \times 1 =$	$9 \times 2 =$		$5 \times 5 =$
$9 \times 1 =$		$6 \times 6 =$	$6 \times 5 =$
	$7 \times 7 =$	$7 \times 6 =$	$7 \times 5 =$
$8 \times 8 =$	$8 \times 7 =$	$8 \times 6 =$	$8 \times 5 =$
$9 \times 8 =$	$9 \times 7 =$	$9 \times 6 =$	$9 \times 5 =$

$$9 \times 9 =$$

66. EXERCISES IN MULTIPLICATION AT SIGHT.

1	2	0	8	3	6	4	5	7	1	9 2
2	5	3	2	0	7	9	8	1	6	4 3
3	1	9	7	8	5	0	4	6	3	2 4
4	9	2	7	1	6	5	4	0	8	3 5
5	4	6	2	9	1	8	5	3	0	7 6
6	8	5	6	2	0	7	3	9	1	4 7
7	3	9	1	6	2	5	0	8	4	7 8
8	6	1	0	5	3	9	2	4	8	7 9

NOTE.—The preceding exercises are to be written upon the board, and used in class drill daily, until every pupil can give, at sight, the product of the numbers expressed by any two digits.

67. A number is either ***concrete*** or ***abstract.***

68. A ***concrete number*** is a number whose unit is named.

69. An ***abstract number*** is a number whose unit is not named.

    a. 5 apples, 70 days, $658 are concrete numbers.
    b. One, sixty-five, 19, 432 are abstract numbers.

a. Three, seven, four books, nine men.

b. 13 boys, 50, 72 hours, 365 days, 10,243.

1. In line **a** which numbers are abstract? Which are concrete? Why?

2. In line **b** which numbers are concrete? Which are abstract? Why?

3. What is the unit of each number in line **a**? In line **b**? Is it abstract or concrete?

EXERCISES.

Oral Work.—1. Five weeks are how many days?

2. How many hills of corn are there in 8 rows of 10 hills each? In 5 rows of 7 hills each?

3. $5 \times 8 =$ how many?   *5.* Multiply 15 by 4.
4. $3 \times 50 =$ how many?   *6.* Multiply 9 by 100.

How much must be paid for

7. 8 oranges, at 5 cents apiece?   *9.* 2 coats, at 15 dollars each?
8. 4 readers, at $.50 apiece?   *10.* 100 sheep, at $3 a head?

11. In each of these ten exercises, which number is the multiplicand? Is it an abstract or a concrete number?

12. In which of these exercises is the product an abstract number?

13. In which exercises is it a concrete number?

In each of the ten exercises,

14. Which number is the multiplier?

15. Is it abstract or concrete?

The multiplier is always considered an abstract number.

What is the product

16. Of 4 times 3 ?	*18.* Of 5 times 9 ?	*20.* Of 15×50 ?
17. Of 3 times 4 ?	*19.* Of 9 times 5 ?	*21.* Of 50×15 ?

In written work, either factor may be used as the multiplier.

70. PRINCIPLE I. *The multiplicand and product are like numbers.*

CASE I. **The multiplier a digit.**

71. *1.* Multiply 20 by 4.	*2.* Multiply 32 by 3.	*3.* Multiply 53 by 5.
4 times 2 tens or 20 are 8 tens or 80.	**3 times 2 are 6, 3 times 30 are 90, and 90+6 are 96.**	**5 times 3 are 15, 5 times 50 are 250, and 250 + 15 are 265.**

Multiply

4. 30, 50, 70, and 40 by 4.	*8.* $36 by 7, 4, 3, and 9.
5. 13, 24, 51, and 32 by 5.	*9.* $ .25 by 8, 5, 7, and 3.
6. 17, 47, 77, and 87 by 7.	*10.* 48 pounds by 3, 6, and 8.
7. 25, 75, 19, and 69 by 9.	*11.* 54 yards by 4, 7, and 9.

72. *A.* *1.* If a man can cut 8 acres of grass with a reaper in one day, how many acres can he cut in 3 days?

In 3 days he can cut 3 times as many acres as in one day, and 3 times 8 acres are 24 acres.

2. How much will 4 saddles cost, at $9 apiece?

3. A shipper of Western beef ships 4 car loads a day. How many car loads does he ship in 7 days?

4. If 8 bushels of apples will make a barrel of cider, how many bushels will make 9 barrels?

5. How much are 3 acres of hay worth, at $20 an acre?

6. How many yards are there in three pieces of carpeting of 60 yards each?

7. How many gallons of molasses are there in 5 casks of 40 gallons each?

B. 1. How much will 4 pounds of raisins cost, at 22 cents a pound?

2. How many yards are there in 3 pieces of linen, each piece containing 42 yards?

3. At $35 apiece, how much will 2 cutters cost?

4. If 32 quarts of milk are used in a hotel daily, how many quarts are used in 5 days? In a week? In 9 days?

5. How many hours are there in 3 days? In 8 days?

6. How much will 7 bushels of potatoes cost, at $.44 a bushel? At $.56? At $.63?

7. At 25 bushels to the acre, how many bushels of wheat can be raised on 5 acres? On 6 acres? On 8 acres?

C. 1. 4 times 2, plus 4 times 20 equal 4 times what number?

2. 3 times 2, plus 3 times 40 equal 3 times what number?

3. 2 times $5 + 2 times $30 = 2 times how many dollars?

4. 5 times 2 quarts + 5 times 30 quarts = 5 times how many quarts?

5. In finding 9 times 32 quarts, what is the first step? The second? The third?

6. In multiplying $16 by 9, how many steps are there, and what are they?

Give the steps, in order, in multiplying

7. 24 hours by 3; by 4; by 7.

8. In finding 7 times $.44; 7 times $.56; 7 times $.63.

9. In finding the product of 25 bushels multiplied by 5; by 6; by 8.

Written Work.—**73.** Ex. Multiply 473 by 9.

EXPLANATION.—I write the multiplier under the ones of the multiplicand, and begin at the right to multiply.

9 times 3 ones are 27 ones, or 7 ones and 2 tens. I write the 7 ones for the ones of the product;—the 2 tens are a part of the tens of the product.

PROCESS.

$$\begin{array}{r} 473 \\ 9 \\ \hline 4,257 \end{array}$$

9 times 7 tens plus the 2 tens are 65 tens, or 5 tens and 6 hundreds. I write the 5 tens for the tens of the product;—the 6 hundreds are a part of the hundreds of the product.

9 times 4 hundreds plus the 6 hundreds are 42 hundreds, or 2 hundreds and 4 thousands, which I write for the hundreds and thousands of the product.

The result, 4,257, is the required product.

PROBLEMS.

A	1	2	3	4	5
Multiply 246	543	3,269	9,624	18,932
by 3	7	5	8	4

6	7	8	9	10
$491	$5,427	$7,057	$108.94	$1,962.40
8	6	4	5	9

11	12	13	14
20,356 yards	257,008 feet	108,094 pounds	40,007 tons
7	3	2	9

B. 1. A carriage maker sold 7 covered carriages, at $325 each. How much did he receive for them?

2. A railroad company bought 6 locomotives, at $12,675 each. How much did they cost?

3. In one week a newsboy sold 246 papers, at 5 cents each. How much did he receive for them?

4. How much will 244 pairs of boots cost, at $4 a pair?

5. How many pounds are there in 3 barrels of salt, each barrel containing 280 pounds?

C 2

6. A mile is 5,280 feet. 8 miles are how many feet?

7. What will be the cost of building a horse railroad 4 miles long, at $12,768 a mile?

8. How many gallons are 8 times 27,645 gallons?

9. How many pounds are 5 times 32,051 pounds?

10. What is the product of 6 times 1,026,348?

11. How much will a laborer earn in 6 months, at $17.50 a month? At $18.75 a month?

12. How much will 7 tons of coal cost, at $6.34 a ton?

Case II. **The multiplier a digit with a cipher or ciphers on the right.**

Oral Work.

74. How much is   What is the product

1. 10 times 5 barrels?   *5.* Of 5 multiplied by 10?

2. 100 times 5 barrels?   *6.* Of 5 multiplied by 100?

3. 10 times 25 peaches?   *7.* Of 25 multiplied by 10?

4. 100 times 25 peaches?   *8.* Of 25 multiplied by 100?

Annexing a cipher to a number multiplies the number by 10. Hence,

75. Principle II. *Each removal of a number one place to the left multiplies the number by 10.*

1. At the rate of 4 bushels an hour, how many bushels of potatoes can a man dig in 10 hours? How many bushels in 10 days of 10 hours each?

2. In measuring depths at sea, 6 feet are a fathom. How many feet are 10 fathoms? Are 100 fathoms?

3. When the street-car fare is 5 cents, how much will 10 rides cost? How much will 100 rides cost?

4. If a joiner can make 8 window-frames in a week, how many can he make in 10 weeks?

5. How much will 10 barrels of beef cost, at $23 a barrel? At $27 a barrel?

6. A field of 10 acres of wheat yielded 36 bushels to the acre. What was the total yield?

7. How many barrels of flour will a teamster draw at 86 loads, if he draws 10 barrels at a load?

8. 32 quarts are a bushel. How many quarts are 10 bushels? Are 100 bushels? Are 1,000 bushels?

9. A box of 8 by 12 window-glass contains 75 panes. How many panes of glass are there in 10 boxes? In 100 boxes? In 1,000 boxes?

10. There are 98 pounds of flour in a half-barrel. How many pounds are there in 1,000 half-barrels?

11. What is the cost of 10,000 sewing-machines, at $24 apiece?

How is a number multiplied

12. By 10? Why?

13. By 10 × 10, or 100? Why?

14. By 10 × 100, or 1,000? Why?

15. By 10,000? By 100,000? By 1,000,000? Why?

76. How much is | What is the product of

1. 3 times 5 barrels?

2. 30 times 5 barrels?

3. 300 times 5 barrels?

4. 3 times 25 peaches?

5. 30 times 25 peaches?

6. 300 times 25 peaches?

7. 5 multiplied by 3?

8. 5 multiplied by 30?

9. 5 multiplied by 300?

10. 25 multiplied by 3?

11. 25 multiplied by 30?

12. 25 multiplied by 300?

13. At 9 cents a box, how much must I pay for 4 boxes of table salt? How much for 40 boxes?

14. At the rate of 7 miles an hour, how many miles will a boat sail in 10 hours? In 60 hours?

15. If 16 poles are required for a mile of telegraph line, how many poles will be required for 10 miles? How many for 30 miles? For 100 miles? For 300 miles?

16. 4 pecks are a bushel. How many pecks are 10 bushels? 50 bushels? 100 bushels? 500 bushels? 1,000 bushels? 5,000 bushels?

17. How much will 9,000 cords of wood cost, at $5 a cord?

Written Work.

77. Ex. Multiply 291 by 60.

PROCESS.

$$\begin{array}{r} 291 \\ 60 \\ \hline 17,460 \end{array}$$

EXPLANATION.—Since 60 is 10 times 6, I multiply 291 by 6, and to the product annex a cipher.

PROBLEMS.

In each of the next eight problems, write the product without writing the factors.

1. 100 times 75 =

2. 1,000 times 75 =

3. 100 times 392 =

4. 1,000 times 1,839 =

5. 392 × 10,000 =

6. 2,893 × 10,000 =

7. 478 × 1,000,000 =

8. 1,000,000 × 58,054 =

9	10	11
567	682	1,908
80	400	7,000

12	13	14
6,947	17,398	90,086
90,000	700,000	5,000,000

15. What is the product of 30 times 254?

16. Multiply 249 by 4,000. By 4,000,000.

17. What is the product of 600 × 972? Of 600,000 × 972?

18. Find the product of the factors 90,000 and 2,165.

19. How many bushels of oats will 800 horses eat in a year, allowing 183 bushels for each horse?

20. A tea merchant bought 700 chests of tea, each containing 42 pounds. How many pounds of tea did he buy?

21. How many gallons are there in a cargo of 7,000 barrels of kerosene, of 42 gallons each?

22. In 214 barrels of fish, containing 200 pounds each, are how many pounds?

23. Sixty minutes are one hour. How many minutes are twenty-four hours, or one day?

Find the cost

24. Of 300 hogsheads of molasses, @ $65.

25. Of 125 barrels of pork, @ $20.

26. Of 176 acres of land, @ $50.

27. Of 70 bushels of wheat, @ $1.25.

28. Of 500 bushels of corn, @ $.70.

29. Of 18 piano-fortes, at $270 each.

30. Of 150 chairs, at $.65 each.

31. Of 600 sheep, at $4.25 a head.

CASE III. **The multiplier two or more digits.**

Oral Work.—**78. A.** *1.* At 8 cents apiece, how much will 4 cocoa-nuts cost? How much will 20 cost? How much will 24 cost?

2. A cooper made 9 barrels a day for 32 days. How many barrels did he make in 2 days? How many in 30 days? How many in the 32 days?

3. At 6 cents for the use of 1 dollar for a year, how much must I pay for the use of 7 dollars? How much for the use of 30 dollars? For the use of 37 dollars?

How much is the cost

4. Of 84 pairs of boots, at $5 a pair?

5. Of 69 yards of cassimere, at $2 a yard?

6. Of 98 miles of railroad fare, at $.03 a mile?

7. Of 54 reams of book paper, at $7 a ream?

8. What is the product, when the multiplicand is ones?

9. When it is tens? | 10. Hundreds? | 11. Thousands?

B. 1. 5 times 25, plus 10 times 25 are how many times 25?

2. Then, how is 25 multiplied by 15?

3. How is any number multiplied by 15?

4. 2 times any number, plus 20 times the same number are how many times the number?

5. Then, how is any number multiplied by 22?

6. 5 times any number, plus 70 times the same number are how many times the number?

7. Then, how is any number multiplied by 75?

How is any number multiplied

8. By 36?	10. By 17?	12. By 215?	14. By 4,215?
9. By 84?	11. By 91?	13. By 975?	15. By 2,047?

79. Principle III. *The product resulting from multiplying one number by the ones, tens, hundreds, etc., of another, is the sum of the several products.*

These several products are called *partial products.*

1. 7 times 13,528 + 40 times 13,528 + 2,000 times 13,528 are how many times 13,528?

2. 7 + 40 + 2,000 times 13,528 are how many times 13,528?

Written Work.—80. Ex. Multiply 13,528 by 2,047.

<table>
<tr><td colspan="2" align="center">FULL PROCESS.</td><td align="center">COMMON PROCESS.</td></tr>
<tr><td></td><td align="right">13,528</td><td align="right">13,528</td></tr>
<tr><td></td><td align="right">2,047</td><td align="right">2,047</td></tr>
<tr><td rowspan="3">Partial products.</td><td align="right">94696 =   7 times 13,528 =</td><td align="right">94696</td></tr>
<tr><td align="right">541120 =   40 times 13,528 =</td><td align="right">54112</td></tr>
<tr><td align="right">27056000 =   2,000 times 13,528 =</td><td align="right">27056</td></tr>
<tr><td></td><td align="right">27,691,816 =   2,047 times 13,528 =</td><td align="right">27,691,816</td></tr>
</table>

EXPLANATION.—Writing the factors with the ones of the multiplier under the ones of the multiplicand, I multiply first by 7 ones, next by 4 tens or 40, and then—as there are no hundreds —by 2 thousands or 2,000, and write the first figure of each partial product under the figure of the multiplier used to obtain it.

I then add the partial products, and obtain 27,691,816, the required product.

PROBLEMS.

A.

1	2	3	4.	5
74	281	2,976	426	4,306
23	54	81	315	284

6	7	8	9	10
13,008	50,028	4,765	29,872	8,009
472	974	807	5,008	6,003

a. *Multiplying any number by 0 produces 0.*

b. *Multiplying 0 by any number produces 0.*

11. What is the product of 58 times 157?

12. 73 × 593 = how many? Multiply 17,248 by 9,005.

13. What is the product of 4,293 multiplied by 2,726?

14. 308 times 203 times 69 yards are how many yards?

15. A load of 74 bushels of oats, weighing 32 pounds to the bushel, weighs how many pounds?

16. In a barrel containing 87 dozens of eggs, are how many eggs?

17. A hoe factory that makes 1,396 hoes per week, makes how many hoes in a year, or 52 weeks?

18. A certain daily newspaper office uses 217 reams of paper per day. How many reams does it use in the 308 business days of a year?

19. If one mile of telegraph wire weighs 489 pounds, what will be the weight of the wire for a line of telegraph 138 miles long?

B 1	2	3	4	5
$31,075	$310.75	$50.44	$243.75	$1,274.09
36	36	705	215	8,047

6. A wholesale dealer sold 80 watches, at $75 each. How much did he receive for them?

7. The yearly wages of 307 men in a coal mine are $736 each. What is the amount of their wages for the year?

8. What is the value of 132 ounces of gold, at $16 an ounce?

9. One year the repairs on a canal 203 miles long, cost $382.75 per mile. What was the total expense?

10. What is the value of the 735 horses of a city horse-car line, at $149 each?

11. One week a butcher bought 356 lambs, at $3.56 a head. How much did they cost him?

12. At $.18 a gallon, what is the cost of a barrel of kerosene containing 42 gallons?

13. How much will 28 bushels of turnips cost, at $.31 a bushel?

How much must I pay

14. For 369 pounds of wool, @ $.64?

15. For 32 yards of body-Brussels carpeting, @ $2.19?

16. For 23 rolls of paper-hangings, @ $.27?

17. A milkman sells 219 quarts a day, at $.05 a quart. How much do his sales amount to in a year?

CASE IV. Each factor a digit or digits, with a cipher or ciphers on the right.

Oral Work.—**81.** *A.* Find the cost

1. Of a turkey that weighs 10 pounds, at $.20 a pound.

2. Of 50 pounds of sugar, at $.10 a pound.

3. Of 30 pounds of chickens, at $.20 a pound.

4. Of 20 pounds of salmon, at $.30.

5. Of 30 barrels of apples, at 150 cents, or $1.50.

6. Of 200 acres of land, at $10. At $20. At $50.

7. A barrel of pork weighs 200 pounds. What is the weight of 3 barrels? Of 30 barrels? Of 300 barrels?

8. There are 160 acres in a quarter-section of government land. How many acres are in 4 quarter-sections? In 40 quarter-sections?

9. How many pounds of butter are there in 40 fifty-pound tubs? In 400 fifty-pound tubs?

10. One year a grocer sold 80 thirty-pound tin cans of maple sugar. How many pounds of sugar did he sell?

B. How many are   What is the product

1. 3 times 20 windows?   *2.* Of 3 times 20, or 20 times 3?

3. 10 times 3 times 20 boards?   *4.* Of 30 times 20?

5. 4 times 200 bricks?   *6.* Of 4 times 200, or 200 times 4?

7. 10 times 4 times 200 shingles?

8. Of 40 and 200?

9. 100 times 3 times 50 rails?   *10.* Of 50 and 300?

How many ciphers are on the right of both factors, and how many are on the right of the product

11. In questions 1 and 2 ?	*13.* In questions 5 and 6 ?
12. In questions 3 and 4 ?	*14.* In questions 7 and 8 ?

15. In questions 9 and 10 ?

82. PRINCIPLE IV. *There are at least as many ciphers on the right of a product, as there are on the right of the factors which produce it.*

Written Work.—Ex. Multiply 7,200 by 160.

EXPLANATION.—Writing the factors with the right-hand digit of the multiplier under the right-hand digit of the multiplicand, I multiply the 72 hundreds of the multiplicand by the 16 tens of the multiplier, and obtain 1,152. To this I annex three ciphers—one for the cipher on the right of the multiplier, and two for the two ciphers on the right of the multiplicand.

```
PROCESS.

  7,200
    160
   432
  72
 1,152,000
```

The result, 1,152,000, is the required product.

PROBLEMS.

1	2	3	4	5
168	1,760	270	1,920	428,000
2400	39	960	650,000	720

6	7	8	9
480	9906432	4893700	596802
7000	789600	536000	307020

10. One month a rolling-mill made 5,800 bars of railroad iron, each bar weighing 402 pounds. How much did the whole weigh?

11. At the rate of 1,400 words an hour, how many words can be sent over a telegraph line in 30 hours?

12. How much will a yearly salary of $1,700 amount to in 12 years?

13. How much will it cost to fence 800 miles of railroad, at $150 a mile?

14. If a rope-maker can spin 19,240 feet of rope in a week, how many feet can he spin in 50 weeks?

15. A barge was loaded with 600 bales of hay, weighing 290 pounds each. What was the weight of the load?

16. How many grape-vines will be required for a vineyard of 40 acres, allowing 1,280 vines to the acre?

17. A nursery-man sold 2,800 young apple-trees, at $.17 apiece. How much did he receive for them?

18. How much will 50 bushels of peaches cost, at $2.50 a bushel?

19. How much must be paid for transporting 450 tons of freight from New York to St. Louis, at $27.50 a ton?

20. In a barrel of beef are 200 pounds. How many pounds are there in 37 barrels?

21. A planter raised 94 acres of cotton, which yielded 460 pounds to the acre. What was the total yield?

22. In a ream of paper are 480 sheets. How many sheets are there in 260 reams?

23. Required the cost of building a line of telegraph 680 miles long, at $1,250 a mile.

24. A manufacturer of reapers and mowers sold in one year 2,500 machines, at $130 each. How much did he receive for them?

25. The factors are three hundred ninety-seven thousand five hundred, and nine thousand eight hundred. What is the product?

83. RULES FOR MULTIPLICATION OF INTEGERS.

I. The multiplier a digit.

1. *Write the multiplier under the ones of the multiplicand.*

2. *Beginning at the right, multiply the units of each order in the multiplicand by the multiplier; in the product write the ones of each result, and add the tens to the next result.*

II. The multiplier a digit, with a cipher or ciphers on the right.

1. *Write the factors—the digit of the multiplier under the ones of the multiplicand.*

2. *Multiply the multiplicand by the digit of the multiplier, and to the product annex the ciphers.*

When the digit is 1—i.e., when the multiplier is 10, 100, 1,000, etc., —perform the process mentally.

III. The multiplier two or more digits.

1. *Write the multiplier under the multiplicand—ones under ones, tens under tens, and so on.*

2. *Beginning at the right, multiply the multiplicand by the ones, tens, hundreds, etc., of the multiplier, place the right-hand figure of each partial product under the figure of the multiplier used to obtain it, and add the partial products.*

IV. Each factor a digit or digits, with a cipher or ciphers on the right.

1. *Write the factors—the right-hand digit of the multiplier under the right-hand digit of the multiplicand.*

2. *Omitting the ciphers on the right of the factors, multiply as in Case III; and to the product thus obtained annex the ciphers.*

PROBLEMS.

A. 1	2	3	4	5
1,026,348	1,327	2,076	175,941	9,654
6	246	382	400,000	21,800

6	7	8	9	10
64	58,000	49,500	1,850	53,276
70,000	73	400	63,000	5,002

Ex. Multiply 654 by 9.

PROCESS.	MAKING THE COMPUTATION.
654	9 4's are 36; write 6 (add 3).
9	9 5's and 3 are 48; write 8 (add 4).
5,886	9 6's and 4 are 58; write 58.
	Result, 5,886.

11. An excursion train of 9 cars has 84 passengers in each car. How many passengers are on the train?

12. Every mile of a road 4 rods wide contains 8 acres. How many acres are there in 168 miles of such a road?

13. If 290 pounds of cheese are made from the milk of one cow, how many pounds can be made from the milk of 470 cows?

14. If a miller grinds 150 barrels of flour in a day, how many barrels will he grind in 56 days?

15. How many tons of iron will be required for 359 miles of railroad, at 97 tons to the mile?

16. How much will 282 street-cars cost, at $825 each?

17. One season a steamboat on the Hudson made 234 trips, and the average number of persons carried per trip was 108. How many persons did the boat carry during the season?

18. How many feet of lumber can be cut from 1,000 logs, each log making 642 feet?

Oral Work.—B. *1.* Ten kits of mackerel of twenty-five pounds each are how many pounds? One hundred kits are how many pounds?

2. A furrier sold 4 muffs at $30 apiece. How much did he receive for them?

3. How much must I pay for 5 pounds of beefsteak, at 16 cents a pound?

4. How many pounds of butter are there in 3 four-gallon jars of 32 pounds each?

5. How many miles will a steamboat run in 24 hours, if she runs 8 miles an hour?

6. How much will 40 silk hats cost, at $6 apiece?

7. Six spoons are a set. How many spoons are seventy-five sets?

8. What is the cost of 20 paper-weights, at $ .60 each?

Written Work.—C. Multiply

1. 7,945 and 70,087 by 7. | *3.* 4,386 by 9; by 800; by 3,764.
2. 4,670 and 37,500 by 40. | *4.* 89,760 by 787; by 20,960.

	5	**6**	**7**	**8**
Multiplicands,	6,597	892,367	84,720	967,008
Multipliers,	9	1,000	326,000	30,854

Find the product of the factors

9. 3,156, 592, and 8. | *12.* 47, 3,400, and $697.48.
10. $5,120, 786, and 25. | *13.* 90,876, 3,008, 90, and 45.
11. 98, $1.63, 39, and 9. | *14.* $897.28, 500, 17, 36, and 24.

15. If 245 pounds of charcoal are used in making 1 ton of gunpowder, how many pounds are used in making 1,056 tons?

16. A common clock strikes 156 times every day. How many times does it strike in a year?

17. A hotel keeper bought 23 barrels of eggs, each barrel containing 83 dozen. How many eggs did he buy?

18. A mail agent made 225 round trips each year for 13 years, over a railroad 108 miles long. How many miles did he travel?

19. 24 sheets of paper are a quire, and 20 quires are a ream. How many sheets are there in 45 reams?

20. How many buttons are there in 7 dozen packages, each package containing 10 cards, and each card 3 dozen buttons?

21. A shoe dealer bought 45 cases of ladies' French kid boots, each case containing 12 pairs, at $3 a pair. What was the amount of the purchase?

22. A Pennsylvania oil well flowed 237 days, at the rate of 345 barrels of oil per day. How much oil did it yield?

23. A manufacturer sold 319 sets of chairs, at $.65 apiece. How much did he receive for them?

NOTE.—For *outlines of multiplication* for review, see page 270.

Review Problems.

Oral Work.—*1.* A man built a fence in 10 days, building 32 rods each day. What was the length of the fence?

2. How far will an express train run in 9 hours, running 34 miles an hour?

3. A steamboat plies between two places that are 50 miles apart. How many miles does she run in 12 trips?

4. If a house rents for $60 a month, how much does the rent amount to in 10 months?

5. A merchant bought 5 pieces of cambric, of 44 yards each, at 10 cents a yard. How much did it cost him?

6. A fruit dealer bought 20 crates of peaches for $48, and sold them at $3 a crate. How much was his gain?

7. Mabel bought 10 yards of calico at 13 cents a yard, and 8 yards of ribbon at 20 cents a yard. How much did her purchases amount to?

8. 8 fields, of 80 acres each, contain how many acres?

9. In a flouring mill are 8 pairs of millstones, and each pair will grind 100 bushels of wheat per day. How many bushels of grain can the mill grind in a week?

10. A hatter bought 8 silk hats for $40, and sold them at $6 apiece. How much did he gain?

Written Work.—*1.* How many square miles are there in 25 townships of 36 square miles each?

2. In a factory are 10 lines of shafting; one of them weighs 882 pounds, and the other 9 weigh 462 pounds each. What is their total weight?

3. If you have $127 when you are 16 years old, and you save $39 each year until you are 21, how much money will you then have?

4. A book-keeper's wages are $56 a month, and his expenses for a year, or 12 months, are $608. How much does he save in a year?

5. A Government surveyor receives $150 a month, and expends $68. How much does he save in a year?

6. How many pickets will be required for the fence that encloses a lot 198 feet long, and 143 feet wide, allowing 3 pickets to the foot?

7. How much must I pay for 25 thousand feet of walnut lumber, at $41.81 per thousand?

8. At $6 per week, how much will 36 boarders pay for board in one year, or 52 weeks?

9. A stock train consists of 17 cars, each car containing 179 sheep. How much do all the sheep weigh, their average weight being 95 pounds?

10. A merchant bought 37 cases of prints, each case containing 12 pieces of 42 yards each. How many yards of print did he buy?

11. If I buy 40 horses at $120 each, and sell all of them for $5,000, how much do I gain?

12. A farmer raised 2 fields of potatoes. The first field, of 5 acres, yielded 102 bushels to the acre; and the second field, of 8 acres, yielded 119 bushels to the acre. How many bushels of potatoes did he raise?

13. A manufacturer pays 125 workmen $39 a month each. How much do their wages amount to in a year?

14. A farmer who raised 1,221 bushels of oats, kept 85 bushels for seed, and enough to winter 9 horses, allowing 50 bushels to each horse, and sold the balance. How many bushels did he sell?

15. Of 5 hogsheads of sugar, billed at 1,125 pounds each, the first was 72 pounds short, the second 56 pounds, the third 38 pounds, the fourth 112 pounds, and the fifth 47 pounds. How many pounds were in the 5 hogsheads?

16. A merchant bought 24 sets of crockery of 45 pieces each, 29 sets of 37 pieces each, and 36 sets of 80 pieces each. How many sets did he buy? How many pieces?

17. A drover bought 69 cattle, at $28.75 a head. He sold 27 of them, at $37.75 a head; and the remainder, at $36.50 a head. Did he gain or lose, and how much?

18. A provision dealer bought 806 barrels of fish, at $16.50 a barrel; and sold the lot at $1,847 more than cost. How much did he receive for it?

19. An agent sold 3 farms. For the first he received $675, for the second twice as much as for the first, and for the third 4 times as much as for the first and second. How much did he receive for the second? For the third? For the 3 farms?

Note.—Teachers who prefer that decimals should be studied in connection with integers, will now require their pupils to study multiplication of decimals, pages 126–129.

D

SECTION V.

DIVISION.

Oral Work.—**84.** How many   How many times

1. Are 2 — 2 ?   2. Can 2 be taken from 2 ?
3. Are 4 — 2 — 2 ?   4. Can 2 be taken from 4 ?
5. Are 6 — 2 — 2 — 2 ?   6. Can 2 be taken from 6 ?
7. Are 8 — 2 — 2 — 2 — 2 ?   8. Can 2 be taken from 8 ?
9. 4 is how many 2's?   How many times 2 ?
10. 6 is how many 2's?   How many times 2 ?
11. 8 is how many 2's?   How many times 2 ?
12. How many times is 2 contained in 4?   In 6?   In 8?

85. To *divide* a number is to separate it into equal parts.

When any number is divided

Into *two* equal parts, one of the parts is *one half* of the number ;

Into *three* equal parts, one of the parts is *one third* of the number ;

Into *four* equal parts, one of the parts is *one fourth* of the number ;

Into *five* equal parts, one of the parts is *one fifth* of the number ;

Into *six* equal parts, one of the parts is *one sixth* of the number ; and so on.

Divide

1. 2 into 2 equal parts.   7. 21 into 3 equal parts.
2. 4 into 2 equal parts.   8. 8 into 4 equal parts.
3. 6 into 2 equal parts.   9. 24 into 4 equal parts.
4. 8 into 2 equal parts.   10. 15 into 5 equal parts.
5. 3 into 3 equal parts.   11. 40 into 5 equal parts.
6. 12 into 3 equal parts.   12. 42 into 6 equal parts.

86. The equal parts into which any number is divided, are commonly called *fractional parts*, or *fractions*.

Halves, thirds, fourths, and fifths are written

$$\frac{1}{2} \qquad \frac{1}{3} \qquad \frac{2}{3} \qquad \frac{1}{4} \qquad \frac{2}{4} \qquad \frac{3}{4} \qquad \frac{1}{5} \qquad \frac{2}{5} \qquad \frac{3}{5} \qquad \frac{4}{5}$$

a. To find one half of a number:—*Divide the number by 2.*

b. To find one third of a number:—*Divide the number by 3.*

c. To find one fourth of a number:—*Divide the number by 4.*

d. To find one fifth of a number:—*Divide the number by 5.*

How much is

1. 1 half of 2?	*5.* 1 third of 21?	*9.* $\frac{1}{2}$ of 6?	*13.* $\frac{1}{3}$ of 54?
2. 1 half of 4?	*6.* 1 fourth of 8?	*10.* $\frac{1}{3}$ of 12?	*14.* $\frac{1}{5}$ of 80?
3. 1 half of 8?	*7.* 1 fourth of 24?	*11.* $\frac{1}{4}$ of 16?	*15.* $\frac{1}{4}$ of 72?
4. 1 third of 3?	*8.* 1 fifth of 15?	*12.* $\frac{1}{5}$ of 40?	*16.* $\frac{1}{6}$ of 42?

87. *A. 1.* When 2 quarts of milk cost 12 cents, how much does 1 quart cost?

1 quart costs 1 half as much as 2 quarts, and 1 half of 12 cents is 6 cents.

2. 2 pounds of crackers cost 16 cents. How much does 1 pound cost?

3. I paid $12 for 6 barrels of potatoes. What was the price per barrel?

4. If a steam-engine in a factory burns 27 tons of coal in 3 days, how many tons does it burn in 1 day?

5. In a garden are 20 trees in 4 equal rows. How many trees are in each row?

6. If I feed my chickens 1 bushel, or 32 quarts, of corn in 4 days, how many quarts will I feed them in a day?

7. If I divide 25 almonds equally among 5 children, how many almonds shall I give to each child?

B. *1.* At 2 cents apiece, how many peaches can I buy for 8 cents?

First Solution.—**At 2 cents apiece, I can buy as many peaches for 8 cents as the times 2 cents can be taken from 8 cents. 2 cents from 8 cents leave 6 cents, 2 cents from 6 cents leave 4 cents, 2 cents from 4 cents leave 2 cents, and 2 cents from 2 cents leave 0. Since 2 cents can be taken from 8 cents 4 times, . I can buy 4 peaches.** *Or,*

Second Solution.—**At 1 cent apiece, for 8 cents I can buy 8 peaches; and at 2 cents apiece, for 8 cents I can buy 1 half of 8 peaches, which is 4 peaches.**

2. How many boys' suits can be made from 18 yards of cloth, allowing 3 yards for a suit?

3. How many days will 20 pounds of flour last a family that uses 4 pounds a day?

4. How much shall I receive for 24 pairs of hose, at the rate of 4 pairs for a dollar?

5. If I drive my horse 5 miles an hour, how many hours will it take me to drive him 15 miles?

88. ***Division*** is the process of separating a number into equal parts.

    a. The number to be separated into equal parts is the ***dividend.***

    b. The number that expresses how many equal parts the dividend is to be separated into, is the ***divisor.***

    c. The number obtained by dividing is the ***quotient.***

When the numbers to be used for dividend and divisor are like numbers, the process of division is a short method of subtraction.

EXERCISES.

A. *1.* The dividend is 54 and the divisor is 6. What is the quotient?

2. What is the quotient of 63 divided by 7?

3. If 32 yards of carpeting be divided into breadths of 6 yards each, how many yards will there be of the remnant?

4. 56 loaves of bread are how many times 8 loaves?

5. How many times can you take 5 cents from 38 cents, and how many cents will remain?

6. Divide $40 into 8 equal parts.

7. Which number is the dividend, which the divisor, and which the quotient, in exercise 2? In exercise 4? In exercise 6?

8. In which of the exercises 1–6 is there no remainder?

9. What kind of a number is the quotient, in exercise 2? In exercise 4? In exercise 6?

B. Divide by 2 every second number	Divide into 2 equal parts every second number
1. From 2 to 20. *2.* From 20 to 2.	*3.* From 2 to 20. *4.* From 20 to 2.
Thus, 2 in 2 once, 2 in 4 2 times, and so on. **2 in 20 10 times, 2 in 18 9 times,** and so on.	**Thus, 1 half of 2 is 1, 1 half of 4 is 2,** and so on. **1 half of 20 is 10, 1 half of 18 is 9,** and so on.
Divide by 3 every third number	Divide into 3 equal parts every third number
5. From 3 to 30. *6.* From 30 to 3.	*7.* From 3 to 30. *8.* From 30 to 3.

89. The *sign of division* is a short horizontal line with a dot above, and a dot below it, $\div$. It is read *divided by.*

Division is also expressed by writing the dividend above, and the divisor below, a horizontal line.

$72 \div 6$ and $\dfrac{72}{6}$ are each read "72 divided by 6."

Read

1. $99 \div 9 = 11$	*3.* $\$513 \div 3 = \$171$	*5.* $\dfrac{315}{35} = 9$
2. $567 \div 81 = 7$	*4.* $81 \div 9 = 27 \div 3$	

Written Work.*—*A. Use the proper sign, and write

1. The quotient of 18 divided by 3 is 6.
2. 1 fourth of 60 quarts is 15 quarts.
3. 42 divided by 6 equals 7.
4. \$11.25 divided by 5 equals \$2.25.
5. 78 bushels divided by 6 equals 13 bushels.
6. Dividend, 120; divisor, 12; quotient, 10.

B. Copy and complete

1. $36 \div 9 =$	5. 45 melons $\div 5 =$ melons	9. $\$80 \div 4 = \$$
2. $56 \div 8 =$	6. 36 pears $\div 4 =$ pears	10. $\$.40 \div 5 = \$$
3. $42 \div 6 =$	7. 36 apples $\div 4 =$ apples	11. $\$1.50 \div 3 = \$$
4. $70 \div 7 =$	8. 72 cherries $\div 8 =$ cherries	12. $\$12.40 \div 2 = \$$

Oral Work.*—90. *A. Divide by 4 every fourth number

    1. From 4 to 40.
    2. From 40 to 4.

Divide into 4 equal parts every fourth number

    3. From 4 to 40.
    4. From 40 to 4.

Divide by 5 every fifth number

    5. From 5 to 50.
    6. From 50 to 5.

Divide into 5 equal parts every fifth number

    7. From 5 to 50.
    8. From 50 to 5.

Divide by 6 every sixth number

    9. From 6 to 60.
    10. From 60 to 6.

Divide into 6 equal parts every sixth number

    11. From 6 to 60.
    12. From 60 to 6.

B. I divided, equally, 12 plums between 2 girls, 12 pears among 3 girls, 12 peaches among 4 boys, and 12 apples among 6 boys.

1. Each girl had what part of the 12 plums? Of the 12 pears?

2. Each girl had how many plums? How many pears?

3. Each boy had what part of the 12 peaches? Of the 12 apples?

4. Each boy had how many peaches? How many apples?

5. If 9 curtains cost $36, what part of $36 does 1 curtain cost? How many dollars does 1 curtain cost?

6. One seventh of a farm of 70 acres is woodland. How many acres are woodland?

7. Five boys gathered forty quarts of chestnuts, which they shared equally. How many quarts had each boy?

8. How many hours must a man work each day, to do 80 hours' work in 8 days? In 10 days?

9. $.45 for 9 quarts of currants is how much a quart?

10. $56 for 8 weeks' board is how much a week? How much a day?

11. 100 bushels of wheat from 10 acres are how many bushels to the acre?

91. *A.* Copy, complete, learn, and recite the

TABLE OF PRIMARY COMBINATIONS IN DIVISION.

$2 \div 2 =$	$12 \div 3 =$	$24 \div 8 =$	$40 \div 8 =$
$3 \div 3 =$	$12 \div 4 =$	$24 \div 4 =$	$42 \div 6 =$
$4 \div 2 =$	$14 \div 2 =$	$24 \div 6 =$	$42 \div 7 =$
$4 \div 4 =$	$14 \div 7 =$	$25 \div 5 =$	$45 \div 5 =$
$5 \div 5 =$	$15 \div 3 =$	$27 \div 3 =$	$45 \div 9 =$
$6 \div 2 =$	$15 \div 5 =$	$27 \div 9 =$	$48 \div 6 =$
$6 \div 3 =$	$16 \div 2 =$	$28 \div 4 =$	$48 \div 8 =$
$6 \div 6 =$	$16 \div 8 =$	$28 \div 7 =$	$49 \div 7 =$
$7 \div 7 =$	$16 \div 4 =$	$30 \div 5 =$	$54 \div 6 =$
$8 \div 2 =$	$18 \div 2 =$	$30 \div 6 =$	$54 \div 9 =$
$8 \div 4 =$	$18 \div 9 =$	$32 \div 4 =$	$56 \div 7 =$
$8 \div 8 =$	$18 \div 3 =$	$32 \div 8 =$	$56 \div 8 =$
$9 \div 3 =$	$18 \div 6 =$	$35 \div 5 =$	$63 \div 7 =$
$9 \div 9 =$	$20 \div 4 =$	$35 \div 7 =$	$63 \div 9 =$
$10 \div 2 =$	$20 \div 5 =$	$36 \div 4 =$	$64 \div 8 =$
$10 \div 5 =$	$21 \div 3 =$	$36 \div 9 =$	$72 \div 8 =$
$12 \div 2 =$	$21 \div 7 =$	$36 \div 6 =$	$72 \div 9 =$
$12 \div 6 =$	$24 \div 3 =$	$40 \div 5 =$	$81 \div 9 =$

B. Copy, complete, learn, and recite the

TABLE OF EQUAL PARTS.

$\frac{1}{2}$ of 2 is	$\frac{1}{4}$ of 12 is	$\frac{1}{4}$ of 24 is	$\frac{1}{8}$ of 40 is
$\frac{1}{3}$ of 3 is	$\frac{1}{6}$ of 12 is	$\frac{1}{6}$ of 24 is	$\frac{1}{6}$ of 42 is
$\frac{1}{2}$ of 4 is	$\frac{1}{2}$ of 14 is	$\frac{1}{8}$ of 24 is	$\frac{1}{7}$ of 42 is
$\frac{1}{4}$ of 4 is	$\frac{1}{7}$ of 14 is	$\frac{1}{5}$ of 25 is	$\frac{1}{5}$ of 45 is
$\frac{1}{5}$ of 5 is	$\frac{1}{3}$ of 15 is	$\frac{1}{3}$ of 27 is	$\frac{1}{9}$ of 45 is
$\frac{1}{2}$ of 6 is	$\frac{1}{5}$ of 15 is	$\frac{1}{9}$ of 27 is	$\frac{1}{6}$ of 48 is
$\frac{1}{3}$ of 6 is	$\frac{1}{2}$ of 16 is	$\frac{1}{4}$ of 28 is	$\frac{1}{8}$ of 48 is
$\frac{1}{6}$ of 6 is	$\frac{1}{4}$ of 16 is	$\frac{1}{7}$ of 28 is	$\frac{1}{7}$ of 49 is
$\frac{1}{7}$ of 7 is	$\frac{1}{8}$ of 16 is	$\frac{1}{5}$ of 30 is	$\frac{1}{6}$ of 54 is
$\frac{1}{2}$ of 8 is	$\frac{1}{2}$ of 18 is	$\frac{1}{6}$ of 30 is	$\frac{1}{9}$ of 54 is
$\frac{1}{4}$ of 8 is	$\frac{1}{3}$ of 18 is	$\frac{1}{4}$ of 32 is	$\frac{1}{7}$ of 56 is
$\frac{1}{8}$ of 8 is	$\frac{1}{6}$ of 18 is	$\frac{1}{8}$ of 32 is	$\frac{1}{8}$ of 56 is
$\frac{1}{3}$ of 9 is	$\frac{1}{9}$ of 18 is	$\frac{1}{5}$ of 35 is	$\frac{1}{7}$ of 63 is
$\frac{1}{9}$ of 9 is	$\frac{1}{4}$ of 20 is	$\frac{1}{7}$ of 35 is	$\frac{1}{9}$ of 63 is
$\frac{1}{2}$ of 10 is	$\frac{1}{5}$ of 20 is	$\frac{1}{4}$ of 36 is	$\frac{1}{8}$ of 64 is
$\frac{1}{5}$ of 10 is	$\frac{1}{3}$ of 21 is	$\frac{1}{6}$ of 36 is	$\frac{1}{8}$ of 72 is
$\frac{1}{2}$ of 12 is	$\frac{1}{7}$ of 21 is	$\frac{1}{9}$ of 36 is	$\frac{1}{9}$ of 72 is
$\frac{1}{3}$ of 12 is	$\frac{1}{3}$ of 24 is	$\frac{1}{5}$ of 40 is	$\frac{1}{9}$ of 81 is

92. Divide by 7
every seventh number
 1. From 7 to 70.
 2. From 70 to 7.

Divide into 7 equal parts
every seventh number
 3. From 7 to 70.
 4. From 70 to 7.

Divide by 8
every eighth number
 5. From 8 to 80.
 6. From 80 to 8.

Divide into 8 equal parts
every eighth number
 7. From 8 to 80.
 8. From 80 to 8.

Divide by 9
every ninth number
 9. From 9 to 90.
 10. From 90 to 9.

Divide into 9 equal parts
every ninth number
 11. From 9 to 90.
 12. From 90 to 9.

93. Exercises in Division at Sight.

÷									
2) 6	12	18	4	10	16	2	8	14	20
3) 9	15	21	6	18	12	24	3	30	27
4)16	8	40	12	24	32	20	36	4	28
5)45	15	35	40	10	20	50	30	25	5
6)24	30	42	36	48	12	54	18	6	60
7)56	28	49	21	70	35	42	7	63	14
8)80	48	16	56	32	40	24	72	64	8
9)72	36	54	9	63	81	45	27	18	90

Note.—The preceding exercises are to be written upon the board, and used in class drill daily, until every pupil can give, at sight, the result in any one of the exercises.

***Oral Work.*—94. *A. 1.* How many five-dollar bills will pay for a cow that costs forty dollars?

2. At the rate of 4 quarts an hour, in how many hours will a boy pick 32 quarts of strawberries? 40 quarts?

3. Last winter Eliza attended school 50 days—5 days each week. How many weeks did she attend school?

4. A carpenter built a house in 54 days. How many weeks was he in building it?

5. When rice is 7 cents a pound, how many pounds can be bought for 35 cents?

6. At the rate of 9 plums for a cent, how much must I pay for 36 plums? For 54 plums?

B. 1. $80 for 10 stoves is how much for 1 stove?

2. 70 cents for 7 slates is how much for 1 slate?

3. A blacksmith used 32 nails in setting 8 horseshoes. How many nails did he use for each shoe?

4. In an orchard are 90 peach-trees in 9 equal rows. How many trees are there in a row?

5. A woman bought a sewing-machine for $36, and paid for it in 6 equal payments. How much was each payment?

6. One man can do a certain piece of work in 45 days. In how many days can 5 men do the same work?

95. Factor or Division Table.

4 is 2 times 2.	32 is 8 times 4, or 4 times 8.
6 is 3 times 2, or 2 times 3.	35 is 7 times 5, or 5 times 7.
8 is 4 times 2, or 2 times 4.	36 is 9 times 4, or 4 times 9, or
9 is 3 times 3.	6 times 6.
10 is 5 times 2, or 2 times 5.	40 is { 10 times 4, or 4 times 10;
12 is { 6 times 2, or 2 times 6;	8 times 5, or 5 times 8.
4 times 3, or 3 times 4.	42 is 6 times 7, or 7 times 6.
14 is 7 times 2, or 2 times 7.	45 is 9 times 5, or 5 times 9.
15 is 5 times 3, or 3 times 5.	48 is 8 times 6, or 6 times 8.
16 is 8 times 2, or 2 times 8, or	49 is 7 times 7.
4 times 4.	50 is 10 times 5, or 5 times 10.
18 is { 9 times 2, or 2 times 9;	54 is 9 times 6, or 6 times 9.
6 times 3, or 3 times 6.	56 is 8 times 7, or 7 times 8.
20 is { 10 times 2, or 2 times 10;	60 is 10 times 6, or 6 times 10.
5 times 4, or 4 times 5.	63 is 9 times 7, or 7 times 9.
21 is 7 times 3, or 3 times 7.	64 is 8 times 8.
24 is { 8 times 3, or 3 times 8;	70 is 10 times 7, or 7 times 10.
6 times 4, or 4 times 6.	72 is 9 times 8, or 8 times 9.
25 is 5 times 5.	80 is 10 times 8, or 8 times 10.
27 is 9 times 3, or 3 times 9.	81 is 9 times 9.
28 is 7 times 4, or 4 times 7.	90 is 10 times 9, or 9 times 10.
30 is { 10 times 3, or 3 times 10;	100 is 10 times 10.
6 times 5, or 5 times 6.	

Note.—The numbers in this table are to be written upon the board, and used in class drill daily, until every pupil can give, at sight, the factors of any number in the table.

1. Divide 72 feet by 9 feet.

1 foot is contained in 72 feet 72 times; and 9 feet are contained in 72 feet 1 ninth of 72 times, which is 8 times.

<table>
<tr><td>Divide</td><td>Find</td></tr>
<tr><td>*2.* 32 nails by 4 nails.</td><td>*7.* 1 seventh of 35 cents.</td></tr>
<tr><td>*3.* 90 trees by 10 trees.</td><td>*8.* 1 fifth of 30 quarts.</td></tr>
<tr><td>*4.* 45 days by 9 days.</td><td>*9.* 1 fourth of 40 pounds.</td></tr>
<tr><td>*5.* $36 by $6.</td><td>*10.* 1 eighth of $40.</td></tr>
<tr><td>*6.* 70 by 7.</td><td>*11.* 1 tenth of 80.</td></tr>
</table>

12. In which of the preceding exercises are the quotients abstract numbers?

13. In which are the quotients concrete numbers?

Principle I. *The dividend and quotient are always like numbers.*

The divisor must always be regarded as an abstract number.

What is the quotient of

<table>
<tr><td>*14.* $36 divided by $4?</td><td>*18.* $5 divided by $.20?</td></tr>
<tr><td>*15.* $120 divided by $30?</td><td>*19.* $25 divided by $.50?</td></tr>
<tr><td>*16.* $.75 divided by $.15?</td><td>*20.* $2.40 divided by $.08?</td></tr>
<tr><td>*17.* 150 cents divided by 25 cents?</td><td>*21.* $12.50 divided by $1.25?</td></tr>
</table>

If the given divisor is cents, and the dividend dollars, or dollars and cents, reduce the dividend to cents before dividing.

Case I. **The divisor ending with a digit.**

96. *A. 1.* A boy earned 80 cents in 4 days. How much did he earn in 1 day?

In one day he earned 1 fourth as much as in four days; and 1 fourth of 80 cents is 20 cents.

2. $90 for 3 cows is how much for 1 cow?

3. 120 hours of work in 10 days is how many hours per day?

4. 128 cents for 4 ducks is how much for 1 duck?

5. A farmer received $140 for wood, at $7 a cord. How many cords did he sell?

At $1 a cord, for $140 he would sell 140 cords; and at $7 a cord, for $140 he sold 1 seventh of 140 cords, which is 20 cords.

6. If a factory girl can weave 180 yards of carpeting in 6 days, how many yards can she weave in a day?

7. A teacher paid $3.60 for writing-books, at $.09 apiece. How many books did she buy?

8. How many suits of clothes can be made from 84 yards of cloth, allowing 4 yards to a suit?

9. A farm of 405 acres is to be divided equally among 5 heirs. How many acres will each heir receive?

B. 1. If a boy can gather 96 bushels of apples in 6 days, how many bushels can he gather in 1 day?

He can gather 1 sixth as many bushels in one day as in six days; *i. e.,* 1 sixth of 96 bushels.

96 bushels are 60 bushels plus 36 bushels; 1 sixth of 60 bushels is 10 bushels; 1 sixth of 36 bushels is 6 bushels; and 10 bushels plus 6 bushels are 16 bushels.

2. A merchant sold 144 spoons in sets of 6 spoons each. How many sets of spoons did he sell?

3. How many cars will be required to transport 280 tons of coal, at 8 tons to the car?

4. A farmer put up 272 gallons of cider in 8 casks. How many gallons did he put into each cask?

5. A gardener received $4.95 for radishes, at $.05 a bunch. How many bunches did he sell?

6. $276 for 4 acres is how much for 1 acre?

7. A printer uses 8 sheets of paper in making a book of 384 pages. How many pages of the book does 1 sheet make?

8. If 9 pounds of crushed sugar cost $1.35, how much does 1 pound cost?

9. 184 yards for 8 silk dresses is how many yards for 1 dress?

10. 1,080 bushels of oats from 20 acres is how many bushels from an acre?

C. 1. 1 fourth of 80, plus 1 fourth of 8 is 1 fourth of what number?

2. 60 divided by 3, plus 9 divided by 3 equals what number divided by 3?

3. $\frac{1}{7}$ of 140, plus $\frac{1}{7}$ of 28 equals $\frac{1}{7}$ of what number?

4. 80÷8, plus 48÷8 equals what number divided by 8?

Into what two parts will you separate the dividend,

5. In finding $\frac{1}{4}$ of 180?	*9.* In dividing 130 by 2?
6. $\frac{1}{6}$ of $2.22?	*10.* $275 by $5?
7. $\frac{1}{8}$ of 168 pails?	*11.* 864 yards by 9 yards?
8. $\frac{1}{8}$ of 384 brooms?	*12.* 546 pens by 7 pens?

D. What is each partial dividend, and what each remainder, in dividing

1. 215 soldiers into 8 squads?	*3.* 531 acres by 6 acres?
2. $4.32 into 5 equal parts?	*4.* 372 pounds by 9 pounds?

In problem 1, of what order of units is

5. The first partial dividend?	*8.* The second partial dividend?
6. The first quotient?	*9.* The second quotient?
7. The first remainder?	*10.* The second remainder?

Note.—Ask similar questions on each of the problems 2, 3, 4.

When a quotient contains two or more orders of units, the part of the dividend used to obtain the units of any order is a *partial dividend.*

Written Work.—**97.** Ex. Divide 936 by 3.

The divisor is commonly written at the left of the dividend, with a short vertical curve between them.

Divisor, *3)936* Dividend.

312 Quotient.

1	2	3	4	5
3)696	$4)$848	3 cents)639 cents	5)2,055	4)1,648

6   **7**   **8**   **9**

8)1,648   2)840 papers   6)1,260 bricks   7 tons)3,542 tons

98. Ex. Divide 36,824 by 8.

FIRST PROCESS.

$$8\,)\,36,824\,(\,4,603$$

EXPLANATION.— 1 eighth of 36 thousand, the first partial dividend, is 4 thousand and a remainder; and I write 4 for the thousands of the quotient. 4 thousand times 8 are 32 thousand, the part of 36 thousand divided; 32 thousand from 36 thousand leaves 4 thousand, the part of 36 thousand undivided; and 4 thousand (=40 hundred), plus the 8 hundred of the given dividend, is 48 hundred, the second partial dividend.

1 eighth of 48 hundred is 6 hundred; and I write 6 for the hundreds of the quotient. 6 hundred times 8 are 48 hundred, the partial dividend used; and as 0 hundreds remain undivided, the 2 tens of the given dividend is the third partial dividend.

1 eighth of 2 tens is 0 tens; and I write 0 for the tens of the quotient. The 2 tens (=20) undivided, plus the 4 ones of the given dividend, is 24 ones, the fourth partial dividend.

1 eighth of 24 is 3; and I write 3 for the ones of the quotient. 3 times 8 are 24, the partial dividend used; and there is no remainder.

The result, 4,603, is the required quotient.

SECOND PROCESS.

$$8\,)\,36,824$$
$$4,603$$

In the first process, the result of each step is written. This process is called *long division.*

In the second process, only the final result or quotient is written. This process is called *short division.*

Long division may be used with any divisor, large or small; short division should be used whenever the divisor is expressed by one figure.

99. The steps, in finding the units of each order in a quotient, are

   *1st. **Dividing**,* to find the number of units.

   *2d. **Multiplying**,* to find the part of the dividend divided.

   *3d. **Subtracting**,* to find the part of the dividend undivided.

   *4th. **Annexing*** to the remainder the units of the next lower order of the dividend, to form the next partial dividend.

NOTE.—In long division both divisor and quotient may be written at the right of the dividend; or the quotient may be written over the dividend, and the divisor at the left, as here shown (**1, 2**). In **1**, the factors of each partial dividend used are brought near together, and no space is occupied at the left of the dividend. In **2**, the place in which each figure of the quotient stands determines its local value.

```
        1                        2
                               273
 6825 | 25              25)6825
   50 | 273                 50
 ----                      ----
  182                       182
  175                       175
 ----                      ----
    75                        75
    75                        75
```

PROBLEMS.

Solve the first 14 of the following problems by long division, and then by short division.

1. If 4 tons of coal are used each day in an iron foundery, how many days will 3,284 tons last?

2. How many days will it take a girl to braid 1,203 straw hats, if she braids 3 hats each day?

3. A city fire department bought 3 fire-engines for $14,064. What was the cost of each?

4. Six men owning a coal bed, sold it to nine others for $39,150. How much did each seller receive, and how much did each buyer pay?

5. If you buy a store for $3,624, and pay for it in 3 equal yearly payments, how much will you pay each year?

6. A plantation of 1,845 acres was divided equally among 9 heirs. How many acres did each heir receive?

7. A business block of 7 stores cost $8,652. How much did each store cost?

8. An iron founder received $12.55 for castings, at $ .05 a pound. How many pounds did he sell?

9. An estate of $32,184 was shared equally among 4 heirs. What was the share of one heir?

10. $4,627 is the cost of how many tons of coal, at $7 a ton?

At $1 a ton $4,627 is the cost of 4,627 tons; and at $7 a ton $4,627 is the cost of 1 seventh of 4,627 tons, which is 661 tons.

PROCESS.

$$\$4,627 = 4,627 \text{ tons.}$$
$$7) \, 4,627 \text{ tons.}$$
$$661 \text{ tons.}$$

11. A boatman carried 5,688 barrels of Onondaga salt to New York, in 6 loads. How many barrels did he take in each load?

12. In how many days will a cooper make 2,712 barrels, if he makes 8 barrels each day?

13. If a teamster draws 5 loads of freight daily, in how many days will he draw 1,215 loads?

14. How many miles must I drive my horse each day, to drive 222 miles in 6 days?

15. My front fence is 10 rods long, and it cost me $130. How much did it cost per rod?

16. A stable keeper pays $576 for the hay to winter 32 horses. What does the hay for one horse cost?

17. 10,304 pounds of corn are how many bushels of 56 pounds each?

18. How many cars, each carrying 48 passengers, will be required to carry 384 passengers?

19. If the cost of constructing 42 miles of railroad is $2,032,632, what is the cost of constructing 1 mile?

20. In how many days can a paper-mill make 10,080 reams of note paper, if it makes 96 reams a day?

21. A manufacturer, having 1,096 ounces of silver, made from it as many coffee urns as possible, each weighing 45 ounces, and a salver of the silver that he had left. How much did the salver weigh?

22. A miller packed 13,475 pounds of flour in sacks, putting 49 pounds into each. How many sacks did he fill?

23. How much must a man earn in each of the 313 working days of a year, to earn $1,252?

24. A butcher paid $11,616 for 352 beeves. What was the cost per head?

25. Into how many farms, of 156 acres each, can 798 acres of land be divided?

26. A telegraph line 441 miles long was constructed at a cost of $443,205. What was the cost per mile?

27. A forwarder ships 93,000 barrels of flour from St. Paul to Pittsburgh, in cargoes of 5,136 barrels each. How many full cargoes does he ship?

28. How many bales, of 396 pounds each, can be made from 84,000 pounds of cotton?

29. At what price per head must I sell 105 sheep, to receive $563.85?

30. A stationer paid $228 for gold pens, at $1.90 apiece. How many pens did he buy?

31. For how many months must I rent a house, at $23.50 per month, to cancel a debt of $423?

32. A chair maker received $172.50 for chairs, at $7.50 a set. How many sets did he sell?

33. The salary of the President of the United States is $50,000 a year. How much is that a day?

34. If the directors of a railroad company appropriate $30,000 for the purchase of passenger cars, at $1,875 each, how many cars can be bought with the appropriation?

35. 1,405,169÷2,376=how many?

36. One year a manufacturer received $2,009 for gloves, at the rate of $12.25 per dozen pairs. How many dozen pairs did he sell?

37. A grocer paid $5,166 for sugar, at $30.75 per box. How many boxes did he buy?

38. How many steamboat bells, each weighing 649 pounds, can be made from 15,576 pounds of bell-metal?

39. Divide 919,734,140 by 22,705.

40. What is the quotient of 18,382,959÷56,217?

CASE II. **The divisor ending with a cipher or ciphers.**

Oral Work.

100. *A.* How much is

1. $\frac{1}{10}$ of 50 figures?
2. $\frac{1}{10}$ of 500 figures?
3. $\frac{1}{100}$ of 500 figures?
4. $\frac{1}{10}$ of 250 letters?
5. $\frac{1}{10}$ of 2,500 letters?
6. $\frac{1}{100}$ of 2,500 letters?

What is the quotient

7. Of 50 divided by 10?
8. Of 500 divided by 10?
9. Of 500 divided by 100?
10. Of 250 divided by 10?
11. Of 2,500 divided by 10?
12. Of 2,500 divided by 100?

B. *1.* In the number 25,000, what value is expressed by the 5?

What value will be expressed by the 5,

2. If it be removed one place to the right?

3. If it be removed two places to the right?

4. If it be removed three places to the right?

NOTE.—Ask questions similar to the last four concerning the 2 in this number, then concerning the 25.

How is the number 25,000 affected

5. By removing one cipher from the right?

6. By removing two ciphers from the right?

7. By removing three ciphers from the right?

PRINCIPLE II. *Each removal of a number one place to the right divides the number by 10.*

101. *A.* What is the quotient

1. Of $ .50 divided by $ .10 ?
2. Of $5 divided by $ .10 ?
3. Of $5 divided by 100 cents ?
4. Of $2.50 divided by $ .10 ?
5. Of $25 divided by $ .10 ?
6. Of $25 divided by 100 cents ?

How much is

7. $\frac{1}{10}$ of $ .50, or 50 cents ?
8. $\frac{1}{10}$ of $5, or 500 cents ?
9. $\frac{1}{100}$ of $5 ?
10. $\frac{1}{10}$ of $2.50, or 250 cents ?
11. $\frac{1}{10}$ of $25 ?
12. $\frac{1}{100}$ of $25 ?

a. To change dollars to cents :—*Multiply by 100.*

b. To change dollars and cents to cents :—*Omit the dollar mark and the decimal point.*

What is the quotient of

13. $7 ÷ 10 ?
14. $72 ÷ 10 ?
15. $725 ÷ 10 ?
16. $7 ÷ 100 ?
17. $72 ÷ 100 ?
18. $725 ÷ 100 ?
19. $7.20 ÷ 10 ?
20. $72.50 ÷ 10 ?
21. $725.40 ÷ 10 ?

a. To divide a number expressing dollars by 10 :—*Place a decimal point before the ones.*

b. To divide a number expressing dollars by 100 :—*Place a decimal point before the tens.*

B. 1. A farmer sowed 30 bushels of plaster on a field of 10 acres. How many bushels did he sow to the acre ?

2. In a regiment are 900 soldiers, in companies of 100 each. How many companies are in the regiment ?

3. How much is 1 tenth of 720 boxes of figs ?

Divide

4. $40 by 10.
5. $27 by 10.
6. $150 by 10.
7. $21.50 by 10.
8. $15.80 by 10.
9. $134.20 by 10.
10. $275 by 100.
11. $830 by 100.
12. $506 by 100.

13. A wheelwright received $60 for wagon wheels, at $10 a set. How many sets did he sell ?

14. A housekeeper paid one dollar for strawberries, at 10 cents a quart. How many quarts did she buy ?

15. I have 84 hours' work to do.   If I work 10 hours a day, how many full days shall I work, and how many hours shall I work the last day?

16. At $.10 apiece, how many pine-apples can I buy for $.47, and how much money will I have left?

17. $1.50 for 10 melons is how much for 1 melon?

18. $15 for 10 days' work is how much a day?

19. $84 for 100 straw hats is how much for one hat?

20. $6,250 for 100 acres of land is how much an acre?

21. A plasterer earned $36.50 in 10 days.   How much was that per day?

Written Work.

102. Ex. Divide 2,764 by 10, and by 100.

EXPLANATION.—I divide 2,764 by 10, by cutting off one figure from the right; and by

PROCESSES.

$$2{,}764 \div 10 = 276 \mid 4 = 276\tfrac{4}{10}$$

$$2{,}764 \div 100 = 27 \mid 64 = 27\tfrac{64}{100}$$

100, by cutting off two figures from the right.

The figures of the dividend not cut off express the integers of the quotient, and those cut off express the part of the dividend remaining undivided.   This remainder, written over the divisor, expresses the fractional part of the quotient.

The results, $276\tfrac{4}{10}$ and $27\tfrac{64}{100}$, are the quotients required.

What is the divisor, what figures express the integers of the quotient, and what figures the fractional part,

1. When you cut off one figure from the right of a number?

2. When you cut off two figures from the right?

3. When you cut off three figures from the right?

4. When you cut off four figures?   Five figures?   Six figures?

5. When you cut off any number of figures?

PROBLEMS.

Divide

1. 647,500 by 100.
2. 1,627,000 by 1,000.
3. 76,275 by 1,000.
4. 324,700,000 by 10,000.
5. 725,000,000 by 100,000.
6. 32,967,816 by 10,000.

Find the price of 1, when

7. 10 cost $43.
8. 10 cost $.80.
9. 10 cost $262.50.
10. 100 cost $375.
11. 100 cost $1,850.
12. 1,000 cost $560.

13. A farmer having $1,807, bought horses at $100 each. How many horses did he buy, and how many dollars had he left?

14. A capitalist invests $375,000 in United States Government bonds, at $1,000 each. How many bonds does he buy?

15. How many freight-cars will be required to transport 58,293 barrels of flour, if 100 barrels make one car load?

Oral Work.—**103. A.** How much is

1. $\frac{1}{10}$ of 60?
2. $\frac{1}{2}$ of $\frac{1}{10}$ of 60?
3. $\frac{1}{20}$ of 60?
4. $\frac{1}{10}$ of 70?
5. $\frac{1}{2}$ of $\frac{1}{10}$ of 70?
6. $\frac{1}{20}$ of 70?
7. $\frac{1}{100}$ of 2,400?
8. $\frac{1}{6}$ of $\frac{1}{100}$ of 2,400?
9. $\frac{1}{600}$ of 2,400?
10. $\frac{1}{100}$ of 2,485?
11. $\frac{1}{6}$ of $\frac{1}{100}$ of 2,485?
12. $\frac{1}{600}$ of 2,485?
13. $\frac{1}{100}$ of 2,785?
14. $\frac{1}{6}$ of $\frac{1}{100}$ of 2,785?
15. $\frac{1}{600}$ of 2,785?

B. What is the quotient

1. Of $\frac{1}{10}$ of 60 ÷ 3?
2. Of 60 ÷ 30?
3. Of $\frac{1}{10}$ of 80 ÷ 3?
4. Of 80 ÷ 30?
5. Of $\frac{1}{10}$ of 84 ÷ 3?
6. Of 84 ÷ 30?
7. Of $\frac{1}{100}$ of 4,800 ÷ 8?
8. Of 4,800 ÷ 800?
9. Of $\frac{1}{100}$ of 4,837 ÷ 8?
10. Of 4,837 ÷ 800?
11. Of $\frac{1}{100}$ of 5,137 ÷ 8?
12. Of 5,137 ÷ 800?

13. What is the fractional part of the quotient in problem 4, and how is it formed?

NOTE.—Ask similar questions concerning problems 6, 10, and 12.

C. 1. A milkman paid $320 for cows, at $40 apiece. How many cows did he buy?

2. At $50 a light, how many lights of French plate window-glass can be bought for $400?

3. At $.60 a bushel, how many bushels of potatoes can be bought for $15?

4. A merchant tailor sold 50 coats for $450. How much did he receive apiece for them?

5. A milliner received $7.50 for ribbon, at $.30 a yard. How many yards did she sell?

6. At $.20 apiece, how many water-melons can I buy for $1.38, and how much money will I have left?

7. $720 for 300 yards of cloth is how much a yard?

8. A fruit dealer packed 2,250 bushels of apples in 900 barrels. How many bushels did he put in a barrel?

9. How much is 1 fortieth of 2,800 barrels of flour?

10. 1,600 pounds of pork are how many barrels of 200 pounds each?

11. 5,400 pounds of wheat are how many bushels of 60 pounds each?

Written Work.—**104.** Ex. Divide 53,485 by 700.

EXPLANATION.—Since $700 = 7$ times 100, I first divide by 100, and the result thus obtained by 7.

Dividing 53,485 by 100, I have 534, with 85 remaining undivided.

PROCESS.

$$7|00\,)\,5\,3,4\,|\,8\,5$$
$$7\,6\;\tfrac{285}{700}$$

Dividing 534, the integral part of the first quotient, by 7, I have 76, with 2 remaining undivided. This 2 is a part of the 4 hundred of the given dividend, and therefore is 2 hundred. Annexing the first remainder, 85, to this 2 hundred, I have 285, the whole remainder; and this, written over the given divisor, 700, forms $\tfrac{285}{700}$, the fractional part of the quotient.

The final result, $76\tfrac{285}{700}$, is the quotient required.

PROBLEMS.

1. At $1,200 each, how many steam-tugs can be bought for $18,000?

2. A lumberman received $3,840 for lumber, at $20 per thousand feet. How many thousand feet did he sell?

3. A company purchase a railroad for $1,656,750, and the payments are to be $250,000 annually. How many payments do they make, and how much is the last payment?

4. A miller purchased 9,478 pounds of wheat. How many bushels did he buy, allowing 60 pounds to the bushel?

5. In one ream of paper there are 20 quires. How many full reams are there in 1,976 quires?

6. An agent sold parlor organs at $130 each, and received $6,240. How many organs did he sell?

7. A wholesale grocer bought 3,440 pounds of tea, in 80-pound chests. How many chests did he buy?

8. There are 60 minutes in an hour. 1,440 minutes are how many hours?

Divide

9. 387,695 by 4,500.
10. 382,775 by 2,500.
11. 8,329,659 by 365,000.
12. 255,837,432,000 by 700,000.

What is the quotient of

13. $299,392 \div 24,000$?
14. $87,693,275 \div 41,700$?
15. $10,735,000 \div 75,000$?
16. $12,600,000 \div 120,000$?

17. If I pay $13,750 for a farm of 550 acres, how much do I pay per acre?

18. The dividend is 87,693,275, and the divisor is 41,700. Find the quotient and the remainder.

19. A Government agent bought cavalry horses at $160 apiece, and expended $60,160. How many horses did he buy?

105. Rules for Division of Integers.

I. The divisor ending with a digit.

1. *Write the divisor at the left of the dividend, and draw a line between them; also a line either under or at the right of the dividend, to separate it from the quotient.*

2. *Divide the first partial dividend by the divisor, and place the result in the quotient; multiply the divisor by this quotient, and subtract the product from the partial dividend.*

3. *Annex to the remainder the units expressed by the next figure of the dividend, and divide the partial dividend thus formed as before.*

4. *Proceed in the same manner with each partial dividend; and, in the quotient, place the final remainder over the divisor.*

II. The divisor ending with a cipher or ciphers.

1. *Cut off the cipher or ciphers, and an equal number of figures from the right of the dividend.*

2. *Divide the remaining part of the dividend by the remaining part of the divisor, and to the last remainder annex the figures cut off from the dividend, for the final remainder.*

  a. When any partial dividend is less than the divisor, place 0 in the quotient; then, to this partial dividend annex the units expressed by the next figure of the dividend, to form the next partial dividend.

  b. When the divisor is 10, 100, 1,000, etc., perform the process mentally.

Note.—Show pupils how to proceed

1. When any product is greater than the partial dividend from which it is to be taken.

2. When the remainder is equal to, or greater than the divisor.

3. To find a quotient figure *by trial*, when the divisor is expressed by more than one figure; *i. e.*, to use the first one or two left-hand figures of the divisor for a *trial divisor*, and an equal number, or one more, of the left-hand figures of the dividend for a *trial dividend.*

PROBLEMS.

A.

1	**2**	**3**	**4**	**5**
6)4,986	8)7,300,528	29)70,235(	10)87,690	100)37,296

6	**7**	**8**
2,500)998,600(	500,000)725,000,000	705)806,450(

9

468)908,808(

10. Divide 4,368 by 6, and by 24.

MAKING THE COMPUTATIONS.

PROCESSES.

1

6)4,368

6 in 43, 7 times (1 remaining); write 7.
6 in 16, 2 times (4 remaining); write 2.
6 in 48, 8 times; write 8. Result, 728.

728

2

24)4,368(182

24 in 43, once; write 1. Once 24 is 24; 24
   from 43 leaves 19; annex 6.
24 in 196, 8 times; write 8. 8 times 24 are
   192; 192 from 196 leaves 4; annex 8.
24 in 48, 2 times; write 2. 2 times 24 are 48;
   48 from 48 leaves 0.
     Result, 182.

24
196
192
48
48

Divide

11. 3,279 by 6; by 8; by 7.

12. 41,220 by 10; by 15; by 20.

13. $408.75 by $3.27; by $1.25.

14. 1,050, 22,365, and 50,000 by 700.

15. $25.25, $100.75, and $492.50 by 25.

16. 996, 48,009, and 65,525 by 150.

Dividends.	Divisors.	Quotients.
17. 1,458	9	—
18. $763	5	—
19. 1,728	6	—
20. $8.64	$.08	—

21. 493 ÷ 12 =

22. 518 ÷ 32 =

23. 674 ÷ 13 =

24. $72.60 ÷ 15 =

25. $5,500 ÷ $1.25 =

26. $\dfrac{8,654,300}{9,000} =$

27. $\dfrac{7,000,888}{758} =$

28. $\dfrac{4,235,262}{1,294} =$

Oral Work.*—*1. A furrier received $400 for buffalo-robes, at $10 apiece.   How many robes did he sell?

2. Carrie paid $.90 for needles, at $.06 a paper.   How many papers did she buy?

3. $588 for 6 lumber wagons is how much apiece?

4. $475 for 5 acres of land is how much per acre?

5. $3.76 for 4 baskets of peaches is how much a basket?

6. A lumberman banked 110 logs in 5 days.   How many logs was that per day?

7. If a Mississippi steamboat burns 7 cords of wood per day, in how many days will she burn 301 cords?

8. How many hours will it take a steamboat to run 270 miles, running 9 miles an hour?

9. A joiner cut a strip of moulding 168 inches long, into 7 equal pieces.   How long was each piece?

10. At $.10 apiece, how many copy-books can I buy with $.75, and how much money will I have remaining?

Written Work.*—*B.* *1. How many sheep are 1 fourth of 16,236 sheep?

2. An Ohio farmer exchanged his wheat crop of 1,965 bushels, for flour, receiving 1 barrel of flour for every 5 bushels of wheat.   How much flour did he receive?

3. If a ship sails from New York to Greece—4,800 miles—in 25 days, what is her daily rate of speed?

4. A company of 96 immigrants purchased a tract of 43,200 acres of Texas lands, which they shared equally. How many acres did each immigrant receive?

5. How many dress patterns of 13 yards each, can be cut from a piece of mohair containing 43 yards?

6. A dealer received $1,680 for sewing-machines, at $35 apiece.   How many machines did he sell?

7. In how many days can 112 men do 4,928 days' work?

8. A fruit dealer sold 686 baskets of peaches for $1,543.50. What was the price per basket?

9. A nursery-man sold 6,872 young apple-trees for $1,030.80. How much did he receive apiece for them?

10. 1 hundredth of 50,000 oranges are how many oranges?

11. A pork buyer packed 237,600 pounds of pork in barrels of 200 pounds each. How many barrels did he fill?

12. If a factory makes 275 yards of cloth daily, in how many days will it make 57,475 yards?

13. The expenses of a party of 8 men on a journey to California, were $1,072. What was each man's share?

14. A farmer harvested 2,520 bushels of oats from 36 acres. What was the yield per acre?

15. A forwarder shipped 74,232 bushels of grain in 18 equal cargoes. How many bushels were in each cargo?

16. A farmer made 962 gallons of cider, which he put into casks holding 41 gallons each. How many full casks had he?

17. An army contractor paid $39,865 for 2,345 barrels of beef. How much did the beef cost him per barrel?

18. A miller purchased 1,157 bushels of wheat weighing 69,420 pounds. What was the weight of one bushel?

19. The yearly cost of keeping a turnpike-road in repair is $1,407.60, at the rate of $30.60 per mile. How many miles long is the road?

20. 39,520 quires of paper are 1,976 reams. How many quires are one ream?

21. How many kettles, each weighing 348 pounds, can be made from 20,000 pounds of iron?

106. The average of two numbers is one half of their sum; of three numbers, one third of their sum; of four numbers, one fourth of their sum; and, in general,

The ***average of two or more numbers*** is the quotient of their sum divided by the number of numbers.

PROBLEMS.

What is the average

1. Of 284 and 150?
2. Of 375 and 645?
3. Of 49, 196, and 442?
4. Of 266, 55, and 738?
5. Of 84, 79, 263, and 590?
6. Of 808, 103, and 643?

7. The ages of 3 boys are 6, 9, and 12 years. What is the average of their ages?

8. What is the average width of a board that is 8 inches wide at one end and 14 inches wide at the other?

9. A man walked in 3 successive days 47 miles, 29 miles, and 17 miles. What was his average daily distance?

10. A grocer bought 3 hogsheads of molasses containing, respectively, 135 gallons, 143 gallons, and 127 gallons. What was the average number of gallons to a hogshead?

11. In a village school the number of pupils in attendance Monday was 134, Tuesday 128, Wednesday 143, Thursday 133, and Friday 147. What was the average daily attendance?

12. At a carpet manufactory 19,110 yards of carpet were woven in 78 days. What was the average number of yards woven daily?

13. Find the average price of 28 acres of land at $36 an acre, and 35 acres at $27 an acre.

14. A merchant's sales Monday amounted to $348.91, Tuesday to $317.07, Wednesday to $294.63, Thursday to $336, Friday to $332.87, and Saturday to $369. How much were his average daily sales?

NOTE 1.—For *outlines of division* for review, see page 270.

NOTE 2.—Teachers who prefer that decimals should be studied in connection with integers, will now require their pupils to study division of decimals, pages 130–138.

SECTION VI.

SIXTEEN GENERAL PROBLEMS IN INTEGERS.

Oral Work.—**107. A. 1.** The parts are 21, 7, 5, and 9.   What is the sum?

2. Charles has 17 cents, James has 13 cents, John has 25 cents, and Luke has 20 cents.   What sum of money have the four boys?

3. The sum of two numbers is 48, and one of the numbers is 18.   What is the other number?

4. In two nests are 27 eggs, and 9 of them are in one nest.   How many eggs are in the other nest?

5. The sum of five numbers is 56, and four of the numbers are 12, 7, 8, and 11.   What is the other number?

6. I have a farm of 80 acres, divided into seven fields. Six of the fields contain, respectively, 15 acres, 10 acres, 13 acres, 7 acres, 18 acres, and 9 acres.   How many acres does the seventh field contain?

Note.—Require pupils to state, briefly and accurately, the process called for by each of the sixteen problems in this section.

Problem I. *The parts given; to find their sum.*

Problem II. *The sum of two numbers, and one of them given; to find the other number.*

Problem III. *The sum of more than two numbers, and all but one of them given; to find that one.*

B. 1. What is the difference between 75 and 89?

2. The greater of two numbers is 51, and the less is 30.   What is the difference?

3. The foremast of a ship is 83 feet high, and the mainmast is 99 feet high.   What is the difference in their heights?

4. The minuend is 42, and the subtrahend is 25. What is the remainder?

5. I have 36 bushels of apples. If I keep 22 bushels, and sell the remainder, how many bushels shall I sell?

6. The minuend is 42, and the remainder is 17. What is the subtrahend?

7. A butcher having $63, paid a part of his money for sheep, and had $18 remaining. How much did the sheep cost him?

8. The greater of two numbers is 89, and the difference is 55. What is the less number?

9. A, who has more money than B, has $125; and the difference between his money and B's is $82. How much money has B?

10. The subtrahend is 32, and the remainder is 68. What is the minuend?

11. How many chestnuts must a boy have, that he may eat 75 of them, and have a remainder of 45?

12. The less of two numbers is 130, and their difference is 95. What is the greater number?

13. In the less of two piles of wood are 135 cords, and the difference between the piles is 45 cords. How many cords of wood are in the greater pile?

PROBLEM IV. *Two numbers given; to find their difference.*

PROBLEM V. *The minuend and subtrahend given; to find the remainder.*

PROBLEM VI. *The minuend and remainder given; to find the subtrahend.*

PROBLEM VII. *The subtrahend and remainder given; to find the minuend.*

PROBLEM VIII. *The greater of two numbers, and their difference given; to find the less number.*

PROBLEM IX. *The less of two numbers, and their difference given; to find the greater number.*

C. 1. The multiplicand is 16, and the multiplier is 7. What is the product?

2. The factors are 2, 8, 5, and 4. What is the product?

3. In 8 windows of 12 panes of glass each, are how many panes of glass?

4. At 3 cents each, how much will 1 dozen lemons cost? How much will 5 dozen cost?

5. The product is 72, and the multiplier is 4. What is the multiplicand?

6. The product is 96, and the multiplicand is 16. What is the multiplier?

7. I paid $72 for 4 tons of hay. What was the price of 1 ton?

8. 96 tons of freight will make how many car loads, of 16 tons each?

9. The product of four factors is 320, and three of the factors are 2, 5, and 4. What is the other factor?

10. I pay 5 carpenters $180, at the rate of $2 a day. How many weeks do they work?

PROBLEM X. *The multiplicand and multiplier given; to find the product.*

PROBLEM XI. *Any number of factors given; to find the product.*

PROBLEM XII. *The product of two factors, and either factor given; to find the other factor.*

PROBLEM XIII. *The product of more than two factors, and all the factors but one given; to find that factor.*

D. *1.* The dividend is 144, and the divisor is 8. What is the quotient?

2. 360 bushels of oats will fill how many 3-bushel bags?

3. 96 panes of glass for 8 windows, are how many panes for 1 window?

4. The divisor is 7, and the quotient is 14. What is the dividend?

5. The divisor is 8, and the quotient is $6\frac{5}{8}$. What is the dividend?

What is the dividend

6. If the divisor is 8 miles, and the quotient is 15?

7. If the divisor is 12 dozen, and the quotient is $9\frac{7}{12}$?

How much money must I have, that I may divide it

8. Among 16 persons, and give each person $10?

9. Among 16 persons, and give each person $10\frac{11}{16}$?

10. The dividend is $2.25, and the quotient is 25. What is the divisor?

11. The dividend is 147 hours, and the quotient is 21 hours. What is the divisor?

Problem XIV. *The divisor and dividend given; to find the quotient.*

Problem XV. *The divisor and quotient given; to find the dividend.*

Problem XVI. *The dividend and quotient given; to find the divisor.*

Written Work.—*1.* The parts are 954, 3,420, 75, 3,659, 251, 8,000, 11,756, 8, 9,999, 730, and 28,028. What is the sum?

2. The minuend is 9,000,001, and the subtrahend is 365,497. What is the difference?

3. Take $324.09 from $1,000. What is the remainder?

4. The multiplicand is 72,394, and the multiplier is 3,600.   What is the product?

5. The sum of two numbers is 31,654, and one of the numbers is 2,870.   What is the other number?

6. What number is that, the factors of which are 93,268 and 50?

7. The quotient is 94, and the divisor is 317.   What is the dividend?

8. The divisor is $25.50, and the dividend is $1,810.50. What is the quotient?

9. 8,400 + 9 + 55,374 + 286 + 6,857 + 2,002 + how many = 100,000?

10. $25,408 − $18,976 = how many times $24?

11. 36 × 25 × 300 × 46 is 50 times what number?

12. The minuend is 875,004, and the remainder 208,365. What is the subtrahend?

13. From what number must $964.87 be taken, to leave $215.13?

14. By what number must 23,040 be divided, to obtain 36?

15. Dividing a certain number by 70,000, I obtain 66 for the integer of the quotient, and 60,000 for a final remainder.   What is the number divided?

16. 100 + 67 + 229 + 80 + 924 = $\frac{1}{5}$ of what number?

17. 527 × 55 × 9 − 253,974 = 3 times how much?

18. 17,984 ÷ 281 = 28 + how many?

19. 809 times the quotient of $525.75 ÷ $21.03 is how much more than 5,000?

20. What number is that to which if 267 be added, from the sum 438 be subtracted, the remainder be multiplied by 6, and the product be divided by 12, the quotient will be 491?

E 2

SECTION VII.

GENERAL REVIEW PROBLEMS IN INTEGERS.

***Oral Work.*—1.** How much can a boy earn in 5 days, at $ .31 a day?

2. Find the cost of 10 yards of calico, at 13 cents a yard; and 8 yards of ribbon, at 20 cents a yard.

3. At ten cents a pound, how much will a grocer pay for 5 barrels of crackers of 41 pounds each?

4. A fruiterer bought 48 boxes of lemons, at $2 a box, and sold them all for $125. How much did he gain?

5. How many pews are there in a church that seats 300 persons, 5 persons in a pew?

6. If I owe $54, $21, and $15, and I pay all but $25. how much do I pay?

7. If 5 cords of wood are worth 15 dollars, how much are 7 cords worth?

8. A butcher killed 8 sheep, the total weight of which was 720 pounds. What was their average weight?

9. A dealer sells melons at 10 cents, 13 cents, 15 cents, and 18 cents apiece, according to size. What is the average price?

10. If the attendance at school Monday is 38, Tuesday 43, Wednesday 39, Thursday 40, and Friday 45, what is the average attendance for the week?

***Written Work.*—1.** A salary of $1,000 per year is how much per month? How much per week?

2. A grain buyer receives an order for 12,500 bushels of wheat, and he has only 7,645 bushels in store. How many bushels must he purchase to fill the order?

3. At $6 a week for board, how much are the receipts from 45 boarders in 26 weeks?

4. One week a fruit dealer bought 123 barrels, 1,075 barrels, 3,550 barrels, 1,805 barrels, 987 barrels, and 562 barrels of apples. How many barrels of apples did he buy?

5. A ship and cargo are valued at $130,480.50, and the cargo is worth $55,297.50. What is the value of the ship?

6. How many bales will 1,072,512 pounds of cotton make, allowing 400 pounds to the bale?

7. If I travel west from Philadelphia 8 hours, at the rate of 34 miles an hour, and then travel east 176 miles, how far will I be from Philadelphia?

8. In building a barn I used 7 thousand feet of lumber, that cost me $15 a thousand; and I paid $139 for other materials and labor. How much did the barn cost me?

9. In a factory 432,740 yards of cassimere were made in 308 days. How many yards were made daily?

10. In the manufacture of this cloth 616,000 pounds of wool were used. How many pounds were used daily?

11. If 1,071,399 yards of cotton cloth are made from 357,133 pounds of cotton, how many yards of cloth are made from one pound of cotton?

12. Three men buy a lot of land for $6,000, and build a store upon it at a cost of $7,281. How many dollars does each man pay?

13. A coal dealer bought 1,050 tons of coal, receiving 2,240 pounds for a ton, and sold it at 2,000 pounds for a ton. How many tons did he sell?

14. What is the average weight of 8 bales of cotton which weigh respectively 385, 367, 418, 374, 396, 405, 373, and 402 pounds?

15. I buy real-estate for $16,575, agreeing to pay for it in yearly payments of $1,200 each. How many payments will I make, and how much will be the last payment?

16. In June a dairyman made 355 pounds, 424 pounds, 391 pounds, and 330 pounds of butter; and packed it in tubs of 50 pounds each.   How many tubs did he fill?

Oral Work.—B. 1. Ira's age is 6 years, and Paul's is 20.   In how many years will Paul be twice as old as Ira?

2. In a certain school are 50 boys, and 4 times as many girls lacking 17.   How many pupils are in the school?

3. If 11 apples cost $ .07, how many apples can I buy for $ .28?

4. If 6 bananas cost $ .42, what do 15 bananas cost?

5. How many tons of hay at 6 dollars a ton, will pay for 8 yards of cloth at $3 a yard?

6. A wood dealer sold to three persons 12 cords, 10 cords, and 36 cords of wood, and had 29 cords left.   How many cords had he at first?

7. From a stock of 100 thousand shingles, 53 thousand were sold to one builder, and 31 thousand to another. How many shingles were unsold?

8. A merchant has 74 yards of cloth in three pieces, one of which contains 29 yards, and another 32 yards. How many yards are there in the third piece?

9. In how many days will 8 men do as much work as 12 men can do in 10 days?

10. In how many weeks will 14 cattle eat as much as 6 cattle will eat in 7 weeks?

11. A man has a job of work that he can do in 192 days.   If he employs 5 men to assist him, in how many days will the work be completed?

12. If 15 men can clear an acre of ground in 8 days, in how many days can 12 men clear it?

13. If a stage coach runs 54 miles in 9 hours, in how many hours will it run 96 miles?

***Written Work.*—1.** A farmer had 3 flocks of sheep, the first containing 184, the second 218, and the third 65. He sold 114 from the first flock, 189 from the second, and 48 from the third. How many sheep had he then?

2. A grocer bought two tubs of maple sugar — one weighing 67 and the other 93 pounds—at $ .15 a pound, and sold it at $ .18 a pound. How much did he gain?

3. I bought a farm wagon for $92, and a family carriage for $172; and paid for them with beef, at $12 a hundred pounds. How many hundred pounds of beef did it take?

4. Find the cost of 115 pounds of hams, at $ .11 a pound; and 43 pounds of bacon, at $ .13 a pound.

5. A fruit dealer having 2,468 barrels of apples, sold 1,382 barrels for $4,146, and the remainder for $4,344. How much did he receive per barrel for each of the two lots?

6. A farmer sold his farm of 36 acres at $40 per acre, and invested the proceeds in Western lands at $2.25 per acre. How many acres did he buy?

7. A drover bought cattle at $49.63 per head, and sold them at $63.50 per head, thereby gaining $1,511.83. How many head of cattle did he buy?

8. Last year a bank teller received a salary of $1,250, and his personal expenses were $753. He bought a village lot for $225, and paid $149 for improvements upon it. How much of his year's salary had he left?

9. I bought a stock of goods for $15,284, paying $2,684 cash, and the balance in monthly payments of $1,575 each. How many monthly payments did I make?

10. 52 ladies and 39 gentlemen went on an excursion, and their expenses, which were $3 each, were paid by the gentlemen. How much did each gentleman pay?

11. A young man worked a year at $26 a month. He paid $13 a month for board, and his other expenses were $100. How much money did he save?

12. A merchant bought 16 pieces of dress flannels, of 43 yards each. After selling 155 yards, how many dress patterns of 13 yards each had he?

13. A man contracted to deliver at a steamboat landing 5,000 cords of wood. He delivered 76 cords each day for 35 days, and 54 cords each day for 24 days. How many cords were yet to be delivered?

14. A captain, mate, and 12 sailors captured a prize of $2,240; the captain took 14 shares, the mate 6 shares, and each of the sailors 1 share. How much did each receive?

15. A farm-house is worth $2,450; the farm is worth 12 times as much, less $600; and the stock is worth twice as much as the house. How much are house, stock, and farm worth?

16. I paid $48 an acre for a wood lot of 60 acres. I sold the wood for $2,378, and the land for $18 an acre. Did I gain or lose, and how much?

17. A clothier invested $3,000 in business. The first year he gained $756, and the second year he lost $1,652. The next three years his average yearly gain was $748. How much was he worth at the end of the five years?

18. Monday morning Mr. D. had in bank $5,878.50. During the week he drew checks for $360.25, $145, and $75.50; and deposited $1,250, $750, $1,000, and $1,500. What was his balance in bank at the close of the week?

19. A farmer's wheat crop brought him $650, his barley $205, his corn $97, and his oats $150. He paid a farm hand $13 per month for 9 months, paid $250 for fertilizers, and $65.75 for utensils and repairs. How much did he clear from his farm that year?

CHAPTER II.
DECIMALS.

SECTION I.

NOTATION AND NUMERATION.

108. *A.* *One tenth* is one of the ten equal parts into which the unit one is divided.

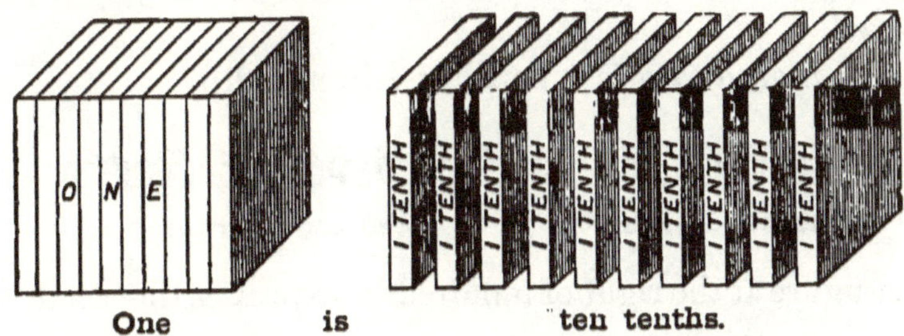

One   is   ten tenths.

A figure at the right of ones expresses tenths.
Tenths are written

1 tenth, .1	4 tenths, .4	7 tenths, .7
2 tenths, .2	5 tenths, .5	8 tenths, .8
3 tenths, .3	6 tenths, .6	9 tenths, .9

B. Dividing each of the 10 tenths of a 1 into 10 equal parts divides the 1 into 10 times 10, or 100 equal parts.

One hundredth is 1 tenth of 1 tenth.

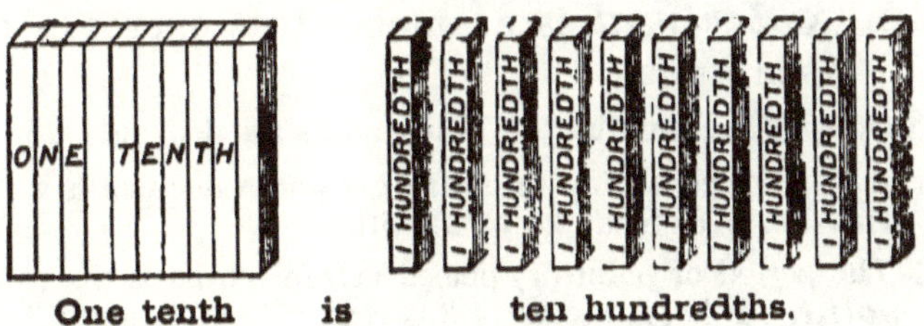

One tenth   is   ten hundredths.

A figure at the right of tenths expresses hundredths.

Hundredths are written

1 hundredth, .01	4 hundredths, .04	7 hundredths, .07
2 hundredths, .02	5 hundredths, .05	8 hundredths, .08
3 hundredths, .03	6 hundredths, .06	9 hundredths, .09

C. Dividing each of the 100 hundredths of a 1 into 10 equal parts divides the 1 into 10 times 100, or 1,000 equal parts.

One thousandth is 1 tenth of 1 hundredth.

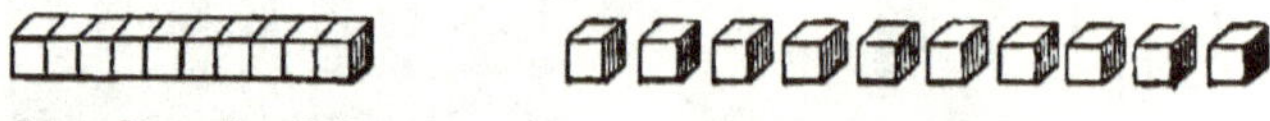

A figure at the right of hundredths expresses thousandths.

Thousandths are written

1 thousandth, .001	4 thousandths, .004	7 thousandths, .007
2 thousandths, .002	5 thousandths, .005	8 thousandths, .008
3 thousandths, .003	6 thousandths, .006	9 thousandths, .009

109. A *decimal unit* is one of the equal decimal parts into which the unit 1 is divided.

> 1 tenth, 1 hundredth, 1 thousandth, 1 ten-thousandth, and so on, are decimal units.

110. A *decimal* is a number that expresses one or more decimal units.

> 7 tenths, 36 hundredths, 258 thousandths are decimals.
>
> *a.* A number consisting of an integer and a decimal is a *mixed number;* as 8 and 25 hundredths.
>
> *b.* The period or point (.) placed before tenths is the *decimal point.* It is read *and.* 4.5 is read "4 and 5 tenths."

111. Tenths and hundredths are read together as hundredths; and tenths, hundredths, and thousandths are read together as thousandths.

EXERCISES.

A. Write and read the numbers expressed by

1. 8 tenths; 3 tenths; 6 tenths; 2 ones and 5 tenths.

2. 1 tenth and 1 hundredth, or 11 hundredths.

3. 3 ones and 27 hundredths; 18 and 2 hundredths.

4. 4 tenths 5 hundredths and 6 thousandths, or 456 thousandths.

5. 8 tens 3 tenths and 5 thousandths.

6. 50 and 16 thousandths; 87 and 87 thousandths.

7. 500 and 4 thousandths; 504 thousandths.

8. 9,000 and 9 thousandths; 101,000 and 101 thousandths.

B. Read

1. .9; 5.2; .07; 8.05; 50.5.

2. .08; .83; 200.09; .002; .901.

3. 4.023; 6.400; .365; 500.5.

Write in words

4. .5; 6.4; 40.6; .03; 3.27; .009.

5. 298.02; .063; .175; 19.02.

6. 80.001; 9.018; 300.300.

C. Express by figures

1. Five tenths; nine hundredths; thirteen hundredths.

2. Forty-eight hundredths; two thousandths; fifty-one thousandths.

3. Eighty thousandths; six hundred five thousandths.

4. Three and nine tenths; twenty-five and fifty-two hundredths; sixty-two and ninety-five thousandths.

5. Seven and seven hundredths; one and eleven hundredths; five and three hundred seventy-six thousandths.

112. A decimal expressed by

one figure		tenths,	1 tenth,
two figures		hundredths,	1 hundredth,
three figures	is	thousandths,	1 thousandth,
four figures		ten-thousandths,	1 ten-thousandth,
five figures		hundred-thousandths,	1 hundred-thousandth,
six figures		millionths,	1 millionth.

and its unit is

And similarly for any greater number of decimal figures.

3. Five thousand eighteen hundred-thousandths.

4. Two thousand sixteen ten-thousandths.

5. One hundred fifteen ten-thousandths.

6. 97 thousand and 18 ten - thousandths; 12 hundred-thousandths; 600 thousand and 284 hundred-thousandths.

7. Six hundred thousand two hundred four millionths.

8. One hundred ninety-seven ten-millionths.

9. Five hundred ninety-one millionths.

10. Two hundred seven thousand fifty-six ten-millionths.

11. 46 million 274 thousand 508 hundred-millionths.

12. 17 and 1,425 hundred-millionths.

13. Ninety million and forty-one ten-millionths

14. Thirty-four million seventeen hundred-millionths.

116. Rule for Decimal Notation.

Write the decimal point, and after it the figures that express the units of each order.

117. Rule for Decimal Numeration.

Read the decimal as an integer, and give to it the name of its lowest order.

Exercises in Decimal Notation and Numeration.

Write and read the numbers expressed by

1. 9 thousandths; 23 thousandths; 35 and 7 tenths; 4 and 276 thousandths.

2. 9 and 18 ten-thousandths; 55 and 5 hundredths; 2,987 ten-thousandths; 4 and 68,001 ten-millionths.

3. 400,000 and 4 hundred-thousandths.

4. 1 thousand and 20 thousand 84 hundred-thousandths; 7 thousand 17 and 4 millionths.

5. 78 thousand and 219 millionths; 106,204 hundred-millionths; 6 and 49 hundred-millionths.

Express by figures

6. Forty-one thousand thirty-six and two hundred seventy-three thousandths.

7. Fourteen hundred-thousandths.

8. Forty-four and forty-four hundred-thousandths.

9. Two hundred six thousand four hundred seventy and three tenths.

10. 50 million and 50 thousand 5 hundred 12 hundred-thousandths.

11. 101 million 101 thousand 101 and 1 million 1 thousand 1 hundred-millionths.

12. Sixty-one million thirty-two thousand eight hundred seventy-six and two million eight hundred fifty thousand forty-one ten-millionths.

13. One hundred seventy-two and eight tenths; six hundred twenty-four hundred-thousandths.

14. One hundred fifty-two million six hundred fifty and fifty million forty thousand thirty-six hundred-millionths.

15. Sixty-five thousand and seven ten-thousandths.

16. Thirty and six thousand eight ten-thousandths.

118. *Currency* is the money used in trade and commerce.

The currency of the United States is a *decimal currency.* It is sometimes called *Federal Money.*

119. The *money units* in common use are the *dollar,* the *cent,* and the *mill.*

a. A cent is 1 hundredth of a dollar ; and

A mill is 1 tenth of a cent, or 1 thousandth of a dollar. Hence,

10 mills are 1 cent.

100 cents " 1 dollar.

Write 1 mill, $.001.	5 dollars 56 cents 8 mills, $5.568.
" 6 mills, $.006.	20 dollars 20 cents 1 mill, $20.201.
" 10 cents 5 mills, $.105.	7 dollars 4 cents 3 mills, $7.043.

$.0006 is 6 tenths of a mill; $.0085 is 8 and 5 tenths mills.
$.2943 is 29 cents 4 and 3 tenths mills.
$15.65425 is 15 dollars 65 cents 4 and 25 hundredths mills.

    b. *Write cents as hundredths, and mills as thousandths, of a dollar.*

    c. *Read decimal parts of a dollar less than mills as decimals of a mill.*

120. Halves, fourths, and eighths of a cent are extensively used in business computations.

$$\tfrac{1}{2}\ \text{cent or}\ \$.00\tfrac{1}{2}\ \text{is } 5\ \text{mills or}\ \$.005$$
$$\tfrac{1}{4}\ \text{``}\quad\text{``}\quad \$.00\tfrac{1}{4}\ \text{`` } 2.5\ \text{``}\quad\text{``}\quad \$.0025$$
$$\tfrac{3}{4}\ \text{``}\quad\text{``}\quad \$.00\tfrac{3}{4}\ \text{`` } 7.5\ \text{``}\quad\text{``}\quad \$.0075$$
$$\tfrac{1}{8}\ \text{``}\quad\text{``}\quad \$.00\tfrac{1}{8}\ \text{`` } 1.25\ \text{``}\quad\text{``}\quad \$.00125$$
$$\tfrac{3}{8}\ \text{``}\quad\text{``}\quad \$.00\tfrac{3}{8}\ \text{`` } 3.75\ \text{``}\quad\text{``}\quad \$.00375$$
$$\tfrac{5}{8}\ \text{``}\quad\text{``}\quad \$.00\tfrac{5}{8}\ \text{`` } 6.25\ \text{``}\quad\text{``}\quad \$.00625$$
$$\tfrac{7}{8}\ \text{``}\quad\text{``}\quad \$.00\tfrac{7}{8}\ \text{`` } 8.75\ \text{``}\quad\text{``}\quad \$.00875$$

EXERCISES.

Copy and read

1. $.225   *4.* $300.567

2. $.007   *5.* $12.108

3. $5.751   *6.* $90.025

Write

7. 8 mills; 15 cents 6 mills.

8. 83 dollars 12 cents 5 mills.

9. 400 dollars 8 cents 1 mill.

Write in decimal form and read

    10. $12\tfrac{1}{2}$ cents; $6\tfrac{1}{4}$ cents; $18\tfrac{3}{4}$ cents.

    11. $65\tfrac{3}{8}$ cents; $85\tfrac{5}{8}$ cents; $2\tfrac{7}{8}$ cents; $\tfrac{1}{8}$ cent.

Write the decimal parts less than cents in fractional form, and read

    12. $.375; $.2025; $1.09125; $10.00625; $105.56875.

    13. Seventy-five dollars thirty-seven and 1 half cents.

    14. One thousand dollars one cent one mill.

    15. Nine dollars nine and one eighth cents.

    16. Fifteen dollars forty-three cents seven and five tenths mills; four dollars three and one eighth cents.

    17. Twelve and one half cents; thirty-one and one fourth cents.

SECTION II.

REDUCTION.

121. *Reduction* is the process of changing num-bers from given to required units, without changing their values.

> Changing tenths to hundredths or thousandths; thousandths to hundredths, tenths, or ones; dollars to cents or mills; mills or cents to dollars, are examples of reduction.

The same values are expressed

1. By .5, .50, and .500.
2. By 2, 2.0, and 2.00.
3. By 7.3, 7.30, and 7.300.
4. By .6300, .630, and .63.
5. By 9.00, 9.0, and 9.
6. By 3.400, 3.40, and 3.4.

122. Reduction of decimals is based upon the following

PRINCIPLE. *Annexing decimal ciphers to a number, or removing decimal ciphers from the right of a number, does not change its value.*

Reduce

1. .7 to hundredths.
2. .025 to millionths.
3. 62 to ten-thousandths.
4. .930 to hundredths.
5. .003000 to thousandths.
6. 800 hundredths to ones.
7. 75 tenths to ones.
8. 368 hundredths to ones.

How are hundredths reduced { *9.* To thousandths? *10.* To ten-millionths? *11.* To tenths? *12.* To ones?

13 How are tenths, hundred-thousandths, thousandths, ones, and ten-thousandths reduced to millionths?

Reduce

14. 5.3 to thousandths.
15. .07 to millionths.
16. 18.602 to ten-thousandths.

Reduce to the same decimal unit

17. 1.2, 4.37, 192, and .0001.
18. 30.251, .0089, and 3.000004.
19. 6.0108, 57.8, 234, and 2.34.

123. The same values are expressed

1. By $5, $5.00, and 500 cents. | *4.* By 200 cents and $2.
2. By $5, $5.000, and 5,000 mills. | *5.* By 675 cents and $6.75.
3. By $.37, $.370, and 370 mills. | *6.* By 953 mills and 95.3 cents.

  7. By 4,621 mills, 462.1 cents, and $4.621.

  8. By 15 mills, 1.5 cents, and $ .015.

  9. By $31.25 and 3,125 cents.   Hence,

In decimal currency,

  a. To reduce dollars to cents:—*Annex two ciphers.*

  b. To reduce dollars to mills:—*Annex three ciphers.*

  c. To reduce cents to mills :—*Annex one cipher.*

  d. To reduce dollars and cents to cents; or dollars, cents,. and mills to mills:—*Remove the dollar mark and the decimal point.*

  e. To reduce dollars and cents to mills:—*Annex one cipher, and remove the decimal point.*

  f. To reduce cents to dollars:—*Point off two decimal places, and prefix the dollar mark.*

  g. To reduce mills to cents:—*Point off one decimal place.*

  h. To reduce mills to dollars :—*Point off three decimal places, and prefix the dollar mark.*

Reduce

  1. 93 dollars to cents. | *2.* 86,000 cents to dollars.
  3. 57 cents to mills. | *4.* 359 mills to cents.
  5. 218 dollars to mills. | *6.* 9,274 mills to dollars.
  7. $.40 to mills. | *8.* 6,000 cents to dollars.
  9. $3 to cents; to mills. | *10.* 3,219 mills to cents.
  11. $3.40 to mills. | *12.* 3,219 mills to dollars.

Reduce to mills	Reduce to cents	Reduce to dollars
13. $.09 ; $.83.	*16.* $4 ; $15.	*19.* 300 cents.
14. $.213 ; $.605.	*17.* $3.27 ; $10.50.	*20.* 4,275 cents.
15. $7 ; $32 ; $.082.	*18.* 875 mills.	*21.* 2,047 mills.

SECTION III.

ADDITION.

124. *The principles for addition of integers, page 23, apply equally to addition of decimals.*

Written Work.—Ex. What is the sum of 7.4875, 836.5, .34, 85.075, and 973?

PROCESS.

$$7.4875$$
$$836.5$$
$$.34$$
$$85.075$$
$$973$$
$$\overline{1,902.4025}$$

EXPLANATION.—I write the numbers so that units of the same order stand in the same column.

I begin at the right and add as in integers, and place a decimal point in the result under the decimal points in the parts.

Always place the decimal point in the result, when the tenths of the result are written.

PROBLEMS.

1	2		3	4
.967	.125	tons	800.1	$121.10
.00054	1.25	tons	9.60	38.47
953.5	12.5	tons	2,064.25	92.86
7.375	.0125	tons	167.4	582.79
6.75	.00125	tons	283	810.04

5	6	7	8	
$ 7.28	$.58	$2,000	47.25	days
241.09	.145	5.75	5.00695	days
.42	.0275	48.01	193.9	days
.96	.5625	.495	5.876	days
44.52	.095	359.17	9.00005	days

9. A silversmith used 4.75 ounces of silver in making vases, 8.65 ounces in making goblets, and 10.6 ounces in making napkin rings. How much silver did he use?

F

10. A family used .732 of a ton of coal in February, .824 of a ton in March, .688 of a ton in April, and .595 of a ton in May.   How many tons of coal did they use?

11. In four meadows containing 11.25 acres, 6.75 acres, 13.33 acres, and 8.72 acres, are how many acres?

12. A boy sold 3.75 bushels, 5.625 bushels, 9.5 bushels, and 6.25 bushels of pears.   How many bushels did he sell?

13. A seedsman sold to five farmers 2.25 bushels, 1 bushel, 3.5 bushels, 4.75 bushels, and 3.225 bushels of grass seed.   How many bushels did he sell?

14. Find the sum of two hundred and four hundredths, five thousand one hundred eight and seven thousand three millionths, one hundred thirteen thousand seven hundred six and two thousand five hundred four ten-thousandths, and ten and fifty-five millionths.

15. By selling a horse for $183.75, I lost $24.50.   For how much should I have sold him, to gain $39.70?

16. A mechanic earned $56.25 in January, $45.63 in February, $67.50 in March, $65.87½ in April, and $75 in May.   How much did he earn in the five months?

17. A lady bought 3 dozen buttons for $1.08, 2 yards of ribbon for $.37½, 6 yards of muslin for $1.18¾, some needles for $.31¼, a belt for $.75, and a dress for $10.62½. How much did her purchases amount to?

18. A grocer bought six hogsheads of molasses, containing 117.5 gallons, 124 gallons, 129.3175 gallons, 104.75 gallons, 130.0625 gallons, and 131.5625 gallons.   How many gallons of molasses did he buy?

19. What is the sum of 967 thousandths, 54 hundred-thousandths, 953 and 5 tenths, 7 and 375 thousandths, 1,000 and 1 ten-thousandth, 6 and 75 hundredths, 8 and 80,808 hundred-thousandths, and 483?

SECTION IV.

SUBTRACTION.

125. *The principle for subtraction of integers, page 40, applies equally to subtraction of decimals.*

Ex. Subtract 16.78 from 38.25; 23.51 from 257.142; and 93.1875 from 130.5.

PROCESSES.

EXPLANATION.—I write the numbers in each example so that units of the subtrahend are under units of like orders in the minuend.	1	2	3
	38.25	257.142	130.5
	16.78	23.51	93.1875
	21.47	233.632	37.3125

I begin at the right and subtract, as in integers, and place a decimal point in the result under the decimal point in the minuend and subtrahend.

In the third process, I suppose three decimal ciphers to be annexed to the minuend, when I perform the subtraction.

Always place the decimal point in the result, when the tenths of the result are written.

PROBLEMS.

1	2	3	4	5
325.48	87.006	1.03045	374	20,000.2875
199.56	9.84	.0009	.125	482.52006

6	7	8	9	10
$250.35	$ .104	$100.000	$1.000	$50
187.50	.087	5.875	.065	2.875

11. From a piece of linen containing 43.5 yards, a clerk sold 26.8 yards. How many yards remained?

12. 362.413 miles — 81.0064 miles = how many miles?

13. At night the snow was 11.37 inches deep, and in the morning it was 13.03 inches deep. How much snow fell during the night?

14. Of a railroad 240.475 miles long, 168.025 miles are double track. How many miles are single track?

15. From a barrel of kerosene containing 42 gallons, 31.25 gallons were drawn. How many gallons remained?

16. Two men built 134 rods of stone fence, one of them building 65.87 rods. How many rods did the other build?

17. From a 5-pound box of starch, a grocer sold 2.0625 pounds. How many pounds remained in the box?

18. From ninety-five and eight thousand five ten-thousandths take ten and forty-four hundredths.

19. A tree 79.95 feet high broke off 4.7 feet above the ground. What was the length of the part broken off?

20. A silver dollar weighs 412.5 grains, and contains 41.25 grains of copper. How much pure silver does it contain?

21. From eight hundred sixty and four hundredths take nineteen and nine thousand fifty-four hundred-thousandths.

22. A cubic foot of gold weighs 1,203.625 pounds, and a cubic foot of iron 450.4375 pounds. How much more does the gold weigh than the iron?

23. If wheat is worth \$1.18¾ per bushel in Milwaukee and \$1.87½ in New York, how much is added to its value by transportation?

24. In a cistern that will hold 320.5 barrels, are 192.8125 barrels of water. How much more water will the cistern hold?

25. Mr. Brown exchanged a silver watch worth \$18.75, for a gold watch worth \$80, paying the difference in money. How much money did he pay?

26. A merchant sold a piece of damaged cloth that cost him $94.37, at a loss of $26.75. For how much did he sell it?

27. A vessel sailed from Portland, Me., for Mobile, with a cargo of 1,438.275 tons of ice, and 561.895 tons of it melted on the voyage. How much more ice reached Mobile than melted on the voyage?

28. A merchant bought a jar of butter for $15.37½, paying $6.87½ in cloth, $4.62½ in groceries, and the balance in money. How much money did he pay?

29. A farmer raised 32.25 bushels of timothy-grass seed. He sowed 4.03125 bushels, and sold 12.125 bushels. How many bushels had he left?

30. A laborer received $6 for his week's work. He paid $1.62½ for flour, $.85 for tea, $.75 for sugar, and $.37½ for butter. How much money had he left?

31. From an ice-house containing 500 tons of ice, a dealer sold 18.263 tons, 15.967 tons, 17.4 tons, and 16.48 tons. How much ice was left in the ice-house?

32. From a cask containing 37.175 gallons of alcohol, a druggist drew at different times .125 of a gallon, 1.5 gallons, .25 of a gallon, and .75 of a gallon. How many gallons remained in the cask?

33. A butcher killed an ox that cost him $63.37. He retailed the meat for $61.96, sold the tallow for $6.08, and the hide for $8.55. How much were his profits?

34. C has 53.843 acres of land in one field, 75.364 acres in another, and 15.527 acres in a third. How much must he purchase of a neighbor, to have a farm of 200 acres?

35. B invests $1,750.25 in oats, $786.37½ in corn, and $2,648.62½ in wheat. He sells the oats for $2,022.45, the corn for $831.50, and the wheat for $2,331.30. Does he gain or lose, and how much, on the oats? On the corn? On the wheat? On the three investments?

SECTION V.

MULTIPLICATION.

126. The methods of written work in multiplication of decimals are based upon the following

PRINCIPLE. *There must be as many decimal places in the product as there are in both factors.*

Ex. 1. The factors are .24 and 39. What is the product?

EXPLANATION.—I write the factors and multiply as in integers; and, since one factor is an integer, and there are two decimal places in the other factor, I point off two decimal figures in the product.

FIRST PROCESS.

$$\begin{array}{r} .24 \\ 39 \\ \hline 216 \\ 72 \\ \hline 9.36 \end{array}$$

SECOND PROCESS.

$$\begin{array}{r} 39 \\ .24 \\ \hline .156 \\ 78 \\ \hline 9.36 \end{array}$$

When one factor is an integer, the product has the same number of decimal places as the other factor.

Ex. 2. Multiply 5.63 by .8.

EXPLANATION.—I write the numbers and multiply as in integers; and, since there are three decimal places in the factors, I point off three decimal figures in the product.

PROCESS.

$$\begin{array}{r} 5.63 \\ .8 \\ \hline 4.504 \end{array}$$

PROBLEMS.

1	2	3	4	5
210.735	634.04	.19125	250,375	47,232
9	76	108	.07	7.38

6	7	8	9	10
$194.17	$310.75	$5,044	$24,960	$74,809
18	236	7.5	.25	17.05

	11	12	13	14	15
Multiply	4.29	9432.6	$647.89	$296.07	5.01234
by	.27	55.55	20.009	65.33	.8007

16. How many feet is it across a street 5 rods wide?
(1 rod is 16.5 feet.)

17. How many bushels of oats are there in 4 bins, each bin containing 20.75 bushels?

18. How many days are there in 10.7 years?

19. What is the weight of 47 reams of printing-paper, each ream weighing 38.125 pounds?

What is the value
20. Of 37 thousand feet of lumber, @ 28.25?
21. Of 29 rolls of wall paper, @ 44c.?
22. Of 125 pounds of nails, @ 6c.?
23. Of 148 yards of broadcloth, @ $3.87½?
24. Of 55.3 acres of land, @ $118?

25. If one ton of lead ore yields .765 of a ton of lead, 372.084 tons of ore will yield how many tons of lead?

26. How many tons of flax can be raised on .85 of an acre of land, if 1.8764 tons are raised on one acre?

27. If .35 of a pound of butter is made from 1 gallon of milk, how many pounds of butter can be made from 2,245.5 gallons of milk?

28. If 22.73 gallons of brine are required for 1 bushel of salt, how many gallons are required for 83.25 bushels?

127. Ex. Multiply .75 by .003.

PROCESS.

EXPLANATION.—I write the numbers and multiply as in integers; and, since there are five decimal places in the factors, I prefix two decimal ciphers to the product of 75 and 3, thus making the number of decimal places in the product equal to the number in both factors.

$$.75$$
$$.003$$
$$\overline{.00225}$$

When there are not as many figures in the written result as there are decimal places in the factors, supply the deficiency by prefixing decimal ciphers.

PROBLEMS.

1	2	3	4	5
.0854	.084	.00393	.00049	.06052
.032	.07	.006	.057	.066

6. How much grass seed will be required for .05 of an acre, at the rate of .3 of a bushel to the acre?

7. How far will a locomotive run in .25 of a minute, at the rate of .36 of a mile per minute?

8. How much will .375 of a pound of bicarbonate of soda cost, at $.18¾ a pound?

9. Find the cost of 15.5 yards of tape, at $.00½ a yard.

10. A cook used .09 of .31 of a gallon of molasses. How much molasses did she use?

11. Multiply 32 ten-thousandths by 7 hundredths.

128. Ex. Multiply 35.827 by 10, by 100, by 1,000, and by 100,000.

PROCESSES.

$$35.827 \times \qquad 10 = \qquad 358.270 = \qquad 358.27$$
$$35.827 \times \qquad 100 = \qquad 3,582.700 = \qquad 3,582.7$$
$$35.827 \times \quad 1,000 = \qquad 35,827.000 = \qquad 35,827$$
$$35.827 \times 100,000 = 3,582,700.000 = 3,582,700$$

Each removal of the decimal point in a number one place to the right, multiplies the number by 10. (See **25.**)

PROBLEMS.

Multiply

1. 53.78 by 10.	*3.* 6.8794 by 100.	*5.* $.0625 by 100.
2. $2.31 by 10.	*4.* 59.6043 by 1,000.	*6.* $37.81¼ by 10,000.

7. What is the total length of 1,000 bars of railroad iron, each bar being .00062 of a mile long?

Find the cost
{ *8.* Of 1,000 fat cattle, @ $42.69¾.
{ *9.* Of 100 days' board, @ 75c.
{ *10.* Of 10,000 quart bottles, @ 7⅛c.

129. RULE FOR MULTIPLICATION OF DECIMALS.

I. *Write the numbers and multiply as in integers.*

II. *Point off as many decimal figures in the product as there are decimal places in both factors.*

Problems.

1. Multiply 172.84 by 50.

2. Multiply $2.73 by 8,600.

3. Multiply .12815 by 93.7.

4. Multiply $.84½ by .946.

5. Multiply .0062 by .0008.

6. $400,000 \times .00004 =$ how many?

7. $397,654 \times 380.07 =$ how many?

8. $100,000 \times 5.875 =$ how many?

9. $2,500 \times .25 =$ how many?

10. $.000007 \times 7,000,000 =$ how many?

11. How much silk will be required for 9 yards of ribbon, if .085 of a pound is required for one yard?

12. How many yards are there in 25 pieces of tapestry carpeting, each piece containing 62.75 yards?

13. How many rods of stone fence will a man lay in 128 days, if he lays 3.69 rods each day?

14. If a rolling-mill makes 94.2 tons of iron per day, how many tons will it make in 164.25 days?

15. If 3.75 gallons of cider can be made from one bushel of apples, how much cider can be made from 38.5 bushels?

Find the cost

16. Of .84 of a ton of plaster, at $4.25 a ton.

17. Of 15,000 bushels of wheat, at $1.06¼ a bushel.

18. Of 18.4 tons of straw, at $3.12½ a ton.

19. Of 7 pieces of lace, 39 yards each, at $ .37½ a yard.

20. How much is the freight on .456 of a ton of goods from New York to Toledo, by railroad, at $28.60 a ton?

21. What is the value of a million pins, at one-ten-thousandth of a dollar each?

22. I bought 2.5 yards of broadcloth, at $3.75; 1 yard of cashmere for $ .87½; 26 yards of calico, at $ .12½; and 14 yards of muslin, at $ .35. What was the cost of the whole?

23. A mechanic earns $2.75 per day, and his expenses are $1.40 per day. How much does he save in a week?

24. I bought 42.5 gallons of linseed-oil for $37.18¾, and sold it at $1.12½ per gallon. How much did I gain?

SECTION VI.

DIVISION.

130. The methods of written work in division of decimals are based upon the following

PRINCIPLE. *There must be as many decimal places in
the quotient as the number of decimal places in the dividend exceeds the number in the divisor.*

Ex. Divide 1,947.15 by 9.

PROCESS.

EXPLANATION.—I divide as in integers; and,
since there are two decimal places in the
dividend and none in the divisor, I point
off two decimal places in the quotient.

$$9)\,\underline{1,947.15}$$
$$216.35$$

*When the divisor is an integer, the quotient has the same number of
decimal places as the dividend.*

PROBLEMS.

1	**2**	**3**	**4**
9).396	39).897(	55)33.440(	105)7.89285(

5. My horse eats .324 of a ton of hay in 9 weeks. How
much hay does he eat in a week?

6. If a boarding-house keeper uses 2.1875 barrels of
flour in a week, how much flour does she use in a day?

7. A fruit dealer sold 686 boxes of oranges for $1,543.50.
What was the price per box?

8. A gentleman bought a parlor carpet containing 43
yards, for $96.75. How much did he pay per yard?

9. If 55 peach baskets hold 34.375 bushels, how much
does each basket hold?

131. Ex. Divide 15.695 by 7.3.

EXPLANATION.—I divide as in integers; and, since there are three decimal places in the dividend and one decimal place in the divisor, I point off two decimal places in the quotient, and I have 2.15, the required quotient.

PROCESS.

$$7.3\,)\,15.695\,(\,2.15$$
$$\underline{146}$$
$$109$$
$$\underline{73}$$
$$365$$
$$\underline{365}$$

NOTE.—To secure accuracy in pointing off decimal figures in the quotient, many teachers prefer the following method:

1. *Before beginning to divide, cut off, by a line, as many places to the right of the decimal point in the dividend as there are decimal places in the divisor, as shown in the example in the margin.*

2. *In dividing, write the decimal point in the result when all the orders to the left of the line have been used.*

$$7.3\,)\,15.6|95\,(\,2.15$$
$$\underline{146}$$
$$109$$
$$73$$
$$365$$
$$365$$

PROBLEMS.

1. How many times is 16.54 contained in 611.98?

2. What is the quotient of .3264 divided by .0034?

3. If one barrel of flour is made from 4.5 bushels of wheat, how many barrels will be made from 67.5 bushels?

4. How many sheets of Russia iron, each weighing 3.31 pounds, will a workman use in making 76.13 pounds of stove-pipe?

5. If one overcoat is made from 3.25 yards of cloth, how many overcoats can be made from 61.75 yards?

6. How many casks, each holding 41.315 gallons, will be required, to hold 11,278.995 gallons of alcohol?

7. 15.9392 tons of iron ore will make how many loads, each weighing .9376 of a ton?

8. A carriage ironer paid $24.72¼ for bar steel, at $.07¼ a pound. How many pounds of steel did he buy?

9. If an acre of land produces 1.92 tons of hay, how much land will produce .9024 of a ton?

132. Ex. 1. Divide 18.24 by 6.4.

PROCESS.

EXPLANATION.—I divide as in integers; and when all the figures expressing the dividend have been used, I form a new partial dividend,—by annexing a cipher to the remainder,—and continue the division.

$$6.4\,)\,18.24\,(\,2.85$$
$$128$$
$$\overline{544}$$
$$512$$
$$\overline{320}$$
$$320$$

Counting the cipher annexed to form the last partial dividend as a decimal place of the given dividend, I point off two decimal places in the quotient.

The result, 2.85, is the required quotient.

a. When there is a remainder after all the orders of the dividend have been used, form a new partial dividend by annexing a cipher, and continue the division.

b. Decimal ciphers annexed to form a partial dividend, must be counted as decimal places of the given dividend.

NOTE.—Proceeding as directed in Note, page 131, the decimal point is placed in the quotient before writing the first decimal figure.

$$6.4\,)\,18.2|4\,(\,2.85$$
$$128$$
$$544$$
$$512$$
$$320$$
$$320$$

PROBLEMS.

1. $7854 \div 5.6 =$	*4.* $7.854 \div 5.6 =$	*7.* $.7854 \div .56\ =$
2. $785.4 \div 5.6 =$	*5.* $.7854 \div 5.6 =$	*8.* $.7854 \div .056 =$
3. $78.54 \div 5.6 =$	*6.* $.7854 \div 56 =$	*9.* $.7854 \div .0056 =$

10. Divide 76.94 by 4.9.

$$76.94 \div 4.9 = 15.702\tfrac{2}{49}\,;\ or\ 76.94 \div 4.9 = 15.702+.$$

When the division does not terminate, or when it has been carried as far as is desirable, express the remainder fractionally, as a part of the quotient; or, write + after the quotient.

Divide, carrying the division to three decimal places,

11. 1.264 by 3. | *12.* 3,156.293 by 25.17. | *13.* $650 by 313.

14. A baker paid $103.60 for 21.25 cords of wood. How much did he pay per cord?

15. A manufacturer made 25 sets of table-spoons that weighed 231 ounces. How much did one set weigh?

16. If .38 of a bushel of grass seed will seed one acre of land, 15.39 bushels will seed how many acres?

17. An Iowa farmer raised 3,045 bushels of corn from 56 acres. How much was the yield to the acre?

18. A bookseller sold 25 arithmetics for $8.43. How much did he receive apiece for them?

19. Divide an estate of $31,723.25 equally among 7 heirs.

133. Ex. Divide 42 by .56.

PROCESS.

$$.56)42.00(75$$
$$\underline{392}$$
$$\underline{280}$$
$$280$$

EXPLANATION.—Since there are two decimal places in the divisor and none in the dividend, I annex two decimal ciphers to the dividend before dividing.

There must be at least as many decimal places in the dividend as in the divisor, before beginning to divide.

PROBLEMS.

1. Divide 5,463.9 by 42.02.

2. $875 ÷ $3.12½ = how many?

3. A farmer exchanged 15 bushels of wheat for flour, receiving 1 sack of flour for every 1.25 bushels of wheat. How many sacks of flour did he receive?

4. If a factory girl weaves 6.25 yards of sheetings in an hour, in how many hours can she weave 40 yards?

5. When the price of rice is $ .06¼ a pound, how many pounds can be bought for $3.50?

6. A stationer sold .875 of a gallon of ink, in bottles holding .0625 of a gallon each. How many bottles of ink did he sell?

7. A druggist puts up 23 gallons of cologne in 736 bottles. How much cologne does each bottle contain?

134. Ex. Divide .002 by .08.

PROCESS.

$$.08\overline{)\,.002}$$
$$.025$$

EXPLANATION. — After dividing, I find that there are five decimal places in the dividend used, and two in the divisor. I therefore point off three decimal places in the result.

NOTE.—The process is more readily performed by the method given in Note, page 131.

$$.08\overline{)\,.00\,|\,2}$$
$$.025$$

PROBLEMS.

1. Divide .897 by 39.   *2.* .27 by 4.32.   *3.* .7 by 112.
4. .0016 by .512.   *5.* .07 by 12.8.   *6.* 2 by 53.1.   *7.* .1537 by 29.

8. Divide $8 into 200 equal parts.

9. If .7505 of an ounce of gold-leaf will cover 79 square feet, how much gold-leaf will gild one square foot?

10. $2.47½ for 275 lemons is how much apiece?

135. Ex. 1. Divide 582.7 by 10, by 100, by 1,000, and by 100,000.

PROCESSES.

$$582.7 \div 10 = 58.27$$
$$582.7 \div 100 = 5.827$$
$$582.7 \div 1,000 = .5827$$
$$582.7 \div 100,000 = .005827$$

Each removal of a decimal point in a number one place to the left divides the number by 10.

Ex. 2. Divide 3,725.4 by 700.

PROCESS.

$$7\,00\overline{)\,37\,|\,25.4}$$
$$5.322$$

EXPLANATION.—Since 700=7 times 100, I divide the dividend by 100, and obtain 37.254; and this result I divide by 7, and obtain 5.322, the required result.

PROBLEMS.

1. Divide 537.8 by 10.
2. Divide 62.5 by 50.
3. Divide 5,960.43 by 900.

4. $.75 ÷ 100 =
5. $437.50 ÷ 1,000 =
6. $30,943.20 ÷ $15,000 =

7. 434.5 acres of land were divided equally among 10 persons. How much land had each person?

8. An Ohio farmer raised 2,175 bushels of corn from 40 acres of land. How much was the yield to the acre?

9. In how many months will a man whose wages are $100 per month, earn $937.50?

10. A railroad 200 miles long was constructed, at a cost of $8,263,860.50. What was the cost per mile?

136. RULE FOR DIVISION OF DECIMALS.

I. *Annex decimal ciphers to the dividend, when necessary, and divide as in integers.*

II. *Point off as many decimal figures in the quotient as the number of decimal places in the dividend exceeds the number in the divisor.*

  a. *Count decimal ciphers annexed to form a partial dividend, as decimal places of the given dividend.*

  b. It is necessary to annex decimal ciphers to the dividend
    1. *When it has a less number of decimal places than the divisor.*
    2. *When the dividend, considered as an integer, is less than the divisor considered as an integer.*
    3. *When there is a remainder after all the orders of the dividend have been used.*

PROBLEMS.

1. .1632 divided by 3.4 = how many?

2. How many times is .0753 contained in 1,385.52?

3. What is the quotient of 5 divided by 64?

4. Divide 90.5 into 14,480 equal parts.

5. 639 cords ÷ 11.25 = how many cords?

6. 15.39 bushels are how many times .38 of a bushel?

7. How many pounds of wool will be required for 264 yards of cloth, at the rate of 1 pound for .625 of a yard?

8. If in an hour 18.75 barrels of water run into a cistern that holds 204 barrels, in how many hours will the cistern be filled?

9. In what time will a railroad train run 16 miles, if it runs at the rate of 31.25 miles an hour?

10. I raised 147 bushels of oats on 2.24 acres of land. At what rate did the land yield per acre?

11. If one gallon of sap makes .18 of a pound of maple sugar, how many gallons of sap will make 112.59 pounds of sugar?

12. If 1 bushel of charcoal is made from .0196 of a cord of wood, how many bushels can be made from 5.831 cords?

13. $564.37½ for 105 sheep is how much a head?

14. $35 buys how many pounds of sugar, at $.12½?

15. $172.50 buys how many lounges, at $7.50?

16. $59.06¼ for 31.5 gallons is how much per gallon?

17. $1.87½ buys how many bushels of plums, at $2.50 a bushel?

18. At $.56 a yard, $24.36 buys how many yards of muslin?

19. How many goblets, each weighing 7.5 ounces, can be made from 176 ounces of silver?

20. 815,105 pounds of hay are how many tons of 2,000 pounds each, and how many pounds over?

21. 124.2 tons of coal will make how many full car loads of 9.5 tons each?

22. 134 bushels of wheat will pay for how many sheep, at 2.5 bushels for 1 sheep?

23. I sold .95 of an acre of land in building-lots of .125 of an acre each. How many lots did I sell?

24. A baker has 834.25 pounds of lard, and he uses 23.75 pounds daily. How many full days will the lard last him, and how many pounds over?

Accounts and Bills.

137. A *debt* is money, goods, or services due from one party to another.

a. A *debtor* is a person from whom a debt is due.

b. A *creditor* is a person to whom a debt is due.

138. A *bill of goods* is a written statement given by the seller to the buyer, containing the date of the purchase; the names of buyer and seller; a list of the goods bought, with their prices; and the total amount or cost.

a. An *item* is each particular in a bill.

b. *Extending an item* is finding the cost of the item.

c. The *footing* is the total cost of all the items in a bill.

139. An *account,* in business transactions, is a written statement of debits and credits between two parties.

a. The *balance of an account* is the difference between the sums of the debits and credits.

b. When a bill or account is paid, the party to whom the payment is made should write at the bottom of the same, *Received payment*, or *Paid*, followed by his name.

PROBLEMS.

Extend the items, and find the footings in the following bills:

1.
Buffalo, June 17, 1882.

Mr. *Arthur Newman*

Bought of B. F. Brown & Co.

4 papers Garden Seeds,	@ $ .10 . . $	
5 Lamp Chimneys,	" .09 . .	
4 sacks Flour,	" 2.12½ .	
1 Corn Cultivator, ...	.	9.25
1 Spade, $ .75; 1 Spading Fork, $1.25		
2 Hoes, $ .63 and $ .81		

$22.04

2.   **Cleveland,** *Sept. 6, 1882.*

Mr. *James W. Graham*

                      Bought of Henry Arnold,

5 *lb. Java Coffee,*	@ *28¢* . . . $	
10 " *Crackers,*	" *11¢* . . .	
6 " *Butter,*	" *30¢* . . .	
1 *doz. Oranges,*		.28
1 *lb. Japan Tea,*		1.10
1 *Willow Basket,*		.35

                      Rec'd payment, $

                                          Henry Arnold.

Put the following narrations of business transactions into bills of proper forms:

3. Philadelphia, December 6, 1882, Charles Roberts & Co. sold to Mrs. Eliza Williams, for cash, 2 doz. silver table forks, at \$37.50 per dozen; 1 dozen silver table-spoons for \$33; 3 sets of silver tea-spoons, at \$9.25 per set; and 1 silver cake basket for \$37.50.

4. Albany, N. Y., November 1, 1882, Joseph Daniels bought of James Riley & Co. 15.5 tons of stove coal, at \$4.75; 19 tons of grate coal, at \$5.12½; and 14 cords of wood, at \$5.25.

5. Springfield, December 24, 1881, Jones & Bogart sold to Lyman A. Moore, on account, 1 piece of Lonsdale cotton, 42 yards, at \$ .12½; 5 yards of French broadcloth, at \$4.75; 16 yards of Merrimac prints, at \$ .09; 8 yards of Irish linen, at \$ .68¾; and 12 yards of Hamburg edging, at \$ .37½.

    Note.—For *outlines of decimals* for review, see page 271.

General Review Problems in Decimals.

1. Multiply twelve thousandths by twelve hundredths, and divide the product by six ten-thousandths.

2. From nine hundred and nine ten-thousandths subtract nine hundred nine ten-thousandths, and divide the remainder by nine hundred thousandths.

3. What is the quotient of .01 divided by 12.8?

4. If a clerk wishes to save $100 a year out of a salary of $900, how much can he spend per week?

5. If 105.6 tons of rails are required for 1 mile of railroad track, how many tons are required for 137.55 miles?

6. How much is the freight on a cargo of 25,380 bushels of wheat, from Chicago to Buffalo, at $.04½ per bushel?

7. A half-dime a day is how much a year?

8. 31 laborers received $1,046.25 for working 22.5 days. What were the average daily wages?

9. When tomatoes are worth $3 a bushel, what part of a bushel can be bought for $.37½?

10. I sowed 2.736 quarts of clover seed in my orchard, at the rate of 5.76 quarts to the acre. How much land is there in my orchard?

11. The taxes paid in a certain school-district one year were as follows: By A, $38.75; B, $10.50; C, $132.50; D, $6; E, $58.75; F, $2.50; Glass Manufactory, $1,057.50; H, $30; I, $1.50; J, $8.60; K, $141.80; L, $3.75; M, $530; National Bank, $1,515; O, $137.60; P, $6.70; Q, $199.60; Railroad Company, $895; S, $9.60; T, $3.50; U, $266.75; V, $176.25; and W, $2.75. What was the amount?

12. A housekeeper uses .375 of a pound of sugar to a jar of fruit. If she has 25 pounds of sugar, how many jars can she put up, and how much sugar will she have left?

13. A farmer raised 823.3 bushels of oats on 15 acres, and 466.45 bushels on 7 acres. What was the average yield per acre from the two pieces of land?

14. 25 miles of a railroad 57.36 miles long cost $13,758.40 per mile, 17 miles cost $16,521.72 per mile, and the remainder cost $18,125.12$\frac{1}{2}$ per mile. What was the average cost per mile of the entire road?

15. A laborer earns 1.31\frac{1}{4}$ per day, his wife $ .62$\frac{1}{2}$, and each of 3 children $ .37$\frac{1}{2}$. What are the earnings of the family per week?

16. If 100 sheep cost $437.50, what is the price per head?

17. How many bushels of onions can be raised on 3.27 acres, at the rate of 415 bushels to the acre?

18. How many tons of broom-corn can be raised from .85 of an acre, if 1.876 tons can be raised from one acre?

19. The owner of a schooner sold .3125 of her to the captain. What part of the vessel did he still own?

20. A contractor built a house for $3,725. The materials cost him $2,641.37$\frac{1}{2}$, and he paid $1,796.50 for labor. Did he make or lose money, and how much?

21. What is the cost of 32.5 bushels of oats, at $ .56$\frac{1}{4}$?

22. To-day Mary Morton bought of me 15 yards of dress silk, at $1.75; 3 yards of satin, at 1.87\frac{1}{2}$; 6 yards of French lace, at $ .81$\frac{1}{4}$; and 12 yards of gingham, at $ .28. Make out the bill.

23. On the 1st day of May last, Andrew Erwin bought of Potter & Co., of Philadelphia, 6 pairs of calf boots, @ $4.50; 8 pairs of kip boots, @ 3.62\frac{1}{2}$; 4 pairs of ladies' kid boots, @ $2.75; and 12 pairs of ladies' cloth boots, @ 2.12\frac{1}{2}$. Make out and receipt the bill.

CHAPTER III.

PROPERTIES OF NUMBERS.

SECTION I.

FACTORS AND DIVISORS.

140. The *integral factors* of a number are those integers of which the number is the product.

> One integer is *exactly divisible* by another when the quotient is an integer.

141. A *composite number* is a number that has other integral factors besides itself and 1.

142. A *prime number* is a number that has no integral factors besides itself and 1.

> *a.* A *prime factor* is a factor that is a prime number.
>
> *b.* An *even number* is a number that is exactly divisible by 2.
>
> *c.* An *odd number* is a number that is not exactly divisible by 2.

Oral Work.—*1.* Name all the composite numbers between 30 and 75, and tell why they are composite.

2. Name all the prime numbers from 1 to 50.

3. What integers less than the number 20 are even? Why?

4. What integers between 30 and 50 are odd? Why?

143. *Factoring* is the process of finding the integral factors of a number.

> An *exact divisor* of a number is any integral factor of that number.

A. What are the integral factors

1. Of 21? | *2.* Of 35? | *3.* Of 18? | *4.* Of 29? | *5.* Of 63?

What numbers are exact divisors

6. Of 15?	*9.* Of 24?	*12.* Of 77?	*15.* Of 64?
7. Of 27?	*10.* Of 56?	*13.* Of 49?	*16.* Of 75?
8. Of 35?	*11.* Of 45?	*14.* Of 95?	*17.* Of 108?

What are the prime factors

18. Of 8?   *19.* Of 36?   *20.* Of 50?   *21.* Of 72?   *22.* Of 128?

Any number is exactly divisible

By 2, if it is an even number.

By 3, if the sum of its digits is exactly divisible by 3.

By 4, if the number expressed by its two right-hand figures is exactly divisible by 4.

By 5, if its right-hand figure is 5 or 0.

By 6, if it is even, and the sum of its digits is exactly divisible by 3.

By 8, if the number expressed by its three right-hand figures is exactly divisible by 8.

By 9, if the sum of its digits is exactly divisible by 9.

By 10, if its right-hand figure is 0.

B. Of the twelve numbers in the margin,

1. Which are exactly divisible by 2?			78	416	656
2. By 3?	*4.* By 5?	*7.* By 9?	95	360	777
3. By 4?	*5.* By 6?	*8.* By 10?	168	595	1,260
	6. By 8?		252	423	2,520

Case I. **Prime factors.**

Written Work.—Ex. Find the prime factors of 210.

Explanation.—Since 210 is an even number, I divide it by the prime factor 2. Since the sum of the digits of 105 is exactly divisible by 3, I divide 105 by the

Process.

210	*105*	*35*	*7*
2	*3*	*5*	*7*

prime factor 3. Since the right-hand figure of 35 is 5, I divide 35 by the prime factor 5, and obtain the prime number 7.

2, 3, 5, and 7 are the prime factors required.

144. Rule for Prime Factors.

I. *Divide the given number by any prime factor.*

II. *If the quotient is a composite number, divide it in like manner; and so continue to divide, till the quotient is a prime number.*

The divisors and the last quotient are the prime factors.

Problems.

Find the prime factors of
1. 315.
2. 436.
3. 555.
4. 863.
5. 729.
6. 954.
7. 2,838.
8. 9,765.

Case II. Common Prime Factors.

***Oral Work.*—145.** What number is an exact divisor of

1. 9 and 15?
2. 16 and 28?
3. 45 and 63?
4. 19 and 72?
5. 9, 12, and 15?
6. 18, 30, and 42?
7. 36, 84, and 120?
8. 27, 45, and 72?
9. 54, 36, and 81?
10. $30, $75, and $90?
11. $.27, $.63, and $.81?
12. $50 and $90?

***Written Work.*—Ex.** Find all the common prime factors of 90, 120, and 210.

Explanation.—I write the numbers in columns, as for addition, and divide successively by the common prime factors 2, 3, and 5, and write the quotients in columns at the right of the numbers divided.

Process.

90	45	15	3
120	60	20	4
210	105	35	7
2	3	5	

The factors 2, 3, and 5 are the common prime factors required.

Problems.

Find all the common prime factors

1. Of 36 and 80.
2. Of 64 and 96.
3. Of 72 and 240.
4. Of 120 and 400.
5. Of 45, 105, and 180.
6. Of 52, 72, and 148.

Case III. Greatest Common Divisor.

***Oral Work.*—146.** What is the greatest exact divisor

1. Of 27 and 36?
2. Of 42 and 70?
3. Of 66 and 99?
4. Of 80 and 108?
5. Of 24, 40, and 56?
6. Of 75, 45, and 120?

147. A *common divisor* of two or more numbers is any factor common to those numbers.

148. The *greatest common divisor* of two or more numbers is the greatest factor common to those numbers.

1. What composite number is the greatest common divisor of 24, 60, and 96?

2. Of what prime factors is this greatest common divisor the product?

3. The prime factors of this greatest common divisor are also prime factors of how many of the numbers 24, 60, and 96?

4. The product of any two or more numbers is the greatest common divisor of what numbers?

149. PRINCIPLE. *The greatest common divisor of two or more numbers is the product of all their common prime factors.*

Written Work.—Ex. Find the greatest common divisor of 105, 525, and 315.

EXPLANATION. — I find the common prime factors of 105, 525, and 315 to be 3, 5, and 7. I then multiply these common prime factors together, and obtain 105, which is the greatest common divisor of the given numbers.

PROCESS.

$$\begin{array}{c|c|c|c}
105 & 35 & 7 & 1 \\
525 & 175 & 35 & 5 \\
315 & 105 & 21 & 3
\end{array}$$

$$3 \times 5 \times 7 = 105$$

PROBLEMS.

Find the greatest common divisor

1. Of 96 and 128.	*6.* Of 105, 135, and 180.
2. Of 240 and 1,200.	*7.* Of 288, 216, and 504.
3. Of 196 and 84.	*8.* Of 280, 196, and 112.
4. Of 102 and 153.	*9.* Of 168, 280, 182, and 252.
5. Of 351 and 3,861.	*10.* Of 2,835, 5,670, and 4,455.

150. Rule for Greatest Common Divisor.

I. *Divide the given numbers by any common prime factor; divide the results in the same manner; and so continue, till results are obtained that have no common prime factor.*

II. *Multiply together all the numbers used as divisors.*

Problems.

Find the greatest common divisor

1. Of 28 and 98.
2. Of 116 and 732.
3. Of 252 and 280.
4. Of 450 and 792.
5. Of 18, 27, and 45.
6. Of 78, 90, and 378.
7. Of 2,835, 2,455, and 5,670.
8. Of 3,150, 4,050, and 4,950.

9. What is the length of the longest chain that will exactly measure the length and width of a piece of land which is 160 rods long and 100 rods wide?

10. A farmer draws to market 1,200 bushels of wheat, 864 bushels of corn, 784 bushels of barley, and 1,786 bushels of oats—each kind by itself—in bags of the greatest possible equal number of bushels. How many bushels does he put into a bag? How many bags of each kind of grain does he draw to market?

11. If 1,080 yards, 360 yards, 680 yards, and 480 yards of carpeting are laid on the floors of rooms of equal size in a hotel, and the largest size possible that exactly uses all the carpeting of each kind, how much carpeting is used for a room? How many rooms are carpeted?

12. A merchant tailor used three pieces of cloth containing 95, 205, and 380 yards in making suits, using the same amount of cloth for each suit, and the greatest amount possible without leaving remnants. How many suits did he make?

SECTION II.

MULTIPLES.

151. A *multiple* is any integer of which a given integer is a factor.

Oral Work.—*1.* Name some number that is a multiple of 4.

A multiple of 4 is any number of which 4 is an integral factor; and 4 is an integral factor of 2 times 4 or 8, 3 times 4 or 12, 4 times 4 or 16, and so on.

Name three numbers } *2.* Of 7. | *4.* Of 6. | *6.* Of 15.
that are multiples } *3.* Of 5. | *5.* Of 9. | *7.* Of 40.

CASE I. **Common multiples.**

152. *1.* Name the first four multiples of 3.

2. Name the first three multiples of 4.

3. Which one of these multiples is a multiple of 3 and 4?

4. What number is a multiple of 4 and 6?

A multiple of 4 and 6 is a number of which 4 and 6 are integral factors; and 4 and 6 are integral factors of 4 times 6 or 24.

What number is a multiple

5. Of 3 and 8? | *7.* Of 4 and 7? | *9.* Of 3, 2, and 11?
6. Of 2 and 5? | *8.* Of 6 and 25? | *10.* Of 4, 7, and 5?

153. A *common multiple* of two or more numbers is any integer of which each of the given numbers is an integral factor.

1. What are the prime factors of 12?

2. What are the other factors of 12?

3. Then, of what numbers is 12 a multiple?

4. Of what numbers is 40 a multiple?

5. Of what numbers is 21 a multiple?

6. Find a common multiple of 6 and 10.

Find a common multiple

7. Of 9 and 4.	9. Of 6 and 3.	11. Of 3, 5, and 4.
8. Of 7 and 12.	10. Of 8 and 20.	12. Of 8, 10, and 7.

13. What number is a common multiple of 9, 10, and 12?

Written Work.—Ex. Find a common multiple of 16 and 25.

EXPLANATION.—I multiply 16 and 25 together, and obtain their common multiple, 400.

PROCESS.

$$16 \times 25 = 400$$

PROBLEMS.

Find a common multiple

1. Of 9 and 16.	3. Of 5, 12, and 19.	5. Of 10, 11, 3, and 31.
2. Of 17 and 22.	4. Of 8, 13, and 50.	6. Of 6, 29, and 67.

CASE II. **Least common multiple.**

Oral Work.—**154.** What number is a multiple, and what is the least number that is a multiple, of

1. 2 and 6?	4. 6 and 9?	7. 2, 4, and 12?	10. 20 and 30?
2. 3 and 6?	5. 4 and 10?	8. 2, 6, and 5?	11. 10 and 25?
3. 4 and 6?	6. 6 and 8?	9. 3, 12, and 10?	12. 3, 4, 6, and 8?

155. The *least common multiple* of two or more numbers is the least integer of which each of the given numbers is an integral factor.

1. What number is a common multiple of 8 and 12?

2. What are the prime factors of 8? Of 12?

3. What number is a common multiple of all the prime factors of 8 and 12?

4. What number is the least common multiple of 8 and 12?

156. PRINCIPLE. *The least common multiple of two or more numbers is a multiple of all the prime factors of each of those numbers, and of no other prime factors.*

Written Work.—Ex. Find the least common multiple of 20, 48, and 56.

EXPLANATION.—I first separate
each of the numbers into its
prime factors.

Then, comparing separately the
prime factors of 20 and 48
with the prime factors of 56
—the greatest given number,
—I find that in the prime fac-
tors of 56 I have all the prime factors of 20 but 5, and all the
prime factors of 48 but 2 and 3; and I write these prime factors
and 56 in a line, as factors of the required least common multiple.
Multiplying these factors together, I obtain 1,680, which is the
least common multiple of the given numbers.

PROCESS.

$$20 = 2 \times 2 \times 5$$
$$48 = 2 \times 2 \times 2 \times 2 \times 3$$
$$56 = 2 \times 2 \times 2 \times 7$$
$$\overline{56 \times 5 \times 2 \times 3 = 1,680}$$

PROBLEMS.

What is the least common multiple of

1. 24 and 66 ?	*5.* 9, 21, 27, and 63 ?	*9.* 54, 72, and 126 ?
2. 15 and 100 ?	*6.* 32, 56, 96, and 72?	*10.* 75, 225, and 400 ?
3. 8, 12, and 48 ?	*7.* 36, 18, and 24 ?	*11.* 16, 81, 49, and 25 ?
4. 6, 15, and 90 ?	*8.* 115, 30, and 75 ?	*12.* 216, 132, and 1,728?

157. Ex. Find the least common multiple of 6, 24,
96, 15, and 60.

EXPLANATION.—I write the
numbers in a line, in or-
der, from least to greatest.
Since 6 and 15 are factors
of 60, and 24 is a factor of
96, I strike out the num-
bers 6, 15, and 24, and find
the least common multiple
of the remaining numbers 60 and 96.

PROCESS.

$$\cancel{6} \quad \cancel{15} \quad \cancel{24} \quad 60 \quad 96$$
$$60 = 2 \times 2 \times 3 \times 5$$
$$96 = 2 \times 2 \times 2 \times 2 \times 2 \times 3$$
$$\overline{96 \times 5 = 480}$$

This least common multiple, 480, is the least common multiple of
all the given numbers.

*When any of the given numbers are factors of other given numbers,
omit those numbers that are factors, and find the least common multiple of the other numbers.*

158. RULES FOR MULTIPLES.

I. To find a common multiple:—

Multiply the numbers together.

II. To find the least common multiple:—

1. *Separate the numbers into their prime factors.*

2. *Multiply together the largest given number and those prime factors of the other given numbers not found among the factors of this largest number.*

PROBLEMS.

Find a common multiple	Find the least common multiple
1. Of 50 and 81.	*5.* Of the first nine integers.
2. Of 3, 8, and 70.	*6.* Of 5, 51, 10, 34, and 85.
3. Of 20 and 67.	*7.* Of 9, 60, 45, 72, 15, 35, 18, and 12.
4. Of 135 and 318.	*8.* Of 21, 35, 7, 100, 15, 28, and 125.

9. What is the least sum of money with which I can purchase melons at 45 cents each, or plums at 27 cents a peck, or peaches at 90 cents a basket, or oranges at 36 cents a dozen?

10. D can pick 40 bushels of apples in a day, E 48 bushels, and F 64 bushels. What is the least number of bushels that will make a number of full days' work for any one of the three men?

11. A can walk round a mile course in 12 minutes, B in 16 minutes, and C in 20 minutes. If they all start together, and walk till they are again together, how many minutes will each walk? How many miles will each walk?

12. What is the least number of gallons of petroleum that will fill, some exact number of times, any one of five casks that hold respectively 34, 54, 68, 108, and 238 gallons?

***Oral Work.*—159.** What factor will remain, if I remove or strike out

   1. From 21 the factor 7? The factor 3?

   2. From 18 the factor 3? The factor 6? The factor 2?

   3. What is the quotient of 75 divided by 15?

   4. Of $\frac{1}{3}$ of 75 divided by $\frac{1}{3}$ of 15?

   5. Of $\frac{1}{5}$ of 75 divided by $\frac{1}{5}$ of 15?

   6. What factors are common to 15 and 75?

   7. If I strike out from 75 all the factors of 15, what factors will remain?

Divide
8. 4×6 by 4×3.	*12.* $6 \times 9 \times 8$ by $8 \times 6 \times 3$.
9. 8×7 by 2×7.	*13.* $4 \times 10 \times 7 \times 12$ by $4 \times 10 \times 12$.
10. 5×12 by 10×6.	*14.* 3×9 or 27 by 2×9 or 18.
11. 9×8 by 3×12.	*15.* $7 \times 2 \times 6$ by 2×7.

   16. If I omit all the common factors from 60 (the dividend), and 24 (the divisor), what factor of the dividend will remain? What factor of the divisor will remain?

   17. If from the number 28 I strike out the factor 7, what is the result? What has been done to the number?

   18. The dividend is 64 and the divisor is 16; what is the quotient? Strike out the common factor 8 from dividend and divisor; what is the quotient?

160. ***Cancellation*** is the process of omitting or striking out equal factors from the dividend and divisor.

   The solution of problems requiring both multiplication and division, may often be shortened by cancellation.

161. PRINCIPLE I. *Cancelling a factor from a number divides the number by that factor.*

PRINCIPLE II. *Cancelling a common factor from dividend and divisor does not change the value of the quotient.*

Written Work.—Ex. 1. Divide $6 \times 9 \times 20$ by 6×4.

EXPLANATION.—In dividend and divisor are the common factors 6 and 4 ($20 = 5 \times 4$). I cancel these factors, and I have remaining the factors 1, 9, and 5 of the dividend, and 1 and 1 of the divisor.

FIRST PROCESS.

$$\frac{6 \times 9 \times 20}{6 \times 4} = \frac{1 \times 9 \times 5}{1 \times 1} = \frac{45}{1} = 45$$

I multiply together the remaining factors of the dividend, and also the remaining factors of the divisor, and obtain 45 for a new dividend and 1 for a new divisor; and completing the division, I have 45, the quotient required.

The work is commonly written as shown in the second process.

SECOND PROCESS.

$$\frac{6 \times 9 \times 20}{6 \times 4} = \frac{45}{1} = 45$$

Ex. 2. Divide 16×21 by 7×8.

PROCESS.

$$\frac{16 \times 21}{7 \times 8} = \frac{6}{1} = 6$$

Ex. 3. Divide $8 \times 25 \times 45$ by $15 \times 24 \times 2$.

PROCESS.

$$\frac{8 \times 25 \times 45}{15 \times 24 \times 2} = \frac{25}{2} = 12\frac{1}{2}$$

a. Cancelling any factor or number leaves 1 in the place of the factor or number cancelled.

b. *When all the other factors of either dividend or divisor are cancelled, write the 1. In all other cases omit it.*

PROBLEMS.

Divide
{
1. 72 by 3×8.
2. $5 \times 5 \times 5$ by 25.
3. 10×12 by 5×6.

4. $14 \times 16 \times 18$ by $7 \times 8 \times 9$.
5. 240×99 by 80×33.
6. $20 \times 32 \times 44$ by $5 \times 6 \times 11$.

7. What is the quotient of 35×17 divided by 5×7?

8. What is the quotient of $8 \times 5 \times 3 \times 6 \div 9 \times 10 \times 4$?

9. What is the quotient of $7 \times 12 \times 6 \times 16 \div 72 \times 32$?

	10	11	12	13
Divide	$\dfrac{975}{13 \times 15}$	$\dfrac{1365}{13 \times 15}$	$\dfrac{5 \times 28 \times 5}{175}$	$\dfrac{5 \times 9 \times 5 \times 7}{175}$

	14	15	16
Divide	$\dfrac{200 \times 24 \times 36}{144 \times 60}$	$\dfrac{7800}{390 \times 4 \times 3}$	$\dfrac{27 \times 55 \times 96 \times 84}{33 \times 132 \times 28 \times 15}$

17. The factors of a dividend are 4, 15, and 27; and of a divisor, 3, 3, 4, and 45. What is the quotient?

18. The dividend is $24 \times 9 \times 15 \times 21$, and the divisor is $5 \times 7 \times 36 \times 108$. What is the quotient?

19. How much coffee, at 30 cents a pound, must be given in exchange for 6 pounds of butter, at 40 cents a pound?

20. A farmer exchanged 360 sheep, valued at $2.75 per head, for cows at $45 each. How many cows did he buy?

21. How many bushels of turnips, at $.25 per bushel, will pay for 36 pounds of tea at $.75 per pound?

22. If a boat sails 24 miles in 4 hours, how many miles will it sail in 2×8 hours?

23. How many tons of hay at $20 a ton, are worth as much as 60 bushels of wheat at $2 a bushel?

24. If a laborer can earn $64 in 30 days, how much can he earn in 35 days?

25. If 12 men can do a piece of work in 30 days, in what time can 9 men do the same work?

26. If 12 men can do a piece of work in 30 days, working 10 hours a day, in what time can 15 men do the same, working 8 hours a day?

Note.—For *outlines of properties of numbers* for review, see page 271.

CHAPTER IV.

FRACTIONS.

SECTION I.

NOTATION AND NUMERATION.

162. *1.* What is the name of one of the parts, when any thing or a *one* is divided into two equal parts?

2. Into three equal parts? | *4.* Into eight equal parts?
3. Into five equal parts? | *5.* Into ten equal parts?
6. Into any number of equal parts?

Any thing or a *one* is how many

7. Halves? | *9.* Eighths? | *11.* Sixths? | *13.* Fourths? | *15.* Tenths?
8. Fifths? | *10.* Thirds? | *12.* Ninths? | *14.* Sevenths? | *16.* Twelfths?

When any thing or a *one* is divided into nine equal parts,
17. What is the name of the parts?

18. Of one part? | *20.* Of two parts? | *22.* Of seven parts?
19. Of four parts? | *21.* Of five parts? | *23.* Of three parts?

163. *Fractional parts* are parts obtained by dividing any thing or a *one* into any number of equal parts.

Halves, fifths, eighths, twelfths are fractional parts.

164. A *fractional unit* is one of the equal fractional parts into which a thing or the unit 1 is divided.

1 half, 1 fifth, 1 eighth, 1 twelfth are fractional units.

165. A *fraction* is a number that expresses one or more fractional units.

1 sixth, 5 eighths, 9 tenths are fractions.

A fraction is expressed by two numbers, written one under the other, with a horizontal line between them, thus: 1 eighth, $\frac{1}{8}$; 3 eighths, $\frac{3}{8}$; 1 fifteenth, $\frac{1}{15}$; 11 fifteenths, $\frac{11}{15}$.

G 2

1. What numbers express the fraction five eighths?

Which number determines	What is
2. The size of the parts?	*5.* The fractional unit?
3. The number of the parts?	*6.* The number of fractional units?
4. The value of one part?	*7.* The value of the fraction?

166. The *terms* of a fraction are the two numbers used to express it.

167. The *denominator* is that term which names the parts expressed by the fraction. It is written *below* the horizontal line.

168. The *numerator* is that term which numbers the parts expressed by the fraction. It is written *above* the horizontal line.

   a. The terms of the fraction $\frac{4}{5}$ are 4 and 5; the denominator is 5; and the numerator is 4.

   b. The denominator shows the size of the parts; and the numerator shows the number of parts expressed by the fraction.

169. The numerator of any fraction is a dividend, the denominator is a divisor, and the value expressed by the fraction is the quotient.

   $\frac{9}{16}$ expresses the quotient of 9 divided by 16.

A. Read each of the fractions given below, and name

1. The terms;	*4.* The fractional unit;	*6.* The dividend;
2. The numerator;	*5.* The number of frac-	*7.* The divisor; and
3. The denominator;	tional units;	*8.* The quotient.

$$\frac{3}{5} \qquad \frac{1}{5} \qquad \frac{5}{13} \qquad \frac{15}{4} \qquad \frac{11}{18} \qquad \frac{7}{25} \qquad \frac{37}{8} \qquad \frac{12}{12}$$

B. The fraction $\frac{2}{3}$ expresses 2 of the 3 equal parts into which 1 is divided; or 1 of the 3 equal parts into which 2 is divided.

What is expressed	What do you understand
1. By the fraction $\frac{2}{6}$? *3.* By $\frac{3}{8}$?	*5.* By $\frac{1}{10}$? *7.* By $\frac{9}{16}$ of a pound?
2. By the number $\frac{4}{7}$? *4.* By $\frac{11}{20}$?	*6.* By $\frac{4}{9}$? *8.* By $\frac{8}{12}$ of a dozen?

C. 1. Which of the fractions in the margin express a value equal to 1? Why? $\frac{1}{3}$ $\frac{7}{7}$ $\frac{15}{15}$ $\frac{2\,3\,6}{2\,3\,6}$

2. Which express less than 1? Why? $\frac{3}{3}$ $\frac{7}{12}$ $\frac{15}{16}$ $\frac{2\,3\,6}{1{,}7\,2\,8}$

3. Which express more than 1? Why? $\frac{5\,3}{3}$ $\frac{7}{4}$ $\frac{15}{5}$ $\frac{2\,3\,6}{6\,7}$

170. A *proper fraction* is a fraction that expresses less than 1.

171. An *improper fraction* is a fraction that expresses 1 or more than 1.

   a. $\frac{4}{5}$, $\frac{7}{10}$ are proper fractions; $\frac{8}{5}$, $\frac{10}{5}$ are improper fractions.

   b. The numerator of a proper fraction is *always* a less number than the denominator; the numerator of an improper fraction is *never* a less number than the denominator.

172. A *mixed number* is a number that expresses an integer and a decimal, or an integer and a fraction.

   a. 17.4, 3.65; $12\frac{2}{3}$, $5\frac{9}{16}$ are mixed numbers.

   b. In reading a mixed number, read *and* between the integer and the fraction.

   c. Decimal units, as well as fractional units, are equal parts of a thing, or of the unit 1. Hence,

      1. Decimal parts are fractional parts; and

      2. Decimals are also called *decimal fractions.*

1. Which of the numbers in the margin are proper fractions, and why? $\frac{4}{9}$ $\frac{8}{13}$ $\frac{7}{16}$

2. Which are improper fractions, and why? $\frac{5}{3}$ $\frac{9}{5}$ $\frac{1}{2}$

3. Which are mixed numbers, and why? $\frac{5}{6}$ $\frac{6}{7}$ $4\frac{3}{8}$ $\frac{37}{16}$ $11\frac{2}{3}$ $3\frac{7}{10}$

What is the unit

  4. Of 315?
  5. Of $89?
  6. Of $\frac{1}{5}$?
  7. Of $\frac{3}{8}$?

  8. Of 37 bushels?
  9. Of 45 pounds?
  10. Of $\frac{3}{7}$ of a bushel?
  11. Of $\frac{4}{5}$ of a pound?

  12. Of $\frac{1}{5}$ of an acre?
  13. Of $\frac{1}{6}$ of a yard?
  14. Of $3\frac{1}{4}$ dozen?
  15. Of $16\frac{2}{3}$ miles?

173. The *unit of a fraction* is *one,* of the kind expressed by the fraction.

What is the unit of each of the numbers in the margin?   28 $\frac{1}{16}$ $\frac{9}{16}$ $\frac{10}{27}$ $8\frac{5}{9}$ $3\frac{4}{7}$ weeks.
413   $\frac{1}{5}$ $\frac{3}{8}$ $\frac{83}{144}$ $15\frac{7}{21}$ $18\frac{3}{4}$ gallons.

174. To *analyze a fraction* is to name and describe all its parts, its kind, and its value.

Ex. Analyze the fraction $\frac{3}{4}$ of a mile.

> ANALYSIS.—The *terms* of this fraction are 3 and 4, because they are the two numbers used to express it; the *denominator* is 4, because it names the parts expressed by the fraction; and the *numerator* is 3, because it numbers the parts expressed by the fraction.
>
> The *unit of the fraction* is 1 mile, because it is the *one* divided to form the fraction; and the *fractional unit* is $\frac{1}{4}$, because it is 1 of the 4 equal parts into which 1 mile is divided.
>
> The fraction is *proper*, because it expresses less than 1; and its *value* is $\frac{3}{4}$ of a mile, because $\frac{3}{4}$ expresses the quotient of the numerator 3 divided by the denominator 4.

Analyze				
Analyze the fractions	*1.* $\frac{4}{7}$ of a week. *2.* $\frac{3}{10}$ of a foot.	*3.* \$$\frac{5}{12}$. *4.* \$$\frac{1}{5}$.	*5.* $\frac{2}{3}$. *6.* $\frac{9}{14}$.	*7.* $\frac{15}{2}$. *8.* $\frac{17}{25}$.

<hr>

SECTION II.

REDUCTIONS.

CASE I. **Fractions to lowest terms.**

Oral Work.—**175.** *1.* 1 is how many fifths? How many fifteenths? How many sixtieths?

2. $\frac{60}{60}$ are how many fifteenths? How many fifths? How many ones?

3. How is the fraction $\frac{5}{10}$ reduced to halves?

4. How is the fraction $\frac{64}{120}$ reduced to sixtieths? To thirtieths? To fifteenths?

5. Dividing the terms of a fraction by any number, has what effect upon the value of the fraction?

Which expresses the greater value,

6. $\frac{1}{2}$ or $\frac{2}{4}$? | *7.* $\frac{4}{6}$ or $\frac{8}{12}$? | *8.* $\frac{30}{40}$, $\frac{18}{24}$, or $\frac{3}{4}$?

176. A fraction is in its ***lowest terms,*** when its terms have no common factor.

1. Reduce the fraction $\frac{8}{28}$ to its lowest terms.

I divide the terms 8 and 28 by the common factor 4, and obtain $\frac{2}{7}$; and, since the terms 2 and 7 have no common factor, the lowest terms of the fraction $\frac{8}{28}$ are $\frac{2}{7}$.

Reduce to lowest terms
$\left\{\begin{array}{l}2.\ \frac{4}{20}. \\ 3.\ \frac{6}{14}.\end{array}\right.$ | $\begin{array}{l}4.\ \frac{7}{35}. \\ 5.\ \frac{14}{16}.\end{array}$ | $\begin{array}{l}6.\ \frac{34}{57}. \\ 7.\ \frac{28}{15}.\end{array}$ | $\begin{array}{l}8.\ \frac{40}{25}. \\ 9.\ \frac{56}{28}.\end{array}$ | $\begin{array}{l}10.\ \frac{15}{20}. \\ 11.\ \frac{52}{69}.\end{array}$

12. $\frac{8}{16}$ of a lemon are how many eighths of a lemon? How many fourths? How many halves?

13. Reduce the fractions $\frac{20}{38}$ and $\$\frac{15}{25}$ to lowest terms.

14. James has $\frac{2}{8}$ of an apple, and Charles has $\frac{6}{24}$. Which has the greater fraction?

15. Is $\$\frac{8}{40}$ more or less than $\$\frac{6}{30}$, and how much?

16. In five successive weeks a family uses $\frac{10}{15}$, $\frac{36}{54}$, $\frac{4}{6}$, $\frac{12}{18}$, and $\frac{48}{69}$ of a bushel of apples. In which week do they use the most?

177. PRINCIPLE I. *The value of a fraction is not changed, by dividing its terms by any common factor.*

Written Work.—Ex. Reduce $\frac{105}{175}$ to lowest terms.

EXPLANATION.—I first divide 105 and 175 —the terms of the given fraction—by the common factor 5, and obtain $\frac{21}{35}$. I then divide 21 and 35—the terms of this fraction—by the common factor 7, and obtain $\frac{3}{5}$. Since the terms 3 and 5 have no common factor, the lowest terms of the fraction $\frac{105}{175}$ are $\frac{3}{5}$.

FIRST PROCESS.
$$\frac{105 \div 5}{175 \div 5} = \frac{21 \div 7}{35 \div 7} = \frac{3}{5}$$

SECOND PROCESS.
$$\frac{105 \div 35}{175 \div 35} = \frac{3}{5}$$

The result may be obtained at one division, by dividing the terms 105 and 175 by 35, their greatest common factor.

PROBLEMS.

What are the lowest terms of

1. $\frac{8}{18}$?	*4.* $\frac{24}{36}$?	*7.* $\frac{16}{80}$?	*10.* $\frac{187}{85}$?	*13.* $\frac{39}{143}$?
2. $\frac{15}{27}$?	*5.* $\frac{34}{51}$?	*8.* $\frac{27}{153}$?	*11.* $\frac{207}{99}$?	*14.* $\frac{143}{213}$?
3. $\frac{40}{25}$?	*6.* $\frac{21}{40}$?	*9.* $\frac{60}{165}$?	*12.* $\frac{128}{88}$?	*15.* $\frac{528}{1804}$?

Reduce to lowest terms
16. $\frac{210}{338}$ of a yard.
17. $\frac{3872}{5808}$ of a day.
18. $\frac{81}{108}$ and $\frac{96}{120}$.
19. $\frac{56000}{64000}$ of a pound.
20. $\frac{4082400}{1134000}$.
21. $\frac{10700}{20120}$ of a ton.

Case II. Fractions to other fractions having given denominators.

Oral Work.—**178.** What fraction expresses the result, when each of 2 halves is divided into

1. 2 equal parts?
2. 3 equal parts?
3. 7 equal parts?
4. 5 equal parts?
5. 10 equal parts?
6. 8 equal parts?

Multiply the terms of the fraction

7. $\frac{3}{4}$ by 3.
8. $\frac{2}{5}$ by 4.
9. $\frac{5}{7}$ by 8.
10. $\frac{1}{3}$ by 6.
11. $\frac{10}{13}$ by 9.
12. $\frac{31}{50}$ by 5.
13. $\frac{13}{18}$ by 10.
14. $\frac{22}{33}$ by 7.

By what number must you multiply the terms, to change

15. $\frac{3}{5}$ to twentieths?
16. $\frac{5}{6}$ to forty-eighths?
17. $\frac{3}{7}$ and $\frac{4}{5}$ to thirty-fifths?
18. $\frac{5}{9}$ and $\frac{3}{11}$ to ninety-ninths?

To reduce a fraction to another fraction having a larger denominator:—*Divide the required denominator by the given denominator, and multiply the terms of the given fraction by the quotient.*

19. Reduce the fraction $\frac{2}{7}$ to twenty-eighths.

7, the denominator of $\frac{2}{7}$, is contained in 28, the required denominator, 4 times; hence, I multiply the terms of $\frac{2}{7}$ by 4, and obtain $\frac{8}{28}$.

20. Reduce $\frac{8}{15}$ to 30ths. To 60ths. To 120ths.
21. $\frac{1}{2}$ to fourths. To 16ths.
22. $\frac{3}{8}$ to fortieths. To 64ths.
23. $\frac{5}{7}$ to forty-seconds.
24. $\frac{2}{9}$ and $\frac{1}{6}$ to 54ths.
25. $\frac{1}{3}$ and $\frac{7}{20}$ to 60ths.
26. $\frac{1}{2}$, $\frac{1}{3}$, and $\frac{1}{4}$ to 12ths.

Which is the greater number,
27. $\frac{3}{5}$ of an hour, or $\frac{17}{25}$ of an hour?
28. $\frac{9}{32}$ of a bushel, or $\frac{3}{8}$ of a bushel?
29. $\frac{31}{100}$ of an acre, or $\frac{3}{10}$ of an acre?

179. Principle II. *The value of a fraction is not changed by multiplying its terms by any number.*

Written Work.—Ex. Reduce the fraction $\frac{3}{5}$ to 125ths.

EXPLANATION. — Dividing 125, the required denominator, by 5, the given denominator, I obtain 25, the number by which the terms of the fraction $\frac{3}{5}$ must be multiplied to reduce it to 125ths. I then multiply the terms 3 and 5 by 25, and obtain $\frac{75}{125}$, the required result.

PROCESS.

$$125 \div 5 = 25$$

$$\frac{3 \times 25 = 75}{5 \times 25 = 125}$$

PROBLEMS.

1. Reduce $\frac{1}{8}$ to a fraction having 468 for a denominator.

2. Seven eighths are how many one hundred sixtieths?

Reduce
3. $\frac{3}{40}$ to 600ths.
4. $\frac{3}{25}$ to 275ths.
5. $\frac{1}{2}$ to 900ths.

6. $\frac{4}{9}$ to 297ths.
7. $\frac{7}{15}$ to 285ths.
8. $\frac{5}{12}$ to 1152ds.

9. $\frac{31}{80}$ to 801sts.
10. $\frac{117}{200}$ to 1184ths.
11. $\frac{37}{144}$ to 1728ths.

12. A has $\$\frac{11}{10}$, B has $\$\frac{5}{8}$, and C has $\$\frac{3}{4}$. Which of the three persons has the most money?

13. A grocer has $\frac{5}{12}$ of a barrel of pulverized sugar, $\frac{17}{40}$ of a barrel of granulated, and $\frac{53}{120}$ of a barrel of crushed. Of which kind has he the most?

CASE III. **Dissimilar fractions to similar fractions.**

180. *Similar fractions* are fractions that have the same fractional unit.

181. *Dissimilar fractions* are fractions that have different fractional units.

a. $\frac{2}{7}$, $\frac{4}{7}$ are similar fractions; $\frac{3}{4}$, $\frac{3}{7}$, $\frac{2}{3}$, $\frac{5}{8}$, $\frac{1}{2}$ are dissimilar fractions.

b. Similar fractions have like denominators.

c. A *common denominator* is the denominator of each of two or more similar fractions.

Oral Work.—*1.* Which of the fractions in the margin are similar fractions? Why?

2. Which are dissimilar fractions? Why?

3. Which have a common denominator?

4. Which can be reduced to eighteenths? Why?

$\frac{1}{2}$, $\frac{1}{7}$, $\frac{3}{4}$, $\frac{2}{5}$.

$\frac{7}{8}$, $\frac{4}{5}$, $\frac{1}{4}$, $\frac{5}{7}$.

$\frac{4}{9}$, $\frac{6}{7}$, $\frac{3}{8}$, $\frac{3}{5}$.

$\frac{3}{7}$, $\frac{5}{11}$, $\frac{1}{8}$, $\frac{9}{10}$.

5. The denominators of fractions that can be reduced to fifteenths, must be factors of what number?

What fractions can be reduced

6. To 28ths? Why? | 7. To 40ths? Why? | 8. To 48ths? Why?

What similar fractions are equal in value

9. To $\frac{5}{7}$ and $\frac{2}{9}$? | 10. To $\frac{4}{5}$ and $\frac{1}{2}$? | 11. To $\frac{1}{6}$ and $\frac{4}{11}$? | 12. To $\frac{1}{3}$, $\frac{4}{5}$, and $\frac{7}{8}$?

The product of all the denominators of two or more fractions is a common denominator of the fractions.　Hence,

182. *A common denominator of two or more similar fractions is a common multiple of all their denominators.*

1. Reduce $\frac{5}{7}$ and $\frac{4}{9}$ to similar fractions.

Since the given denominators 7 and 9 are factors of 63, sevenths and ninths can be reduced to sixty-thirds.

Multiplying the terms of $\frac{5}{7}$ by 9, and the terms of $\frac{4}{9}$ by 7, I obtain the similar fractions $\frac{45}{63}$ and $\frac{7}{63}$.

Reduce to similar fractions

2. The fractions $\frac{1}{3}$ and $\frac{2}{5}$.　| 4. $\frac{5}{7}$ and $\frac{3}{4}$.　| 6. $\frac{1}{4}$, $\frac{3}{5}$, and $\frac{7}{9}$.
3. The fractions $\frac{3}{8}$ and $\frac{7}{10}$.　| 5. $\frac{1}{2}$, $\frac{1}{3}$, and $\frac{1}{6}$.　| 7. $\frac{5}{8}$, $\frac{3}{4}$, and $\frac{2}{3}$.

Written Work.—**183.** Ex. Reduce $\frac{2}{3}$, $\frac{1}{2}$, and $\frac{5}{9}$ to similar fractions.

> EXPLANATION.—Since $3 \times 2 \times 9 = 54$, thirds, halves, and ninths can be reduced to fifty-fourths. I therefore multiply the terms of each fraction by the denominators of the other fractions.
>
> The results, $\frac{36}{54}$, $\frac{27}{54}$, and $\frac{30}{54}$ are similar fractions.

PROCESS.

$$\frac{2 \times 2 \times 9}{3 \times 2 \times 9} = \frac{36}{54}$$

$$\frac{1 \times 3 \times 9}{2 \times 3 \times 9} = \frac{27}{54}$$

$$\frac{5 \times 3 \times 2}{9 \times 3 \times 2} = \frac{30}{54}$$

PROBLEMS.

1. Reduce to similar fractions $\frac{1}{7}$, $\frac{1}{2}$, and $\frac{2}{3}$. | 6. $\frac{3}{8}$, $\frac{3}{25}$, and $\frac{7}{81}$.
2. $\frac{3}{8}$ and $\frac{2}{11}$. | 4. $\frac{1}{2}$, $\frac{3}{5}$, $\frac{1}{3}$, and $\frac{3}{4}$. | 7. $\frac{1}{3}$, $\frac{1}{8}$, $\frac{1}{6}$, $\frac{1}{12}$, and $\frac{1}{2}$.
3. $\frac{7}{13}$ and $\frac{17}{18}$. | 5. $\frac{5}{6}$, $\frac{5}{7}$, $\frac{5}{9}$, and $\frac{5}{11}$. | 8. $\frac{2}{11}$, $\frac{2}{3}$, $\frac{2}{13}$, $\frac{2}{7}$, $\frac{2}{5}$, and $\frac{2}{17}$.

9. Reduce $\frac{5}{8}$, $\frac{2}{5}$, $\frac{1}{4}$, and $\frac{5}{9}$ to fractions of equal value having a common denominator.

10. The denominators of several dissimilar fractions are 13, 3, 10, 5, and 12. What is the denominator of the similar fractions of equal value?

11. Reduce $\frac{1}{4}$, $\frac{5}{12}$, $\frac{2}{7}$, $\frac{3}{8}$, and $\frac{8}{9}$ to fractions having a common fractional unit.

CASE IV. **Dissimilar fractions to least similar fractions.**

184. *Least similar fractions* are fractions that have the greatest common fractional unit possible.

The *least common denominator* is the denominator of least similar fractions.

Oral Work.—What number is a common denominator

1. Of $\frac{1}{3}$ and $\frac{1}{8}$?   3. Of $\frac{1}{2}$ and $\frac{1}{4}$?   5. Of $\frac{1}{3}$, $\frac{1}{2}$, and $\frac{1}{7}$?
2. Of $\frac{1}{2}$ and $\frac{1}{5}$?   4. Of $\frac{1}{4}$ and $\frac{1}{6}$?   6. Of $\frac{1}{4}$, $\frac{1}{6}$, and $\frac{1}{8}$?

What number is a common denominator, and what number is the least common denominator

7. Of $\frac{1}{4}$ and $\frac{1}{6}$?   9. Of $\frac{3}{4}$ and $\frac{3}{10}$?   11. Of $\frac{1}{2}$, $\frac{1}{4}$, and $\frac{1}{12}$?
8. Of $\frac{1}{6}$ and $\frac{3}{8}$?   10. Of $\frac{5}{8}$ and $\frac{5}{6}$?   12. Of $\frac{1}{3}$, $\frac{1}{12}$, and $\frac{1}{10}$?

185. *The least common denominator of two or more fractions is the least common multiple of all their denominators.*

By what number must you multiply the terms

1. Of $\frac{1}{8}$ and $\frac{1}{12}$, to reduce the fractions to 24ths?
2. Of $\frac{5}{9}$, $\frac{1}{12}$, and $\frac{7}{18}$, to reduce the fractions to 36ths?
3. Of $\frac{7}{10}$, $\frac{2}{5}$, $\frac{9}{20}$, and $\frac{1}{3}$, to reduce the fractions to 60ths?
4. Of $\frac{3}{8}$, $\frac{7}{16}$, and $\frac{11}{12}$, to reduce to least similar fractions?
5. Of $\frac{4}{15}$, $\frac{11}{20}$, $\frac{3}{10}$, and $\frac{1}{5}$, to reduce to least similar fractions?
6. Reduce $\frac{3}{4}$ and $\frac{5}{6}$ to least similar fractions.

Since 12 is the least common multiple of the denominators 4 and 6, the fractions can be reduced to twelfths. Since 12 equals 4 times 3 or 6 times 2, I reduce $\frac{3}{4}$ to twelfths by multiplying its terms by 3, and $\frac{5}{6}$ to twelfths by multiplying its terms by 2; and I obtain the least similar fractions $\frac{9}{12}$ and $\frac{10}{12}$.

Reduce to least similar fractions

7. The fractions $\frac{1}{9}$ and $\frac{2}{15}$. | 9. $\frac{2}{5}$ and $\frac{5}{6}$. | 11. $\frac{1}{36}$, $\frac{1}{18}$, and $\frac{1}{24}$.
8. The fractions $\frac{3}{8}$ and $\frac{7}{20}$. | 10. $\frac{5}{16}$ and $\frac{7}{24}$. | 12. $\frac{5}{8}$, $\frac{1}{12}$, and $\frac{25}{48}$.

***Written Work.*— 186.** Ex. Reduce the dissimilar fractions $\frac{4}{9}$, $\frac{2}{15}$, and $\frac{11}{18}$ to least similar fractions.

EXPLANATION.—I first find the least common multiple of the given denominators —9, 15, 18—to be 90.

I next divide this 90 by the given denominators 9, 15, 18, and obtain 10, 6, 5.

I then multiply the terms of $\frac{4}{9}$ by 10, the terms of $\frac{2}{15}$ by 6, and the terms of $\frac{11}{18}$ by 5;

PROCESS.

$$\begin{array}{c|c|c} 9 & 3 & 1 \\ 15 & 5 & 5 \\ 18 & 6 & 2 \end{array}$$

$$3 \times 3 \times 5 \times 2 = 90$$

$$90 \div 9 = 10$$
$$90 \div 15 = 6$$
$$90 \div 18 = 5$$

$$\frac{4 \times 10}{9 \times 10} = \frac{40}{90}$$

$$\frac{2 \times 6}{15 \times 6} = \frac{12}{90}$$

$$\frac{11 \times 5}{18 \times 5} = \frac{55}{90}$$

Hence, $\frac{4}{9}, \frac{2}{15}, \frac{11}{18} = \frac{40}{90}, \frac{12}{90}, \frac{55}{90}.$

and obtain $\frac{40}{90}$, $\frac{12}{90}$, and $\frac{55}{90}$, the least similar fractions required.

PROBLEMS.

Reduce to least similar fractions

1. $\frac{7}{12}$ and $\frac{9}{16}$. | 5. $\frac{13}{20}$, $\frac{3}{8}$, and $\frac{2}{5}$.
2. $\frac{6}{25}$ and $\frac{7}{10}$. | 6. $\frac{5}{6}$, $\frac{3}{4}$, and $\frac{11}{12}$.
3. $\frac{5}{12}$, $\frac{1}{8}$, and $\frac{2}{3}$. | 7. $\frac{7}{15}$, $\frac{17}{25}$, $\frac{5}{6}$, and $\frac{11}{24}$.
4. $\frac{1}{6}$, $\frac{3}{4}$, and $\frac{4}{9}$. | 8. $\frac{4}{5}$, $\frac{38}{45}$, $\frac{7}{9}$, and $\frac{11}{15}$, and $\frac{1}{3}$.

9. Reduce $\frac{5}{9}$, $\frac{1}{4}$, $\frac{7}{18}$, and $\frac{5}{6}$ to equivalent fractions having the least common denominator.

10. What is the fractional unit of the least similar fractions to which $\frac{3}{8}$, $\frac{7}{2}$, $\frac{5}{70}$, and $\frac{63}{108}$ can be reduced?

CASE V. **Improper fractions to integers or mixed numbers.**

***Oral Work.*— 187.** 1. $\frac{59}{8}$ are how many ones?

Since 8 eighths are 1, 59 eighths are as many 1's as the times 8 eighths are contained in 59 eighths. 1 eighth is contained in 59 eighths 59 times, and 8 eighths are contained in 59 eighths 1 eighth of 59 times, which is $7\frac{3}{8}$ times.

How many 1's

2. Are 12 fourths? | 4. Are 28 sevenths? | 6. Are 54 ninths?
3. Are 36 sixths? | 5. Are 24 thirds? | 7. Are 55 fifths?

8. How many 1's are $\frac{10}{3}$? | 9. Are $\frac{25}{3}$? | 10. Are $\frac{32}{3}$?

Reduce to an integer	Reduce to a mixed number
11. The fraction $\frac{30}{5}$.	14. The fraction $\frac{33}{5}$.
12. The fraction $\frac{21}{7}$.	15. The fraction $\frac{25}{7}$.
13. The fraction $\frac{18}{2}$.	16. The fraction $\frac{21}{2}$.

17. How is an improper fraction reduced to an integer or a mixed number?

When the denominator is a factor of the numerator, the value of the fraction is an integer.

Written Work.—188. Ex. Reduce $\frac{593}{32}$ to an integer or a mixed number.

Explanation.—Since the numerator of a fraction is a dividend, and the denominator is a divisor, I divide the numerator 593 by the denominator 32, and obtain the mixed number $18\frac{17}{32}$.

Process.

$$\frac{593}{32} = 593 \div 32 = 18\frac{17}{32}$$

Problems.

Reduce to integers or mixed numbers

1. $\frac{528}{3}$.	5. $\frac{375}{32}$.	9. $\frac{587}{54}$.	13. $\frac{35216}{8}$.	17. $\frac{675}{4}$.
2. $\frac{126}{7}$.	6. $\frac{5375}{23}$.	10. $\frac{3402}{9}$.	14. $\frac{1384}{5}$.	18. $\frac{2317}{27}$.
3. $\frac{1596}{6}$.	7. $\frac{176}{3}$.	11. $\frac{1031}{25}$.	15. $\frac{1265}{7}$.	19. $\frac{10000}{16}$.
4. $\frac{207}{11}$.	8. $\frac{704}{16}$.	12. $\frac{2500}{40}$.	16. $\frac{1661}{11}$.	20. $\frac{57642}{133}$.

21. 153 bales of hay, each weighing $\frac{1}{8}$ of a ton, weigh how many tons?

22. In 1,760 baskets, each containing $\frac{1}{3}$ of a bushel of peaches, are how many bushels?

How many dollars are

23. 1,954 quarter-dollars? | 24. $\$\frac{1451}{4}$? | 25. $\$\frac{7563}{8}$?

CASE VI. Integers or mixed numbers to improper fractions.

Oral Work.—**189.** *1.* $5\frac{3}{4}$ are how many fourths?

Since 1 is 4 fourths, 5 are 5 times 4 fourths, or 20 fourths; and $5\frac{3}{4}$ are 20 fourths plus 3 fourths, which are 23 fourths.

2. How many fourths are $8\frac{1}{4}$? Are $20\frac{1}{4}$? Are 15?

3. Reduce 9 to fifths. $6\frac{4}{5}$ to fifths. $20\frac{5}{8}$ to eighths.

Reduce $\begin{cases} 4.\ \text{7 to fifteenths.} \\ 5.\ \text{4 to twelfths.} \end{cases}$ $\Big|$ 6. 8 to fifths. $\Big|$ 8. $5\frac{3}{8}$ to eighths. $\Big|$ 7. $7\frac{2}{3}$ to thirds. $\Big|$ 9. $12\frac{1}{10}$ to tenths.

10. How is an integer reduced to an improper fraction?

11. A mixed number to an improper fraction?

Written Work.—**190.** Ex. Reduce $27\frac{3}{5}$ to an improper fraction.

EXPLANATION.—I multiply 5, the number of fifths in 1, by 27, and obtain 135, the number of fifths in 27. To this result I add the 3 fifths of the given number, and obtain $\frac{138}{5}$, the improper fraction required.

FIRST PROCESS.	SECOND PROCESS.
5 fifths.	$27\frac{3}{5}$
27	5
135 fifths.	$135+3=138$
3 fifths.	
138 fifths.	

Hence, $27\frac{3}{5} = \frac{138}{5}$.

The work is commonly written as shown in the second process.

PROBLEMS.

1. 18 is how many ninths?

2. $24\frac{1}{4}$ are how many fourths?

3. $36\frac{3}{8}$ are how many eighths?

4. How many 53ds are $7\frac{11}{53}$?

5. How many 37ths is 37?

6. Reduce $11\frac{4}{15}$ to fifteenths.

What improper fraction is equal

7. To $17\frac{1}{8}$? | *11.* To $14\frac{3}{20}$? | *15.* To $100\frac{9}{40}$? | *19.* To $31\frac{5}{8}$?

8. To $27\frac{7}{12}$? | *12.* To $75\frac{7}{30}$? | *16.* To $87\frac{3}{50}$? | *20.* To $33\frac{9}{11}$?

9. To $24\frac{3}{8}$? | *13.* To $17\frac{3}{65}$? | *17.* To $5\frac{30}{140}$? | *21.* To $115\frac{18}{237}$?

10. To $2\frac{3}{250}$? | *14.* To $20\frac{7}{81}$? | *18.* To $21\frac{44}{83}$? | *22.* To $86\frac{931}{2007}$?

191. RULES FOR REDUCTIONS OF FRACTIONS.

I. A fraction to lowest terms.

Cancel all the factors common to the terms of the fraction.

II. A fraction to another fraction having a given denominator.

Divide the given denominator by the denominator of the fraction, and multiply both terms of the fraction by the quotient.

III. Dissimilar fractions to similar fractions.

Multiply the terms of each fraction by the denominators of all the other fractions.

IV. Dissimilar fractions to least similar fractions.

1. For the least common denominator;—*Find the least common multiple of all the denominators.*

2. For each new numerator;—*Divide the least common multiple by the denominator of each fraction, and multiply the numerator by the quotient.*

V. An improper fraction to an integer or a mixed number.

Divide the numerator by the denominator.

VI. An integer or a mixed number to an improper fraction.

1. *Multiply the integer by the denominator, and if there be a numerator add it to the product.*

2. *Write this result for the numerator, and the given denominator for the denominator of the required fraction.*

Rules I and V are used for reducing final results to their simplest forms; rules II, III, and IV are used for preparing numbers for addition, subtraction, and division; and rule VI is used for preparing numbers for multiplication and division.

SECTION III.

ADDITION.

Oral Work.—**192.** *1.* What is the sum of $\frac{3}{8}$ and $\frac{1}{8}$?

2. What is the sum of $\frac{2}{7}$, $\frac{1}{7}$, and $\frac{3}{7}$?

3. What is the sum of $\frac{3}{20}$, $\frac{7}{20}$, $\frac{9}{20}$, and $\frac{11}{20}$?

4. To what must halves be added? Ninths? Sixteenths?

5. What similar fractions equal $\frac{2}{5}$ and $\frac{1}{4}$?   What is their sum?

What is the sum of		Add	
6. $\frac{3}{5}$ and $\frac{4}{7}$?	*8.* $\frac{2}{3}$ and $\frac{6}{7}$?	*10.* $\frac{2}{3}$ and $\frac{4}{5}$.	*12.* $\frac{1}{3}$, $\frac{1}{4}$, and $\frac{1}{5}$.
7. $\frac{7}{10}$ and $\frac{5}{8}$?	*9.* $\frac{3}{8}$ and $\frac{1}{12}$?	*11.* $\frac{3}{10}$ and $\frac{4}{5}$.	*13.* $2\frac{1}{4}$ and $\frac{5}{7}$.

When any of the parts are mixed numbers, add the fractions first.

Add $\begin{cases} \textit{14. } 4\frac{7}{12} \text{ and } \frac{4}{5}. & \textit{16. } 15\frac{2}{3} \text{ and } 8\frac{4}{5}. & \textit{18. } \frac{4}{7},\ 2\frac{3}{8},\ \text{and } 17. \\ \textit{15. } 5\frac{4}{11} \text{ and } 7\frac{1}{3}. & \textit{17. } 3\frac{5}{6} \text{ and } 6\frac{4}{7}. & \textit{19. } 5\frac{7}{9},\ 3\frac{5}{6},\ \text{and } 4\frac{2}{3}. \end{cases}$

20. $\$\frac{1}{5}$ for corn and $\$\frac{1}{4}$ for peas is how much for both?

21. Esther paid $\$\frac{5}{8}$ for overshoes, $\$\frac{3}{4}$ for gloves, and $\$\frac{1}{2}$ for handkerchiefs.   How much did she pay for all?

22. Eli paid $\$2\frac{3}{4}$ for a calf, and sold it for $\$\frac{7}{10}$ more than it cost him.   For how much did he sell it?

23. If I burn $\frac{4}{7}$ of a ton of coal one month, and $\frac{3}{5}$ of a ton the next, how much do I burn in the two months?

24 Roger sawed a load of wood in $1\frac{7}{10}$ days, and split it in $1\frac{4}{5}$ days.   How much time did he work?

25. My orchard contains $3\frac{1}{4}$ acres, and my garden $1\frac{1}{3}$ acres.   How much land is there in my orchard and garden?

26. Harry is $3\frac{5}{12}$ years old, Carlos is $6\frac{1}{2}$ years older than Harry, and Hattie is $5\frac{1}{6}$ years older than Carlos.   How old is Hattie?

27. Can $\frac{2}{5}$ of a day and $\frac{3}{8}$ of a day be added? Why?

28. Can $\frac{2}{5}$ of a mile and $\frac{3}{8}$ of a dollar be added? Why?

***Written Work.*—193.** Ex. 1. What is the sum of $\frac{4}{5}$, $\frac{1}{3}$, and $\frac{3}{4}$?

EXPLANATION.—
Fifths, thirds, and fourths can not be directly added. I therefore reduce them to the similar fractions $\frac{48}{60}$, $\frac{20}{60}$, and $\frac{45}{60}$.

FIRST PROCESS.

$$\frac{4}{5} + \frac{1}{3} + \frac{3}{4} = \frac{48}{60} + \frac{20}{60} + \frac{45}{60} = \frac{113}{60} = 1\frac{53}{60}$$

SECOND PROCESS.

$$\frac{4}{5} + \frac{1}{3} + \frac{3}{4} = \frac{48+20+45}{60} = \frac{113}{60} = 1\frac{53}{60}$$

Then, adding the numerators 48, 20, and 45, I obtain 113; and since the parts are sixtieths, I write $\frac{113}{60} = 1\frac{53}{60}$ for the required sum.

The common denominator of the similar fractions need be written but once,—as shown in the second process.

Ex. 2. What is the sum of $2\frac{4}{5}$, 7, and $4\frac{2}{3}$?

EXPLANATION.—Since $\frac{4}{5}$ equal $\frac{12}{15}$, and $\frac{2}{3}$ equal $\frac{10}{15}$, $2\frac{4}{5}$ equal $2\frac{12}{15}$, and $4\frac{2}{3}$ equal $4\frac{10}{15}$. Adding the fractions, I have $\frac{22}{15}$, or $1\frac{7}{15}$; and I write the $\frac{7}{15}$ in the result.

I then add the 1 with the given integers, and write the sum, 14, in the result, making $14\frac{7}{15}$, the required sum.

PROCESS.

$$2\frac{4}{5} = 2\frac{12}{15}$$
$$7 = 7$$
$$4\frac{2}{3} = 4\frac{10}{15}$$
$$\overline{14\frac{7}{15}}$$

PROBLEMS.

Add

1. $\frac{3}{10}$ and $\frac{5}{13}$.
2. $\frac{7}{12}$ and $\frac{9}{10}$.
3. $\frac{6}{7}$, $\frac{1}{5}$, and $\frac{1}{4}$.
4. $2\frac{3}{4}$ and $4\frac{4}{5}$.
5. $5\frac{7}{9}$ and $3\frac{4}{7}$.
6. $\frac{2}{3} + \frac{3}{4} + \frac{1}{6}$.

What is the sum of

7. $25\frac{11}{15} + 1\frac{17}{30}$?
8. $\frac{7}{10} + \frac{2}{3} + \frac{3}{5}$?
9. $\frac{7}{20} + 8\frac{1}{150}$?
10. $241\frac{5}{12} + 4\frac{2}{3} + \frac{3}{5}$?
11. $8\frac{5}{8} + 6\frac{7}{9} + 27\frac{2}{3}$?
12. $3\frac{1}{9} + 5 + 10\frac{2}{35}$?

13. $\frac{11}{12}$ of a yard $+ \frac{17}{18}$ of a yard $+ \frac{1}{6}$ of a yard $+ \frac{35}{36}$ of a yard $+ \frac{1}{4}$ of a yard $+ \frac{3}{8}$ of a yard $+ \frac{7}{16}$ of a yard = how many yards?

14. Add $60\frac{11}{40}$ miles, $75\frac{7}{8}$ miles, and $110\frac{9}{16}$ miles.

15. Add $4\frac{4}{5}$, \$23, $6\frac{7}{8}$, $1\frac{9}{20}$, and $55\frac{17}{100}$.

194. Rule for Addition of Fractions.

Reduce dissimilar to similar fractions, add the numerators, and under the sum write the common denominator.

a. Reduce fractions to lowest terms, before reducing to similar fractions.

b. In all final results, reduce fractions to lowest terms, and improper fractions to integers or mixed numbers.

Problems.

1. $\frac{3}{4}$ of an acre of blackberries, $\frac{1}{3}$ of an acre of raspberries, and $\frac{3}{5}$ of an acre of strawberries are how many acres of berries?

2. A stable keeper bought two loads of straw, weighing $1\frac{3}{20}$ tons, and $\frac{37}{40}$ of a ton. How much straw did he buy?

3. $\frac{7}{10} + \frac{2}{3} + \frac{3}{4} =$ how many?

4. $2\frac{7}{5} + 1\frac{17}{15} + 2\frac{221}{225} =$ how many?

5. $3\frac{3}{4} + 5\frac{5}{6} + 6\frac{6}{7} =$ how many?

6. Add $\frac{87}{144}$, $\frac{7}{12}$, $\frac{17}{24}$, and $\frac{11}{12}$.

7. Add $\frac{7}{8}$, $\frac{9}{10}$, $\frac{11}{12}$, and $\frac{14}{15}$.

8. Add $10\frac{1}{10}$, $8\frac{1}{5}$, $27\frac{1}{20}$, and $14\frac{1}{15}$.

9. A clerk expended $\frac{1}{10}$ of his salary in travel, $\frac{1}{4}$ of it for board, $\frac{3}{6}$ for clothing, and $\frac{3}{20}$ for other purposes. What part of his salary did he expend?

10. A lady paid $\$\frac{3}{10}$ for sewing silk, $\$\frac{7}{20}$ for buttons, $\$\frac{63}{100}$ for ribbon, $\$\frac{2}{5}$ for a silver thimble, and $\$\frac{1}{2}$ for a pair of scissors. How much did her purchases amount to?

11. How much wood is there in $\frac{77}{128}$ of a cord, $3\frac{1}{8}$ cords, $1\frac{1}{16}$ cords, and $\frac{63}{64}$ of a cord?

Add
12. $\frac{3}{16}$, $\frac{8}{9}$, $\frac{87}{64}$, and $\frac{99}{128}$.
13. $\frac{28}{40}$, $\frac{25}{200}$, and $\frac{405}{729}$.
14. $3\frac{4}{7}$, 14, $5\frac{3}{13}$, $\frac{1}{5}$, and $4\frac{1}{2}$.
15. $19\frac{3}{4}$, $\frac{7}{15}$, $65\frac{4}{5}$, $\frac{8}{15}$, and 23.

16. From A to B is $27\frac{3}{10}$ miles, from B to C 30 miles, from C to D $51\frac{13}{40}$ miles, and from D to E $32\frac{17}{100}$ miles. What is the distance from A to E?

17. In three pieces of carpeting that contain $37\frac{4}{9}$ yards, $49\frac{5}{8}$ yards, and $50\frac{3}{4}$ yards are how many yards?

SUBTRACTION.

Oral Work.—**195.** *1.* Subtract $\frac{5}{16}$ from $\frac{9}{16}$.

2. How is one of two similar fractions subtracted from the other?

3. What similar fractions are equal to $\frac{7}{8}$ and $\frac{3}{5}$? What is the difference between $\frac{7}{8}$ and $\frac{3}{8}$? Between $\frac{2}{3}$ and $\frac{2}{5}$?

Subtract		What is the difference between	
4. $\frac{1}{4}$ from $\frac{3}{8}$.	*7.* $\frac{6}{11}$ from $\frac{3}{4}$.	*10.* $1\frac{3}{15}$ and $\frac{8}{15}$?	*13.* $2\frac{1}{2}$ and $7\frac{1}{2}$?
5. $\frac{1}{4}$ from $\frac{8}{3}$.	*8.* $\frac{5}{7}$ from $\frac{5}{6}$.	*11.* $5\frac{1}{3}$ and 2?	*14.* $5\frac{3}{8}$ and $9\frac{7}{8}$?
6. $\frac{4}{9}$ from $\frac{5}{8}$.	*9.* $\frac{1}{3}$ from $\frac{1}{2}$.	*12.* $3\frac{4}{5}$ and $\frac{3}{5}$?	*15.* $8\frac{7}{12}$ and $4\frac{5}{12}$?

When the subtrahend is a mixed number, subtract the fraction first.

How much is

16. $8\frac{7}{10}$ less $3\frac{3}{10}$? | *18.* $7\frac{1}{4}-1\frac{3}{4}$? | *20.* From $9\frac{1}{3}$ take $5\frac{2}{5}$.

17. $12\frac{5}{8}$ less $5\frac{4}{8}$? | *19.* $6\frac{1}{4}-2\frac{1}{2}$? | *21.* From $24\frac{5}{12}$ take $15\frac{5}{6}$.

22. The minuend is $6\frac{1}{7}$ and the subtrahend is $4\frac{5}{7}$. What is the remainder? $(6\frac{1}{7}=5+\frac{8}{7}.)$

23. Ethan gathered $\frac{11}{16}$ of a bushel of walnuts, and sold $\frac{1}{4}$ of a bushel. What part of a bushel had he left?

24. Jennie paid $\frac{3}{7}$ of the yearly cost of *Our Young People*, and her brother Edgar paid the balance. What part of the cost did Edgar pay?

25. One week A worked $5\frac{7}{10}$ days and B $5\frac{3}{4}$ days. Which worked the longer? How much the longer?

How much money shall I have left

26. Of $\$1\frac{3}{4}$, after paying $\$\frac{3}{10}$ for a slate?

27. Of $\$7$, after paying $\$5\frac{1}{4}$ for a pair of boots?

28. Of $\$8\frac{1}{4}$, after paying my grocer $\$6\frac{2}{5}$?

29. I owe $\$5\frac{1}{2}$. If I pay $\$\frac{7}{8}$, how much shall I then owe?

30. Anna will be 13 years old $\frac{3}{5}$ of a year hence. What is her age now? How old was she $2\frac{1}{4}$ years ago?

H

31. A woman having $2\frac{3}{4}$ gallons of boiled cider, used all but $1\frac{1}{8}$ gallons. How much cider did she use?

32. Can $\frac{3}{8}$ of a day be subtracted from $\frac{4}{5}$ of a day? Why?

33. Can $\frac{3}{8}$ of a mile be subtracted from $8\frac{4}{5}$? Why?

Written Work.—**196.** Ex. 1. Subtract $\frac{3}{5}$ from $\frac{13}{16}$.

EXPLANATION.—Fifths can not be directly subtracted from sixteenths. I therefore reduce the given fractions $\frac{13}{16}$ and $\frac{3}{5}$ to the similar fractions $\frac{65}{80}$ and $\frac{48}{80}$.

Then, subtracting the numerator 48 from the numerator 65, I obtain 17; and, since the fractions are eightieths, I write $\frac{17}{80}$ for the required difference.

FIRST PROCESS.
$$\frac{13}{16} - \frac{3}{5} = \frac{65}{80} - \frac{48}{80} = \frac{17}{80}$$

SECOND PROCESS.
$$\frac{13}{16} - \frac{3}{5} = \frac{65 - 48}{80} = \frac{17}{80}$$

Ex. 2. What is the difference between $7\frac{3}{8}$ and $4\frac{4}{5}$?

EXPLANATION.—$7\frac{3}{8}$ equal $7\frac{15}{40}$, and $4\frac{4}{5}$ equal $4\frac{32}{40}$. But $\frac{32}{40}$, the fractional part of the subtrahend, is more than $\frac{15}{40}$, the fractional part of the minuend. I therefore take 1 of the 7, and unite its value, $\frac{40}{40}$, with the $\frac{15}{40}$, thus changing the form of the minuend to $6\frac{55}{40}$.

Then, subtracting $4\frac{32}{40}$ from $6\frac{55}{40}$, I obtain $2\frac{23}{40}$, the required difference.

PROCESS.
$$7\frac{3}{8} = 7\frac{15}{40} = 6\frac{55}{40}$$
$$4\frac{4}{5} = \phantom{7\frac{15}{40} =\;} 4\frac{32}{40}$$
$$\overline{\phantom{7\frac{15}{40} =\;} 2\frac{23}{40}}$$

PROBLEMS.

From	Take	Take	From	Find the difference between	
1. $\frac{13}{16}$	$\frac{1}{2}$.	3. $\frac{13}{16}$	$\frac{23}{25}$.	5. $\frac{3}{11}$ and $\frac{2}{17}$.	7. $\frac{19}{18}$ and $\frac{19}{20}$.
2. $\frac{7}{11}$	$\frac{2}{9}$.	4. $\frac{1}{6}$	$\frac{5}{14}$.	6. $\frac{5}{14}$ and $\frac{17}{66}$.	8. $\frac{7}{8}$ and $\frac{131}{100}$.

9. The minuend is $\frac{52}{110}$ and the subtrahend is $\frac{10}{102}$. What is the remainder?

10. $\frac{15}{16}$ of a mile minus $\frac{3697}{5280}$ of a mile equals what part of a mile?

Subtract

11. $75\frac{1}{4}$ from 99.	14. $7\frac{8}{11}$ from $16\frac{7}{10}$.	17. $15\frac{32}{35}$ from $21\frac{8}{33}$.
12. $40\frac{7}{16}$ from 103.	15. $45\frac{11}{213}$ from $45\frac{1}{2}$.	18. $33\frac{17}{99}$ from $99\frac{9}{100}$.
13. $9\frac{19}{20}$ from $108\frac{7}{40}$.	16. $\frac{23}{30}$ from $19\frac{4}{5}$.	19. $235\frac{54}{60}$ from $532\frac{22}{33}$.

197. Rule for Subtraction of Fractions.

Reduce dissimilar to similar fractions, subtract the numerator of the subtrahend from the numerator of the minuend, and under the difference write the common denominator.

See remarks under Rule for Addition of Fractions, page 168.

Problems.

Find the remainder in each of these six problems:

1. $1\frac{11}{25} - \frac{24}{25}$.
2. $\frac{25}{26} - \frac{25}{36}$.
3. $1\frac{29}{135}$ minus $\frac{77}{81}$.
4. 30 minus $\frac{7854}{10000}$.
5. $87\frac{19}{72}$ less 59.
6. $54\frac{1}{35}$ less $27\frac{1}{34}$.

7. From $\frac{9}{10}$ of a cord of wood a teamster took $\frac{27}{32}$ of a cord. How much wood remained?

8. A farmer bought $\frac{17}{20}$ of a ton of plaster, and sowed $\frac{7}{16}$ of a ton on his clover field. What part of a ton had he left?

9. $4\frac{5}{13}$ is how much greater than $\frac{6}{7}$?

10. $17\frac{4}{15}$ is how much less than $25\frac{4}{17}$?

11. What is the difference between $\frac{213}{579}$ and $\frac{57}{131}$?

12. If I have $5\frac{1}{4}$ and pay out $\frac{4}{5}$, how much money have I left?

13. Frank walked $18\frac{11}{320}$ miles, and Harry walked as far lacking $2\frac{9}{64}$ miles. How far did Harry walk?

14. $37\frac{3}{8}$ yards of white flannel shrank $1\frac{5}{8}$ yards in dyeing. How much did the cloth then measure?

Find the difference between each two numbers following:

15.		17.		19.		21.		23.	
$\frac{4}{15}$	$\frac{9}{32}$	$\frac{24}{40}$	$15\frac{3}{8}$	$9\frac{4}{13}$	$2\frac{1}{8}$	$1\frac{3}{16}$	$\frac{9}{10}$	$5\frac{1}{3}$	$124\frac{3}{11}$	$19\frac{15}{396}$
	16.		18.		20.		22.		24.	

25. From a lot containing $\frac{19}{20}$ of an acre of land I sold $\frac{9}{20}$ of an acre to one man, and $\frac{1}{8}$ of an acre to another. How much land had I left?

26. If $\frac{3}{8}$ be taken from a certain number, the remainder is $\frac{5}{7}$. What is the number?

27. If 5 be added to each term of $\frac{3}{5}$, is the value of the fraction increased or diminished? How much?

28. From the sum of $\frac{5}{7}$ and $3\frac{1}{2}$ subtract the difference between $4\frac{1}{3}$ and $5\frac{1}{4}$.

29. What is the sum of $\frac{4}{5}$ and $\frac{37}{90}$? What is their difference? What is the sum of their sum and difference?

SECTION V.

MULTIPLICATION.

Oral Work.—198. *A.*

How much is
1. 4 times $\frac{5}{6}$?
2. 3 times $\frac{3}{10}$?
3. 7 times $\frac{3}{8}$?
4. 11 times $\frac{6}{7}$?

Multiply
5. $\frac{5}{12}$ by 2; by 3.
6. $\frac{3}{22}$ by 5; by 9.
7. $4\frac{3}{22}$ by 5; by 9.
8. $9\frac{1}{4}$ by 3; by 6.

What is the product of
9. $5\frac{1}{4}$ multiplied by 10?
10. $3\frac{5}{16}$ multiplied by 8?
11. $3\frac{4}{5}$ multiplied by 6?
12. $7\frac{7}{12}$ multiplied by 4?

How much is
13. 4 times $\frac{11}{16}$ of a pound?
14. 8 times $\frac{5}{8}$ of a bushel?
15. 10 times $\frac{3}{4}$ of a gallon?
16. 5 times $7\frac{3}{10}$ miles?
17. 12 times $5\frac{3}{4}$?
18. 10 times $2\frac{1}{4}$ yards?

19. How much do 6 bushels of apples cost, at $\$\frac{3}{5}$ a bushel?

6 bushels cost 6 times as much as 1 bushel, or 6 times $\$\frac{3}{5}$; and 6 times $\$\frac{3}{5}$ are $\$\frac{18}{5}$, or $\$3\frac{3}{5}$.

20. How much do 12 ducks cost, at $\$\frac{11}{20}$ apiece?

21. How many acres of corn will 4 men hoe in a day, if they average $\frac{5}{8}$ of an acre each?

22. In how many minutes can I drive my horse 5 miles, if I drive at the rate of a mile in $7\frac{2}{5}$ minutes?

How much money will buy

23. 15 barrels of XXX flour, at 7\frac{7}{10}$ a barrel?

24. 12 apples, at $\frac{2}{3}$ of a cent apiece?

25. 100 clothes-pins, at $\frac{1}{4}$ of a cent apiece?

26. 7 yards of bleached muslin, at $\$\frac{3}{20}$ per yard?

27. 1 dozen boxes of layer raisins, at 1\frac{7}{10}$ per box?

B. 1. How do 3 fourths of a number compare with 1 fourth of it?

3 fourths of any number are 3 times 1 fourth of the number.

2. How do you find $\frac{1}{4}$ of any number?

3. How do you find $\frac{3}{4}$ of any number?

How much is	Multiply	Find the product of
4. $\frac{1}{4}$ of 20?	*9.* 18 by $\frac{5}{6}$.	*14.* 3 multiplied by $2\frac{1}{2}$.
5. $\frac{3}{4}$ of 20?	*10.* 11 by $\frac{7}{22}$.	*15.* 8 multiplied by $4\frac{2}{3}$.
6. $\frac{4}{5}$ of 25?	*11.* 8 by $\frac{4}{15}$.	*16.* 9 multiplied by $3\frac{3}{4}$.
7. $\frac{3}{8}$ of $9?	*12.* 12 by $\frac{2}{3}$.	*17.* $11\frac{1}{4}$ times 10.
8. $\frac{2}{3}$ of $.16?	*13.* 12 by $5\frac{2}{3}$.	*18.* $2\frac{4}{5}$ times 7.

19. Multiply 32 pounds by $\frac{3}{4}$; *i. e.,* find $\frac{3}{4}$ of 32 pounds.

How much is

20. $\frac{7}{10}$ of 32 yards of ribbon? | *24.* $6\frac{3}{4}$ times 10 dozen eggs?
21. $\frac{3}{8}$ of 50 pounds of nails? | *25.* $7\frac{3}{10}$ times 5 bushels of oats?
22. $\frac{5}{6}$ of 57 feet of gas pipe? | *26.* $15 multiplied by $3\frac{1}{4}$?
23. $\frac{3}{4}$ of 34 days' work? | *27.* $.08 multiplied by $5\frac{5}{16}$?

C. 1. How much will $\frac{3}{8}$ of a yard of linen cost, at $.60 a yard?

3 eighths of a yard will cost 3 times as much as 1 eighth of a yard, or 3 times 1 eighth of 60 cents. 1 eighth of 60 cents is $7\frac{1}{2}$ cents, and 3 times $7\frac{1}{2}$ cents are $22\frac{1}{2}$ cents.

2. At $8 a ton, how much does $\frac{3}{8}$ of a ton cost?

3. A tailor used $\frac{4}{7}$ of 3 yards of silk serge in lining a coat. How many yards of serge did he use?

4. At 10 cents a yard for silk braid, how much will 2 yards cost? How much will $\frac{1}{2}$ yard cost? How much will $2\frac{1}{2}$ yards cost?

5. I burned 12 thousand feet of gas in my store in the summer, and $3\frac{1}{6}$ times as much in the winter. How many thousand feet did I burn in the winter?

6. A hotel in one month used 20 pounds of coffee, and $8\frac{3}{5}$ times as much sugar. How much sugar was used?

7. Two sevenths of the 49 children in a district attend school. How many children attend school?

8. A and B bought a mowing machine for \$145, A paying $\frac{3}{10}$ of the cost, and B $\frac{7}{10}$. How much did each pay?

D. What fraction is equal to | Multiply

1. $\frac{1}{3}$ of 9 tenths? | 3. $\frac{1}{7}$ of $\frac{21}{25}$? | 5. $\frac{8}{15}$ by $\frac{3}{4}$.

2. $\frac{2}{3}$ of 9 tenths? | 4. $\frac{4}{7}$ of $\frac{21}{25}$? | 6. $\frac{18}{20}$ by $\frac{5}{6}$.

How much is

7. $\frac{3}{5}$ of $2\frac{1}{2}$ bushels? $(2\frac{1}{2}=\frac{5}{2})$ | 11. $\frac{3}{4}$ of $12\frac{28}{33}$ rods?

8. $\frac{3}{8}$ of $1\frac{1}{2}$ pounds? | 12. $\frac{3}{5}$ of $27\frac{27}{100}$ miles?

9. $\frac{9}{20}$ of $6\frac{2}{3}$ yards? | 13. $\frac{2}{3}$ of $42\frac{1}{2}$ feet? $(42\frac{1}{2}=40+2\frac{1}{2})$

10. $\frac{4}{5}$ of $10\frac{5}{6}$ gallons? | 14. $\frac{4}{5}$ of $15\frac{3}{4}$ weeks?

    a. The word *of* between two numbers, the first or both of which are fractions, signifies multiplication.

    b. A *compound fraction* is two or more numbers connected by the word *of*, the first, at least, of the numbers being a fraction.

E. 1. $\frac{1}{5}$ is how many twentieths? How much is $\frac{1}{4}$ of $\frac{4}{20}$? Then, how much is $\frac{1}{4}$ of $\frac{1}{5}$?

2. How much is $\frac{3}{4}$ of $\frac{1}{5}$? | 3. $\frac{1}{4}$ of $\frac{3}{5}$? | 4. $\frac{1}{5}$ of $\frac{3}{7}$? | 5. $\frac{3}{8}$ of $\frac{7}{8}$?

6. How much is $\frac{2}{3}$ of $\frac{4}{7}$?

2 thirds of 4 sevenths are 2 times as much as 1 third of 4 sevenths. 4 sevenths are 12 twenty-firsts; 1 third of 12 twenty-firsts is 4 twenty-firsts, and 2 times 4 twenty-firsts are 8 twenty-firsts.

Multiply	How much is	What is the product of
7. $\frac{7}{12}$ by $\frac{3}{10}$.	11. $2\frac{2}{3}$ times $\frac{4}{7}$?	15. $\frac{5}{6}$ multiplied by $\frac{7}{11}$?
8. $\frac{5}{8}$ by $\frac{7}{10}$.	12. $1\frac{4}{5}$ times $\frac{6}{11}$?	16. $\frac{9}{20}$ multiplied by $\frac{3}{4}$?
9. $\frac{3}{5}$ by $\frac{4}{7}$.	13. $\frac{4}{7}$ of $2\frac{2}{3}$?	17. $\frac{3}{5}\times\frac{4}{9}$? 19. $\frac{3}{4}\times\frac{2}{5}\times\frac{1}{2}$?
10. $\frac{14}{15}$ by $2\frac{1}{2}$.	14. $\frac{6}{11}$ of $1\frac{4}{5}$?	18. $\frac{24}{25}\times\frac{5}{6}$? 20. $\frac{3}{8}\times\frac{7}{10}\times\frac{2}{3}$?

How much is

21. $\frac{5}{6}$ of \$$2\frac{2}{5}$?	25. $2\frac{1}{2}$ times $\frac{3}{4}$ of a yard?
22. $\frac{2}{3}$ of $7\frac{5}{8}$ barrels?	26. $1\frac{1}{3}$ times $2\frac{1}{4}$ yards?
23. $\frac{7}{8}$ of $30\frac{1}{3}$ dozen?	27. $\frac{4}{5}\times\frac{3}{11}$ of $6\frac{7}{8}$ pounds?
24. $4\frac{4}{7}$ times $\frac{1}{5}$ of a mile?	28. $6\frac{2}{5}$ times $2\frac{1}{2}$ bushels?

199. The general method of written work in multiplication of fractions is based upon the following

Principle. *The product of two fractions equals the product of their numerators divided by the product of their denominators.*

Written Work.—Ex. 1. What is the product of $\frac{2}{3}$ and $\frac{4}{5}$?

Explanation.—I multiply 2 and 4—the numerators of the fractions—together for the numerator of the product; and 3 and 5—the denominators of the fractions—together for the denominator of the product.

Process.

$$\frac{2}{3}\times\frac{4}{5}=\frac{2\times4}{3\times5}=\frac{8}{15}$$

Problems.

Find the product in each of the next twelve problems.

1. $\frac{11}{12}\times\frac{13}{21}=$
2. $\frac{4}{7}\times\frac{24}{25}=$
3. $\frac{5}{6}\times\frac{12}{13}=$
4. $\frac{23}{24}$ of $\frac{25}{26}=$
5. $\frac{21}{72}$ of $\frac{35}{80}=$
6. $\frac{14}{25}$ of $\frac{4}{7}=$
7. $\frac{19}{27}\times\frac{31}{48}=$
8. $\frac{218}{427}\times\frac{103}{159}=$
9. $\frac{9}{10}\times\frac{15}{33}=$
10. $\frac{1}{3}$ of $\frac{2}{7}$ of $\frac{5}{9}=$
11. $\frac{7}{12}\times\frac{5}{8}\times\frac{11}{16}=$
12. $\frac{2}{3}$ of $\frac{12}{15}\times\frac{15}{16}=$

Ex. 2. Find the product of $\frac{5}{9}\times\frac{6}{7}\times\frac{63}{65}$.

I cancel all factors common to both numerators and denominators, before multiplying.

$$\frac{5}{9}\times\frac{6}{7}\times\frac{63}{65}=\frac{6}{13}$$

13. How much is $\frac{5}{7}\times\frac{2}{3}\times\frac{21}{25}$?
14. How much is $\frac{5}{51}\times\frac{17}{35}\times\frac{27}{2}$?
15. What number equals $\frac{5}{6}$ of $\frac{3}{8}\times\frac{1}{2}$ of $\frac{18}{25}$?
16. $\frac{2}{19}\times\frac{57}{60}\times\frac{3}{10}=$ how much?
17. $7\frac{1}{2}$ times $\frac{5}{7}$ of $\frac{8}{9}$ of $\frac{7}{15}\times\frac{27}{35}=$ what number?
18. $\frac{16}{35}\times\frac{7}{24}\times\frac{1}{2}$ of $\frac{15}{1}=$ how many?

19. What is the product of $\frac{4}{5}$ of $6\frac{2}{3}$ times 8?

$6\frac{2}{3} = \frac{20}{3}$, and $8 = \frac{8}{1}$. Hence, $\frac{4}{5}$ of $6\frac{2}{3} \times 8 = \frac{4}{5}$ of $\frac{20}{3} \times \frac{8}{1}$.

20. Multiply $3\frac{1}{8}$ times $\frac{11}{50}$ by 16. | *21.* Multiply $\frac{13}{18}$ by 15 times $32\frac{7}{52}$.

22. What part of a melon is $\frac{2}{3}$ of $\frac{4}{5}$ of $\frac{5}{6}$ of $1\frac{2}{17}$ of a melon?

23. A man who owned $\frac{7}{16}$ of a factory, sold $\frac{8}{21}$ of his share. What part of the factory did he sell?

24. Find the cost of $\frac{11}{16}$ of a yard of silk, at $\$2\frac{3}{8}$ a yard.

25. I planted $\frac{87}{480}$ of 3 acres to potatoes, and $13\frac{3}{25}$ times as much to corn. How many acres did I plant to corn?

26. If a man can paint $4\frac{2}{3}$ rods of picket-fence in a day, how many rods can he paint in $17\frac{1}{4}$ days?

200. Ex. Multiply $13\frac{2}{11}$ by 8.

PROCESSES.

EXPLANATION.—I multiply $\frac{2}{11}$ and 13, separately, by 8; then, adding the results, I have $105\frac{5}{11}$, the required product.

1

$$\frac{2}{11} \times \frac{8}{1} = \frac{16}{11} = 1\frac{5}{11}$$
$$13 \times 8 = 104$$
$$13\frac{2}{11} \times 8 = 105\frac{5}{11}$$

2

$$13\frac{2}{11}$$
$$8$$
$$105\frac{5}{11}$$

The work is commonly written as shown in the second process.

When the multiplicand is a mixed number and the multiplier an integer, multiply the fractional and integral parts separately, and then add the products.

PROBLEMS.

Multiply

1. $\frac{5}{38}$ by 17. | 3. $\frac{15}{26}$ by 13. | 5. $\frac{37}{100}$ by 1,000. | 7. $34\frac{3}{28}$ by 7.
2. $\frac{16}{17}$ by 12. | 4. $\frac{17}{18}$ by 36. | 6. $\frac{9}{689}$ by 588. | 8. $875\frac{1}{4}$ by 53.

9. How many bushels of peaches are there in 75 baskets, each basket containing $\frac{9}{10}$ of a bushel?

10. A house painter's wages are $\$1\frac{3}{8}$ per day. How much do his wages amount to in a month, or 26 days?

11. How many days' work can 54 men do in $\frac{7}{10}$ of a day?

12. How much will it cost to keep my horse a year, or 52 weeks, at $\$2\frac{4}{25}$ per week?

201. Ex. What is the product of 128 multiplied by $5\frac{2}{3}$?

PROCESSES.

EXPLANATION.—I multiply 128 by $\frac{2}{3}$ and by 5 separately; then, adding the partial products, I have $725\frac{1}{3}$, the required product.

$$\tfrac{128}{1} \times \tfrac{2}{3} = 85\tfrac{1}{3}$$
$$128 \times 5 = 640$$
$$128 \times 5\tfrac{2}{3} = 725\tfrac{1}{3}$$

$$\begin{array}{r} 128 \\ 5\frac{2}{3} \\ \hline 85\frac{1}{3} \\ 640 \\ \hline 725\frac{1}{3} \end{array}$$

The work is commonly written as shown in the second process.

When the multiplicand is an integer and the multiplier a mixed number, multiply by the fractional and integral parts separately, and then add the products.

PROBLEMS.

Multiply

1. 44 by $\frac{9}{88}$.
2. 98 by $\frac{45}{49}$.
3. 57 by $\frac{7}{15}$.
4. 23 by $\frac{19}{20}$.
5. \$9 by $3\frac{3}{4}$.
6. \$3.50 by $7\frac{3}{8}$.
7. 4,765 by $13\frac{7}{25}$.
8. 13,672 by $28\frac{3}{17}$.

9. I bought 300 pounds of nails, and used $\frac{7}{8}$ of them in building a barn. How many pounds of nails did I use?

10. An ox weighed 1,172 pounds, and, when killed, the beef weighed $\frac{11}{16}$ as much. How much did the beef weigh?

Find the cost of

11. $81\frac{1}{4}$ pounds of sugar, @ 12¢.
12. $37\frac{5}{8}$ bushels of oats, @ 44¢.
13. $72\frac{5}{6}$ barrels of oil, @ \$5.31.
14. $67\frac{37}{80}$ tons of iron, @ \$62.50.

202. RULE FOR MULTIPLICATION OF FRACTIONS.

I. *Reduce mixed numbers to improper fractions, and integers to the form of fractions.*

II. *Multiply all the numerators together for the numerator, and all the denominators together for the denominator, of the product.*

PROBLEMS.

1. What is the value of $\frac{4}{7}$ of $\frac{9}{20}$ of $\frac{15}{16}$ of $\frac{14}{17}$ of \$34?

2. How much can a dress-maker save in $5\frac{1}{2}$ days, if she saves $\$\frac{7}{8}$ a day?

Find the cost

3. Of $\frac{3}{4}$ of a yard of oil-cloth, at $\$\frac{3}{4}$ a yard.

4. Of $\frac{5}{8}$ of a bushel of clover seed, at $\$7\frac{7}{10}$ per bushel.

5. Of $66\frac{2}{3}$ yards of flannel, at $\$.12\frac{1}{2}$ per yard.

6. Of $125\frac{3}{4}$ pounds of mutton, at $5\frac{7}{8}$ cents a pound.

7. Of a lot of goods that cost $\frac{2}{3}$ of $\frac{3}{4}$ of 6 times $\$18\frac{3}{4}$.

8. Multiply $\frac{7}{8}$ of $\frac{5}{9}$ of $\frac{11}{15}$ by $\frac{4}{21}$ of $\frac{27}{40}$.

9. A carpenter built 15 lengths of board fence, and each length was $\frac{32}{33}$ of a rod long. How long was the fence?

10. Suppose a coat costs $\frac{3}{4}$ of $\$12\frac{7}{8}$, and a hat costs $\frac{2}{5}$ as much; how much is paid for the hat?

11. If 4 barrels of apples cost $\$4\frac{3}{4}$, how much will 6 barrels cost?

12. At the rate of $13\frac{7}{30}$ miles per hour, how many miles will a steamboat run in $2\frac{3}{4}$ hours?

13. What is $\frac{1}{2}$ of the sum of $\frac{1}{8}$, $\frac{1}{12}$, and $\frac{1}{16}$?

14. Find the cost of $\frac{3}{4}$ of a dozen eggs, at $\$\frac{3}{10}$ per dozen; and $\frac{1}{8}$ of a barrel of flour, at $\$11$ per barrel.

15. From $\frac{3}{4}$ of $\frac{7}{8}$ take $\frac{2}{3}$ of $\frac{2}{5}$.

16. A man who owned $\frac{2}{3}$ of a ship, sold $\frac{4}{8}$ of his share. What part of the ship did he then own?

17. How much more will $\frac{7}{8}$ of a yard of cloth cost, at $\$4.50$ per yard, than $\frac{3}{8}$ of a yard, at $\$3.75$ per yard?

18. I bought 10 pounds of sugar, @ $11\frac{1}{4}$ cents; and 5 pounds of tea, @ $87\frac{1}{2}$ cents. How much did I expend?

— 19. How much will a turkey, weighing $8\frac{11}{16}$ pounds, cost, at $\$\frac{3}{20}$ a pound?

20. From 12 pieces of cloth of $40\frac{1}{4}$ yards each, a merchant tailor made 48 suits, using $5\frac{3}{8}$ yards of cloth for each suit. How much cloth had he left?

SECTION VI.

DIVISION.

Oral Work.*—203. *A. Divide — What is the quotient of

1. $\frac{8}{9}$ by 4.
2. $\frac{9}{10}$ by 3.
3. $2\frac{2}{11}$ by 8.
4. $2\frac{5}{8}$ by 7.
5. $7\frac{6}{7}$ by 11.
6. $\frac{10}{12}$ by 2.
7. $\frac{28}{35}$ by 7.
8. $\frac{15}{22}$ by 5.
9. $15\frac{15}{22}$ by 5.
10. $27\frac{3}{4}$ by 3.
11. $51\frac{1}{5}$ divided by 10?
12. $27\frac{1}{5}$ divided by 8?
13. $30\frac{6}{11}$ divided by 14?
14. $22\frac{4}{5}$ divided by 6?
15. $216\frac{2}{3}$ divided by 50?

16. Divide $2\frac{1}{16}$ pounds into 11 equal parts—*i. e.*, find $\frac{1}{11}$ of $2\frac{1}{16}$ pounds.

Divide

17. $3\frac{1}{2}$ dozen by 6.
18. $2\frac{1}{4}$ bushels by 8.
19. $7\frac{1}{2}$ gallons by 10.
20. $\$\frac{3}{4}$ by 12.
21. $\frac{3}{10}$ of a mile by 5.
22. $2\frac{1}{4}$ yards by 12.
23. $\frac{1}{2}$ ton by 10.
24. $\$1\frac{1}{2}$ by 4.
25. $6\frac{2}{3}$ feet by 5.

B. *1.* $\$2\frac{2}{5}$ for 6 chickens is how much for 1 chicken?

1 chicken costs 1 sixth as much as 6 chickens, or 1 sixth of $\$2\frac{2}{5}$; and 1 sixth of $\$2\frac{2}{5}$ is 1 sixth of $\$\frac{12}{5}$, which is $\$\frac{2}{5}$.

2. $\$2\frac{4}{5}$ for 8 yards of muslin is how much for 1 yard?

3. If 11 persons eat $9\frac{5}{8}$ pounds (or $\frac{77}{8}$ pounds) of butter in a week, how much butter does 1 person eat?

4. I bought 4 pounds of fresh fish for $\$\frac{3}{5}$ (or $\$\frac{12}{20}$). How much was the fish per pound?

5. Julia picked $\frac{7}{8}$ of a bushel of strawberries in 4 hours. How many berries did she pick in an hour?

6. $\$2\frac{4}{5}$ for 7 bushels of oats is how much per bushel?

7. $\$2\frac{1}{2}$ per dozen for photographs is how much apiece?

8. How many weeks will $35\frac{4}{5}$ pounds of butter last a family that uses 4 pounds per week?

9. $17\frac{3}{4}$ yards for 8 coats is how much for 1 coat?

C. *1.* 4 is $\frac{1}{5}$ of what number?

4 is 1 fifth of 5 times 4; and 5 times 4 are 20.

What is the number of which

2. 6 is $\frac{1}{3}$?	*4.* $\frac{1}{10}$ is $\frac{1}{8}$?	*6.* $4\frac{4}{5}$ is $\frac{1}{9}$?	*8.* $17\frac{2}{5}$ is $\frac{1}{2}$?
3. 12 is $\frac{1}{5}$?	*5.* $1\frac{3}{15}$ is $\frac{1}{4}$?	*7.* $3\frac{1}{3}$ is $\frac{1}{6}$?	*9.* $9\frac{3}{4}$ is $\frac{1}{7}$?

10. 4 is $\frac{2}{5}$ of what number?

**4 is 2 fifths of 5 times 1 half of 4; 1 half of 4 is 2, and 5 times
2 are 10.**

What is the number of which

11. 6 is $\frac{2}{3}$?	*13.* 45 is $\frac{5}{6}$?	*15.* $3\frac{1}{8}$ is $\frac{5}{8}$?	*17.* 22 is $\frac{4}{9}$?
12. 9 is $\frac{3}{4}$?	*14.* 24 is $\frac{9}{7}$?	*16.* $4\frac{2}{3}$ is $\frac{7}{10}$?	*18.* 35 is $\frac{3}{5}$?

19. \$2 for $\frac{1}{4}$ of a barrel of flour is how much for 1 barrel?

20. \$.12$\frac{1}{2}$ for $\frac{1}{2}$ quire of paper is how much for a quire?

21. After paying \$$\frac{3}{4}$ for railroad fare, I had $\frac{2}{7}$ of my
money left. How much money had I at first?

22. $7\frac{2}{3}$ yards are $\frac{1}{5}$ of the distance across a bridge.
What is the length of the bridge?

23. \$.16 for $\frac{2}{5}$ of a pound of figs is how much for 1 pound?

24. \$16 for $\frac{4}{5}$ of a ton of hay is how much for 1 ton?

25. 6 days are $\frac{2}{7}$ of how many days?

26. 9 bushels of plums are $\frac{2}{5}$ of how many bushels?

D. *1.* What is the quotient of 5 divided by $\frac{2}{3}$?

**5 is 15 thirds; 1 third is contained in 15 thirds 15 times,
and 2 thirds are contained in 15 thirds 1 half of 15 times, which
is $7\frac{1}{2}$ times.**

Divide	What is the quotient of	Divide
2. 4 by $\frac{2}{5}$.	*6.* 3 divided by $\frac{3}{4}$?	*10.* 6 by $1\frac{2}{3}$.
3. 2 by $\frac{4}{9}$.	*7.* 10 divided by $\frac{5}{8}$?	*11.* 15 by $3\frac{3}{4}$.
4. 5 by $\frac{6}{7}$.	*8.* 4 divided by $\frac{1}{6}$?	*12.* 10 by $2\frac{6}{7}$.
5. 5 by $\frac{1}{4}$.	*9.* 8 divided by $2\frac{1}{2}$ (or $\frac{5}{2}$)?	*13.* 9 by $1\frac{1}{10}$.

To what must 12 be reduced, before it can be divided

14. By $\frac{2}{3}$? | *15.* By $\frac{2}{6}$? | *16.* By $\frac{4}{11}$? | *17.* By $\frac{7}{16}$? | *18.* By $\frac{7}{12}$?

19. To what must any integer be reduced, before it can be divided by a fraction?

20. At $\$\frac{1}{5}$ apiece, how many hats will $\$2$ buy?

21. At $\$\frac{1}{4}$ a bushel, how many bushels of lime will $\$5$ buy?

22. How many yards of cambric can I buy for $\$4$, at $\$\frac{2}{5}$ a yard?

23. In how many days will a horse eat 9 bushels of oats, if he eats $\frac{3}{8}$ of a bushel daily?

24. How many scarfs, each $2\frac{1}{4}$ yards long, can be made from 18 yards of lace?

25. How many hours will it take you to walk 20 miles, if you walk $2\frac{2}{5}$ miles an hour?

26. In how many days can a man mow 15 acres, if he mows $1\frac{3}{8}$ acres per day?

E. 1. Reduce $\frac{2}{5}$ and $\frac{3}{7}$ to thirty-fifths.

2. Divide 14 thirty-fifths by 15 thirty-fifths.

To what fractional unit are the given fractions reduced,

To divide $\begin{cases} \textit{3. Sevenths by fifths?} & \textit{5. Fourths by eighths?} \\ \textit{4. Fourths by ninths?} & \textit{6. Twelfths by eighths?} \end{cases}$

Divide

7. $\frac{3}{20}$ by $\frac{1}{5}$.	11. $\frac{7}{40}$ by $\frac{1}{8}$.	15. $5\frac{3}{5}$ by $\frac{4}{5}$.	19. $\frac{2}{7}$ by $3\frac{1}{4}$.
8. $\frac{3}{20}$ by $\frac{3}{5}$.	12. $\frac{1}{2}$ by $\frac{2}{3}$.	16. $4\frac{2}{7}$ by $\frac{5}{7}$.	20. $\frac{5}{9}$ by $1\frac{3}{4}$.
9. $\frac{3}{20}$ by $\frac{3}{4}$.	13. $\frac{3}{5}$ by $\frac{4}{7}$.	17. $4\frac{1}{3}$ by $\frac{2}{15}$.	21. $6\frac{2}{3}$ by $16\frac{2}{3}$.
10. $\frac{7}{40}$ by $\frac{3}{5}$.	14. $\frac{5}{9}$ by $\frac{3}{8}$.	18. $\frac{5}{6}$ by $2\frac{1}{2}$.	22. $2\frac{1}{2}$ by $1\frac{1}{3}$.

23. How many hours must a boy work to earn $\$\frac{3}{4}$, if he earns $\$\frac{3}{50}$ an hour?

24. In how many days will a hotel use $\frac{5}{8}$ of a barrel of sweet-potatoes, if it uses $\frac{1}{4}$ of a barrel daily?

25. How many pounds of mixed candies can I buy for $\frac{3}{4}$ of a dollar, at $\frac{1}{6}$ of a dollar per pound?

26. A woman received $\$7\frac{1}{2}$ for chickens, at $\$\frac{3}{4}$ apiece. How many chickens did she sell?

27. At the rate of 1 pound of cheese for $\frac{3}{4}$ of a pound of honey, how many pounds of cheese must a grocer give in exchange for $4\frac{5}{8}$ pounds of honey?

28. If a cook uses $2\frac{1}{4}$ pounds of soda in a month, in what part of a month will she use $\frac{9}{10}$ of a pound?

29. A wood sawyer sawed and split $12\frac{1}{3}$ cords of wood in $6\frac{1}{3}$ days. How many cords did he average per day?

30. A hop grower picked $7\frac{1}{2}$ tons of hops, from a yard which averaged $1\frac{1}{3}$ tons to the acre. How many acres were there in the hop-yard?

204. The process of dividing by a fraction is based upon the following

PRINCIPLE. *Multiplying a number by the denominator of a fraction and dividing the product by the numerator, divides the number by the fraction.*

A *fraction is inverted,* by interchanging the places of its terms. Hence,

To divide by a fraction :—*Invert the divisor, and proceed as in multiplication.*

Written Work.—Ex. Divide $\frac{5}{12}$ by $\frac{15}{16}$.

FIRST PROCESS.	SECOND PROCESS.
$\frac{5}{12} \div \frac{15}{16} = \frac{5}{12} \times \frac{16}{15} = \frac{80}{180} = \frac{4}{9}$	$\frac{5}{12} \div \frac{15}{16} = \frac{5}{12} \times \frac{16}{15} = \frac{4}{9}$

PROBLEMS.

Divide
1. $\frac{11}{14}$ by $\frac{8}{9}$.
2. $\frac{19}{20}$ by $\frac{7}{8}$.
3. $\frac{19}{67}$ by $12\frac{2}{11}$.
4. $\frac{52}{10000}$ by $\frac{13}{100}$.
5. $\frac{17}{24}$ by $3\frac{2}{5}$. $(3\frac{2}{5}=\frac{17}{5}.)$
6. $5\frac{3}{7}$ by $\frac{3}{8}$. $(5\frac{3}{7}=\frac{38}{7}.)$
7. $7\frac{1}{5}$ by $\frac{6}{7}$.
8. $1\frac{1}{15}$ by $\frac{4}{5}$.
9. $5\frac{3}{10}$ by $\frac{7}{10}$.

Divide
10. $7\frac{7}{11}$ by $6\frac{3}{10}$.
11. $16\frac{4}{5}$ by $10\frac{1}{2}$.
12. $3\frac{1}{4}$ by $10\frac{2}{5}$.
13. $10\frac{1}{2}$ by $16\frac{4}{5}$.
14. $3\frac{1}{5}$ by $4\frac{2}{3}$.
15. $13\ (\frac{13}{1})$ by $7\frac{4}{5}$.
16. $20\frac{3}{4}$ by $8\frac{1}{5}$.
17. $40\frac{5}{8}$ by $5\frac{4}{5}$.
18. 25 by $\frac{7}{12}$.

19. If $\frac{1}{12}$ of a bushel of mortar covers 1-square yard of wall, how many square yards will $5\frac{1}{4}$ bushels cover?

20. I paid $\$\frac{3}{5}\frac{9}{8}$ for $8\frac{2}{3}$ quarts of strawberries. What was the price per quart?

21. In how many days, of $9\frac{1}{5}$ hours each, can a man perform $738\frac{3}{10}$ hours' work?

205. Ex. Divide $2,786\frac{3}{4}$ by 6.

PROCESS.

$$6\,)\,2786\tfrac{3}{4}$$
$$\overline{\quad 464\tfrac{11}{24}}$$

EXPLANATION.—Dividing the integer by 6, I obtain 464, with a remainder of $2\frac{3}{4}$, or $\frac{11}{4}$.

Then dividing the $\frac{11}{4}$ by 6, I obtain $\frac{11}{24}$, which with the 464 makes $464\frac{11}{24}$, the required quotient.

When the dividend is a large mixed number and the divisor an integer, divide the integral part as in integers, and the remainder as in fractions.

PROBLEMS.

Divide

1. $\frac{6}{7}$ by 7.
2. $\frac{9}{11}$ by 5.
3. $\frac{24}{25}$ by 16.
4. $\frac{3825}{4371}$ by 25.
5. $2\frac{4}{5}$ by 8.
6. $8\frac{2}{9}$ by 37.
7. $15\frac{1}{8}$ by 18.
8. $41\frac{5}{7}$ by 9.
9. $400\frac{7}{12}$ by 23.
10. $2,506\frac{3}{5}$ by 12.
11. $2,000\frac{5}{7}$ by 20.
12. $5,678\frac{9}{10}$ by 27.

13. If $\frac{5}{6}$ of a ton of hay can be bought for $15, what part of a ton can be bought for $1?

14. A butcher packed $\frac{4}{5}$ of a ton of beef in 8 barrels. How much did he put into each barrel?

15. I bought 9 cakes of maple sugar that weighed $4\frac{3}{8}$ pounds. How much did each cake weigh?

16. A broom maker used $22\frac{1}{2}$ pounds of broom-corn for 72 brooms. How much broom-corn did he use for 1 broom?

17. $27\frac{3}{5}$ for 18 turkeys is how much for 1 turkey?

18. What is the average weight of 11 men, whose united weight is $1,758\frac{7}{8}$ pounds?

206. Ex. Divide 31 by $\frac{7}{9}$.

PROCESS.

$$31 \div \frac{7}{9} = \frac{31}{1} \times \frac{9}{7} = \frac{279}{7} = 39\frac{6}{7}$$

PROBLEMS.

Divide

1. 12 by $\frac{7}{9}$.
2. 9 by $\frac{2}{5}$.
3. 153 by $\frac{8}{11}$.
4. 62 by $\frac{38}{45}$.
5. 18 by $10\frac{1}{2}$.
6. 80 by $2\frac{1}{7}$.
7. 625 by $6\frac{1}{4}$.
8. 8 by $2\frac{4}{5}$.
9. $41 by $\frac{3}{4}$.
10. 16 hours by $7\frac{2}{3}$.
11. 28 yards by $5\frac{2}{9}$.
12. 84 dozens by $1\frac{5}{12}$.

13. A shoe dealer paid $15 for a case of overshoes, at $\frac{5}{8}$ a pair. How many pairs of shoes were in the case?

14. How many yards of silk will $24 buy, at $1\frac{1}{25}$ a yard?

15. A stick of timber 24 feet long can be cut into how many blocks, each $\frac{3}{4}$ of a foot long?

16. A yield of 93 bushels of wheat from $4\frac{1}{2}$ acres, is how many bushels to the acre?

17. A lawyer's clerk wrote 36 pages in $6\frac{2}{3}$ hours. How many pages did he write in 1 hour?

18. How many steps of $2\frac{1}{2}$ feet each will a soldier take, in marching a mile, or 5,280 feet?

19. $423 for the rent of a house $18\frac{4}{5}$ months, is how much per month?

20. $1,500 for $2,707\frac{1}{2}$ feet of sewer pipe is how much a foot?

207. RULE FOR DIVISION OF FRACTIONS.

I. *Reduce mixed numbers to improper fractions, and integers to the form of fractions.*

II. *Invert the divisor, and proceed as in multiplication.*

PROBLEMS.

Divide

1. $\frac{11}{25}$ by 9.
2. 29 by $\frac{4}{7}$.
3. $200\frac{1}{11}$ by 5.
4. 360 by $12\frac{6}{7}$.
5. $\frac{27}{32}$ by $18\frac{7}{10}$.
6. $1,811\frac{7}{15}$ by $\frac{17}{18}$.
7. $1\frac{2}{13}$ by $\frac{6}{65}$.
8. $3\frac{1}{27}$ by $45\frac{5}{8}$.

9. A seamstress used $\frac{5}{8}$ of a yard of linen in making 9 collars. How much linen did she use for each collar?

10. 7 men harvested $22\frac{3}{5}$ acres of wheat in a day. How many acres was that for each man?

11. How many quarts of oysters can be bought for $11, at $\frac{2}{7}$ a quart?

12. A teamster draws $3\frac{2}{5}$ cords of stone at 15 loads. How many cords does he draw at each load?

13. How much candy will $\$\frac{5}{8}$ pay for, at $\$\frac{2}{3}$ a pound?

14. At $\$5\frac{1}{3}$ a bushel, how much clover seed will $\$\frac{11}{12}$ buy?

15. 12 tea-spoons weigh $\frac{9}{20}$ of a pound. How much does 1 spoon weigh?

16. If in 1 day a carpenter can build $4\frac{2}{5}$ rods of picket-fence, in how many days can he build 33 rods?

17. $\$\frac{21}{50}$ will pay for how much tea, at $\$\frac{7}{8}$ a pound?

18. A mechanic whose wages are $\$2\frac{1}{4}$ a day, receives $12 at the end of the week. How many days has he worked?

19. In how many minutes will a locomotive run $22\frac{1}{2}$ miles, running at the rate of $\frac{9}{14}$ of a mile per minute?

20. When $14\frac{2}{3}$ quarts of vinegar cost $\$\frac{22}{25}$, how much does 1 quart cost?

21. If a farm hand breaks $\frac{7}{8}$ of an acre of fallow in a day, in how many days can he break $13\frac{15}{32}$ acres?

22. $\$1\frac{9}{16}$ for $12\frac{1}{2}$ pounds of rice is how much for 1 pound?

23. How many tons of coal must 2 men load per hour, to load $23\frac{7}{32}$ tons in $9\frac{3}{8}$ hours?

24. $\frac{7}{12}$ of $2\frac{5}{8} \div \frac{5}{8}$ of $8\frac{3}{4} =$ what number?

25. Divide $\frac{3}{8}$ of $3\frac{1}{8}$ by $7\frac{1}{2}$ times 15.

26. Find the quotient of $15\frac{2}{7}$ times $4\frac{2}{3} \div 24\frac{1}{2}$ times $\frac{3}{7}$ of $7\frac{2}{7}$.

27. Divide $2\frac{7}{8}$ times $1\frac{11}{16}$ by $\frac{3}{7}$ of $\frac{5}{18}$ of $2\frac{1}{10}$.

A *complex fraction* has a fraction or a mixed number in one or both terms.

What is the value of | Simplify the complex fractions

28. $\dfrac{\frac{5}{6}\text{ of }3\frac{3}{5}}{\frac{7}{45}\text{ of }8\frac{1}{10}}$ | *29.* $\dfrac{7\frac{1}{12}\text{ times }\frac{8}{17}\times\frac{6}{25}}{7\frac{1}{7}\times 1\frac{24}{25}}$ | *30.* $\dfrac{\frac{5}{7}-\frac{5}{9}}{\frac{5}{7}+\frac{5}{9}}$ | *31.* $\dfrac{16}{24\frac{4}{5}}\div\dfrac{12\frac{2}{5}}{18}$

32. Divide the sum of $9\frac{3}{5}\times\frac{15}{8}$ and $\frac{6}{11}$ of $2\frac{1}{5}\times 75$ by their difference.

NOTE.—For *outlines of fractions* for review, see page 272.

SECTION VII.

GENERAL REVIEW PROBLEMS IN FRACTIONS.

Oral Work.—*1.* Add $18\frac{4}{11}$ and $7\frac{2}{3}$.

2. I sold my horse for \$25 more than I paid for him, and gained $\frac{1}{4}$ of his cost. For how much did I sell him?

3. If $\frac{4}{15}$ of \$30 is the cost of 5 bushels of tomatoes, what is the cost of 6 bushels?

4. A gentleman paid $\$362\frac{1}{2}$ for a pair of horses. How much did each horse cost him?

5. 144 is $\frac{9}{10}$ of 10 times what number?

6. One week a mechanic lost $\frac{5}{12}$ of his time. How many days did he work?

7. $\frac{2}{3}$ of 27 is what part of 54?

8. $\frac{5}{6}$ of 18 is $\frac{3}{4}$ of what number?

9. 48 is 2 times $\frac{1}{5}$ of what number?

10. A owns $\frac{2}{5}$ of an iron mine, B owns $\frac{3}{8}$ of it, and C the remainder. What part of the mine does C own?

11. A man owning $\frac{2}{3}$ of a boat, sold $\frac{3}{8}$ of his share for \$10. What was the value of the boat, at the same rate?

12. A fruit grower sold 9 bushels of plums, and had $\frac{1}{6}$ of his plums left. How many bushels of plums did he raise?

13. \$15 are $\frac{3}{8}$ of the monthly rent of a house. How much is that a year?

14. If 2 boxes of lemons cost $\$5\frac{1}{3}$, how many boxes can be bought for $\$16\frac{2}{3}$?

15. James hoed a piece of corn in $5\frac{5}{6}$ days, hoeing $\frac{2}{5}$ of an acre each day. How many acres were in the piece?

16. Emma is $\frac{3}{8}$ as old as her mother, her mother is $\frac{4}{5}$ as old as her grandmother, and her grandmother is 70 years old. How old is Emma?

***Written Work.*—1.** Change $\frac{3}{17}$ to 85ths; to 153ds.

2. Reduce to mixed numbers $\frac{13293}{47}$, $\frac{37419}{83}$, and $\frac{42763}{234}$.

3. Reduce $\frac{4}{7}$, $\frac{4}{5}$, and $\frac{4}{9}$ to similar fractions.

4. The sum of three numbers is $357\frac{5}{16}$, and two of them are $256\frac{5}{8}$ and $\frac{11}{12}$. What is the third number?

5. The minuend is $103\frac{5}{7}$, and the remainder is $21\frac{2}{3}$. What is the subtrahend?

6. The quotient is 335, and the divisor is $23\frac{1}{15}$. What is the dividend?

7. The dividend is $\frac{7}{12}$ of $1\frac{5}{7}$, and the divisor is $\frac{5}{9}$ of $87\frac{3}{4}$. What is the quotient?

8. If $13\frac{3}{4}$ dozens of eggs cost $\$3\frac{17}{20}$, how much will $11\frac{2}{3}$ dozen cost?

9. How many pounds of butter, at $18\frac{3}{4}$ cents, will pay for $15\frac{1}{2}$ pounds of sugar, at $10\frac{1}{2}$ cents?

10. F sold $\frac{2}{5}$ of his land, then bought $37\frac{3}{4}$ acres, and then had $112\frac{2}{20}$ acres. How much land had he at first?

11. Divide $\frac{7}{8}$ of $\frac{1}{2}$ of $42\frac{3}{5}$ by $\frac{1}{6}$ of $\frac{4}{9}$ of 27.

12. I owned $\frac{3}{4}$ of a fruit farm, and sold $\frac{3}{7}$ of my part for \$3,405. What was the whole farm worth?

13. If $\frac{7}{8}$ of a yard of silk is worth $\$\frac{7}{8}$, what is the value of $16\frac{1}{2}$ yards?

14. A grocer, after selling $\frac{1}{8}$, $\frac{2}{5}$, $\frac{3}{20}$, and $\frac{1}{4}$ of a hogshead of sugar, had 102 pounds left. How many pounds did the hogshead contain at first?

15. A saleswoman earns $\$\frac{7}{8}$ a day, and her expenses are $\$3\frac{1}{4}$ a week. How much money will she save in 52 weeks?

16. How much will $\frac{7}{8}$ of $3\frac{1}{3}$ tons of coal cost, at $\frac{2}{3}$ of $\$8\frac{5}{8}$ per ton?

17. Reduce $\frac{48}{84}$, $\frac{35}{215}$, $\frac{105}{441}$, $\frac{1575}{1225}$, and $\frac{11907}{17199}$ to lowest terms.

18. If 4 be subtracted from both terms of the fraction $\frac{9}{15}$, is its value increased or diminished? How much?

19. What fraction added to $\frac{1}{3}$ of $10\frac{1}{2}$ times $\frac{1}{14}$, equals 1 ?

20. The product of four factors is $207\frac{2}{3}$, and three of them are $10\frac{1}{8}$, $116\frac{10}{16}$, and $3\frac{2}{3}$. What is the fourth factor? Find the sum, the difference, and the product of

21. $\frac{4}{5}$ and $\frac{2}{3}$. | *22.* $\frac{7}{8}$ and $2\frac{3}{5}$. | *23.* $\frac{6}{7}$ and $\frac{4}{7}$. | *24.* $5\frac{1}{8}$ and $7\frac{7}{8}$.

25. What part of $19\frac{2}{3}$ is $18\frac{1}{12}$?

26. Reduce to similar fractions $17\frac{1}{3}$, $\frac{1}{5}$ of $\frac{9}{11}$, and 12.

27. Bought 3 crocks of butter weighing $25\frac{7}{16}$, $29\frac{3}{4}$, and $27\frac{1}{8}$ pounds. The empty crocks weigh $5\frac{9}{16}$, $5\frac{5}{8}$, and $7\frac{1}{2}$ pounds. How many yards of muslin will pay for the butter, at the rate of $1\frac{1}{4}$ yards per pound ?

28. Find the difference between $\frac{7}{12}$ of $18\frac{3}{4}$ and $\frac{2}{3}$ of $17\frac{3}{4}$.

29. Of a 50-acre farm $\frac{3}{7}$ was planted to corn, $\frac{1}{4}$ of the remainder to potatoes, and the balance was sown to wheat. How many acres were there of each kind of crop ?

30. A makes a boot in $\frac{2}{3}$ of a day, and B makes one in $\frac{3}{5}$ of a day. How many boots can the two men make in a day ?

31. I paid 12 cents a pound for a live turkey that weighed $11\frac{3}{4}$ pounds, and the waste in dressing was $\frac{2}{7}$ of its weight. How much a pound did the dressed turkey cost me ?

32. B walked $3\frac{7}{8}$ miles per hour for $7\frac{4}{15}$ hours, and A walked $4\frac{1}{5}$ miles per hour for $3\frac{1}{6}$ hours. Which walked the greater distance? How much the greater?

33. If a man can earn \$31.25 in 26 days, working 10 hours a day, how much can he earn in 19 days, working 12 hours a day ?

34. Divide the product of 9 times $\dfrac{1\frac{1}{3}}{2\frac{2}{3}}$ and $\dfrac{\frac{1}{2}\text{ of }1\frac{1}{8}}{\frac{2}{7}-\frac{3}{5}}$ by their sum.

35. A merchant paid out $\frac{1}{3}$ of his money, then $\frac{1}{3}$ of what remained, and then $\frac{1}{3}$ of $\frac{4}{5}$ of what then remained. What part of his money had he left ?

CHAPTER V.

COMPOUND NUMBERS.

SECTION I.

MEASURES OF EXTENSION AND CAPACITY.

208. A *simple number* is a number that expresses units of the same kind.

A simple number may be either abstract or concrete.

209. A *denominate number* is a concrete number that expresses measure, weight, or money value.

210. A *compound number* is a number that expresses units of different kinds or denominations.

a. 38, 49 apples, 25 bushels, $362 are simple numbers.

b. 17 yards, 40 days, 271 pounds, $362 are denominate numbers.

c. 3 feet 5 inches, 7 gallons 2 quarts 1 pint, 81 pounds 6 ounces are compound numbers.

Which of the numbers in the margin	51 yards; 36 men; 12 acres.
	125 trees; 21 dozen; 258 sheep.
1. Are simple numbers?	5 bushels 3 pecks; 13 miles 215 rods.
2. Are denominate numbers?	
3. Are compound numbers?	18 days 6 hours 30 minutes.

211. The quantity of all articles bought and sold is determined by *measuring, weighing,* or *counting* them.

212. *Linear* or *line measures* are the measures used in measuring distances,—as length, width, thickness.

The denominations are the *mile* (mi.), the *rod* (rd.), the *yard* (yd.), the *foot* (ft.), and the *inch* (in.).

Table of Linear Measures.

12 in.	are 1 ft.	In measuring goods sold by the
3 ft.	" 1 yd.	yard in length,
5½ or 5.5 yd., or 16¼ or 16.5 ft.	" 1 rd.	4½ or 4.5 in. are 1 eighth.
320 rd., or 1,760 yd., or 5,280 ft.	" 1 mi.	9 in. or 2 eighths } " 1 qr. (quarter).
		4 qr. " 1 yd.

213. A *surface* is a figure that has length and width.

The *area* of a figure is the extent of its surface.

a. A surface 1 inch long and 1 inch wide is a *square inch;*

b. A surface 1 foot long and 1 foot wide is a *square foot;*

c. A surface 1 yard long and 1 yard wide is a *square yard;* etc.

214. *Surface measures* are the measures used in computing the area of surfaces,—such as land, lumber, flooring, and plastering.

The denominations are the *square mile* (sq. mi.), the *acre* (A.), the *square rod* (sq. rd.), the *square yard* (sq. yd.), the *square foot* (sq. ft.), and the *square inch* (sq. in.).

Table of Square Measures.

144 sq. in.	are 1 sq. ft.	In surveys of Government lands
9 sq. ft.	" 1 sq. yd.	160 A. are 1 qr. sec. (section).
30¼ or 30.25 sq. yd.	" 1 sq. rd.	320 A. " 1 half sec.
160 sq. rd.	" 1 A.	640 A. " 1 sec. (or 1 sq. mi.).
640 A.	" 1 sq. mi.	36 sec. " 1 Tp. (township).

215. A *solid* or *body* is a portion of matter or of space that has length, width, and thickness.

a. A solid whose surfaces are each 1 inch square is a *cubic inch;*

b. A solid whose surfaces are each 1 foot square is a *cubic foot;*

c. A solid whose surfaces are each 1 yard square is a *cubic yard.*

216. *Solid measures* are the measures used in computing the solid contents of bodies,—such as timber, wood, stone, and earth;—and the capacity of bins, boxes, etc.

The denominations are the *cord* (cd.), the *cubic yard* (cu. yd.), the *cubic foot* (cu. ft.), and the *cubic inch* (cu. in.).

Table of Cubic Measures.

1,728 cu. in. are 1 cu. ft.
27 cu. ft. " 1 cu. yd.
128 cu. ft. " 1 cd.

a. On public works, a cubic yard of earth is a standard load.

b. A pile of wood or of rough stone 8 feet long, 4 feet wide, and 4 feet high is 1 cord.

217. *Liquid measures* are the measures used in measuring water, oil, milk, molasses, wines, and other liquids.

The denominations are the *gallon* (gal.), the *quart* (qt.), the *pint* (pt.), and the *gill* (gi.).

218. *Dry measures* are the measures used in measuring grain, seeds, fruits, berries, most kinds of vegetables, lime, charcoal, and some other articles.

The denominations are the *bushel* (bu.), the *peck* (pk.), the *quart*, and the *pint*.

Table of Liquid Measures.

4 gi. are 1 pt.
2 pt. " 1 qt.
4 qt. " 1 gal.

Table of Dry Measures.

2 pt. are 1 qt.
8 qt. " 1 pk.
4 pk. " 1 bu.

Case I. Reduction Descending.

219. *Reduction Descending* is the process of changing a number to another of less unit value.

Changing rods to yards, feet, or inches is Reduction Descending.

Oral Work.—*1.* How many inches are 9 ft.?

2. How many inches are 9 ft. 6 in.?

3. Reduce 2 yards 1 foot 8 inches to inches.

2 yards are 2 times 3 feet, or 6 feet; and 2 yards 1 foot are 6 feet plus 1 foot, or 7 feet. 7 feet are 7 times 12 inches, or 84 inches; and 7 feet 8 inches are 84 inches plus 8 inches, or 92 inches. Hence; 2 yards 1 foot 8 inches are 92 inches.

4. How many rods are 3 mi. ?

5. Are 3 mi. 40 rd. ?

6. Change 6 yards to feet.

7. Change 6 feet to inches.

Reduce

8. 1 A. 40 sq. rd. to square rods.

9. 12 gal. 2 qt. to pints.

10. 9 bu. 2 pk. to half-pecks.

11. 2 bu. 1 pk. 3 qt. to quarts.

12. 2 cu. yd. 8 cu. ft. to cubic feet.

13. 4 yd. 2 ft. to inches.

14. 5 gal. 1 qt. of catsup will fill how many quart bottles? How many pint bottles?

15. How many quart boxes will 2 bu. 2 pk. 5 qt. of strawberries fill?

16. A dealer sold 3 bu. 4 qt. of chestnuts by the pint. How many pints did he sell?

Reduction Descending is performed by multiplication.

Written Work.—220. Ex. Reduce 17 yd. 1 ft. 5 in. to inches.

EXPLANATION. —1 yard is 3 feet, 17 yards are 17 times 3 feet, and 17 yards 1 foot are 17 times 3 feet, plus 1 foot, or 52 feet.

1 foot is 12 inches, 52 feet are 52 times 12 inches, and 52 feet 5 inches are 52 times 12 inches, plus 5 inches, or 629 inches.

Hence, 17 yd. 1 ft. 5 in. = 629 in.

PROCESS.

$$17 \text{ yd. } 1 \text{ ft. } 5 \text{ in.}$$
$$\underline{3}$$
$$52 \text{ ft.}$$
$$\underline{12}$$
$$629 \text{ in.}$$

In Reduction Descending, the true multiplicand is commonly used as a multiplier, and the true multiplier as a multiplicand.

PROBLEMS.

1. Reduce 5 mi. 187 rd. 2 yd. 1 ft. 9 in. to inches.

2. Reduce 25 sq. rd. 3 sq. yd. 8 sq. ft. to square inches.

Reduce to units of the lowest denomination named

3. 63 rd. 4 yd. 2 ft.

4. 84 sq. rd. 4 sq. ft.

5. 275 bu. 3 pk. 7 qt.

6. 5 cu. yd. 848 cu. in.

7. 42 yd. 3 qr. to inches.

8. $34\frac{3}{10}$ sq. mi. to square rods.

9. 4.375 sq. mi. to acres.

10. $7\frac{5}{8}$ cd. to cubic feet.

Case II. **Reduction Ascending.**

221. *Reduction Ascending* is the process of changing a number to another of greater unit value.

Changing feet to yards, rods, or miles is Reduction Ascending.

Oral Work.—*1.* 72 inches are how many feet?

2. 72 inches are how many yards?

3. 96 inches are how many yards and feet?

4. Reduce 207 inches to yards.

1 inch is $\frac{1}{12}$ of a foot, and **207** inches are $\frac{207}{12}$ feet, or **17 feet 3 inches**; 1 foot is $\frac{1}{3}$ of a yard, and **17 feet** are $\frac{17}{3}$ yards, or **5 yards 2 feet**; and **5 yards 2 feet plus 3 inches are 5 yards 2 feet 3 inches.**

Change
5. 124 inches to yards.
6. 35 yards to rods.
7. 103 pints to gallons.
8. 150 cubic feet to cords.
9. 1,000 rods to miles.
10. 320 pints to bushels.

11. 100 cubic feet are how many cubic yards?

12. A well that is 40 feet deep is how many rods deep?

13. If you buy 1 pint of milk a day, how many quarts will you buy in 60 days? How many gallons?

Reduction Ascending is performed by division.

Written Work.—**222.** Ex. Reduce 1,532 ft. to units of higher denominations.

Explanation.—I divide 1,532 feet by 3, the number of feet in 1 yard, and obtain 510 yards 2 feet. I divide the 510 yards of this result by 5.5, the number of yards in 1 rod, and obtain 92 rods 4 yards. To this result I annex 2 feet, the first remainder, and I have 92 rods 4 yards 2 feet, the required result.

Process.

$$3)\,\overline{1,532\ ft.}$$
$$5.5)\,\overline{510\ yd.}\ 2\ ft.\ (92\ rd.\ 4\ yd.$$
$$\underline{495}$$
$$\overline{15.0}$$
$$\underline{11.0}$$
$$\overline{4.0}$$

Hence, $1,532\ ft. = 92\ rd.\ 4\ yd.\ 2\ ft.$

I

Problems.

1. How many feet and inches are 925 inches?

2. How many miles and rods are 2,000 rods?

3. How many square miles are 312,000 square rods?

Reduce
4. 297 sq. ft. to sq. yd.
5. 398 yd. to rods.
6. 17,283 qt. to bushels.
7. 1,535 pt. to gallons.
8. 3,236 A. to sq. mi.
9. 185,520 cu. in. to cu. yd
10. 334,970 sq. in. to sq. rd.
11. 4,713,256 cu. in. to cd.

12. 3,825 quarts of wheat are how many bushels?

13. 2,469 cubic feet of wood are how many cords?

14. 1,727 pints of milk are how many gallons?

223. Rules for Reductions of Compound Numbers.

I. For Reduction Descending.

1. *Multiply the units of the highest denomination given, by that number of the next lower denomination which equals 1 of this higher, and to the product add the units of the lower denomination.*

2. *In like manner, reduce this result to units of the next lower denomination; and so continue until the given number is reduced to units of the required denomination.*

II. For Reduction Ascending.

1. *Divide the given number by that number of the same denomination which equals 1 of the next higher; writing the quotient as units of the higher denomination, and the remainder as units of the denomination divided.*

2. *In like manner, reduce this quotient to units of the next higher denomination; and so continue until the given number is reduced to units of the required denomination.*

3. *Write the last quotient and the several remainders in their order, for the required result.*

PROBLEMS.

1. How many tiles, each 1 foot long, will be required for 1 mi. 68 rd. 2 yd. of tile-drain?

2. 7 bu. 3 pk. 6 qt. of chestnuts are how many pints?

3. How many rods of fence will it take to inclose a tract of land 2 mi. 45 rd. long and $\frac{7}{8}$ mi. wide?

4. How many hills of corn are there in a 10-acre field, if there is a hill on every square yard?

5. How many acres are there in an orchard of 6,386 peach-trees, each tree occupying 1 square rod of land?

6. One year a fruit grower had a crop of 305 quarts of cherries. How many bushels had he?

7. A perfumer put up 10 gallons of cologne in bottles that held 1 gill each. How many bottles did he fill?

8. How many pint papers of seed-corn are equal to 7 bu. 3 pk. 5 qt. 1 pt. ?

9. Christmas week a grocer sold 365 quart cans of oysters. How many gallons of oysters did he sell?

10. A seedsman put up 353 pint papers of marrowfat peas. How many bushels did he put up?

CASE III. Addition.

***Oral Work.*—224.** *1.* The sum of 9 in., 5 in., 11 in., 7 in., 3 in., and 10 in. is how many inches? How many feet and inches? How many yards, feet, and inches?

2. The sum of 7 ft., 12 ft., 1 ft., 6 ft., and 8 ft. is how many rods, yards, and feet?

3. Add 7 gal. 3 qt. and 2 gal. 2 qt. 1 pt.

4. What is the sum of 3 pk. 5 qt. and 2 pk. 7 qt. ?

5 quarts plus 7 quarts are 12 quarts, or 1 peck 4 quarts; this 1 peck plus the 3 pecks and 2 pecks are 6 pecks, or 1 bushel 2 pecks; and 1 bushel 2 pecks plus 4 quarts are 1 bu. 2 pk. 4 qt

5. Add 2 yd. 1 ft., 1 yd. 2 ft., and 5 yd. 2 ft.

6. What is the sum of 5 sq. yd. 7 sq. ft., 2 sq. yd. 5 sq. ft., and 4 sq. yd. 8 sq. ft.?

7. 4 yd. + 2 yd. + 13 yd. + 8 yd. + 3 yd. = how many rd., yd., ft., and in.?

8. In 3 hours a butcher drove an ox 1 mi. 200 rd., 1 mi. 160 rd., and 2 mi. 40 rd. How far was the ox driven?

***Written Work.*—225.** Ex. Add 4 yd. 2 ft. 3 in., 1 yd. 1 ft. 9 in., 2 yd. 1 ft., 2 ft. 11 in., and 5 yd. 5 in.

EXPLANATION.—I write the parts with units of like denominations in the same columns, and begin at the right to add.

PROCESS.

yd.	ft.	in.
4	2	3
1	1	9
2	1	0
	2	11
5	0	5

2 rd. 3 yd. 2 ft. 4 in.

The sum of the inches is 28, or 2 feet 4 inches; and I write the 4 inches in the result.

The sum of the 2 feet and the feet in the given numbers is 8, or 2 yards 2 feet; and I write the 2 feet in the result.

The sum of the 2 yards and the yards in the given numbers is 14, or 2 rods 3 yards, which I write in the result.

The entire result, 2 rd. 3 yd. 2 ft. 4 in., is the required sum.

NOTE.—Compare this process and explanation with the process and explanation on page 23.

226. *The processes of addition, subtraction, multiplication, and division of compound numbers are similar to those employed in integers. Hence, special rules for these processes are unnecessary.*

PROBLEMS.

1			2		3		
21 gal.	3 qt.	0 pt.	9 A.	96 sq. rd.	29 cu. yd.	16 cu. ft.	525 cu. in.
17	1	1	11	44	10	14	368
126	0	1	8	108		9	968
43	2	0	10	56	15	3	874

Add $\begin{cases} 4. & \text{4 yd. 2 ft. 4 in., 3 yd. 1 ft. 8 in., 5 yd. 2 ft. 6 in.} \\ 5. & \text{20 gal. 2 qt., 15 gal. 1 qt., and 14 gal. 3 gi.} \\ 6. & \text{13 bu.}+\text{12 bu. 3 pk.}+\text{19 bu. 2 qt.}+\text{36 bu. 2 pk. 2 qt.} \end{cases}$

7. In three piles of wood containing 5 cd. 60 cu. ft., 6 cd. 96 cu. ft., and 9 cd. 68 cu. ft., are how many cords?

8. In four days a telegraph company put up 1 mi. 14 rd. 3 yd., 318 rd. 5 yd., 1 mi. 39 rd. 4 yd., and 1 mi. 67 rd. of wire. How much wire did they put up in the four days?

9. A farmer raised 751 bu. 3 pk. of wheat, 135 bu. 1 pk. 6 qt. of rye, 640 bu. 2 pk. of corn, and 514 bu. 4 qt. of oats. How much grain did he raise?

10. A painter used 5 gal. 3 qt. 1 pt. of raw oil, and 3 gal. 2 qt. 1 pt. of boiled oil. How much oil did he use?

11. There are 35 sq. yd. 5 sq. ft. of plastering in the ceiling of a room, 22 sq. yd. 2 sq. ft. in each of the two side walls, and 17 sq. yd. 7 sq. ft. in each of the two end walls. How much plastering is there in the room?

CASE IV. Subtraction.

Oral Work.—**227.** Subtract

1. 3 in. from 4 ft. 8 in.		4. 7 sq. ft. from 1 sq. yd.
2. 1 ft. from 4 ft. 8 in.		5. 15 cu. ft. from 3 cu. yd.
3. 1 ft. 3 in. from 4 ft. 8 in.		6. 120 sq. rd. from 5 A.

7. Take 10 rd. 5 yd. from 25 rd. 2 yd.

5 yards can not be taken from 2 yards. But 25 rods 2 yards are 24 rods 7½ yards; 5 yards from 7½ yards leave 2½ yards; 10 rods from 24 rods leave 14 rods; and 14 rods plus 2½ yards (2 yards 1 foot 6 inches) are 14 rods 2 yards 1 foot 6 inches.

What is the difference between

8. 6 ft. and 4 ft. 7 in.?	12. 4 cu. yd. and 13 cu. ft. 28 cu. in.?
9. 10 yd. and 2 ft. 9 in.?	13. 12 sq. yd. 3 sq. ft. and 5 sq. ft.?
10. 4 qt. and 2 qt. 3 gi.?	14. 6 sq. ft. and 4 sq. ft. 36 sq. in.?
11. 3 qt. 1 pt. and 1 gal.?	15. ½ bu. and ⅛ pk.?

16. All of a 10-acre lot but 3 A. 75 sq. rd. is meadow. How many acres are meadow?

17. From a barrel containing 30 gal. of turpentine, 14 gal. 3 qt. were drawn. How many gallons were left?

18. On a city lot 30 ft. 6 in. wide, stands a house 19 ft. 10 in. wide. How much wider is the lot than the house?

***Written Work.*—228.** Ex. What is the difference between 8 yd. 1 ft. 11 in. and 3 yd. 2 ft. 5 in.?

EXPLANATION.—I write the units of the subtrahend under units of like denominations of the minuend, and begin at the right to subtract.

PROCESS.

$$8 \text{ yd. } 1 \text{ ft. } 11 \text{ in.}$$
$$3 \qquad 2 \qquad 5$$
$$\overline{4 \text{ yd. } 2 \text{ ft. } 6 \text{ in.}}$$

5 inches from 11 inches leave 6 inches, which I write in the result.

2 feet can not be subtracted from 1 foot; but the 8 yards 1 foot of the minuend are 7 yards 4 feet; and 2 feet from 4 feet leave 2 feet, which I write in the result.

3 yards from the remaining 7 yards of the minuend leave 4 yards, which I write in the result.

The entire result, 4 yards 2 feet 6 inches, is the required difference.

NOTE.—Compare this process and explanation with the process and explanation on page 40.

PROBLEMS.

	1	**2**
From	5 mi. 220 rd. 4 yd. 2 ft. 5 in.	9 sq. rd. 4 sq. yd.
Subtract	2 264 3 2 8	3 5

3. From 1 rd. take 1 in. | *4.* From 8 bu. 3 pk. 2 qt. take 4 bu. 7 qt.

5. From 90 cu. yd. subtract 39 cu. yd. 18 cu. ft. 966 cu. in.

6. 113 cd. of wood have been drawn from a wood yard containing 200 cd. How much wood remains in the yard?

7. Last year 23 mi. 194 rd. 2 yd. of gas pipe were in use in a certain city, and now 25 mi. 49 rd. 1 ft. are in use. How much pipe has been laid during the year?

8. In a 20-gallon can are 5 gal. 2 qt. 1 pt. of kerosene. How much more kerosene will the can hold?

CASE V. Multiplication.

Oral Work.—**229.** *1.* 7 times 9 inches are how many inches? How many feet?

2. 7 times 12 cubic feet are how many cubic yards?

Multiply { *3.* 2 mi. 15 rd. by 4. | *5.* 20 A. 16 sq. rd. by 10.
{ *4.* 5 cd. 20 cu. ft. by 3. | *6.* 7 yd. 3 qr. by 8.

7. 9 times 3 quarts 1 pint are how many gallons, quarts, and pints?

9 times 1 pint are 9 pints, or 4 quarts 1 pint; and 9 times 3 quarts plus 4 quarts 1 pint are 31 quarts 1 pint, or 7 gallons 3 quarts 1 pint.

8. How much is 20 times 9 rd. 5 yd.?

9. How much is 5 times 2 sq. yd. 8 sq. ft.?

10. My horse eats 2 bu. 2 pk. 2 qt. of oats in a week. How many bushels does he eat in 4 weeks?

11. If a farm hand can mow 2 A. 40 sq. rd. of grass in a day, how many acres can he mow in a week?

Written Work.—**230.** Ex. Multiply 5 mi. 72 rd. 8 ft. by 8.

PROCESS.

$$5 \; mi. \quad 72 \; rd. \quad 8 \, ft.$$
$$8$$
$$\overline{41 \; mi. \; 259 \; rd. \; 14 \, ft. \; 6 \; in.}$$

EXPLANATION.—I write the multiplier under the lowest denomination of the multiplicand, and begin at the right to multiply.

8 times 8 feet are 64 feet, or 3 rods 14½ feet (14 ft. 6 in.); and I write 14 feet 6 inches in the result.

8 times 72 rods, plus the 3 rods of the first partial product are 579 rods, or 1 mile 259 rods; and I write 259 rods in the result.

8 times 5 miles, plus the 1 mile of the second partial product are 41 miles, which I write in the result.

The entire result, 41 miles 259 rods 14 feet 6 inches, is the required product.

NOTE.—Compare this process and explanation with the process and explanation on page 57.

PROBLEMS.

Multiply

1. 50 bu. 6 qt. by 17.
2. 9 mi. 6 in. by 122.
3. 129 cu. in. by 384.
4. 36 A. 90 sq. rd. 16 sq. ft. 4 sq. in. by 8.
5. 32 gal. 3 qt. 1 pt. by 7.
6. 3 mi. 280 rd. 2 ft. by 219.

7. How many cords of wood can a team draw at 18 loads, if it draws 1 cd. 44 cu. ft. at each load?

8. How many bushels of potatoes will a family use in a year, at the rate of 3 bu. 5 qt. per month?

9. How much land is there in 38 building lots, each lot containing 5 sq. rd. 24 sq. yd. ?

10. Some track hands with a hand-car pass, 4 times each day, over the road between two railroad stations 5 mi. 213 rd. 1 yd. 2 ft. apart.   How far do they travel in 26 days?

CASE VI. **Division.**

Oral Work.—**231.** *1.* Find 1 half of 6 mi. 40 rd.

2. 1 sixth of 2 ft. (or 24 in.).
3. 1 sixth of 14 ft. (or 12 ft. + 2 ft.).
4. 1 third of 16 sq. yd.
5. 1 ninth of 20 cu. yd.

6. Divide 23 gallons 3 quarts into 5 equal parts.

1 fifth of 23 gallons is 4 gallons, and 3 gallons remainder; this 3 gallons plus the 3 quarts of the given number are 15 quarts; 1 fifth of 15 quarts is 3 quarts; and 4 gallons plus 3 quarts are 4 gallons 3 quarts.

7. Divide 40 sq. yd. 6 sq. ft. into 3 equal parts.

8. Divide 21 cu. yd. 13 cu. ft. by 4. | 9. 3 bu. 3 pk. by 8.

10. If a stone-mason lays 27 cu. yd. 16 cu. ft. of stone in 5 days, how much does he lay per day?

11. A yacht sailed 59 mi. 20 rd. in 7 hours.   What was her average hourly distance?

12. If 7 men can mow 22 A. 29 sq. rd. of grass in a day, how much can 1 man mow?

13. How many barrels, each holding 2 bu. 3 pk., will be required to hold 11 bushels of apples?

***Written Work.*— 232.** Ex. Divide 76 sq. rd. 15 sq. yd. by 6.

PROCESS.

$$6)\overline{76\ sq.\ rd.\ 15\ sq.\ yd.}$$
$$12\ sq.\ rd.\ 22\ sq.\ yd.\ 6\ sq.ft.$$

EXPLANATION. — I write the dividend and divisor as in integers, and begin at the left to divide.

1 sixth of 76 square rods is 12 square rods, and 4 square rods remainder; and I write 12 square rods in the result.

The 4 square rods remainder plus the 15 square yards of the dividend are 136 square yards; 1 sixth of 136 square yards is 22 square yards, with 4 square yards remainder; and I write 22 square yards in the result.

The 4 square yards remainder are 36 square feet, and 1 sixth of 36 square feet is 6 square feet, which I write in the result.

The entire result, 12 sq. rd. 22 sq. yd. 6 sq. ft., is the required result.

NOTE.—Compare this process and explanation with the process and explanation on page 86.

PROBLEMS.

1
9)16 mi. 95 rd. 14 ft.

2
14)36 sq. mi. 74 sq. rd.

3
30)93 cu. yd. 14 cu. ft.(

4. Divide 526 rd. 4 ft. 9 in. into 12 equal parts.

5. Divide 428 A. 50 sq. rd. 4 sq. ft. by 20.

6. How much is 1 twenty-fifth of 19 cu. ft. 675 cu. in.?

7. 52 gal. 2 qt. of sirup will fill how many kegs that hold 8 gal. 3 qt. each?   (Reduce both numbers to quarts.)

÷ *8.* Divide 35 bu. 1 pk. 2 qt. by 17 bu. 2 pk. 5 qt.

9. A workman laid 64 rd. 3 yd. 1 ft. of stone-wall in 26 days.   How much did he lay per day?

10. A bridge pier containing 448 cu. yd. of stone, was built in 36 days.   What was the average amount of stone laid daily?

11. A farmer put 125 bu. 3 pk. 6 qt. of wheat into bags holding 1 bu. 3 pk. 6 qt. each.   How many bags did he fill?

12. If 7 men can mow 26 A. 40 sq. rd. of grass in 10 hours, how much can 1 man mow in 1 hour?

SECTION II.

WEIGHTS.

233. *Weight* is the measure of the quantity of matter in a body.

234. *Avoirdupois weights* are the weights used for all the ordinary purposes of weighing.

The denominations are the *ton* (**T.**), the *hundred-weight* (**cwt.**), the *pound* (**lb.**), and the *ounce* (**oz.**).

Table of Avoirdupois Weights.

16 oz.	are 1 lb.		196 lb. of flour	are 1 bar.
100 lb.	" 1 cwt.		200 lb. of beef,	" 1 bar.
20 cwt., or 2,000 lb.,	" 1 T.		pork, or fish	

In selling coal, coarse metals, and ores at wholesale; and in estimating duties on foreign goods at the U. S. Custom-houses,	28 lb.	are 1 qr.
	4 qr. (112 lb.)	" 1 cwt.
	20 cwt. (2,240 lb.)	" 1 T.

Oral Work.—1. Reduce 50 lb. 8 oz. to ounces.

2. Reduce 168 oz. to pounds.

3. Add 16 cwt. 25 lb., 10 cwt. 70 lb., and 6 cwt. 50 lb.

4. Take 9 cwt. 35 lb. from 2 T. 5 cwt.

5. How much is 6 times 2 lb. 5 oz.?

6. Divide 72 lb. 8 oz. into 5 equal parts.

7. 3 lb. 8 oz. of nutmegs are how many ounces?

8. 43 oz. of cheese are how many pounds?

9. 75 cwt. of coal are how many tons?

10. 5 T. 12 cwt. of iron are how many hundred-weight?

11. One day a grocer sold 6 lb. 8 oz., 4 lb. 4 oz., 10 lb. 5 oz., 9 lb. 7 oz., and 5 lb. of butter. How many pounds of butter did he sell?

PROBLEMS.

***Written Work.*—1.** 4 T. 16 cwt. 83 lb. of hay are how many pounds?

2. 25 lb. 12 oz. of cinnamon are how many ounces?

How many barrels { 3. Are 6,811 pounds of flour?
{ 4. Are 65,015 ounces of beef?

	5					**6**		
Add 3	T. 6	cwt. 5	lb. 7	oz.		From 2 T. 715 lb. 3 oz.		
	4	16	9	12		Take 1	929	7
	24	9	8	10				
	15	12	46	13			**7**	
		7	32	00		Multiply 5 T. 39 lb. 6 oz.		
	9	19	00	15		by	12	

Divide { 8. 7 times 1,285 lb. 8 oz. by 32.
{ 9. 1 T. 968 lb. 14 oz. by 63.

10. A manufacturer put up 5 T. 429 lb. of saleratus in quarter-pound packages. How many packages did he put up?

11. How many tons of bluing will a manufacturer use in putting up 845,000 1-ounce boxes?

12. A freight-car was loaded with 3 T. 8 cwt. 48 lb. of groceries, 3 T. 19 cwt. 40 lb. of hardware, 1 T. 1 cwt. 94 lb. of furniture, and 18 cwt. 64 lb. of dry goods. How much freight was in the car?

13. A crock of butter weighed 44 lb. 6 oz., and the crock weighed 7 lb. 10 oz. How much did the butter weigh?

14. What is the total weight of 45 loads of coal, each weighing 1 T. 375 lb. ?

15. A farmer cut 28 T. 1,375 lb. of hay from 15 acres of meadow. What was the yield per acre?

16. How many days will 6 bar. 84 lb. of flour last a family that uses 3 lb. 8 oz. per day?

17. The total weight of 13 cheeses is 440 lb. 6 oz. What is their average weight?

SECTION III.

TIME.

235. *Time* is a limited portion of duration.

The denominations are the *century*, the *year* (yr.), the *month* (mo.), the *week* (wk.), the *day* (da.), the *hour* (h.), the *minute* (min.), and the *second* (sec.).

Table of Time.

			MONTHS AND DAYS.		
60 sec.	are 1 min.		Nos.	Names.	Days.
60 min.	" 1 h.		1st,	January,	31
24 h.	" 1 da.		2d,	February,	28 or 29
7 da.	" 1 wk.		3d,	March,	31
52 wk. 1 da., or 365 da.,	" 1 common yr.		4th,	April,	30
			5th,	May,	31
52 wk. 2 da., or 366 da.,	" 1 leap-yr.		6th,	June,	30
100 yr.	" 1 century.		7th,	July,	31
			8th,	August,	31
			9th,	September,	30
			10th,	October,	31
			11th,	November,	30
			12th,	December,	31

a. February has 28 days in a common year, and 29 in a leap-year.

b. Every fourth year from the beginning of a century is a leap-year.

c. In most business transactions 30 days are considered a month.

Oral Work.—*1.* Change 5 min. 20 sec. to seconds.

2. Reduce 8 wk. 4 da. to days. To hours.

3. Reduce 150 h. to days. | *4.* Reduce 63 min. to hours.

5. Add 13 h. 17 min., 10 h. 40 min., and 18 min.

6. What is the sum of 8 wk. 5 da., 6 wk. 6 da., 12 wk. 4 da., and 9 wk. 3 da. ?

7. Take 3 h. 5 min. from 8 h. 3 min. | *9.* Multiply 3 wk. 5 da. by 5.

8. Take 5 da. 8 h. from 3 wk. | *10.* Multiply 4 h. 13 min. by 12.

11. How much is 1 eighth of 49 wk. 3 da. ?

12. Divide 2 da. 17 h. 20 min. by 7.

13. From 12 o'clock noon to 6 o'clock 40 min. P.M. is how many minutes?

14. Charles's age is 13 yr. 7 mo., William's is 10 yr. 5 mo., and David's is 12 yr. 7 mo. What is the sum of their ages?

15. If the afternoon is of the same length as the forenoon, what is the time from sunrise to sunset when the sun rises at 5 o'clock 47 minutes?

16. Edwin is 13 yr. 7 mo. old, and his father is 4 times as old. How old is his father?

17. If a railroad train runs 80 mi. in 4 hours, in how many minutes does it run 1 mile?

PROBLEMS.

Written Work.—*1.* Reduce 875,675 seconds to higher denominations.

2. 50,400 minutes are how many weeks?

3. How many hours are there in a leap-year?

4. Reduce 365 da. 5 h. 48 min. 49 sec. to seconds.

<table>
<tr><td>5</td><td>6</td></tr>
</table>

```
          5                              6
Add 280 da. 21 h.        From      8 wk. 3 da. 3 h. 20 min.
    150     16   48 min.  Subtract       5    0    15      9 sec.
    321     12   29
    294     15   37
                                            7
                         27 ) 331 da. 12 h.
```

8. Multiply 9 yr. 54 da. 37 min. by 36.

9. On the 4th day of July at noon, of the year 1876, how many minutes of the year had passed?

10. In how many days will a clock tick 1,000,000 times, if it ticks once every second?

11. The sum of two numbers is 16 yr. 28 da., and one of the numbers is 11 yr. 24 da. What is their difference?

12. An express train runs from Boston to Albany in 6 h. 10 min.; to Buffalo in 9 h. 30 min. more; to Cleveland in 5 h. 35 min. more; to Indianapolis in 8 h. 55 min. more; and to St. Louis in 9 h. 10 min. more. What is the running time of the train from Boston to St. Louis?

13. In how many days of 10 hours each can a man chop 25 cords of wood, if he chops a cord in 3 h. 15 min. ?

14. If a tailor makes 112 military suits in 88 wk. 4 da., working 10 hours a day, in what time does he make 1 suit?

236. Ex. How many years, months, and days from April 15, 1874, to July 4, 1877?

Explanation.—I write the later of the two dates for the minuend, and the earlier for the subtrahend, writing the number of the year, month, and day, in order.

I then subtract as in other compound numbers, calling 30 days a month—as the number of days in the subtrahend is greater than that in the minuend.

Process.

1877 yr.	7 mo.	4 da.
1874	4	15
3 yr.	2 mo.	19 da.

Problems.

1. Benjamin Franklin died April 17, 1790, aged 84 yr. 3 mo. What was the date of his birth?

2. George Washington was born Feb. 22, 1732, and died Dec. 14, 1799. How old was he when he died?

3. A note dated Jan. 7, 1880, was paid Nov. 4, 1881. How long did it remain unpaid?

4. A note was given April 25, 1882, payable Sept. 19, following. How long had it to run?

5. What is the age to-day of a person who was born Oct. 9, 1858?

6. Find the difference in time between July 2, 1881, and Aug. 16, 1885.

SECTION IV.

ENUMERATION OR COUNTING.

237. Many articles are sold by count.

The denominations *dozen* (**doz.**), *gross* (**gro.**), *great gross* (**grt. gro.**), *sheet, quire, ream* (**rm.**), and *score* are in common use.

Table of Counting.

12 things are 1 doz.	24 sheets of paper are 1 quire.	
12 doz. " 1 gro.	20 quires " 1 rm.	
12 gro. " 1 grt. gro.	20 things of a kind " 1 score.	

Oral Work.—*1.* 800 eggs are how many dozen?

2. What is the sum of 48 doz., 28 doz. 6, and 5 doz. 10?

3. How many great gross are 8 times 9 gro. 6 doz.?

4. Divide 32 reams 15 sheets into 9 equal parts.

5. How much is $\frac{1}{6}$ of 32 gro. 6 doz.?

6. A bookseller having 10 rm. 12 quires of letter-paper, sold 16 quires 12 sheets. How much paper had he left?

PROBLEMS.

Written Work.—Reduce

1. 3 grt. gro. 5 gro. 6 doz. to dozens.
2. 7 rm. 15 quires 19 sheets to sheets.

3. 3,872 pens to grt. gro.
4. 5,319 sheets to rm.

5

From   50 rm. 3 quires 5 sheets
Subtract 24   9   13

6

Multiply 3 gro. 9 doz. 4
by   48

7. In a ream of foolscap paper are how many sheets?

8. One week a grocer sold 23 gro. 19 doz. clothes-pins. How many clothes-pins did he sell?

9. 248 pigeons are how many dozen pairs of pigeons?

10. A school that uses 18 crayons a week, will use how many gross of crayons in 40 weeks?

NOTE.—For *outlines of compound numbers* for review, see page 273.

GENERAL REVIEW PROBLEMS IN COMPOUND NUMBERS.

Oral Work.—*1.* How much must I pay for 7 gal. 2 qt. of maple syrup, at 20 cents a quart?

2. 3¢ a quart for tomatoes is how much a bushel?

3. A girl sold 10 quarts of blackberries each day for 18 days. How many bushels did she sell?

4. A farmer sold to one customer 4 bu. of apples, to another 5 bu. 3 pk., and to another 1 bu. 3 pk. 4 qt. How many bushels of apples did he sell?

5. How many hours and minutes are there from 5 o'clock 15 min. A.M., to 6 o'clock 45 min. P.M.?

6. A chain 197 feet long is how many rods long?

7. If a man travels 50 rods in 5 minutes, in what time will he travel a mile?

Find the cost

8. Of 4 quarts of peas, at $1.60 a bushel.

9. Of 2 yards of silver wire, at 2 cents an inch.

10. Of 7 pounds of indigo, at 2 cents an ounce.

11. Of 7 lb. 6 oz. of beef, at 16 cents a pound.

12. How many days were there in the first seven months of the year 1880?

13. If a cooper can make 4 barrels in 5 hours, in what time can he make 1 barrel?

14. When flour is $9 a barrel, how much will a 49-pound sack cost?

15. 4,054 pound bars of lead are how many tons?

16. The fore quarters of a lamb weighed 7 lb. 9 oz. each, and the hind quarters 8 lb. 11 oz. each. How much did the lamb weigh?

17. A blacksmith having 8 lb. 10 oz. of bar steel, used 3 lb. 14 oz. How much had he left?

18. 8 loads of hay, each weighing 1 T. 250 lb., weigh how much?

19. A man killed 7 sheep, and their united weight was 280 lb. 14 oz.   What was their average weight?

20. A man cut 4 T. 7 cwt. of hay from 3 acres.   What was the average yield per acre?

21. I sowed 20 bu. 2 pk. of wheat, and 11 bu. 3 pk. of barley.   How much more wheat than barley did I sow?

22. $28.80 will pay for how many gross of copy-books, at $ .10 apiece?

23. What is the capacity of a cask that holds 10 pailfuls of 2 gal. 3 qt. each?

24. If 7 men can mow 22 A. 20 sq. rd. of grass in a day, how much can 1 man mow?

25. A stationer, by selling paper at a profit of 8 cents a quire, made $2.40.   How many reams did he sell?

Written Work.*—*1. In 6 successive days a fruit canning establishment put up 3 bu. 1 pk., 5 bu. 2 pk. 3 qt., 4 bu. 3 pk. 5 qt. 1 pt., 5 bu. 1 pk., 6 bu. 3 qt., and 6 bu. 7 qt. of strawberries.   How many bushels of berries were canned in the week?

2. From a can containing 8 gal. of milk, a milkman sold 2 qt. to each of 6 customers, 3 pt. to each of 4 others, and $\frac{1}{2}$ gal. to each of 3 others.   How much milk was left?

3. If you can count 75 every minute, how much time would you spend in counting 27,000,000?

4. In one lamp I use 2 qt., and in another 5 pt. of kerosene weekly.   How much kerosene do I use in 9 weeks?

5. A farmer raised 488 bu. 1 pk. of oats from 14 acres of land.   What was the yield per acre?

6. At a spice mill 5,000 doz. 4-oz. packages of spices are put up weekly.   How many pounds are put up?

7. In a bundle of lath are 100 pieces, each 4 ft. long. If laid end to end in a row upon the ground, how many rods would they reach?

8. I own seven city lots which contain 42 sq. rd. 108 sq. ft., 40 sq. rd. 194 sq. ft., 38 sq. rd. 256 sq. ft., 36 sq. rd. 58 sq. ft., 38 sq. rd. 110 sq. ft., 31 sq. rd. 216 sq. ft., and 29 sq. rd. 88 sq. ft.   How much land is there in the seven lots?

9. May 10, C hired a house at $420 per annum, and occupied it until Dec. 10.   How much rent did he pay?

10. If 12 men can chop 132 cords of wood in 4 days, how many cords can 1 man chop in 1 day?

11. One day 5 T. 1,875 lb. of mackerel were taken by a fishing-smack.   How many barrels of fish were caught?

12. If a grocer uses 100 reams 2 quires of wrapping paper in the 308 business days of a year, how much paper does he use daily on an average?

13. If 1 bu. of apples will make 3 gal. 1 qt. of cider, how many bushels will be required to make 926 gal. 1 qt.?

14. In grading 250 rods of a street, 5 cu. yd. 3 cu. ft. of gravel were used to the rod.   How much gravel was used?

15. William lives 93 rods from the school-house.   He attends school regularly for a term of 14 weeks of 5 days each, and goes home to dinner every day.   How many miles does he travel?

16. A farm of 184 A. 46.25 sq. rd. was divided equally among 5 heirs.   How much land did each heir receive?

17. If a horse eats 1 pk. 6 qt. of oats a day, how many days will 5 bu. 1 pk. last him?

18. A train of 63 coal-cars was loaded at a coal-mine in Pennsylvania, 3 T. 550 lb. of coal being put upon each car.   How much coal did the train carry?

CHAPTER VI.

MEASUREMENTS.

SECTION I.

RECTANGLES, TRIANGLES, AND TRAPEZOIDS.

238. *Dimensions* are length, width, and thickness.

a. A *line* has one dimension,—length.

b. A *surface* has two dimensions,—length and width.

c. A *body* has three dimensions,—length, width, and thickness.

239. *Extension* is that which has one or more of the three dimensions—length, breadth, thickness.

240. An *angle* is the opening between two lines, at the point at which they meet.

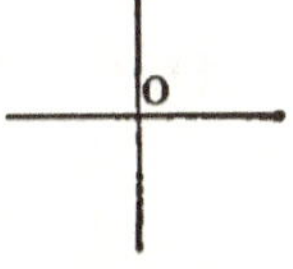

> The opening at the point *c*, between the lines *a c* and *b c*, Figure 1, is an angle.

a. A *right angle* is one of the four equal angles formed by the crossing of two lines.

> The four equal angles about the point O, formed by the crossing of two lines, Figure 2, are right angles.

b. An *acute angle* is less than a right angle.

c. An *obtuse angle* is greater than a right angle.

> In Figure 1, *c* is an acute angle, and *d* is an obtuse angle.

241. *Two lines are perpendicular to each other,* when they form a right angle at the point of meeting.

242. A *parallelogram* is a figure whose four sides are straight lines, and whose opposite sides are parallel and equal.

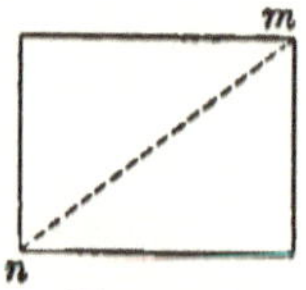

243. A *rectangle* is a parallelogram whose angles are right angles.

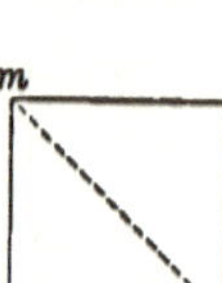
Figure 3.

244. A *square* is a rectangle that has four equal sides.

    a. The *altitude* of a parallelogram is the perpendicular distance between its opposite sides.

    b. The *diagonal* of a parallelogram is a straight line joining opposite angles.

Figure 4.

    c. The *perimeter* of a parallelogram is the total length of its sides.

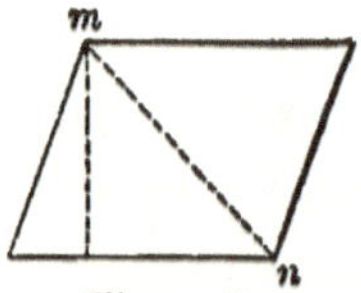

     1. Figures 3, 4, 5 are parallelograms, and the lines *m n* are diagonals.

     2. Figures 3 and 4 are rectangles; figure 4 is a square.

Figure 5.

CASE I. **To find the area of a rectangle.**

Oral Work.—**245.** *1.* Draw a rectangle 8 inches long and 5 inches wide.

2. Divide this figure into squares, by drawing lines 1 inch apart from side to side, and also from end to end.

3. What are the dimensions ⎰
4. What is the name   ⎱ of each of the small squares?

5. Counting from side to side, how many rows of small squares are there in the figure?

6. How many square inches are there in 1 row?

7. In 2 rows?	*9.* In 4 rows?	*11.* In 6 rows?
8. In 3 rows?	*10.* In 5 rows?	*12.* In 7 rows?

13. How many square inches are there in the figure?

How many squares $\begin{cases} \textit{14. } \text{Are 8 times 5 squares ?} \\ \textit{15. } \text{Are 5 times 8 squares ?} \end{cases}$

16. Draw a square foot, and divide it into square inches.

17. Draw a square yard, and divide it into square feet.

18. What are the dimensions, in inches, of a square foot ?

19. A square foot is how many square inches ?

20. What are the dimensions, in inches, of a square yard ?

A square yard is $\begin{cases} \textit{21. } \text{How many square feet ?} \\ \textit{22. } \text{How many square inches ?} \end{cases}$

The number of units in the area of a rectangle equals the product of the numbers expressing its two dimensions.

Written Work. — 246. Ex. What is the area of a field 36 rd. long and 32 rd. wide ?

PROCESS.

EXPLANATION.—Since the field is 36 rods long and 32 rods

$$32 \times 36 \ sq. \ rd. = 1,152 \ sq. \ rd.$$

wide, its area consists of 32 strips of land of 36 square rods each. I therefore multiply 36 square rods by 32, and obtain 1,152 square rods, the required area.

a. Numbers expressing width and length are frequently written with the word "by," or the sign of multiplication, between them.

b. 7 by 9 inches, or 7×9 inches, means 7 inches wide and 9 inches long.

247. Dimensions are always expressed in one or more of the denominations of linear measure.

a. When the dimensions are given $\begin{cases} \text{1. In inches,} \\ \text{2. In feet,} \\ \text{3. In yards,} \\ \text{4. In rods,} \\ \text{5. In miles,} \end{cases}$ the area is $\begin{cases} \text{in square inches.} \\ \text{in square feet.} \\ \text{in square yards.} \\ \text{in square rods.} \\ \text{in square miles.} \end{cases}$

b. In computations in measurements, the dimensions given must be of the same denomination; *i. e.*, they must have the same unit.

PROBLEMS.

What is the area of a figure

1. 27 rods long and 12 rods wide?
2. 215 yards long and 140 yards wide?
3. 57.25 feet long and 38 feet wide?
4. 31.7 inches long and 0.56 inches wide?
5. 15 feet 3 inches long and $8\frac{3}{8}$ inches wide?

6. 137 by 28.5 rd.?
7. 45.3 by 32 yd.?
8. 56×18 in.?
9. 321×94 ft.?
10. 87.5×15.31 mi.?

11. What is the difference in the areas of two rectangles, one 15 rd. long and $18\frac{1}{2}$ ft. wide, and the other 71 yd. long and 3 rd. wide?

12. A tinsmith covered a roof with 1,152 sheets of tin, each sheet covering 40 by 20 inches. How many square feet of roof were there?

13. How many acres are there in 100 mi. of a 4-rd. road?

CASE II. **To find either dimension of a rectangle.**

248. Ex. The area of the floor of a room is 864 sq. ft., and its width is 24 ft. What is its length?

PROCESS.

$$864 \; sq. \, ft. = 864 \, ft. \; long \; and \; 1 \, ft. \; wide; \; and$$
$$864 \, ft. \div 24 = 36 \, ft.$$

EXPLANATION.—The area of a surface 864 feet long and 1 foot wide, is 864 square feet; and the length of a floor that has the same area and is 24 feet wide, is 1 twenty-fourth of 864 feet.

I therefore divide 864 feet by 24, and obtain 36 feet, the required length of the floor.

The number of units in either dimension of a rectangle equals the quotient of the number expressing the area divided by the number expressing the other dimension.

NOTE.—Read the problems on the next page as follows:

Problem 1. Read as printed. Problem 2. Read 72 rods in place of 44 rods.

Problem 3. Read 2,175 square rods in place of 1,584 square rods.

Problem 4. Read the numbers which stand at the right of the brace. in their order, in places of the numbers in problem 1.

Read problems 5–8, 9–12, 13–16 in a similar manner.

PROBLEMS.

What is the other dimension of a figure

1– 4. 44 rods long, and containing } 72 rd. 2,175 sq. rd.
1,584 square rods?

5– 8. 15 feet wide, and containing } 21¾ ft. 2,436$\frac{3}{16}$ sq. ft.
17,880 square feet?

9–12. 90.5 rods wide, and containing } 156.15 rd.· 320 A.
172.4 acres?

13–16. 330 feet long, and containing } 111 yd. 2,805 sq. ft.
311⅔ square yards?

17. The area of a blackboard 3¾ ft. wide is 37⅜ sq. ft.
What is its length?

18. A board 8 inches wide contains 8⅓ square feet.
What is its length?

19. 18⅔ square yards of oil-cloth cover the floor of a
room 10½ feet wide. How many feet long is the room?

20. A contractor received $247.50 for flagging a court-
yard 30 feet long, at $2.75 per square yard. What was
the width of the yard?

249. A *triangle* is a figure bounded by
three straight lines, and having three angles.

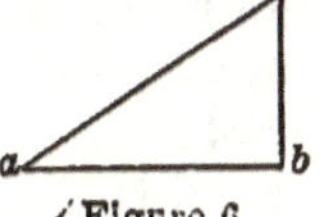
Figure 6.

   a. A *right-angled triangle* has one right
angle. (See Fig. 6.)

   b. An *obtuse-angled triangle* has one obtuse angle. (See Fig. 7.)

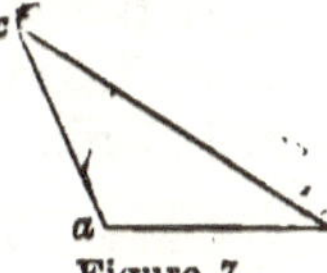
Figure 7.

   c. An *acute-angled triangle* has three acute
angles. (See Fig. 8.)

   d. The *base* of a triangle is the side on which
it is supposed to stand.

   e. The *vertex* is the point opposite to the base.

   f. The *altitude* is the perpendicular height of
the vertex above the base.

Figure 8.

The base of each of the triangles, Figures 6, 7, 8,
is the side *a b*; the vertex of each is the point *c*; and the altitude
of each is the perpendicular height of the vertex above the base.

CASE III. **To find the area, the base, or the altitude of a triangle.**

250. Ex. 1. The altitude of a triangle is 37 inches, and the base is 16 inches. What is the area?

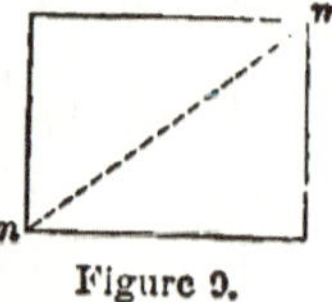
Figure 9.

The diagonal *m n* in Figure 9 divides the parallelogram into two equal triangles. Hence,

The number of units in the area of a triangle equals one half the product of the numbers expressing its base and altitude.

PROCESS.

$$\frac{16 \times 37 \; sq. \; in.}{2} = 296 \; sq. \; in.$$

Ex. 2. The area of a triangle is 2 sq. yd. 3 sq. ft. 92 sq. in., and its altitude is 1 yd. 2 in. What is the length of its base?

PROCESS.

2 sq. yd. 3 sq. ft. 92 sq. in. = 3,116 sq. in.;
and 1 yd. 2 in. = 38 in.
3,116 sq. in. = 3,116 in. long and 1 in. wide;
3,116 in. ÷ 38 = 82 in.; and 82 in. × 2 = 164 in. = 13 ft. 8 in.

PROBLEMS.

Find the area of a triangle,		Given;	
the base being	and the altitude	Area,	to find
1. 42 in.,	54 in.	6. 178 sq. in.; base, 24 in.;	altitude.
2. 96 ft.,	96 ft.	7. 2,861½ sq. in.; base, 8 ft. 1 in.;	altitude.
3. 18 ft. 6 in.,	24 ft. 3 in.	8. 298⅔ sq. yd.; base, 128 ft.;	altitude.
4. 59 ft. 8 in.,	13¼ yd.	9. 12 sq. yd.; altitude, 9 ft.;	base.
5. 141 rd.,	56 rd.	10. 12 A. 56 sq. rd.; altitude, 70½ rd.;	base.

CASE IV. **To find the area of a parallelogram.**

251. Ex. The base of a parallelogram is 123 feet, and its altitude is 96 feet. What is its area?

The area of the parallelogram *a b c d* equals the area of the rectangle *e f c d*. Hence,

Figure 10.

PROCESS.   *96 × 123 sq. ft. = 11,808 sq. ft.*

The number of units in the area of a parallelogram equals the product of the numbers expressing its length and the perpendicular distance between its sides.

PROBLEMS.

Find the areas of the following parallelograms:

	Base.	Altitude.		Base.	Altitude.
1.	18 inches;	15 inches.	*4.*	17 ft. 10 in.;	8 ft. 4 in.
2.	23 feet;	25 feet.	*5.*	5 yd. 2 ft.;	7 ft. 3 in.
3.	231 yards;	155 yards.	*6.*	$32\frac{3}{8}$ ft.;	15.75 ft.

CASE V. **To find the area of a trapezoid.**

252. A *trapezoid* is a figure that has four sides, two of which are parallel.

> The *altitude* of a trapezoid is the perpendicular distance between its parallel sides.

> In Figure 11 *a b c d* is a trapezoid, and *e h* or *f g* is its altitude

Ex. 1. The two parallel sides of a trapezoid are 24 and 18 inches, and the altitude is 15 inches.   What is the area?

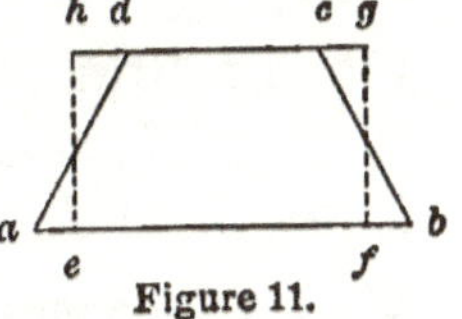

The area of the trapezoid *a b c d* equals the area of the rectangle *e f g h*. Hence,

PROCESS.

$$\frac{18\ in. + 24\ in.}{2} = 21\ in.; \text{ and } 15 \times 21\ sq.\ in. = 315\ sq.\ in.$$

The number of units in the area of a trapezoid equals the product of the two numbers that express one half the sum of the two parallel sides and the perpendicular distance between them.

Ex. 2. The area of a trapezoid is 7 sq. ft. 99 sq. in., and the parallel sides are 32 and 50 inches long.   How far apart are they?

PROCESS.

$$7\ sq.\ ft.\ 99\ sq.\ in = 1,107\ sq.\ in.;$$
$$\frac{32\ in. + 50\ in.}{2} = 41\ in.; \text{ and } 1,107\ in. \div 41 = 27\ in.$$

K

PROBLEMS.

Find the areas of the following trapezoids :

Parallel sides.	Distance apart.		Parallel ends.	Distance between.
1. 10 in., and 27 in. ;	13 in.		*4.* ½ ft., and 5 rd. ;	40 rd.
2. 40 yd., and 22 yd. ;	25 yd.		*5.* 13 ft., and 17 ft. ;	9¼ yd.
3. 63 mi., and 1.35 mi.;	300 rd.		*6.* 10 ft., and 2½ ft. ;	14 ft. 8 in.

253. RULES FOR MEASUREMENTS OF RECTANGLES, TRI-
ANGLES, AND TRAPEZOIDS.

I. To find the area of a rectangle :—
Multiply the length by the width.

II. To find either dimension of a rectangle :—
Divide the area by the given dimension.

III. To find the area of a triangle :—
*Multiply the base by the altitude, and divide the prod-
uct by 2.*

IV. To find the area of a parallelogram :—
*Multiply the base by the perpendicular distance be-
tween the sides.*

V. To find the area of a trapezoid :—
*Multiply one half the sum of the parallel sides by the
perpendicular distance between them.*

PROBLEMS.

1. In a farm 225 rods long and 145 rods wide are how
many acres ?

2. How many yards of carpeting ¾ yd. wide will carpet
a parlor 26 ft. long and 21¼ ft. wide ?

3. The area of the floor of a school room 6¼ yd. wide is
83⅓ sq. yd.   What are its dimensions, in feet and inches ?

4. The parallel sides of a trapezoid are 44 and 32 yards,
and the distance between them is 20 feet.   What is the
area, in square yards ?

5. A building lot has a frontage of 121 ft., and its area is 4,719 sq. yd. What is its other dimension?

6. The base of a triangle is 10 ft. 10 in., and its altitude is 9 ft. 2 in. What is its area?

7. Find the base of a triangle whose altitude is 50 feet and area 115 square yards.

8. S bought $33\frac{1}{2}$ acres of land for $225 per acre, and laid it out into lots 5 by 8 rods, which he sold at $100 each. How much did he gain by the transaction?

9. The area of a meadow in the form of a trapezoid is 3 A. 68.8 sq. rd., and its parallel sides are 21 and $38\frac{1}{2}$ rd. What is its altitude?

10. How many feet of boards are there in the four sides of a barn 30 by 40 feet, 16 feet high to the eaves, and $24\frac{1}{2}$ feet high to the gable peaks?

SECTION II.

THE CIRCLE.

254. A *circle* is a surface bounded by a curved line, every part of which is equally distant from a point within, called the centre.

   a. The **circumference** or **periphery** of a circle is the line that bounds it.

   b. An **arc** of a circle is any part of its circumference.

   c. The **diameter** of a circle is the distance across it through its centre.

   d. The **radius** of a circle is a straight line that joins its centre and circumference.

The radius of a circle is equal to one half of its diameter.

Figure 12 is a circle; a, b, c, d is its circumference; a, b, c and $d c$ are arcs; o is its centre; $a c$ is its diameter; and $a o, b o, c o$, or $d o$ is a radius.

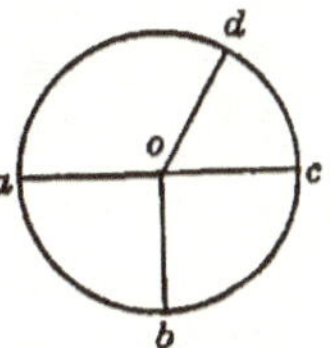

Figure 12.

CASE I. To find the circumference or the diameter of a circle.

255. The circumference of a circle is about $3\frac{1}{7}$ times its diameter. Hence,

For ordinary purposes,—*Estimate the circumference of a circle at $3\frac{1}{7}$ times the diameter.*

> Where greater accuracy is required—as in circles more than 100 feet in diameter:—*Estimate the circumference at $3\frac{16}{113}$ times the diameter.*

Ex. 1. The diameter of a carriage wheel is 5 ft. 3 in. What is its circumference?

PROCESS.

$$5 \text{ ft. } 3 \text{ in.} = 63 \text{ in.}$$
$$3\tfrac{1}{7} \times 63 \text{ in.} = 198 \text{ in.} = 16 \text{ ft. } 6 \text{ in.}$$

Ex. 2. The circumference of the top of a cistern is 29 ft. 8 in. What is the diameter?

PROCESS.

$$29 \text{ ft. } 8 \text{ in.} = 356 \text{ in.}$$
$$356 \text{ in.} \div 3\tfrac{1}{7} = 113\tfrac{3}{7} \text{ in.} = 9 \text{ ft. } 5\tfrac{3}{7} \text{ in.}$$

PROBLEMS.

Find the circumference

1. Of a circle 8 ft. in diameter.
2. Of a log 32 in. through.
3. Of a tank 17 ft. in diameter.
4. Of a globe 13 in. in diameter.

Find the diameter

5. Of a circle 359 inches in circumference.
6. Of a wheel 16 feet 6 inches in circumference.
7. Of a mound 534.5 yards in circumference.
8. Of a clock dial $16\frac{1}{2}$ inches in circumference.

CASE II. To find the area of a circle.

256. Any circle may be supposed to be divided into equal triangles, the bases forming the circumference of the circle, and the altitudes being the radius of the circle. Hence,

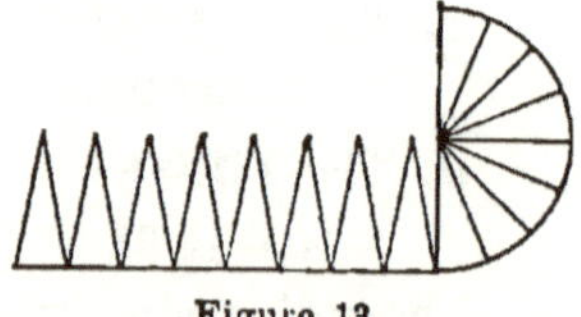

Figure 13.

The number of units in the area of a circle equals the product of the numbers expressing the radius and one half the circumference.

Ex. What is the area of a circle 20 feet in diameter?

FULL SOLUTION.

$$3\tfrac{1}{7} \times 20 \text{ ft.} = 62\tfrac{6}{7} \text{ ft., circumference.}$$
$$\tfrac{1}{2} \text{ of } 62\tfrac{6}{7} \text{ ft.} = 31\tfrac{3}{7} \text{ ft., } \tfrac{1}{2} \text{ of circumference.}$$
$$\tfrac{1}{2} \text{ of } 20 \text{ ft.} = 10 \text{ ft., radius.}$$
$$10 \times 31\tfrac{3}{7} \text{ sq. ft.} = 314\tfrac{2}{7} \text{ sq. ft., area.}$$

PROBLEMS.

1. What is the area of a circle 113 feet in diameter?

2. Of a barrel head 16 inches in diameter?

3. Of a disc of 15 inches radius?

4. Of a lake 721 rods in circumference?

5. Of a race-course 1 mile in circumference?

6. Of a circle 1,000 yards in circumference?

257. RULES FOR MEASUREMENTS OF CIRCLES.

I. To find the circumference:—
Multiply the diameter by $3\tfrac{1}{7}$.

II. To find the diameter:—
Divide the circumference by $3\tfrac{1}{7}$.

III. To find the area:—
Multiply one half of the circumference by the radius.

PROBLEMS.

1. What is the difference between the perimeter of a square $19\tfrac{5}{8}$ miles on each side, and the circumference of the largest circle that can be inscribed in it?

2. The perimeter of a square and the circumference of a circle are each 100 feet. Find the difference in their areas.

Find the area

3. Of the bottom of a RR. water tank 18 ft. in diameter.

4. Of a circular pond 93 rods in circumference.

5. Of a disc $50\tfrac{5}{7}$ inches in circumference.

SECTION III.

RECTANGULAR SOLIDS.

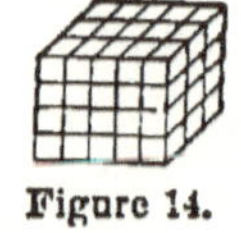

Figure 14.

258. A *rectangular solid* is a body bounded by six rectangles.

259. A *cube* is a rectangular solid whose sides are equal squares.

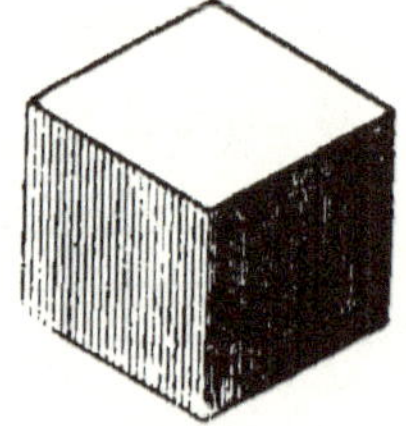

Figure 15.

The solid contents of a body, and the capacity of a portion of space are also called *cubic contents* and *volume*.

CASE I. **To find the cubic contents of a rectangular solid.**

If you place 5 rows of 8 cubic blocks each, side by side, how many blocks do you use

1. For 2 of the rows? | *3.* For 4 of the rows?
2. For 3 of the rows? | *4.* For the 5 rows, or the layer?

If you place 3 layers in a pile, how many blocks do you use

5. For 2 of the layers? | *6.* For the 3 layers?

How many cubic inches are there in a block of wood

7. 8 inches long, 5 inches wide, and 1 inch thick?

8. 8 inches long, 5 inches wide, and 2 inches thick?

9. 8 inches long, 5 inches wide, and 3 inches thick?

10. What are the dimensions, in inches, of a cubic foot?

What are the dimensions of a cubic yard,

11. Expressed in feet? | *12.* Expressed in inches?

How many cubic inches are there in a body that is 12 inches long, 12 inches wide, and

13. 1 inch thick? | *15.* 5 inches thick? | *17.* 10 inches thick?
14. 3 inches thick? | *16.* 8 inches thick? | *18.* 12 inches thick?

260. Ex. Find the cubic contents of a block of wood 18 inches long, 13 inches wide, and 9 inches thick.

Since the block is 18 inches long and 13 inches wide, the contents of a portion 1 inch thick are 13 times 18 cubic inches; and the contents of the entire block are 9 times 13 times 18 cubic inches. Hence,

PROCESS.

$$9 \times 13 \times 18 \ cu. \ in. = 2,106 \ cu. \ in.$$

The number of units in the cubic contents of a rectangular solid equals the product of the numbers expressing its three dimensions.

When the dimensions are given
1. In inches,
2. In feet,
3. In yards,
4. In rods,
5. In miles,
the volume is
cubic inches.
cubic feet.
cubic yards.
cubic rods.
cubic miles.

NOTE.—For manner of reading the following problems, see note, page 214.

PROBLEMS.

What are the cubic contents of a body

1– 5. 14 feet long, 11 feet wide, and 7.5 feet deep?   37 feet. 8.2 feet. 13 feet.

6–10. 27 inches long, 16 inches wide, and 12 inches high?   5.21 inches. 4.25 inches. 2.9 inches.

11–15. 576 ft. by 125 ft. by 87 ft.?   72 yd. 61 yd. 45 yd.

CASE II. **To find any one dimension of a rectangular solid.**

261. Ex. The capacity of a bin 16 feet wide and $7\frac{1}{2}$ feet deep is 2,280 cubic feet. What is its length?

The capacity of a portion of the bin 1 foot long is $7\frac{1}{2}$ times 16 cubic feet. 2,280 cubic feet

PROCESS.

$$7\frac{1}{2} \times 16 \ cu. \ ft. = 120 \ cu. \ ft.$$
$$2,280 \ cu. \ ft. = 2,280 \ ft. \ by \ 1 \ ft. \ by \ 1 \ ft.$$
$$2,280 \ ft. \div 120 = 19 \ ft.$$

is the capacity of a bin 2,280 feet long, 1 foot wide, and 1 foot deep; and $\frac{1}{120}$ of 2,280 feet is the length of a bin 16 feet wide and $7\frac{1}{2}$ feet deep. Hence,

The number of units in any one of the three dimensions of a rectangular solid, equals the quotient obtained by dividing the number expressing the cubic contents by the product of the numbers expressing the other two dimensions.

PROBLEMS.

What is the third dimension of a body

1– 5. 4 in. wide and 5 in. high, and containing 1,280 cu. in.? } { 5.6 in. wide. $7\frac{1}{4}$ in. high. 1 cu. ft.

6–10. 12 ft. high and 4 ft. thick, and containing 6,000 cu. ft.? } { 8 ft. high. 6.375 ft. thick. 200 cu. yd.

11–15. 4 yd. deep and 12.3 yd. wide, and containing 196.8 cu. ft.? } { $3\frac{1}{2}$ in. deep. $3\frac{1}{2}$ ft. wide. $3\frac{1}{2}$ cu. yd.

16. 56 ft. long and 8 ft. high, and containing 12.25 cd.?

262. RULES FOR MEASUREMENTS OF RECTANGULAR SOLIDS.

I. To find the cubic contents:—

Multiply the length, width, and thickness together.

II. To find one dimension:—

Divide the cubic contents by the product of the two given dimensions.

PROBLEMS.

1. How many loads of earth must be removed, in digging a cellar 21 ft. long, 18 ft. wide, and 6 ft. deep?

2. How many cords of wood are there in a pile 45 ft. long, 4 ft. wide, and 7 ft. high?

3. How many half-inch cubes can be put into a box, the inside measurements of which are 12 by 6 by 3 inches?

4. If 100,000 bricks, each 2 by 4 by 8 inches, are piled together, how many cubic yards are there in the pile?

5. A mow of hay 25.5 ft. wide, and 12 ft. 5 in. high contains $422\frac{1}{3}$ cu. yd. How many feet long is it?

SECTION IV.

MEASUREMENTS APPLIED TO BUSINESS AFFAIRS.

263. Volume is measured by the units given in the following

Table of Standard Units for Measures of Volume.

1 cubic foot	is 1,728 cu. in.
1 cubic yard	" 27 cu. ft.
1 bushel—even or stricken measure	" 2,150.42 cu. in.
1 bushel—heaped measure	" 2,688 " "
1 gallon—liquid measure	" 231 " "
1 gallon—dry measure ($\frac{1}{2}$ peck)	" 268.8 " "

264. In business transactions, quantities and values are associated with certain units suited to the various departments of business.

In estimating materials and labor, mechanics, artizans, engineers, and laborers use the following units:

I. For measures of surface.

1. The *square foot,*—for stone-cutting, flagging, lumber, sawed timber, and masonry.

> In estimating quantity and cost of *matched lumber,* .25 is added to the surface measure.

2. The *square yard,*—for painting, plastering, ceiling, paving, bricklaying, and masonry.

3. The *square,* of 100 square feet,—for flooring, roofing, and bricklaying.

> *a.* Shingles are estimated to average 4 inches wide across the butt. 9 shingles laid 4 inches to the weather cover 1 square foot.
>
> *b.* 1,000 shingles laid 4 inches to the weather, without waste, cover 111 square feet. Allowing for waste and imperfections, 1,000 shingles are estimated to cover a square.
>
> *c.* In estimating by the square yard and by the square, the **wall** is supposed to be 12 inches or 1½ bricks thick.

4. The ***bunch*** of lath,—100 pieces, each 4 feet long.

A bunch of lath covers 5 square yards of surface.

II. For measures of volume.

1. The ***cubic foot,***—for bricklaying, masonry, and hewn timber.

2. The ***cubic yard,***—for masonry, excavations, and embankments.

a. On public works a cubic yard of earth is a standard load.

b. In computing the cubic contents of walls, of foundations, and of buildings, the length of each wall is measured on the outside. The wall at each corner is thus measured twice.

3. The ***barrel,*** of $31\frac{1}{2}$ gallons ; and

4. The ***hogshead,*** of 63 gallons,—for the capacity of cisterns and reservoirs.

a. The barrels and hogsheads used for commercial purposes are not fixed measures,—a barrel containing from 30 to 40 gallons, and a hogshead from 60 to 125 gallons.

b. In the petroleum trade 42 gallons are a barrel.

5. The ***perch*** of stone,—$16\frac{1}{2}$ cubic feet.

There is no standard perch of masonry. Architects and builders in different sections of the country estimate the perch variously, the range being from 22 to 27 cubic feet. The perch of $24\frac{3}{4}$ cubic feet—$16\frac{1}{2}$ feet long, $1\frac{1}{2}$ feet thick, and 1 foot high—is more extensively adopted than any other.

6. The ***brick.***

Bricks are made of different sizes, as follows :

Common brick, $8 \times 4 \times 2$ in.	Philadelphia and Baltimore brick, } $8\frac{1}{4} \times 4\frac{1}{8} \times 2\frac{3}{8}$ in.
Maine " $7\frac{1}{2} \times 3\frac{3}{8} \times 2\frac{3}{8}$ "	
North River " $8 \times 3\frac{1}{2} \times 2\frac{1}{4}$ "	Milwaukee " $8\frac{1}{2} \times 4\frac{1}{8} \times 2\frac{3}{8}$ "

a. 27 common bricks piled solid, or $22\frac{1}{2}$ laid in mortar, are estimated as a cubic foot.

b. Bricklaying is also estimated by *the thousand*, by actual count, or by measure in the wall.

265. ALLOWANCES OR DEDUCTIONS.

In painting, plastering, ceiling, bricklaying, and masonry, the following deductions are made:

1. *Materials,*—for openings in walls (doors and windows).

2. *Labor,*—for $\frac{1}{2}$ the openings, and $\frac{1}{2}$ the corners (by special contract only).

> *a.* Materials are commonly estimated by solid measures; and the work, by either solid or surface measures.
>
> *b.* IN THE LUMBER TRADE a square foot is called a *board foot;* and a cubic foot is called a *timber foot.*
>
> *c.* Lumber 1 inch thick or less is sold by surface measure; if more than 1 inch thick, it is computed at this thickness.
>
> *d.* The average width of a tapering board is one half the sum of the widths of the two ends; or, it is the width of the board at one half the distance between the ends.
>
> *e.* In writing dimensions, the accent mark (') is often used instead of the abbreviation in. Thus, 6 in. = 6'.
>
> *f.* Per C or @ C means *per hundred;* and per M or @ M means *per thousand.*

PROBLEMS.

1. 568.5 gallons liquid measure are how many cubic inches less than the same number of gallons dry measure?

2. If 8 gallons of water are in a tub that will hold 1 bushel of wheat, how much more water will the tub hold?

3. A tank that will hold 15,000 gallons of oil will hold how many bushels of potatoes?

4. A roofer used 840 sheets of 16' by 24' tin in roofing a house. What was the area of the roof? How many squares of roofing were covered?

5. The floor of a public hall 44 × 75 feet contains how many squares of flooring? How many feet of flooring $1\frac{1}{2}$ inches thick will be required for the floor?

6. How many slates will be required for 11.52 squares of roofing, allowing 3 slates to cover a square foot?

7. How many bunches, of 500 shingles each, will cover a roof, each side of which is 67.5 ft. long and 25 ft. wide?

8. How much will it cost to lath and plaster a room 36 ft. by 24 ft. by 12 ft., at $.30 per square yard?

9. A plasterer lathed a room 14 ft. by 20 ft., and 11 ft. 6 in. high. How many bunches of lath did he use?

10. How many square yards are there in the four walls and ceiling of a church 70 ft. long, 30 ft. wide, and 20 ft. high?

11. What will be the expense of ceiling the sales room of a store 24 ft. by 87 ft. 6 in., at $1.00 per square yard?

12. The grade of a portion of street 126 ft. long and 60 ft. wide, is to be raised 1 ft. 8 in. How many cubic yards of earth will be required?

13. At $.81¼ a sq. yd., how much will it cost to pave a street ¼ mi. long and 49½ ft. wide?

14. A box of glass contains 50 sq. ft. How many panes are there in a box of 9×16 glass?

15. How many boxes of 12×20 glass will be required to glaze 32 windows, each requiring 3 ft. by 6 ft. 8 in. of glass?

16. A stone-cutter dressed the tops, front side, and two ends of three stone steps 8×11 in. and 4 ft. 8 in. long; and of a broad step of the same length and height and 2 ft. 9 in. wide. How much did he receive for the work, at $.21 per sq. ft.?

17. A school-house 24×32 feet on the ground, the side walls 16 feet high, and the gable peaks 9 feet higher than the side walls, was painted three coats, at 31½ cents per square yard. Allowing for one half of 8 windows each $3 \times 6½$ feet, what was the cost of the job?

18. How many cubic yards of earth must be removed, in digging a cellar 52 ft. × 28 ft. × 8 ft.?

19. How many wagon loads of earth will be removed, in digging a ditch 2,000 ft. long, 4 ft. wide, and 18 in. deep?

20. A breakwater at the entrance to a harbor is 1,400 ft. long, 13 ft. wide, and 20 ft. high. How many cubic yards of masonry does it contain?

21. In digging a cellar 45 ft. long and 6 ft. deep, 270 loads of earth were removed. How wide was the cellar?

22. How many hogsheads of water will fill a cistern 10 ft. 6 in. long, 8 ft. 3 in. wide, and 7 ft. deep?

23. A rectangular cistern 12 ft. long, 10 ft. wide, and 9 ft. deep will hold how many barrels of water?

24. How much lumber is there in 5 boards, each 14 ft. long, 15′ wide at one end, and 8′ wide at the other?

25. How many common bricks will make a pile 12 feet long, 9 feet wide, and 5 feet high?

26. How many feet of 9′ by 13′ timber will be required for the sills of a 30 by 40-foot barn?

27. A pile of rough stone 47 feet × 14 feet × 5.5 feet contains how many perches? How many cords?

28. Find the cost of calcimining the walls and ceiling of a room 18 by 15 by 10½ feet, at 15⅛ cents per square yard.

29. In a stick of timber 12′ by 18′ and 30 ft. long, are how many feet of timber? How many feet of lumber?

30. How many common bricks, laid flatwise, will be required for a sidewalk 100 ft. 4 in. long and 4 ft. wide?

31. At $9.50 per M for materials and labor, and allowing .025 for openings, how much must I pay for the brick-work in the walls of a square-roofed house 48 ft. long, 25 ft. wide, and 18 ft. high, the walls being 12¼′ thick?

32. How many cubic yards of earth must be removed, to grade down $1\frac{1}{2}$ A. of ground 1 ft. 4 in. ?

33. At \$.10$\frac{1}{2}$ per sq. ft., what will it cost to flag a walk 2 ft. wide surrounding a grass plat 20 ft. square ?

34. How many perches of stone are required for stoning a well 30 feet deep, the diameter of the excavation being 6 ft., and of the well hole 3 ft. ?

35. In a stock of 12 boards 16 ft. long and 10 in. wide, are how many feet of lumber ?

36. A 4-inch plank 18 ft. long and 16' wide contains how many feet of lumber ?

37. A stick of ship timber 25 ft. long, 1 ft. 2' wide, and 10' thick contains how many timber feet ?

38. A stick of timber 48 ft. long and 10 in. square contains how many board feet ?

39. In 18 pieces of studding, each 15 ft. long and 2' by 4', are how many feet of lumber ?

40. A man used 7 cd. of stone in building a wall 4 ft. high and 2 ft. thick. What was the length of the wall ?

41. At \$15 per M, how much must I pay for $2\frac{1}{2}$-inch plank for a 4-foot walk on the street sides of a corner lot 4 rd. by 7 rd. 12 ft. 6', the walk to be placed 2 ft. 3' from the fence ?

III. **Units for farm products.**

1. A ***bushel*** of grain, seed, fruit, vegetables, and root crops.

> A cubic foot is .8 of a bushel *even measure;* it is also a small fraction more than .64 of a bushel *heaped measure.* Hence,

To find the capacity, in bushels, of any granary, bin, box, cask, or other portion of space.

> I. Even measure,—*Multiply the contents in cubic feet by .8.*
>
> II. Heaped measure,—*Multiply the contents in cubic feet by .64*

a. The *even bushel* is the unit of measure for wheat and other kinds of grain; and for seeds and small fruits,—such as clover seed, berries, plums, cherries, etc.

b. The *heaped bushel* is the unit of measure for coal, lime, and corn in the ear; and for large fruits, root crops, and garden vegetables,—such as apples, peaches, potatoes, turnips, tomatoes, snap beans, green peas, etc.

2. A *ton of hay.*

Farmers estimate the volume of hay that will weigh a ton, by the following units:

550 cu. ft. of clover or meadow hay loose, or in loads, or on scaffolds.

450 cu. ft. of meadow hay in bays, or mows.

270 cu. ft., or 10 cu. yd., well settled in large mows or stacks.

Problems.

There are how many bushels

42. Of wheat, in a freight-car 33 ft. long and 8 ft. wide, the wheat being 2 ft. $4\frac{1}{2}'$ deep in the car?

43. Of potatoes, in a bin 5 ft. by 16 ft. and 20 ft. deep?

44. Of coal, in a wagon box 10 ft. $6' \times 3$ ft. $4' \times 1$ ft. $3'$, the box being even full?

45. Of corn in the ear, in a crib 100 ft. long, 12 ft. high, 7 ft. wide at the bottom, and 10 ft. wide at the top?

46. In three bins—(*a*) of wheat, 6 ft. by 8 ft. by $4\frac{1}{2}$ ft.; (*b*) of oats, 6 ft. by $9\frac{1}{4}$ ft. by $4\frac{1}{2}$ ft.; and (*c*) of shelled corn, 6 ft. by 6 ft. by $4\frac{1}{2}$ ft.?

How many tons are there

47. Of old hay, in a mow 40 ft. $\times 25$ ft. $\times 18$ ft.?

48. In a load of hay 15 ft. by 8 ft. $4'$ by 7 ft. $3'$?

49. Of clover hay, on a scaffold over a barn floor, 30 ft. long, 12 ft. wide, and 9 ft. high to the peak of the roof?

Note.—For *outlines of measurements* for review, see page 273.

SECTION V.

GENERAL REVIEW PROBLEMS IN MEASUREMENTS.

1– 4. A field 72 rods long and 21 rods wide $\Big\}$ $43\frac{3}{4}$ rd. long. contains how many square rods? 37.7 rd. wide.

5– 8. A carpet $7\frac{1}{2}$ yards long and $4\frac{3}{4}$ yards $\Big\}$ $6\frac{2}{3}$ yd. long. wide contains how many square yards? 5.625 yd. wide.

9–12. A ceiling 87.3 feet $\times$ 21.55 feet contains $\Big\}$ $34\frac{7}{12}$ ft. by how many square yards? 25.5 ft.

What are the cubic contents of a body

13–17. 5 yd. long, 5 ft. wide, and 5′ high? $\Big\}$ $8\frac{1}{4}$ yd.; $8\frac{1}{4}$ ft.; $8\frac{1}{4}′$.

18–22. 12 ft. 8′ by 5 ft. 6′ by 4 ft. 2′? $7\frac{1}{2}$ ft.; $4\frac{5}{6}$ ft.; $3\frac{1}{12}$ ft.

23. A girl covered a box, 4′ by 7′ by $9\frac{1}{2}′$, with gilt paper. How many square inches of paper did she use?

24. The base of the Great Pyramid of Cheops is 763 ft. square. How many acres does it cover?

25. What is the difference between a figure that contains $\frac{1}{4}$ of a square foot, and one that is $\frac{1}{4}$ of a foot square?

26. How many persons can be seated in a hall 120 ft. long and 64 ft. 6′ wide, allowing 5 persons to 2 square yards?

27. How much will it cost me to carpet a parlor 15 ft. 9′ by 22 ft. 6′, with tapestry carpeting $\frac{3}{4}$ yd. wide, at $ .95 a yard, running measure?

28. At 1.12\frac{1}{2}$ per sq. yd., how much must I pay for oil-cloth for the hall of my house, which is $2\frac{3}{4}$ by $8\frac{1}{2}$ yd.?

29. The ceiling of a room is 18 feet long, and its area is 288 sq. ft. What is its width?

30. What is the length of a carpet for a flight of stairs of 18 steps, each $10\frac{1}{2}$ in. wide and $7\frac{1}{4}$ in. high?

31. What must be the width of a board 16 feet long, to contain 12 square feet?

32. What length of a board 8 in. wide will make a box cover 2 ft. 8 in. square?

33. A certain rectangular tract of land 32 rods wide contains 120 acres. What is its length?

34. If 64 yd. of carpeting $\frac{3}{4}$ yd. wide will carpet a room 24 ft. long, what is the width of the room?

35 A window curtain 3 ft. 3 in. wide contains 2 sq. yd. 2 sq. ft. 84 sq. in. What is its length?

36. How many pickets 3 in. wide, and placed 3 in. apart, will be required for a fence around a lot 16 rd. long and 15 rd. wide?

37. What is the area of the two gables of a barn 32 ft. wide, the ridge being 9 ft. higher than the plates?

38. What are the contents of a triangular piece of land, the longest side of which is 141 rods, and the perpendicular distance to the angle opposite 56 rods?

39. The area of a triangle is 108 sq. ft., and its altitude is 9 ft. What is the length of its base?

40. At the side of a staircase is a triangular piece of wall 18 ft. long and 13 ft. high. What is its area, in square yards?

41. Find the area of a cubical block whose edge measures 10 inches.

42. A 100-acre farm is a trapezoid, the two parallel sides of which are 64.7 rd. and 135.3 rd. How far apart are these two sides?

43. A lot of land lying between two parallel streets 3 rods apart, measures 200 ft. on one street and 160 feet on the other. How many sq. rd. does it contain?

44. Find the cost, at $28 per M, of 1$\frac{1}{4}$-inch matched flooring for a two-story house 32 by 24 ft., making the customary allowance for matched lumber.

45. Find the area of a field 40 rd. long, 15 rd. wide at one end, and $\frac{1}{2}$ rd. wide at the other.

46. What is the volume of a space 22.5 ft. by 6.4 ft. by 3.25 ft. ?

47. Find the cubic contents of a marble slab 6 ft. long, 2 ft. 6' wide, and $3\frac{1}{4}'$ thick.

48. In a school room 32 ft. long, 24 ft. wide, and 12 ft. 6' high are 60 pupils, each breathing $12\frac{1}{2}$ cu. ft. of air per hour. In what time will they breathe as much air as the room contains?

49. In digging a mill-race 120 rd. long and 30 ft. wide, 5,500 cu. yd. of earth were removed. What was the depth of the race?

50. A pile of 4-foot wood 24 rods long contains 100 cords. What is its height?

51. How many more bushels of barley than of corn in the ear, can be stored in a bin $12\frac{2}{3}$ ft. long, 8 ft. wide, and 5.5 ft. deep?

52. How many sheets of roofing tin, each covering 14' by 22', will cover 3.5 squares of roof?

53. At $.25 per sq. yd. for plastering, and $.50 per roll for paper-hanging, what will it cost to plaster and paper a room 18 ft. by 16 ft. by 9.5 ft., the paper being $\frac{1}{2}$ yd. wide, and 9 yd. in a roll; and making allowance, in papering, for 2 windows, each 3 ft. by 6 ft., and 3 doors, each 3 ft. 6' by 7 ft. 6'?

54. A sewer $2\frac{2}{3}$ mi. long, 5 ft. wide, and 12 ft. deep, cost $6,468. What did it cost per cubic yard?

55. Find the cost of digging a cellar 27 ft. by 19 ft. by 7 ft., at $.18 per cubic yard.

56. A rock excavation 20 ft. long, 10 ft. wide, and 9 ft. deep will hold how many barrels of water?

57. What depth of rain-fall upon a roof 30 by 40 feet will fill an 80-hogshead cistern?

58. How many bricks are in the walls of a church 60 ft. long, 40 ft. wide, the side walls 28 ft. high, the gable peaks 46 ft. 6′ high, and the walls 1 ft. thick; allowances being made for one half of the openings, which are (*a*) one door-way 7 ft. by 12 ft., (*b*) two door-ways each 8 ft. 2′ by 8 ft. 6′, (*c*) ten windows each 3 ft. by 8 ft. 6′, and (*d*) ten windows each 3 ft. by 7 ft. 6′?

59. Allowing 22½ bricks to make a cubic foot of brick wall, what part of the wall consists of mortar?

60. At 33⅓¢ per sq. yd. for labor, and $7.50 per M for brick, what will a contractor receive for a brick pavement in a court 3 rd. long and 40 ft. wide, the brick being laid flatwise?

61. At $.93¾ per perch for the stone, and $1.25 per cubic yard for the mason work, what is the cost of a partition wall between the cellars of two stores, the wall being 72 ft. long, 8 ft. high, and 18′ thick, and 1 perch of stone making 22 cubic feet of masonry?

62. Find the cost of 9 pieces of floor joists 13 ft. long and 2′ by 9′, at $14.50 per M.

63. How many tons are there in a stack of hay 22 ft. by 35 ft. on the ground, 12 ft. high to the slope, and the ridge of the roof-shaped top,—which extends lengthwise,—15 ft. higher than the sides?

64. How much 1½′ matched flooring will be required for a school room 32 ft. by 48 ft., and a class room ⅓ as long and ½ as wide?

65. At $16.25 per M, what must I pay for 8 boards 18 feet long, 14 inches wide at one end, and tapering to a point?

66. I am building a carriage - house 19 by 28 feet. How much will the 2-inch plank for the floor cost me, at $17.50 per M?

67. A wagon box is 9 ft. 9' long, 3 ft. 4' wide, and 2 ft. 2' deep, inside measurements. How many bushels of wheat will it hold, if filled even full? How many bushels of potatoes?

68. A cellar, 21.5 ft. by 29.5 ft. has a cement floor. How much did it cost, at $1.15 per sq. yd.?

69. What is the value of a stick of ship timber 32 ft. long and 16' by 20', at $18 per C?

70. At 1.18\frac{3}{4}$ per perch for stone and labor, what will be the cost of the two abutments of a bridge, each 24 ft. long, 11 ft. wide at the bottom, 7 ft. wide at the top, and 15 ft. high?

71. A farmer built a stone fence 72 rd. long, 3 ft. 6' high, 2 ft. thick at the bottom, and 1 ft. thick at the top. How many cords of stone did he use?

72. A mow of hay 1 rd. square at the ends and 33 ft. long, contains how many tons?

73. A coal-house 15 ft. by 8 ft. by 7$\frac{1}{2}$ ft. will store how many bushels of coal?

74. At 40¢ per bunch for lath, and 22¢ per square yard for lathing and plastering, what will it cost to lath and plaster this room, making the customary allowance for openings?

75. What must be the length of a bin 6$\frac{1}{4}$ ft. wide and 4$\frac{1}{2}$ ft. deep, to contain 2$\frac{1}{4}$ times as much as a bin 7 ft. long, 5 ft. wide, and 3$\frac{2}{3}$ ft. deep?

76. A packing-box made of 1-inch lumber is 2 ft. 4$\frac{1}{4}$ wide and 1 ft. 6$\frac{1}{2}$' deep, inside measurement; and its capacity is 12 cu. ft. 587.1 cu. in. What are the outside dimensions of the box?

CHAPTER VII.
PERCENTAGE.

SECTION 1.
NOTATION.

266. The term *per cent* means by the hundred.

1 per cent is one of every hundred, or one hundredth.
6 per cent is 6 of every hundred, or 6 hundredths.
$16\frac{2}{3}$ per cent is $16\frac{2}{3}$ of every hundred, or $16\frac{2}{3}$ hundredths.

A. How many hundredths of a number

1. Is 1 per cent of it?	*3.* 5 per cent?	*5.* 8 per cent?
2. Are 3 per cent of it?	*4.* 7 per cent?	*6.* 10 per cent?

What fractional part of a number, in its lowest terms,

7. Is 20 per cent of it?	*10.* $6\frac{1}{4}$ per cent?	*13.* 100 per cent?
8. Is 25 per cent of it?	*11.* $12\frac{1}{2}$ per cent?	*14.* 140 per cent?
9. Is 50 per cent of it?	*12.* $33\frac{1}{3}$ per cent?	*15.* $116\frac{2}{3}$ per cent?

B. *1.* What per cent of any number is $\frac{1}{2}$ of it?

2. $\frac{1}{3}$ of it?	*7.* $\frac{1}{7}$ of it?	*12.* $\frac{1}{15}$ of it?	*17.* $\frac{11}{25}$ of it?
3. $\frac{2}{3}$ of it?	*8.* $\frac{5}{8}$ of it?	*13.* $\frac{4}{15}$ of it?	*18.* $\frac{9}{40}$ of it?
4. $\frac{1}{4}$ of it?	*9.* $\frac{4}{9}$ of it?	*14.* $\frac{7}{16}$ of it?	*19.* $\frac{43}{50}$ of it?
5. $\frac{3}{5}$ of it?	*10.* $\frac{7}{10}$ of it?	*15.* $\frac{5}{18}$ of it?	*20.* $\frac{79}{100}$ of it?
6. $\frac{5}{6}$ of it?	*11.* $\frac{5}{12}$ of it?	*16.* $\frac{3}{20}$ of it?	*21.* The whole of it?

C. *1.* What decimal part of a number is $\frac{1}{2}$ per cent of it?   *8.* What fractional part of a number is $\frac{1}{4}$ per cent of it?

2. $\frac{1}{4}$ per cent?	*5.* $\frac{3}{4}$ per cent?	*9.* $\frac{1}{5}$ per cent?	*12.* $\frac{2}{5}$ per cent?
3. $\frac{1}{6}$ per cent?	*6.* $\frac{5}{6}$ per cent?	*10.* $\frac{1}{8}$ per cent?	*13.* $\frac{3}{8}$ per cent?
4. $\frac{1}{10}$ per cent?	*7.* $\frac{7}{10}$ per cent?	*11.* $\frac{1}{3}$ per cent?	*14.* $\frac{3}{3}$ per cent?

267. The *commercial sign,* %, signifies per cent.

15% signifies 15 hundredths, and is read "15 per cent."

Per cent may be applied to any number.

40 per cent of 1 bushel $= .40$ bu. $= \frac{40}{100}$ bu. $= \frac{2}{5}$ bu.

$14\frac{1}{2}$ "   "   " 365 days $= .145$, or $\frac{29}{200}$ of 365 days.

7 "   "   " $85.42 = .07$, or $\frac{7}{100}$ of $85.42.

$16\frac{2}{3}$ "   "   " $93\frac{1}{4} = .16\frac{2}{3}$, or $\frac{50}{300}$, or $\frac{1}{6}$ of $93\frac{1}{4}$.

125% is 1.25, or $\frac{5}{4}$. $\qquad$ $12\frac{1}{2}$% is $.12\frac{1}{2}$, or .125, or $\frac{1}{8}$.

308% is 3.08, or $\frac{77}{25}$. $\qquad$ $\frac{1}{4}$% is .25%, or $.00\frac{1}{4}$, or .0025.   Hence,

268. I. *To express per cent decimally, two decimal figures are required.*

II. *To express 100 per cent or more, an integer or a mixed decimal number is required.*

III. *To express parts of 1 per cent, either decimal figures, or fractions at the right of hundredths, are required.*

$\frac{1}{2}$% or .5% is $.00\frac{1}{2}$ or .005. $\qquad$ $\frac{3}{8}$% or .375% is $.00\frac{3}{8}$ or .00375.

$\frac{1}{5}$% or .20% is $.00\frac{1}{5}$ or .002. $\qquad$ $\frac{1}{3}$% or $.33\frac{1}{3}$% is $.00\frac{1}{3}$.

Write decimally { 8 per cent   5 per cent   40 per cent   33 per cent.
                   3 per cent   10 per cent   14 per cent   65 per cent.

Read and write decimally { 12%   10%   56% $16\frac{7}{8}$%   31.25%   200%
                        9%   90%   64%   18.7%   114% $\frac{1}{4}$% $\frac{1}{8}$%.

Read as per cent   .07   .30   .19   1.37   2.038 $.44\frac{3}{8}$ $.08\frac{1}{3}$.

269. *Percentage* is the process of finding any number of hundredths of a number.

In this process three elements are considered, viz., the *per cent*, the *base*, and the *percentage*.

270. The *per cent* is the decimal that expresses the number of hundredths of the base to be found.

271. The *base* is the number the hundredths of which are to be found.

272. The *percentage* is the result obtained by finding the required number of hundredths of the base.

273. The *amount* is the base plus the percentage.

274. The *difference* is the base minus the percentage.

SECTION II.

THE FIVE GENERAL CASES OF PERCENTAGE.

CASE I. **Base and per cent given, to find percentage.**

Oral Work.—**275.** *1.* How much is 7% of 50 bushels?

7 per cent of a number is 7 times 1 hundredth of it; 1 hundredth of 50 bushels is .5 of a bushel, and 7 times .5 of a bushel are 3.5 bushels.

2. 15% of 80 boxes of raisins are how many boxes?

15 per cent of a number is 15 hundredths, or 3 twentieths, of it; and 3 twentieths of 80 boxes of raisins are 12 boxes.

How much is	How much is

How much is			How much is	
3– 7. 1 per cent		⎫	*28–32.* 25%	⎫
8–12. 4 per cent		⎪	*33–37.* 12½%	⎪
13–17. 5 per cent	of	⎬	*38–42.* 50%	of
18–22. 8 per cent		⎪	*43–47.* 66⅔%	⎪
23–27. 6 per cent		⎭	*48–52.* 80%	⎭

	500?		400 acres?
	150?		75 melons?
	70?		120 horses?
	36?		9 days?
	325?		5.5 dollars?

Find	*53.* 5% of 140 cd. of wood.	*56.* 12½% of $75.
	54. 8% of 250 yd. of sheetings.	*57.* 30% of 190 mi.
	55. 3% of 50 thousand shingles.	*58.* 6¼% of 240 bu.

59–67. The base is ⎧ 25, ⎫ and the per cent is ⎧ 6. ⎫ What is the ⎨ 60, ⎬ ⎨ 15. ⎬ percentage? ⎩ 7.5, ⎭ ⎩ 33⅓. ⎭

276. *The percentage is the product of the base multiplied by the per cent.*

PROBLEMS.

Written Work.—*1.* 8% of a flock of 475 sheep are black. How many black sheep are in the flock?

2. At a school of 125 pupils, the average daily attendance is 88% of the whole number. What is the daily attendance?

3. From a cask of 44 gallons of oil, 7½% leaked out. How much oil leaked out?

4. 62½% of a township of Western land is prairie. How many acres of land in the township are prairie?

5. A farmer raised 9,875 bushels of grain, 12½% of which was barley. How many bushels of barley did he raise?

6. 11⅔% of an army of 63,000 men are riflemen. How many men are riflemen?

7. A dealer bought 6,250 tons of coal, 33% of which was Lehigh, 46% Lackawanna, and the balance Pittston. How many tons of each kind of coal did he buy?

8. A man thrashed 6,319 bushels of oats for 12½% of them. How many bushels of oats did he receive?

Case II. **Percentage and base given, to find per cent.**

Oral Work.—**277.** *1.* 3 is what per cent of 15?

3 is 3 fifteenths or 1 fifth of 15. Since 15 is 100 per cent of itself, 1 fifth of 15 is 1 fifth of 100 per cent, or 20 per cent.

2. What per cent of 18 is 9? | What per cent

3. Of 25 is 10?	*7.* Of 2 is ⅓?	*11.* Of 500 bu. are 50 bu.?
4. Of 46 is 7?	*8.* Of ⅘ is ⅖?	*12.* Of 75 gal. are 15 gal.?
5. Of 120 is 12?	*9.* Of $72 are $6?	*13.* Of 30 mo. are 10 mo.?
6. Of 22.5 is 7½?	*10.* Of $52 are $13?	*14.* Of 380 ft. are 19 ft.?

15. Of 6 bu. 1 pk. are 1 bu. 3 pk.? | *16.* Of ⅘ h. is ⅗ h.?

17–25. The base is $\left. \begin{matrix} 25, \\ 60, \\ 7.5, \end{matrix} \right\}$ and the percentage is $\left. \begin{matrix} 1.5. \\ 9. \\ 2.5. \end{matrix} \right\}$ What is the per cent?

278. *The per cent is the quotient of the percentage divided by the base.*

Problems.

Written Work.—*1.* $15 per acre for the use of garden land valued at $250 per acre, is what % on the value of the land?

2. 25 bushels of oats are what % of 5,000 bushels?

3. A farmer harvested 270 bushels of potatoes from 18 bushels of seed. The seed was what % of the yield?

4. The yield was what % of the seed?

5. A sheep grower sold 95 sheep from a flock of 475. What % of the flock did he sell?

6. $119 are what % of $340?

7. A house, worth $7,500, rents for $600 a year. What % on its value does it rent for?

8. A fruit grower transplanted 250 peach-trees, and 45 of them died. What % of them died?

9. 975 acres of a Southern plantation of 12,350 acres are marsh. What % of the plantation is marsh?

10. A fruit dealer bought a cargo of 85,744 oranges, and lost 5,359 of them. What % of the cargo did he lose?

Case III. **Percentage and per cent given, to find base.**

*Oral Work.—***279.** *1.* 21 is 6 per cent of what number?

21 is 6 per cent of 100 times 1 sixth of 21; 1 sixth of 21 is 3.5, and 100 times 3.5 are 350.

2. 75 is 10 per cent of what number?

Since 10 per cent of any number is 1 tenth of the number, 75 is 10 per cent, or 1 tenth, of 10 times 75, or 750.

What is the number of which

3. 10 is 40%?	*8.* $2\frac{1}{2}$ is $16\frac{2}{3}$%?	*13.* 30 lb. are 5%?
4. 12 is 10%?	*9.* $\frac{1}{3}$ is 50%?	*14.* 13 da. are 26%?
5. 9 is $33\frac{1}{3}$%?	*10.* $\frac{4}{5}$ is 75%?	*15.* 25 T. are $62\frac{1}{2}$%?
6. 8 is 25%?	*11.* $60 are 120%?	*16.* $\frac{1}{4}$ rd. is .3%?
7. 4 is $8\frac{1}{3}$%?	*12.* $\frac{7}{8}$ mi. is 175%?	*17.* $7\frac{7}{8}$ gal. are $2\frac{1}{4}$%?

18–26. The percentage is $\left\{\begin{matrix} 7.5, \\ 42, \\ 2\frac{1}{3}, \end{matrix}\right\}$ and the per cent is $\left\{\begin{matrix} 6. \\ 8. \\ 7. \end{matrix}\right\}$ What is the base?

280. *The base is the quotient of the percentage divided by the per cent.*

Problems.

Written Work.—*1.* A merchant vessel has 169 tons of hides on board, which are 13% of the whole cargo. How many tons are there in the cargo?

2. The distance between two stations on a railroad is 11.5 miles, and this is $12\frac{1}{2}\%$ of the whole length of the road. What is the length of the road?

3. A gentleman sold his house and lot for 18% above cost, and made $500. How much did the property cost?

4. Monday my sales amounted to $237.50, which was $12\frac{1}{2}\%$ of my sales for the week. How much were my sales for the week?

5. A grocer sold 10 sacks of coffee, which was $\frac{1}{2}\%$ of his whole stock. How many sacks of coffee had he?

6. This year a planter sold his cotton at 9 cents a pound, which was 80% of the price he received last year. At what price did he sell his crop last year?

7. A certain school closed its winter term with 115 pupils, which was 92% of the number with which the term began. With how many pupils did it begin?

8. 7.5 sq. rd. of land are 6% of how many square rods?

9. $.$30\frac{1}{4}$ are 120% of how much money?

10. $\frac{1}{4}$ lb. of tea is $7\frac{1}{2}\%$ of a package of how many pounds?

Case IV. Base and per cent given, to find amount or difference.

Oral Work.—**281.** *1.* The base is 25, and the per cent is 20. What is the amount?   *2.* What is the difference?

For the amount.—**25 plus 20 per cent of 25 is 120 per cent of 25, or 6 fifths of 25, which is 30.**

For the difference.—**25 minus 20 per cent of 25 is 80 per cent of 25, or 4 fifths of 25, which is 20.**

What is the amount, and what is the difference,

  3. When the base is 60, and the per cent is 15 ?

  4. The base being 14 mo., and the per cent 25 ?

  5. The per cent being $33\frac{1}{3}$, and the base 27 cu. ft. ?

  6. If the base is $6.4, and the per cent is $6\frac{1}{4}$?

  7. When $\frac{7}{3}$ yd. is the base, and $8\frac{1}{3}$ the per cent ?

8–25. Given, $\left\{\begin{array}{l}40,\\75,\\1.25,\end{array}\right\}$ and the $\left\{\begin{array}{l}7;\\30;\\140;\end{array}\right\}$ to find $\left\{\begin{array}{l}\text{amount.}\\ \\ \text{difference.}\end{array}\right.$ the base   per cent   the

282. I. *The amount is the product of the base multiplied by 1 plus the per cent;* and

II. *The difference is the product of the base multiplied by 1 minus the per cent.*

Problems.

Written Work.—*1.* If oak bark is worth 25% more than hemlock, and hemlock sells at $6.72 a cord, how much is a cord of oak bark worth?

2. A lady having $600, paid 18% of it for a parlor organ. How much money had she left?

3. Last year a merchant bought table linens at 60¢ a yard, but this year he pays $37\frac{1}{2}$% more for the same class of goods. How much does he pay per yard this year?

4. A gentleman having $876 deposited in a bank, checked out $62\frac{1}{2}$% of it. How much remained on deposit?

5. If a man's income is $800, and he expends $66\frac{2}{3}$% of it, how much does he save?

Case V. Amount or difference and per cent given, to find base.

Oral Work.—**283.** *1.* The amount is 30, and the per cent is 20. What is the base?

Since 30—the amount—is 100 per cent plus 20 per cent, or 120 per cent of the base, the base is the quotient of 30 divided by 1.20 or $\frac{6}{5}$, which is 25.

2. The difference is 24, and the per cent is 25.   What is the base?

Since 24—the difference—is 100 per cent minus 25 per cent, or 75 per cent of the base, the base is the quotient of 24 divided by .75 or $\frac{3}{4}$, which is 32.

Given, $\begin{cases} \textit{3.}\ \text{Amount, 36; per cent, } 12\frac{1}{2}; \\ \textit{4.}\ \text{Amount, 69; per cent, 15;} \\ \textit{5.}\ \text{Amount, } 17\frac{1}{2}; \text{ per cent, 25;} \\ \textit{6.}\ \text{Amount, \$6.8; per cent, } 6\frac{1}{4}; \end{cases}$ to find the base.

7. What number of cows, plus 16% of the number, equals 87 cows?

8. How much money, less 78% of itself, leaves $44?

9. How many yards, less 5% of the number, equals 57 yards?

10. What number, plus 7% of the number, equals 321?

11. Any amount is the base, or 100 per cent, plus what?

12. Any difference is the base minus what?

284. *The base is the quotient*

   1. *Of the amount divided by 1 plus the per cent;* or

   2. *Of the difference divided by 1 minus the per cent.*

PROBLEMS.

Written Work.—*1.* By selling a piano for $540, I gain 20 per cent.   What did it cost me?

2. Sold a carriage for $270, which was 20% less than it cost.   What was the cost?

3. This year a lawyer's receipts from his practice are $2,662.50, which is 42% more than they were last year. How much were his receipts last year?

4. A physician saves $56 a month, and his expenses are 60% of his yearly income.   What is his income?

5. My income is 8% greater this year than it was last, and this year it is $1,890.   How much was it last year?

6. A manufacturer sells reapers at $126 apiece, and gains 40%. How much do they cost him apiece?

7. 44 yards of unsponged cloth measured 2½% more than did the same cloth sponged. What was its length after being sponged?

285. RULES FOR PERCENTAGE.

I. Base and per cent given, to find percentage:—
Multiply the base by the per cent.

II. Percentage and base given, to find per cent:—
Divide the percentage by the base.

III. Percentage and per cent given, to find base:—
Divide the percentage by the per cent.

IV. Base and per cent given, to find amount or difference:—

1. For the amount;—*Multiply the base by 1 plus the per cent.*

2. For the difference;—*Multiply the base by 1 minus the per cent.*

V. Amount or difference and per cent given, to find base:—

1. *Divide the amount by 1 plus the per cent;* or

2. *Divide the difference by 1 minus the per cent.*

   a. *In final results, if the mills are 5 or more, call them 1 cent; and if they are less than 5, reject them.*

   b. The terms base, per cent, and percentage correspond to the terms multiplicand, multiplier, and product. Hence,

Any two of the three terms—base, per cent, percentage—being given, the third term may be found. Thus:

   c. In multiplication   *d.* In percentage

I. *Multiplicand × multiplier = product.* Hence, I. *Base × per cent = percentage.*

II. $\dfrac{Product}{multiplier} = multiplicand.$ Hence, II. $\dfrac{Percentage}{per\ cent} = base.$

III. $\dfrac{Product}{multiplicand} = multiplier.$ Hence, III. $\dfrac{Percentage}{base} = per\ cent.$

SECTION III.

SPECIAL APPLICATIONS OF THE FIVE GENERAL CASES.

I. PROFIT AND LOSS.

286. *Profit* is the sum above cost for which goods are sold.

287. *Loss* is the sum below cost for which goods are sold.

In computations in profit and loss,

    a. *Cost = base;* | *b.* *Profit or loss = percentage;*

    c. *Selling price = amount or difference.*

PROBLEMS.

1. 10% profit on \$2.50 cost, is how much profit?

2. 8% loss on \$7.25 cost, is how much loss?

3. I bought vinegar at \$.16 a gallon, and sold it at a profit of $56\frac{1}{4}\%$. How much did I gain on a gallon?

4. A man sold a city lot that cost him \$160, at an advance of $212\frac{1}{2}\%$. How much did he gain?

5. I bought a carriage for \$187.50, and sold it at a loss of $12\frac{1}{2}\%$. How much did I lose?

6. If a milliner sells ribbon that cost \$.31$\frac{1}{4}$ a yard, at a profit of 20%, how much does she gain on a yard?

7. Cost, \$.40; profit, $62\frac{1}{2}\%$. What is the selling price?

8. Cost, \$1.20; loss, $33\frac{1}{3}\%$. What is the selling price?

9. The bread made from a barrel of flour weighs 40% more than the flour. How many pounds does it weigh?

10. A grocer sold tea that cost him \$.78 a pound, at a loss of 15%. At what price per pound did he sell it?

11. Mark silk that cost \$2.60 per yard, to sell at 20% loss.

12. Mark silk that cost \$2.60 per yard, to sell at 25% gain.

13. Mark gold pens that cost \$1.25, to sell at 60% profit.

14. Mark kid gloves that cost \$.93¾, to sell at 9⅓% loss.

15. \$.87½ profit on \$10.50 cost, is what **per cent**?

16. \$.02½ loss on \$.15 cost, is what per cent?

17. A flour dealer bought flour for \$6.56 a barrel, and sold it for \$7.31. What % did he make?

18. What % do I make, by selling eggs at ⅘ of their cost?

19. If kerosene is bought at ⅚ of the market price, and sold at 10% below the market price, what % is lost?

20. I sell for \$5 what cost me \$4.25. What % do I gain?

21. I sell for \$.30 what cost me \$.37½. What % do I lose?

22. A jeweler sold a watch for \$112.50, which was 15% advance on the cost. How much was the cost?

23. A gentleman sold a horse and harness for \$187.50, which was 10% less than cost. How much was the cost?

24. \$.90, the retail price of a book, is 40% above the wholesale price. What is the wholesale price?

II. COMMISSION.

288. An *agent* is a person authorized to transact business for another.

289. A *commission-merchant* is a merchant who buys or sells goods or other property as an agent for others.

290. *Commission* is a percentage paid to an agent for transacting business.

In computations in commission,

   a. Sum expended or collected by agent = base;

   b. Commission = percentage;

   c. Sum collected, or sum expended plus commission=amount.

Problems.

1. 5% on $415 collections, is how much commission?

2. 2½% on $8,362$\frac{50}{100}$ invested, is how much commission?

3. A real-estate agent sold a house and lot for $2,275. How much was his commission, at 2%?

4. How much commission will an auctioneer receive for selling a stock of goods for $1,975, at 3%?

5. An agent buys 8,040 lb. of wool, at $.37½ a pound. How much is his commission, at 2½%?

6. I sold 15,000 yards of sheetings, at $.11½. How much was my commission, at 1⅓%?

7. $29.80 for collecting $238.40, is at what per cent?

8. $56.33 for investing $2,319, is at what per cent?

9. $1,390 for investment after deducting 5% commission, is how much for investment? How much for commission?

10. $12,400 includes investment, and commission at 3⅓%. What is the investment? What is the commission?

11. A druggist sent his broker or agent $2,630 with which to buy goods, after deducting his commission of 2½%. How much did the broker expend for goods?

12. A wool buyer receives $5,600 with which to purchase wool, less 2% commission on the money paid out. How much money will he expend for wool?

13. A broker received $6,500 with which to buy hops, at $.31¼ a pound, after deducting his commission of 4%. How many pounds of hops did he buy?

On what amount { *14.* Is $41.70 the commission, at 15%?
of sales { *15.* Is $450.30 the commission, at 7½%?

16. A collector received $123.75 for collecting bills, at 5% commission. How much money did he collect?

III. INSURANCE.

291. *Insurance* is a security against loss or damage.
Insurance is of various kinds,—as *fire insurance, marine insurance, life insurance, health insurance, accident insurance.*

292. *Valuation* is the estimated value of the property insured.

293. *Premium* is the sum paid for the insurance.

294. A *policy* is a written contract between the insurer and the insured.

In computations in insurance,

    a. Valuation = base; | *b. Premium = percentage.*

Problems.

1. 4% on \$2,250 valuation, is how much premium?

2. ⅝% on \$6,287 valuation, is how much premium?

—*3.* What premium must a grocer pay for a policy of insurance of \$1,950 on his stock of goods, at 1½%?

4. At ¼% a year, what premium do I pay yearly for an insurance of \$3,750 on my house?

- *5.* What is the annual premium for insuring a steam saw-mill for \$2,250, at 3¾%?

6. Find the premium on a cargo of flour, shipped from New York to Liverpool, insured for \$9,000, at ½%.

7. An ocean steamship is insured for \$97,500, at ¾% a voyage. What is the premium per voyage?

At what { *8.* Is \$31.25 the premium on \$12,500 valuation?
per cent { *9.* Is \$97.50 the premium on \$6,500 valuation?

10. A shipper paid \$37.50 for an insurance of \$7,500 on a cargo of produce. What % premium did he pay?

11. An agent took a risk of \$2,500 on a stock of stoves, and received \$50 premium. What was the per cent?

—*12.* At $\frac{3}{4}\%$, $9.50 is the premium on what valuation?

13. A premium of 28.12\frac{1}{2}$, at $\frac{5}{8}\%$, is on what valuation?

14. An agent received $9.75 for insuring a barn and its contents, at $\frac{1}{2}\%$. What was the valuation of the property?

IV. TAXES.

295. *Taxes* are sums of money levied upon persons and property, to meet public expenses.

A *property tax* is a tax on personal property and real-estate ; a *poll tax* is a tax on the person.

In computations in taxes,

  a. Valuation = base ; | *b. Tax = percentage.*

PROBLEMS.

1. Find the tax on property valued at $2,875, at 1.3%.

2. What is the tax on $932 of valuation, at .4%?

3. $3.57 tax on 277\frac{50}{100}$ valuation, is at what per cent?

4. The tax on $3,200 is $12. What is the per cent?

5. The taxable property in an incorporated village is valued at $500,000, and a tax of $1,875 is voted for school purposes. What is the per cent of the tax?

6. In the same village A's property is assessed at $1,250, B's at $1,500, C's at $2,250, D's at $750, and E's at $4,250. Allowing 5% for collector's fees, how much tax has each one to pay?

7. My tax is $15.25, at 1$\frac{7}{100}\%$. What is the valuation?

8. What is the assessed value of a farm that is taxed 23.37\frac{1}{2}$, at 2$\frac{1}{2}$ mills on the dollar?

9. The capital of a glass factory is owned by 8 partners, whose shares are $3,300, $450, $1,200, $2,250, $750, $1,800, $600, and $900 ; and repairs are made that cost $225. At what per cent must the capital be taxed, to pay for the repairs? How much must each partner pay?

V. CUSTOMS OR DUTIES.

296. *Customs* or *duties* are taxes levied on imported goods and other property, for the support of the General Government.

 a. *Imports* are goods and other property brought into a country.

 b. A *custom-house* is an office at which duties are collected.

 c. A *port of entry* is a seaport in which a custom-house is situated.

297. A *tariff* is a list or schedule of the legal rates of duties on imports.

298. Duties are of two kinds, *ad valorem* and *specific*.

 a. *Ad valorem duties* are duties on the net cost of imports, at the place where they are purchased.

 b. *Specific duties* are duties on the number or quantity.

299. *Tare, leakage,* and *breakage* are deductions made, on certain kinds of goods, before specific duties are computed.

 a. *Tare* is a deduction for the weight of the box, cask, bag, or case that contains the goods.

 b. *Leakage* is a deduction for waste of liquors in casks or barrels.

 c. *Breakage* is a deduction for loss of liquors in bottles.

300. *Gross weight* is the weight without deductions.

301. *Net weight* is the weight less the deductions.

302. An *invoice* is a written list of merchandise, with prices and charges annexed.

 A *manifest* is a complete invoice of a ship's cargo.

303. In computations in duties,

 a. *Net value = base;* | *b.* *Duty = percentage.*

Rules for Computing Duties.

I. For ad valorem duties:—*Multiply the net value of the imports by the tariff per cent of duty.*

II. For specific duties:—*Multiply the tariff rate of duty on a unit by the net number of units.*

Problems.

1. The gross weight of 225 boxes of raisins is $33\frac{1}{3}$ lb. per box, and the tare is 25%. What are the duties, at $2\frac{1}{4}$¢ per lb. ?

2. What are the duties on 316 boxes of lemons, invoiced at \$3.45 per box, at 20% ad valorem ?

3. What are the duties on 25 pieces of Brussels carpeting of 65 yd. each, invoiced at \$.43¾ per yd., the tariff rates being \$.44 per yd. specific and 35% ad valorem ?

4. A sugar refiner imports 72 hhd. of W. I. sugar, gross weight 975 lb. each, tare $12\frac{1}{2}$%, invoice price $6\frac{1}{8}$¢ per lb. The tariff rates are 2¢ per lb. specific and 25% ad valorem. What are the custom-house charges?

VI. STOCKS.

304. *Stock* is the money or other property invested in the business of a corporation.

305. A *share* of stock is one of the equal parts into which the stock of a corporation is divided.

The original value of a share is commonly \$100.

306. The *par value* of stock is 100 per cent.

307. The *market value* of stock is the sum for which it will sell.

a. Stock is *at par,* when its market value is 100 per cent;

b. Stock is *above par,* when its market value is above 100 per cent; and

c. Stock is *below par,* when its market value is below 100 per cent.

308. *Premium* is the excess above 100 per cent in the value of stock that is above par.

309. *Discount* is the deficiency below 100 per cent in the value of stock that is below par.

310. A *stock-broker* is an agent who buys and sells stocks for others.

311. *Brokerage* is the commission paid to stock brokers.

In computations in stocks,

> *a.* *Par value = base;* | *b.* *Premium or discount = percentage;*
> .*c.* *Market value = amount or difference.*

Problems.

What is the market $\begin{cases} 1. & \text{That sells at } 7\frac{3}{8}\% \text{ premium?} \\ 2. & \text{That sells at } 16\% \text{ discount?} \end{cases}$
value of stock

Find the $\begin{cases} 3. & \text{Premium on 7 shares of stock, at } 5\frac{1}{8}\% \text{ above par.} \\ 4. & \text{Discount on 35 shares of stock, at } 3\frac{1}{16}\% \text{ below par.} \end{cases}$

5. If Western Union Telegraph stock is at a premium of 15%, how much must be paid for 75 shares?

6. $8,982\frac{75}{100}$ buys how much stock, at $103\frac{1}{4}$; *i. e.*, at $3\frac{1}{4}\%$ premium?

7. $2,346.87\frac{1}{2}$ buys how much stock, at $93\frac{7}{8}$; *i. e.*, at $6\frac{1}{8}\%$ discount?

8. I sell telegraph stock at par that cost me 94. What % do I gain?

9. I sell stock at 75 that cost me 80. What % do I lose?

10. What is the market value of 50 shares of mining stock, that sells at $32\frac{1}{8}\%$ below par?

11. I bought 15 shares of Novelty Iron Works stock, at $116\frac{1}{8}$. How much did it cost me?

12. A widow invested $937\frac{1}{2}$ in toll-bridge stock, at $37\frac{1}{2}\%$ below par. How many shares did she buy?

VII. PARTNERSHIP.

312. A *partnership* or *company* is an association of persons for the transaction of business.

> A *firm* is the name under which a company transacts business. A firm is also called a *house.*

313. *Partners* are the persons associated in a partnership or company.

> *a.* An *active partner* is one who takes an active part in the management of the business.
>
> *b.* A *silent partner* is one who furnishes capital, but takes no active part in the management of the business.
>
> *c.* A *general partner* is one who is responsible for the debts of the company, to the amount of his entire property.
>
> *d.* A *special partner* is one whose responsibility is limited to a certain amount, specified in the written articles of partnership.

314. *Capital* or *stock* is the money, or its equivalent, invested in business.

> *a.* Capital may be money, real estate, personal property, time, labor, or skill.
>
> *b.* The *resources* or *assets* of a company are its entire property, including capital, and all demands in its favor.
>
> *c.* The *liabilities* or *obligations* of a company are its entire indebtedness, or all demands against it.
>
> *d.* *Net capital* or *surplus* is the excess of resources over liabilities.
>
> *e.* A *deficit* is the excess of liabilities over resources.
>
> *f.* When resources exceed liabilities, the company is *solvent;* and when liabilities exceed resources, the company is *insolvent* or *bankrupt.*

315. *Dividends* are the profits divided among the partners of a company.

316. *Assessments* are sums to be paid by the partners of a company, to meet expenses or cover losses.

317. Each partner's share of a dividend or assessment is such a % of his share of the capital, as the entire dividend or assessment is % of the entire capital.

Ex. M, N, and R are partners; M furnishes $3,500 of the capital, N $2,500, and R $2,000; and their profits are $3,200. What is each partner's share?

FULL SOLUTION.

$$\$3,200, \text{ entire dividend.}$$
$$\$3,500 + \$2,500 + \$2,000 = \$8,000, \text{ entire capital.}$$
$$\$3,200 \div \$8,000 = .40 = 40 \text{ per cent of dividend.}$$
$$40\% \text{ of } \$3,500 = \$1,400, M\text{'s share.}$$
$$40\% \text{ of } \$2,500 = \$1,000, N\text{'s }\text{``}$$
$$40\% \text{ of } \$2,000 = \$\ \ \ 800, R\text{'s }\text{``}$$

318. RULE FOR PARTNERSHIP.

I. For per cent of dividend or assessment:—*Divide the total dividend or assessment by the total capital.*

II. For each partner's dividend or assessment:—*Multiply his capital by the per cent of dividend or assessment.*

PROBLEMS.

1. Reed and Clark form a partnership. Reed furnishes $3,500 of the capital, and Clark $5,000. They gain $2,450. What is each partner's share?

2. A, B, and C hire a pasture for $22.50. A's horse is in the pasture 5 months, B's horse 7 months, and C's horse 6 months. How much of the rent does each pay?

3. A carpet factory was damaged by fire to the amount of $15,180, and it was insured in the Hanover Ins. Co. for $9,000, in the Globe Ins. Co. for $7,200, in the Ætna Ins. Co. for $6,000, and in the Franklin Ins. Co. for $5,400 How much of the loss did each company sustain?

4. Bates and Davis lose $828 in trade. Bates's capital is $1,200, and Davis's $1,600. What is the loss of each?

5. The total capital of a firm is $75,000, of which G's share is ⅓ less than H's, and K's is one half the sum of G's and H's. The year's profits are $18,600. Required, each partner's capital, and each partner's dividend.

6. Four men shipped 6,000 bales of cotton to England, E furnishing 2,100 bales, F 1,250 bales, G 1,725 bales, and H the balance. In a storm 1,920 bales were thrown overboard. What was each man's share of the loss?

7. Williams, Jones, and Brown manufacture parlor organs. Mr. W. furnishes $3,000 of the capital, Mr. J. $6,750, and Mr. B. $8,250, and in four years their profits are $70,200. What is each partner's share?

8. Two men harvest and thrash 945 bushels of wheat for ⅛ of the crop, A furnishing 8 men 7 days, and B 14 men 5 days. How many bushels of wheat does each partner receive?

9. A, B, and C own 100 shares of RR. stock; and A's annual dividend is $210, B's $400, and C's $240. How many shares of stock does each own?

10. Hilton and Roberts hire a pasture for $50. Hilton puts in 25 horses 30 days, and Roberts puts in 20 horses 42 days. How much of the rent ought each to pay?

11. January 1, A, B, and C begin the manufacture of hats, with a capital of $20,400, $\frac{7}{16}$ of which is A's, ⅜ is B's, and the remainder is C's. May 1, C buys ¼ of B's share, and D buys ² of A's share. The profits for the year are $8,420. How much is each partner's share?

12. A, B, C, and D formed a partnership. A furnished 4 times as much of the capital as B, B ½ as much as C, and D as much as A and B together. Their profits were $1,943.76. What was each partner's dividend?

SECTION IV.

INTEREST.

319. *Interest* is the sum paid for the use of money.

320. *Principal* is the money for the use of which interest is paid.

321. *Amount* is the sum of principal and interest.

322. The *rate of interest* is the number of hundredths allowed for the use of $1 of principal for 1 year.

> The *per cent,* in interest, depends upon the rate of interest and the time.

323. In computations in interest,

  a. Principal = the base;

  b. Rate of interest × time (in years) *= per cent;*

  c. Interest = the percentage. Hence,

Interest = principal × rate of interest × time; i. e.,

Interest = principal × per cent.

CASE I. Interest for years.

***Oral Work.*—324. A.** At 6 per cent per annum, the rate of interest on $1 for 1 year is .06 or $\frac{6}{100}$.

What is the per cent on

1. $1 for 3 yr. ?	*4.* $1 for 8 yr. ?	*7.* $10 for 7 yr. ?
2. $3 for 1 yr. ?	*5.* $1 for 4 yr. ?	*8.* $100 for 1 yr. ?
3. $3 for 5 yr. ?	*6.* $5 for 4 yr. ?	*9.* $100 for 2 yr. ?

B. At 6 per cent per annum, the interest of $1 for 1 year is $.06.

What is the interest of

1. $1 for 7 yr. ?	*4.* $50 for 6 yr. ?	*7.* $ .50 for 1 yr. ?
2. $8 for 7 yr. ?	*5.* $15 for 10 yr. ?	*8.* $ .50 for 5 yr. ?
3. $1 for 6 yr. ?	*6.* $300 for 4 yr. ?	*9.* $1.50 for 5 yr. ?

325.
FORMULAS.
I. *Int. for 1 yr. = prin. × rate of int.*
II. *Int. for yr. = prin. × rate of int. for No. of yr.*

Written Work.—Ex. What is the interest of $135.25 for 3 years, at 6%?

EXPLANATION.—*1st. For* 1 *year.* I multiply $135.25, the principal, by .06, the rate of interest, and obtain $8.11½.

2d. For 3 *years.* I multiply $8.11½, the interest for 1 year, by 3, and obtain $24.34½, the required interest.

PROCESS.

$135.25	Principal.
.06	Rate of int.
$8.1150	Int. for 1 yr.
3	
$24.345	Int. for 3 yr.

PROBLEMS.

1. What is the interest of $467 for 1 year, at 6%?

2. Find the interest of $321 for 1 year, at 5%. Find the amount.

3. Find the interest of $167.50 for 5 years, at 7%.

4. What is the interest of $612.75 for 3 years, at 8%?

5. What sum of money will pay a debt of $165.88, 1 year after it is due, with interest at 10%?

6. What is the amount of $3,750 for 3 years, at 5%?

7. February 11, 1880, I borrowed $2,250. How much did the debt amount to, February 11, 1883, interest at 6%?

8. What is the interest of $560.10 for 2 years, at 7%?

CASE II. **Interest for months.**

Oral Work.—**326.** *A. 1.* What part of a year is 1 month?

2. Are 6 mo.?	*4.* Are 4 mo.?	*6.* Are 9 mo.?	*8.* Are 5 mo.?
3. Are 3 mo.?	*5.* Are 2 mo.?	*7.* Are 8 mo.?	*9.* Are 7 mo.?

B. 1. The per cent on $1 for 1 month is what part of the rate on $1 for 1 year?

2. At 6% per annum, what is the per cent on $1 for 6 mo. ?

3. For 3 mo. ? | *5.* For 4 mo. ? | *7.* For 2 mo. ? | *9.* For 7 mo. ?
4. For 9 mo. ? | *6.* For 8 mo. ? | *8.* For 1 mo. ? | *10.* For 11 mo. ?

C. 1. The interest of $1 for 1 month is what part of the interest of $1 for 1 year?

2. The interest of any sum for 1 month is what part of the interest of the same sum for 1 year?

3. At 6% per annum, what is the interest of $1

4. For 1 mo. ? | *6.* For 9 mo. ? | *8.* For 8 mo. ? | *10.* For 7 mo. ?
5. For 3 mo. ? | *7.* For 4 mo. ? | *9.* For 2 mo. ? | *11.* For 11 mo. ?

D. At 6% per annum, what is the interest of

1. $4 for 3 mo. ? | *5.* $20 for 2 mo. ? | *9.* $1 for 1 yr. 6 mo. ?
2. $2 for 9 mo. ? | *6.* $100 for 1 mo. ? | *10.* $8 for 1 yr. 6 mo. ?
3. $7 for 4 mo. ? | *7.* $40 for 7 mo. ? | *11.* $40 for 1 yr. 4 mo. ?
4. $10 for 8 mo. ? | *8.* $12 for 11 mo. ? | *12.* $200 for 3 yr. 7 mo. ?

327.
Formulas.
$\left\{\begin{array}{l} \text{III. } \textit{Int. for 1 mo.} = \tfrac{1}{12} \textit{ of int. for 1 yr.} \\ \text{IV. } \textit{Int. for mo.} = \tfrac{1}{12} \textit{ of int. for 1 yr.} \times \textit{No. of mo.} \end{array}\right.$

Written Work.—Ex. What is the interest of $84.50 for 1 yr. 5 mo., at 6%?

PROCESS.

$84.50
.06
——————
$5.070   Int. for 1 yr.
17
——————
12)$86.19
——————
$7.18   Int. for 1 yr. 5 mo.

EXPLANATION.—*1st. For* 1 *yr.* I multiply $84.50, the principal, by .06, the rate of interest, and obtain $5.07.

2d. For 1 yr. 5 mo., or 17 *mo.* Since 17 months are $\tfrac{17}{12}$ years, I multiply $5.07, the interest for 1 year, by $\tfrac{17}{12}$, and obtain $7.18, the required interest.

a. When the time is expressed in months:—*Divide the interest for 1 year by 12, and multiply the quotient by the number expressing the time in months.*

b. Or, to avoid fractions in the process:—*Multiply the interest for 1 year by the number expressing the time in months, and divide the product by 12.*

Problems.

1. What is the interest of \$952.17 for 3 months, at 6%?

2. What is the interest of \$187.75 for 5 months, at 4%?

3. Find the interest of \$1,168.48 for 1 yr. 4 mo., at $3\frac{1}{2}\%$.

4. If I have \$938.25 on interest for 4 yr. 10 mo., at 6%, how much interest shall I receive?

5. What is the amount of \$294.25 for 6 mo., at 5%?

6. If I give my note for \$3,275, Jan. 11, 1882, and pay it Feb. 11, 1883, with 7% interest, how much do I pay?

7. If I borrow \$2,732, at 12% interest, and pay the debt in 1 month, how much do I pay?

8. How much must I pay for the rent of a store valued at \$3,150, for 1 yr. 4 mo., at 7% on the valuation?

9. How much is the semi-annual interest on a 7% mortgage for \$1,730?

Case III. **Interest for days.**

Oral Work.—**328.**

A. 1. How many days is .1 of a mo.?

How many tenths of a month

9. Is 1 day? | *10.* Are 3 days?

2. Are .3 of a mo.?

3. .2 mo.? | *6.* .9 mo.? | *11.* 15 da.? | *15.* 24 da.? | *19.* 25 da.?

4. .6 mo.? | *7.* $.0\frac{1}{3}$ mo.? | *12.* 9 da.? | *16.* 18 da.? | *20.* 7 da.?

5. .4 mo.? | *8.* $.5\frac{2}{3}$ mo.? | *13.* 6 da.? | *17.* 11 da.? | *21.* 16 da.?

                 14. 12 da.? | *18.* 20 da.? | *22.* 29 da.?

B. 1. The per cent on \$1 for 3 days is what part of the per cent on \$1 for 1 month or 30 days?

2. At 6% per annum, what is the % on \$1 for 3 days?

3. For 15 da.? | *5.* For 12 da.? | *7.* For 1 da.? | *9.* For 20 da.?

4. For 9 da.? | *6.* For 18 da.? | *8.* For 11 da.? | *10.* For 25 da.?

C. 1. The interest of \$1 for 3 days is what part of the interest of \$1 for 1 month?

2. The interest of any sum for 3 days is what part of the interest of the same sum for 1 month?

At 6% per annum, what is the interest of $1

3. For 1 mo.?	*5.* For 24 da.?	*7.* For 1 da.?	*9.* For 20 da.?
4. For 15 da.?	*6.* For 3 da.?	*8.* For 4 da.?	*10.* For 25 da.?

11. Of $6 for 12 da.? | *12.* $25 for 18 da.? | *13.* $100 for 27 da.?

D. How many months and tenths of a month

1. Are 2 mo. 15 da.?	*3.* Are 1 mo. 21 da.?	*5.* Are 7 mo. 25 da.?
2. Are 6 mo. 18 da.?	*4.* Are 10 mo. 6 da.?	*6.* Are 11 mo. 29 da.?

7. Are 1 yr. 3 mo. 12 da.? | *9.* Are 1 yr. 8 mo. 13 da.?
8. Are 2 yr. 1 mo. 27 da.? | *10.* Are 3 yr. 28 da.?

E. At 6% per annum, what is the interest of $1

1. For 2 mo. 15 da.?	*3.* For 1 mo. 21 da.?	*5.* For 7 mo. 25 da.?
2. For 3 mo. 3 da.?	*4.* For 4 mo. 10 da.?	*6.* For 5 mo. 17 da.?

7. Of $10 for 6 mo. 3 da.? | *10.* Of $1 for 1 yr. 3 mo. 12 da.?
8. Of $7 for 10 mo. 18 da.? | *11.* Of $10 for 1 yr. 2 mo. 6 da.?
9. Of $9 for 7 mo. 17 da.? | *12.* Of $5 for 4 yr. 4 mo. 20 da.?

At any rate of interest, how is the interest of any principal found

13. For 3 days? | *14.* For 1 day? | *15.* For any number of days?

329. { V. *Int. for 3 da. = .1 of int. for 1 mo.*
FORMULAS. { VI. *Int. for da. = .1 of int. for 1 mo. × $\frac{1}{3}$ the No. of da.*

Written Work.—Ex. What is the interest of $169.75 for 2 yr. 3 mo. 10 da., at 8%?

FIRST PROCESS.		SECOND PROCESS.	
2 yr. 3 mo. 10 da. = 27.3⅓ mo.		2 yr. 3 mo. 10 da. = 27.3⅓ mo.	
$169.75	Prin.	$169.75	Prin.
.08	Rate of int.	.08	Rate of int.
12)$13.5800	Int. for 1 yr.	$13.5800	Int. for 1 yr.
$1.13⅙	Int. for 1 mo.	27.3⅓	
27.3⅓	No. of mo.	12)$371.187	
$30.932	Required Int.	$30.932	Int. for $\frac{27.33}{12}$ yr.

The second process avoids complicated computations in fractions

PROBLEMS.

1. How much interest will I have to pay, at 7%, on a loan of $1,296 for 9 mo. 15 da. ?

2. What is the interest of $716.25 for 1 yr. 24 da., at 6%?

3. Find the interest of $936 for 3 yr. 2 mo. 29 da., at 10%.

4. What is the interest of $718 for 1 yr. 14 da., at 6%?

5. If I borrow $819 for 20 days, at 8%, how much interest must I pay?

6. What is the interest of $483.70, from Nov. 23, 1882, to Dec. 8, 1883, at 7%?

7. Find the legal interest of $917.50 from Feb. 14 last to this date.

330. RULES FOR INTEREST.

I. To find the interest for 1 year:—
Multiply the principal by the rate of interest.

II. To find the interest for 2 or more years:—
Multiply the interest for 1 year by the number of years.

III. To find the interest for any other time:—
Multiply the interest for 1 year by the time expressed in months and tenths of a month, and divide the product by 12.

IV. To find the amount:—
Add the interest to the principal.

In computations, retain only three decimal places in partial results.

331. All computations of interest come under this

GENERAL FORMULA.

Principal × rate of interest × time = interest.

Problems.

What is the interest

<table>
<tr><td>1– 25. Of $387.50</td><td rowspan="5">for</td><td>5 yr.,</td><td rowspan="5">at</td><td>10% ?</td></tr>
<tr><td>26– 50. Of $293</td><td>2 yr. 9 mo.,</td><td>7% ?</td></tr>
<tr><td>51– 75. Of $7,461.13</td><td>1 yr. 7 mo. 21 da.,</td><td>4½% ?</td></tr>
<tr><td>76–100. Of $12,009.08</td><td>11 mo. 13 da.,</td><td>1¼% per mo. ?</td></tr>
<tr><td>101–125. Of $4,731.87</td><td>3 yr. 28 da.,</td><td>6% ?</td></tr>
</table>

What is the amount

<table>
<tr><td>126–134. Of $82.44</td><td rowspan="3">for</td><td>7 mo. 10 da.,</td><td rowspan="3">at</td><td>5¼% ?</td></tr>
<tr><td>135–143. Of $316.90</td><td>2 yr. 11 mo.,</td><td>7% ?</td></tr>
<tr><td>144–152. Of $2.054</td><td>1 yr. 3 mo. 27 da.,</td><td>6% ?</td></tr>
</table>

153. A contractor, while building a church, borrowed $13,080 for 7 mo. 15 da., at 8%. How much interest did he pay?

154. Find the amount of $180 for 2 yr. 2 mo. 20 da., at 6%.

155. At ¾% a month, how much will a banker receive for the use of $100 for 2 yr. 5 mo. 10 da. ?

156. A mortgage for $375 has been running 4 yr. 4 mo. 15 da. How much interest has accrued on it, at 8% ?

157. What is the interest of $873.60, from Feb. 10, 1881, to Oct. 10, 1882, at 10% ?

158. A note for $1,824.75, dated Oct. 8, 1881, was paid Dec. 23, 1882, with 6% interest. What amount was paid ?

159. $213 50/100.   New York, *July* 1, 1882.

Three months after date, I promise to pay to Richard Carter, or order, Two Hundred Thirteen and 50/100 Dollars, with interest, for value received.   *Henry Seward.*

This note was paid Nov. 17, 1882, with 7% interest. What was the amount?

160. What is the discount on a bill of goods amounting to $237.50, at 30 days, 2½% off for cash ?

161. Draw your note for $956, bearing date Boston, Oct. 9, 1882, payable to James Fields, or bearer, and due June 15, 1883, with interest.

162. Compute the interest on this note, at 6%.

163. Draw your note for $250, bearing date Chicago, Jan. 14, 1882, payable to Thomas Clark, or order, and due in 1 year, with 10% interest after 3 months.
Find the amount due to-day on this note.

164. A debt of $1,000 due Mar. 2, 1881, was paid Apr. 17, 1882, with interest at 8%. What was the amount?

165. At the date last named, a payment of $350 was made. How much was due June 26, 1883?

166. Memorandum:—Note for $1,824, dated Philadelphia, Oct. 10, 1881. Payment made of $550, Apr. 25, 1882. What was due Jan. 2, 1883, interest at 6%?

167.   *$1.650.*   **St. Louis, Mo., Nov. 19, 1880.**

One year after date, I promise to pay Wm. T. Harris, or order, Sixteen Hundred Fifty Dollars, with interest, for value received.   *Edward Jenkins.*

Indorsements:—June 17, 1882, $225 ; Oct. 24, 1882, $475. How much was due on settlement, Mar. 3, 1883, interest at 6%?

168. A wholesale merchant sold a bill of goods amounting to $3,126$\frac{50}{100}$, on a credit of 3 months; and for cash down, he deducted or *discounted* 5% from the amount of the bill. How much did he receive for the goods?

169. An invoice of fancy goods, at retail prices, amounts to $920 ; and the discounts are 25% off from the amount of the invoice, and 3% off from the balance, for cash. What is the cash cost of the goods?

For *outlines of percentage* for review, see page 275.

General Review Problems in Percentage.

1. At an election, the successful candidate received 11,480 votes, and the defeated candidate $87\frac{1}{2}\%$ of the same number. How many votes did both candidates receive?

2. A farmer divided 225 acres of land among his 3 sons, giving 81 acres to the first, 76.5 acres to the second, and the remainder to the third. What % of the whole number of acres did each receive?

3. What is the difference between 33% and $25\frac{1}{2}\%$ of 480 miles?

4. A merchant sold goods at $33\frac{1}{3}\%$ above cost, and received $.45 a yard for them. How much did they cost him per yard?

5. I sold 2 stones for $24 apiece; on one of them I made 20%, and on the other I lost 20%. What was my gain or loss on both?

6. If 10% is lost by selling boards at $7.20 per M, what % would be gained by selling them at $.90 per C?

7. At what price per pound must I sell tea that cost $.75, to make a profit of 20%?

8. A commission-merchant received $157.75 for selling flour, his commission being $2\frac{1}{2}$ per cent. For how much was the flour sold?

9. A lawyer collected $950, and charged $12\frac{1}{2}\%$ commission. What were his fees, and what was the sum to be remitted?

10. If a tax of $387.75 is paid by an assessment of $\frac{7}{8}$ of 1%, what is the assessed valuation?

11. The cost of building a school-house is $935; the assessed valuation of the district is $34,750, and A owns a farm assessed at $9,475. How much is his tax?

M

12. A merchant's store is insured for $7,850, at $\frac{1}{4}$%; and his goods for $12,375, at $\frac{1}{2}$%. What premium does he pay?

13. A steamship was insured for $87,500, the premium being $1,968.75. What was the per cent?

14. If I sell railroad stock which cost me $2,500, at a loss of $8\frac{1}{2}$%, how much do I receive for it?

15. How much are 5 shares of bank stock worth at 118?

16. An account of $45.50 has been due 2 yr. 6 mo. How much interest has accrued on it, at 6%?

17. What is the interest of $735 from April 9, 1882, to July 15, 1884, at 6 per cent?

18. How much will a debt of $385.50, contracted Feb. 15, 1882, amount to Jan. 3, 1884, on interest at 7%?

19. If you save $150 of your salary each year, and put your savings at interest, at 10%, at the end of each year, how much will your savings amount to in 10 years?

20. After spending 25% of my capital, and 25% of the remainder, I had $675. What capital had I at first?

21. A merchant bought cassimere, at auction, at $28\frac{4}{7}$% below the manufacturer's price, paying $1.25 a yard for it. He retailed it at 22% above manufacturer's price. At what price did he retail it?

22. I sell coal at the same price per net ton (2,000 lb.) as I pay for it per gross ton (2,240 lb.). What per cent profit do I make?

23. A market-man sells eggs at $\frac{1}{2}$ cent apiece above cost, and makes 25%. What do the eggs cost him apiece? At what price per dozen does he sell them?

24. The premiums paid for insuring four stores in a block are $147, $97.50, $153.75, and $107.25; and the rate is $1\frac{1}{2}$%. What amount is insured on each store?

25. A commission-merchant in Milwaukee received from an Oswego miller $1,000, to buy wheat, after deducting his commission at 2%. The merchant paid $1.06¼ per bushel. How many bushels did he buy?

26. If I invest $2,500 in bank-stock, and sell it at an advance of 6%, for how much do I sell it?

27. I buy stock at 5 per cent discount, and sell it at 3 per cent premium, gaining $184. How much do I invest?

28. Dec. 15, 1877, a farmer mortgaged his farm for $4,850; and Sept. 15, 1881, he paid the mortgage, with 6% interest. What amount did he pay?

29. A note for $754.19, dated Jan. 10, 1881, was paid Dec. 14, 1882, with 6% interest. What amount was paid?

30. What sum must be paid to cancel a debt of $219.16, which has been due 1 yr. 6 mo. 14 da., at the legal rate of interest in this State?

31. A man who owned ⅝ of a ship, sold 40% of his share. What part of the ship did he then own?

32. A grain dealer bought wheat at $1.25 per bushel, and sold it at a profit of 20%, making $50 by the transaction. How many bushels did he buy?

33. A merchant sells goods at retail at 30% above cost, and at wholesale at 12% less than retail price. What is his gain per cent on goods sold at wholesale?

34. A man 27 years of age took out a life-insurance policy for $8,000 for the benefit of his wife, at the annual rate of $21.70 per $1,000; his death occurred at the age of 33. How much did the widow receive more than had been paid in annual premiums?

35. I sold 375 100-pound sacks of Rio coffee, at $ .17⅛ a pound, and my commission amounted to $80.27. What per cent commission did I receive?

36. A man sold his house for $2,500, payable in one year, with interest at 6%. At the end of 6 months he received a payment of $1,600. What was due him at the end of the year?

37. How much will you gain, if you buy 45 shares of telegraph stock at 27% discount—or 27% below par—and sell it at 12% discount?

38. If goods are bought at $\frac{1}{3}$ of their value, and sold for 10% more than their value, what is the gain per cent?

39. A merchant bought a hogshead of molasses, and lost $\frac{1}{4}$ of it by leakage; he sold the remainder at 20% advance on its cost. What per cent did he lose on the investment?

40. A note for $850, at 6% interest, was given Sept. 15, 1880. April 23, 1881, a payment of $290 was made; and Jan. 3, 1882, a payment of $345. How much was due Sept. 29, 1882?

41. A druggist buys perfumery at $\frac{1}{3}$ off from retail price. What % does he make by selling it at the retail price?

42. A man can hire a farm of 97 acres for $500 per annum, or he can buy it for $70 an acre. If money is worth 6%, which is the cheaper for him, and how much the cheaper?

43. A farmer bought 80 sheep, at $4.20 a head, giving his note payable in 6 months, at 7%. At the end of the 6 months he sold the sheep at $5.25 a head, and paid the note. How much did he get for the keeping of the sheep?

44. If wool that costs $ .60 per pound, shrinks 45% in cleansing, at what price per pound must it be sold, after cleansing, to gain $33\frac{1}{3}$% on the cost?

BLACKBOARD OUTLINES.

FOR REVIEWS AND EXAMINATIONS.

Notation and Numeration.

I. TERMS.
1. *Arithmetic.*
2. *A unit.*
3. *A number.*
4. *Unit of a number.*
5. *An integer.* Whole numbers.
6. *Cipher or zero.*
7. *Digits.*
8. *Periods of figures.*
9. *Order of a unit.*
10. *Values expressed by figures.*
11. *Simple value.*
12. *Local value.*
13. *Notation.*
14. *Numeration.*
15. *Dollar mark.*
16. *Decimal point.*

II. PRINCIPLES.
1. *Values of orders from right to left.*
2. *Values of orders from left to right.*

III. RULES.
1. *For expressing money.*
   a. Dollar mark.
   b. Decimal point.
   c. Less than 10 cents.
2. *For notation.*
3. *For numeration.*

Addition.

I. TERMS.
1. *Like numbers.*
2. *Unlike numbers.*
3. *Addition.*
4. *Parts.*
5. *Sum or amount.*

II. SIGNS.
1. *Of addition.*
2. *Of equality.*

III. PRINCIPLES.
1. *Parts = the whole.*
2. *What units can be added.*

IV. RULE. *Steps* I, II, III.

Subtraction.

I. TERMS.
1. *Subtraction.*
2. *Minuend.*
3. *Subtrahend.*
4. *Difference or remainder.*

II. SIGN.

III. PRINCIPLE.

IV. RULE. *Steps* I, II, III.

Multiplication.

I. TERMS.
1. *Multiplication.*
   Multiplication is addition.
2. *Multiplicand.*
3. *Multiplier.*
4. *Factors.*
5. *Product.*
   Partial products.
6. *A concrete number.*
7. *An abstract number.*

II. SIGN.

III. IMPORTANT FACTS.
1. *Multiplier an abstract number.*
2. *Either factor for multiplier.*
3. *Annexing 0 to a number.*
4. *One factor 0.*

IV. PRINCIPLES.
1. *Product concrete or abstract.*
2. *Removing a number to the left.*
3. *Multiplying by ones, tens, hundreds, etc.*
4. *Number of 0's on right of product.*

V. CASES AND RULES.
1. *The multiplier a digit.*
2. *Ciphers on the right of multiplier.*
3. *The multiplier two or more digits.*
4. *Ciphers on the right of both factors.*

Division.

I. TERMS.
1. *To divide.*
2. *Fractional parts.*
   Halves, thirds, and so on.
3. *Division.*
   Division is subtraction.
4. *Long division.*
5. *Short division.*
6. *Dividend.*
   Partial dividend.
7. *Divisor.*
8. *Quotient.*
9. *Average of numbers.*

II. SIGNS.   *1st; 2d.*

III. IMPORTANT FACTS.
1. *Divisor an abstract number.*
2. *Steps in division.*
3. *How to change dollars and cents to cents.*
4. *When to change dividend to cents.*
5. *How to divide dollars by 10 or 100.*

IV. PRINCIPLES.
1. *Quotient like dividend.*
2. *Removing a number to the right.*

V. CASES AND RULES.
1. *Divisor ending with a digit.*
2. *Ciphers on right of divisor.*

Decimals.

I. Terms.
1. *A decimal unit.*
2. *A decimal.*
3. *A mixed number.*
4. *The decimal point.*
5. *Currency.*
6. *Money units.*
7. *Reduction.*
8. *A debt.*
9. *A debtor.*
10. *A creditor.*
11. *A bill of goods.*
12. *An item.*
13. *Extending an item.*
14. *The footing of a bill.*
15. *An account.*
16. *The balance of an account.*
17. *Receipting a bill.*

II. Important Facts.
1. *How to write cents and mills.*
2. *How to read cents and mills.*
3. *Removal of decimal point to the right.*
4. *Removal of decimal point to the left.*

III. Principles.
1. *Notation.*
   - *1st.* Lower to higher units.
   - *2d.* Higher to lower units.
2. *Reduction.*
   - *1st.* Annexing decimal ciphers.
   - *2d.* Removing decimal ciphers.
3. *Addition.*
4. *Subtraction.*
5. *Multiplication.* Number of decimal places in product.
6. *Division.* Number of decimal places in quotient.

IV. Processes and Rules.
1. *To reduce decimal currency,*—8 processes.
2. *How to add decimal numbers.*
3. *How to subtract decimal numbers.*
4. *Rule for multiplication.*
   Less decimal places in product than in factors.
5. *Rule for division.*
   When annex decimal ciphers to dividend.

Properties of Numbers.

I. Terms.
1. *Integral factors.*
   An integer is exactly divisible.
2. *A composite number.*
3. *A prime number.*
   A prime factor.
4. *An even number.*
5. *An odd number.*
6. *Factoring.*
7. *An exact divisor.*
8. *A common divisor.*
9. *The greatest common divisor.*
10. *A multiple.*
11. *A common multiple.*
12. *The least common multiple.*
13. *Cancellation.*

II. **Principles.**
- 1. *The greatest common divisor the product of what?*
- 2. *The least common multiple a multiple of what?*
- 3. *Cancelling a factor from a number.*
- 4. *Cancelling a common factor.*
     When the factor 1 remains.

III. **Rules.**
- 1. *For finding prime factors.*
- 2. *For finding greatest common divisor.*
- 3. *For finding multiples; 1, 2.*

Fractions.

I. **Terms.**
- 1. *Fractional parts.*
- 2. *A fractional unit.*
- 3. *A fraction.*
- 4. *The terms.*
     Lowest terms.
- 5. *The denominator.*
- 6. *The numerator.*
- 7. *A proper fraction.*
- 8. *An improper fraction.*
- 9. *A mixed number.*
     Decimal fractions.
- 10. *A compound fraction.*
      The word *of.*
- 11. *A complex fraction.*
- 12. *The unit of a fraction.*
- 13. *To analyze a fraction.*
- 14. *Similar fractions.*
- 15. *Least similar fractions.*
- 16. *Dissimilar fractions.*
- 17. *Common denominator.*
- 18. *Least common denominator.*
- 19. *A fraction is inverted.*

II. **Important Facts.**
- 1. *Common denominator a common multiple.*
- 2. *Least common denominator least common multiple.*

III. **Principles.**
- 1. *Dividing terms by a common factor.*
- 2. *Multiplying terms by any number.*
- 3. *What the product of two fractions equals.*
- 4. *The process of dividing by a fraction.*

IV. **Cases and Rules.**

Reductions of
- 1. *Fractions to lowest terms.*
- 2. *Fractions to given fractional units.*
- 3. *Dissimilar to similar fractions.*
- 4. *Dissimilar to least similar fractions.*
- 5. *Fractions to integers or mixed numbers.*
- 6. *Integers or mixed numbers to improper fractions.*
     Use of each case in reduction.

- 7. *Addition.*   Steps 1, 2.
- 8. *Subtraction*   Steps 1, 2.
- 9. *Multiplication.*   Steps 1, 2.
- 10. *Division.*   Steps 1, 2.

Compound Numbers.

I. TERMS.
1. *A simple number.*
2. *A denominate number.*
3. *A compound number.*
4. *A surface.*
5. *Area.*
   Square inch; foot; yard.
6. *A solid or body.*
   Cubic inch; foot; yard.
7. *Weight.*
8. *Linear measures.*
9. *Surface measures.*
10. *Solid measures.*
11. *Liquid measures.*
12. *Dry measures.*
13. *Avoirdupois weights.*
14. *Time.*
15. *Reduction descending.*
16. *Reduction ascending.*

II. TABLES OF MEASURES.
1. *Linear or line.*
2. *Surface.*
3. *Solid.*
4. *Liquid.*
5. *Dry.*
6. *Avoirdupois weight.*
7. *Time.*
8. *Counting.*

III. IMPORTANT FACTS.
1. *How quantities of articles are determined.*
2. *Process used in reduction descending.*
3. *Process used in reduction ascending.*
4. *Special rules omitted, and why.*
5. *Leap-years, how determined.*
6. *A month, in business transactions.*

IV. CASES. *I; II; III; IV; V; VI.*

V. PROCESSES AND RULES.
1. *Rule for reduction descending.*
2. *Rule for reduction ascending.*
3. *How to add, subtract, multiply, and divide compound numbers.*
4. *How to divide by a compound number.*
5. *How to find difference in time between dates.*

Measurements.

I. TERMS.
1. *Dimensions.*
2. *A line.*
3. *A surface.*
4. *A body.*
5. *Extension.*
6. *An angle.*
7. *A right angle.*
8. *An acute angle.*
9. *An obtuse angle.*
10. *Perpendicular lines.*
11. *A parallelogram.*
12. *A rectangle.*
13. *A square.*
14. *Altitude of parallelogram.*
15. *Diagonal of.*
16. *Perimeter of.*
17. *A triangle.*
18. *A right-angled.*
19. *An obtuse-angled.*
20. *An acute-angled.*
21. *Base of triangle.*
22. *Vertex of.*
23. *Altitude of.*
24. *A trapezoid.*
25. *Altitude of.*
26. *A circle.*
27. *Circumference of.*
28. *Arc of.*
29. *Diameter of.*
30. *Radius of.*
31. *A rectangular solid.*
32. *A cube.*
33. *Cubic contents or volume.*

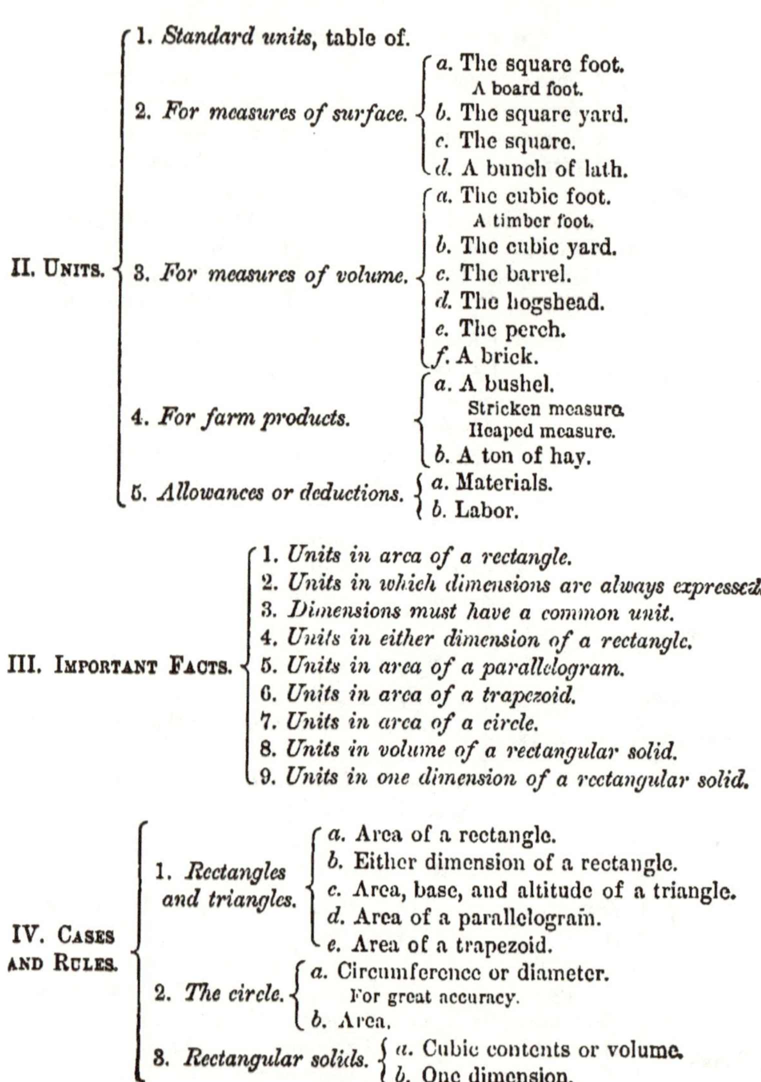

II. UNITS.

1. *Standard units*, table of.

2. *For measures of surface.*
   - a. The square foot.
     - A board foot.
   - b. The square yard.
   - c. The square.
   - d. A bunch of lath.

3. *For measures of volume.*
   - a. The cubic foot.
     - A timber foot.
   - b. The cubic yard.
   - c. The barrel.
   - d. The hogshead.
   - e. The perch.
   - f. A brick.

4. *For farm products.*
   - a. A bushel.
     - Stricken measure.
     - Heaped measure.
   - b. A ton of hay.

5. *Allowances or deductions.*
   - a. Materials.
   - b. Labor.

III. IMPORTANT FACTS.

1. *Units in area of a rectangle.*
2. *Units in which dimensions are always expressed.*
3. *Dimensions must have a common unit.*
4. *Units in either dimension of a rectangle.*
5. *Units in area of a parallelogram.*
6. *Units in area of a trapezoid.*
7. *Units in area of a circle.*
8. *Units in volume of a rectangular solid.*
9. *Units in one dimension of a rectangular solid.*

IV. CASES AND RULES.

1. *Rectangles and triangles.*
   - a. Area of a rectangle.
   - b. Either dimension of a rectangle.
   - c. Area, base, and altitude of a triangle.
   - d. Area of a parallelogram.
   - e. Area of a trapezoid.

2. *The circle.*
   - a. Circumference or diameter.
     - For great accuracy.
   - b. Area.

3. *Rectangular solids.*
   - a. Cubic contents or volume.
   - b. One dimension.

Percentage.

A. Without Time as an Element.

I. TERMS.

1. *Per cent.*
2. *Percentage.*
3. *The per cent.*
4. *The base.*
5. *The percentage.*
6. *The amount.*
7. *The difference.*
8. *Profit.*
9. *Loss.*
10. *An agent.*
11. *A commission-merchant.*
12. *Commission.*
13. *Insurance.*
14. *Valuation.*
15. *Premium.*
16. *A policy*
17. *Taxes.*
18. *A property tax.*
19. *A poll tax.*
20. *Customs or duties.*
21. *Imports.*
22. *A custom-house.*
23. *A port of entry.*
24. *A tariff.*
25. *Ad valorem duties.*
26. *Specific duties.*
27. *Tare.*
28. *Leakage.*
29. *Breakage.*
30. *Gross weight.*
31. *Net weight.*
32. *An invoice.*
33. *A manifest.*
34. *Stock.*
35. *A share.*
36. *Par value.*
37. *Market value.*
    At par.
    Above par.
    Below par.
38. *Premium.*
39. *Discount.*
40. *A stock-broker.*
41. *Brokerage.*
42. *A partnership.*
43. *A firm or house*
44. *Partners.*
    Active.
    Silent.
    General.
    Special.
45. *Capital or stock*
46. *Resources.*
47. *Liabilities.*
48. *Net capital.*
49. *A deficit.*
    Solvency.
    Insolvency.
50. *A dividend.*
51. *An assessment.*

II. NOTATION.

1. *Per cent written as a decimal.*
2. *Per cent written as a fraction.*
3. *The commercial sign.*

III. IMPORTANT FACTS.

1. *Of what factors the percentage is a product.*
2. *Of what the per cent is a quotient.*
3. *Of what the base is a quotient.*
4. *Of what factors the amount is a product.*
5. *Of what factors the difference is a product.*
6. *How to determine a partner's share of a dividend or an assessment.*
7. *Corresponding terms in multiplication and percentage.*

IV. THE FIVE GENERAL CASES.

1. *To find the percentage.*
2. *To find the per cent.*
3. *To find the base.*
4. *To find the amount.*
5. *To find the difference.*

    a. Percentage and per cent given.
    b. Amount and per cent given.
    c. Difference and per cent given

V. SPECIAL APPLICATIONS OF THE FIVE GENERAL CASES.
1. *Profit and loss.*
2. *Commission.* . . { *a.* On money collected. / *b.* On money expended.
3. *Insurance.*
4. *Taxes.*
5. *Duties.* { *a.* Ad valorem. / *b.* Specific.
6. *Stocks.*
7. *Partnership.*

B. With Time as an Element.

I. TERMS.
1. *Interest.*   3. *Amount.*
2. *Principal.*   4. *Rate of interest.*

II. IMPORTANT FACTS.
1. *Upon what the per cent, in interest, depends.*
2. *Corresponding terms in interest and percentage.*
3. *Of what three factors interest is a product.*

III. COMPUTATIONS.
1. *Cases.*
 a. Interest for years.
 b. Interest for months.
 c. Interest for days.
2. *Rules.*
 a. Interest for 1 year.
 b. Interest for 2 or more years.
 c. Interest for any other time.
 d. For amount.

SUPPLEMENT.

---

§ **1.** METHODS OF PROOF.

1. The *fundamental rules of arithmetic* are addition, subtraction, multiplication, and division.

> All arithmetical computations are performed by the use of one or more of these processes.

The methods of proof of the fundamental rules, here given, are based upon the following *truths:*

I. *The sum is not changed by changing the order in which the parts are added.*

II. *A whole equals the sum of all its parts.*

III. *The difference between one of two numbers and their sum equals the other number.*

IV. *The product is not changed by changing the order of the factors.*

V. *The product of two factors divided by either factor equals the other factor.*

VI. *The divisor and quotient are the factors of the dividend.*

2. TO PROVE ADDITION.

First Method.—*Add the given parts in reverse order.*

> The two results must be alike.   (See I.)

Second Method.—*Omit one or more of the parts, and to the sum of the remaining parts add the sum of the parts omitted.*

> This result and the result first obtained must be alike.   (See II.)

3. To Prove Subtraction.

First Method.—*Add the subtrahend and remainder.*
The result must equal the minuend.   (See II.)

Second Method.—*Subtract the remainder from the minuend.*
The result must equal the subtrahend.   (See III.)

4. To Prove Multiplication.

First Method.—*Multiply the multiplier by the multiplicand.*
The two results must be alike.   (See IV.)

Second Method.—*Divide the product by either factor.*
The result must equal the other factor.   (See V.)

5. To Prove Division.

First Method.—*Multiply the divisor and quotient together.*
The result must equal the dividend.   (See VI.)
In integers and decimals, add any final remainder to the product.

Second Method.—*Divide the dividend by the quotient.*
The result must equal the divisor.   (See V.)
In integers and decimals, subtract any final remainder from the dividend, before dividing.

Problems.

Add and prove

1. 2,416 ; 13,892 ; 937 ; 65,429 ; 182,705 ; and 89,076.
2. 95.73 ; 4.067 ; 238.4 ; 25.206 ; 317.0317 ; and 4,404.0404.
3. $\frac{3}{4}, \frac{5}{6}, \frac{13}{20}, \frac{31}{90}, \frac{11}{18}$, and $\frac{1}{2}$.

Subtract and prove
4. \$2,719.37 from \$21,050.
5. 505,992 less 278,059.
6. 83.83 less 8.0383.
7. $\frac{321}{500} - \frac{27}{80}$.

Multiply and prove
8. 4,971 by 628.
9. 32.07 × 5.213.
10. 23.4 times \$189.18$\frac{3}{4}$.
11. $\frac{237}{481} \times \frac{3152}{7440}$.

Divide and prove
12. 4,692 by 69.
13. 5,831 by 84.
14. 24.952 ÷ 4.76.
15. \$293.75 ÷ 45$\frac{3}{4}$.
16. \$518.70 by \$14.25.
17. 3$\frac{11}{64}$ by $\frac{35}{88}$.

§ 2. GENERAL PRINCIPLES OF DIVISION.

6. Any change in either dividend or divisor produces a change in the quotient.

1. With a given divisor, the greater the dividend the greater the quotient; and the less the dividend the less the quotient.

2. With a given dividend, the greater the divisor the less the quotient; and the less the divisor the greater the quotient.

7. The quotient of 72 divided by 12 is 6. Then

$$\overset{\underline{1}}{} \qquad \overset{\underline{2}}{} \qquad \overset{\underline{3}}{} \qquad \overset{\underline{4}}{}$$

A. $\quad 12\overline{)72\times2}\qquad 12\overline{)72\times3}\qquad 12\overline{)72\div2}\qquad 12\overline{)72\div3}\qquad$ Hence,
$$121832$$

*Multiplying the dividend multiplies the quotient; and
Dividing the dividend divides the quotient.*

$$\overset{\underline{1}}{} \qquad \overset{\underline{2}}{} \qquad \overset{\underline{3}}{} \qquad \overset{\underline{4}}{}$$

B. $\quad 12\times2\overline{)72}\qquad 12\times3\overline{)72}\qquad 12\div2\overline{)72}\qquad 12\div3\overline{)72}\qquad$ Hence,
$$321218$$

*Multiplying the divisor divides the quotient; and
Dividing the divisor multiplies the quotient.*

$$\overset{\underline{1}}{} \qquad \overset{\underline{2}}{} \qquad \overset{\underline{3}}{} \qquad \overset{\underline{4}}{}$$

C. $\ 2\times12\overline{)2\times72}\ \ 3\times12\overline{)3\times72}\ \ \tfrac{1}{2}\,of\,12\overline{)\tfrac{1}{2}\,of\,72}\ \ \tfrac{1}{3}\,of\,12\overline{)\tfrac{1}{3}\,of\,72}\ $ Hence,
$$6666$$

*Multiplying dividend and divisor by the same number does not change the quotient; and
Dividing dividend and divisor by the same number does not change the quotient.*

8. GENERAL PRINCIPLES OF DIVISION.

I. Multiplying the dividend or dividing the divisor multiplies the quotient.

II. Dividing the dividend or multiplying the divisor divides the quotient.

III. Multiplying or dividing both dividend and divisor by the same number does not change the quotient.

§ **3.** GENERAL PRINCIPLES OF FRACTIONS.

9. Any change in either term of a fraction produces a change in the value of the fraction.

1. With a given denominator, the greater the numerator the greater the value of the fraction; and the less the numerator the less the value of the fraction.

2. With a given numerator, the greater the denominator the less the value of the fraction; and the less the denominator the greater the value of the fraction.

10. The value of the fraction $\frac{12}{72}$ is $\frac{1}{6}$. Then

A. $\quad \underset{1}{\dfrac{12 \times 2}{72} = \dfrac{2}{6}} \qquad \underset{2}{\dfrac{12 \times 3}{72} = \dfrac{3}{6}} \qquad \underset{3}{\dfrac{12 \div 2}{72} = \dfrac{1}{12}} \qquad \underset{4}{\dfrac{12 \div 3}{72} = \dfrac{1}{18}}$ Hence,

Multiplying the numerator multiplies the fraction; and
Dividing the numerator divides the fraction.

B. $\quad \underset{1}{\dfrac{12}{72 \times 2} = \dfrac{1}{12}} \qquad \underset{2}{\dfrac{12}{72 \times 3} = \dfrac{1}{18}} \qquad \underset{3}{\dfrac{12}{72 \div 2} = \dfrac{1}{3}} \qquad \underset{4}{\dfrac{12}{72 \div 3} = \dfrac{1}{2}}$ Hence,

Multiplying the denominator divides the fraction; and
Dividing the denominator multiplies the fraction.

C. $\quad \underset{1}{\dfrac{12 \times 2}{72 \times 2} = \dfrac{1}{6}} \qquad \underset{2}{\dfrac{12 \times 3}{72 \times 3} = \dfrac{1}{6}} \qquad \underset{3}{\dfrac{12 \div 2}{72 \div 2} = \dfrac{1}{6}} \qquad \underset{4}{\dfrac{12 \div 3}{72 \div 3} = \dfrac{1}{6}}$ Hence,

Multiplying both terms by the same number does not change the value of the fraction; and
Dividing both terms by the same number does not change the value of the fraction.

11. GENERAL PRINCIPLES OF FRACTIONS.

I. *Multiplying the numerator or dividing the denominator multiplies the fraction.*

II. *Dividing the numerator or multiplying the denominator divides the fraction.*

III. *Multiplying or dividing both terms by the same number does not change the value of the fraction.*

§ 4. SHORT METHODS OF COMPUTATION.

Case I. The multiplier a composite number.

12. Ex.   Multiply 83 by 35.

EXPLANATION.—Since 35 is 5 times 7, 35 times any number is 5 times 7 times that number. I therefore multiply 83 by 7 and the result by 5, and obtain 2,905, the required result. Hence,

PROCESS.

$$35 = 5 \times 7$$
$$83 \times 7 = 581$$
$$581 \times 5 = 2,905$$

Rule.

Multiply successively by any set of factors of the number.

Problems.

1. Multiply 4,285 by the factors of 72.

2. 42,196 by 108.

3. 805,061 by 252.

4, 5. 878 by 21, and by 99.

6. 30.54 by 42.

7. 500.05 by 5.6.

8. .00964 by .032.

Case II. The multiplier an aliquot part.

13. An *aliquot part* of a number is any exact divisor of the number.

5, $3\frac{1}{3}$, $2\frac{1}{2}$, and 2 are aliquot parts of 10.

14. The *unit of an aliquot part* is the number divided to obtain the part.

100 is the unit of the aliquot parts 50, $33\frac{1}{3}$, 25, $16\frac{2}{3}$, $12\frac{1}{2}$, etc.

15. TABLE OF ALIQUOT PARTS.

UNITS.	1	10	100	1,000	2,000 lb.	1 ft., or 12 in.	1 doz. or 12	1 lb. or 16 oz.	1 A.
One half	$\frac{1}{2}$	5	50	500	1,000 lb.	6 in.	6	8 oz.	80 sq. rd.
One third	$\frac{1}{3}$	$3\frac{1}{3}$	$33\frac{1}{3}$	$333\frac{1}{3}$	$666\frac{2}{3}$ "	4 "	4		40 "
One fourth	$\frac{1}{4}$	$2\frac{1}{2}$	25	250	500 "	3 "	3	4 "	40 "
One fifth	$\frac{1}{5}$	2	20	200	400 "				32 "
One sixth	$\frac{1}{6}$	$1\frac{2}{3}$	$16\frac{2}{3}$	$166\frac{2}{3}$	$333\frac{1}{3}$ "	2 "	2		
One eighth	$\frac{1}{8}$	$1\frac{1}{4}$	$12\frac{1}{2}$	125	250 "			2 "	20 "
One tenth	$\frac{1}{10}$	1	10	100	200 "				16 "
One twelfth	$\frac{1}{12}$		$8\frac{1}{3}$	$83\frac{1}{3}$		1 "	1		
etc.									

$$\text{Since} \begin{cases} 3\tfrac{1}{3} \text{ is } \tfrac{1}{3} \text{ of } & 10, \\ 25 \text{ is } \tfrac{1}{4} \text{ of } & 100, \\ 500 \text{ is } \tfrac{1}{2} \text{ of } & 1{,}000, \end{cases} \begin{matrix} 3\tfrac{1}{3} \\ 25 \\ 500 \end{matrix} \begin{cases} \text{ times any} \\ \text{number is} \end{cases} \begin{cases} \tfrac{1}{3} \text{ of } & 10 \\ \tfrac{1}{4} \text{ of } & 100 \\ \tfrac{1}{2} \text{ of } & 1{,}000 \end{cases} \begin{matrix} \text{times} \\ \text{that} \\ \text{number.} \end{matrix}$$

$$\text{Since} \begin{cases} 8 \text{ qt. are } \tfrac{1}{4} \text{ bu.} \\ 6 \text{ in. are } \tfrac{1}{2} \text{ ft.,} \\ 400 \text{ lb. are } \tfrac{1}{5} \text{ T.,} \end{cases} \begin{matrix} \text{the} \\ \text{cost} \\ \text{of} \end{matrix} \begin{cases} 8 \text{ qt.} \\ 6 \text{ in.} \\ 400 \text{ lb.} \end{cases} \text{is} \begin{cases} \tfrac{1}{4} \text{ of} \\ \tfrac{1}{2} \text{ of} \\ \tfrac{1}{5} \text{ of} \end{cases} \begin{matrix} \text{the} \\ \text{cost} \\ \text{of} \end{matrix} \begin{cases} 1 \text{ bu.} \\ 1 \text{ ft.} \\ 1 \text{ T.} \end{cases}$$

Hence,

16. RULE.

Multiply by the unit of the aliquot part, and divide the product by the number of aliquot parts in the unit.

PROBLEMS.

What is the product of

1. $3\tfrac{1}{3}$ times 582 ?
2. 25 times 1,735 ?
3. 491×500 ?
4. $364 \times 1\tfrac{1}{4}$?
5. $2.015 \times 2{,}500$?
6. $7.14 \times 16\tfrac{2}{3}$?

How much must I pay

7. For $12\tfrac{1}{2}$ bu. of chestnuts, at \$3.25 a bushel ? $(12\tfrac{1}{2} = \tfrac{1}{8}$ of $100)$
8. For $83\tfrac{1}{3}$ A. of land, at \$75 an acre ? $(83\tfrac{1}{3} = \tfrac{1}{12}$ of $1{,}000)$
9. For 198 bar. of apples, at $3.33\tfrac{1}{3}$ a barrel ?
10. For 1 grt. gro. of clothes-pins, at $1\tfrac{1}{4}$ cents a dozen ?
11. For 625 bu. of potatoes, at \$.75 per bushel ?
12. For 376 bu. of corn, at $\$1.12\tfrac{1}{2}$ a bushel ?

CASE III. The multiplier 9, 99, or any number expressed by 9's.

$10 - 1 = 9$; $100 - 1 = 99$; and so on. Consequently, 10 times any number, less the number, is 9 times the number; 100 times any number, less the number, is 99 times the number ; and so on. Hence,

17. RULE.

Annex as many 0's to the multiplicand as there are 9's in the multiplier, and subtract the multiplicand from this result.

PROBLEMS.

Multiply

1. 7,496 by 99.
2. 6,842 by 999.
3. 16,971 by 9,999.
4. 80,207 by 99,999.
5. 227,641 by 999,999.
6. 26,942,781 by 99,999.

CASE **IV.** The divisor a composite number.

18. Ex.   Divide 2,905 by 35.

EXPLANATION.—Since 35 is 5 times 7, $\frac{1}{35}$ of any number is $\frac{1}{7}$ of $\frac{1}{5}$ of that number. I therefore divide 2,905 by 5 and the result by 7, and obtain 83, the required result.   Hence,

PROCESS.

$$35 = 5 \times 7$$
$$2,905 \div 5 = 581$$
$$581 \div 7 = 83$$

RULE.

Divide successively by any set of factors of the number.

PROBLEMS.

Divide
1. 40,600 by the factors of 56.
2. 2,310 by 35.
3. 179,412 by 48.
4. 27,030 by 5.4.
5. 1,720.32 by 168.
6. 100.625 by 1.25.
7. 87,444 by 2,520.

CASE **V.** The divisor an aliquot part.

Since $3\frac{1}{3}$ is $\frac{1}{3}$ of 10, 25 is $\frac{1}{4}$ of 100, 500 is $\frac{1}{2}$ of 1,000, any number contains $3\frac{1}{3}$ 3 times, 25 4 times, 500 2 times, as many times as it contains 10, 100, 1,000.

Since 1 bu. is 4 times 8 qt., 1 doz. is 3 times 4, 1 T. is 5 times 400 lb., the cost of 1 bu. is 4 times, 1 doz. is 3 times, 1 T. is 5 times the cost of 8 qt. 4. 400 lb.

19. RULE.

Divide by the unit of the aliquot part, and multiply the quotient by the number of aliquot parts in the unit.

PROBLEMS.

What is the quotient of
1. $4,280 \div 2\frac{1}{2}$?
2. $13,450 \div 500$?
3. $66,000 \div 333\frac{1}{3}$?
4. $119 \div 16\frac{2}{3}$?
5. $\$478.50 \div 12\frac{1}{2}$?
6. $\$35.48 \div \$.20$?

Find the cost
7. Of 1 box of oranges, at \$56.75 for 25 boxes.
8. Of 1 yard of muslin, at $\$1.40\frac{7}{8}$ for $12\frac{1}{2}$ yards.
9. Of 1 ton of steel, at $\$8.12\frac{1}{2}$ for 250 pounds.

10. \$4.25 is the yards of cloth, at \$1.25 ?
11. $\$13.18\frac{3}{4}$ value of pounds of butter, at \$.20 ?
12. \$9,641 how many barrels of beef, at $\$16.66\frac{2}{3}$?

§ 5. CONVERSE REDUCTIONS.

20. *Converse operations* are those arithmetical proc-esses that are the reverse of each other.

    a. Subtraction is the reverse of addition ; hence,
      Addition and subtraction are converse operations.

    b. Division is the reverse of multiplication ; hence,
      Multiplication and division are converse operations.

CASE I. **A decimal to a fraction.**

21. Any decimal may be written in two forms.

    7 tenths is .7 or $\frac{7}{10}$; 59 thousands is .059, or $\frac{59}{1000}$; 3 ten-thou-sandths is .0003, or $\frac{3}{10000}$.

In the decimal form, the unit is indicated by the position of the decimal point. In the fractional form, it is expressed by the denominator, which is 1 with as many ciphers an-nexed as there are decimal places in the decimal.

    Ex. 1. Express .125 in fractional form.   PROCESS.

      EXPLANATION.—I write the number without the decimal point for a numerator, and under it I write its denominator, 1,000.

$$.125 = \frac{125}{1000} = \frac{5}{40}$$

    Ex. 2. Reduce .083⅓ to the fractional form.   PROCESS.

$$.083\tfrac{1}{3} = \frac{83\tfrac{1}{3}}{1000} = \frac{250}{3000} = \frac{1}{12}$$

RULE.

Write the given number without the decimal point for a numerator, and under it write its denominator.

PROBLEMS.

    1. Reduce .375 to a fraction. | *4.* .1625 = what fraction ?
    2. Reduce .9125 to a fraction. | *5.* .00064 = what fraction ?
    3. Reduce .85 to a fraction. | *6.* .06875 = what fraction ?
    7. Reduce 18.75 to a mixed fractional number.
    8. .00016 of a mile = what fractional part of a mile ?
    9. .02¾ of a week is what fractional part of a week ?
    10. Reduce $.16⅔ to the fraction of a dollar.

CASE II. A fraction to a decimal.

22. Annexing decimal ciphers to the numerator of a fraction does not change its value.

Ex. Reduce $\frac{11}{16}$ to the decimal form.　　**PROCESS.**

EXPLANATION.—I first reduce the nu-　$\frac{11}{16} = \frac{11.0000}{16} = .6875$
merator 11 to ten-thousandths, by an-
nexing four decimal ciphers.

I then reduce $\frac{11.0000}{16}$, the fraction thus formed, to a decimal, by dividing its numerator 11.0000 by its denominator 16.

The result, .6875, is the required decimal.

RULE.

Annex a decimal cipher or ciphers to the numerator, and divide the number thus formed by the denominator.

When the decimal does not terminate :—
Write a fraction after the decimal figures ; or
Carry the quotient to any desired number of decimal places, and annex the sign + to it, to show that the division is incomplete.

Thus, $\frac{1}{3} = .3\frac{1}{3}$; $\frac{5}{11} = .45\frac{5}{11}$; $\frac{2}{3} = .666 +$; $\frac{3}{7} = .42857 +$.

PROBLEMS.

1. Reduce $\frac{7}{20}$ to a decimal.
2. Reduce $\frac{13}{32}$ to a decimal.
3. What decimal equals $\frac{3}{11}$?
4. Change $\frac{1}{25000}$ to a decimal.
5. Reduce $18\frac{3}{4}$ and $7\frac{3}{40}$ to mixed decimal numbers.
6. $\frac{5}{9}$ of a day is what decimal of a day?
7. Reduce $19\frac{4}{11}$ yards to a mixed decimal number.

CASE III. A denominate decimal to a compound number.

23. Ex. Reduce .75 of a yard to a compound number.

EXPLANATION.—To reduce .75 of a　　　**PROCESS.**
yard to feet, I multiply by 3, and
obtain 2.25 feet.　　　　$.75 \ yd. \times 3 = 2.25 \ ft.$

To reduce the .25 of a foot to inch-　$.25 \ ft. \times 12 = 3.00 \ in.$
es, I multiply by 12, and obtain 3　Hence, $.75 \ yd. = 2 \ ft. \ 3 \ in.$
inches.

Writing the integral parts of the results in order, I have 2 ft. 3 in., the required compound number.

In this process, the decimal part only of any result is reduced to a lower denomination.   In other respects the process is the same as the general process of Reduction Descending (Page 194).

PROBLEMS.

Reduce to compound numbers

1. .8 da.
2. .625 yd.
3. .21875 mi.
4. 21.875 bu.
5. .66⅔ gal.
6. .0019⅖ sq. yd.
7. .75 of the year 1882.
8. ⅔ of a gross ton.

CASE IV. A compound number to a denominate decimal.

24. Ex. Reduce 2 ft. 3 in. to the decimal of a yard.

EXPLANATION.—To reduce 3 inches to the decimal of a foot, I annex decimal ciphers and divide by 12; and I obtain .25 of a foot, which I write at the right of the 2 feet of the given number.

To reduce the 2.25 feet to the decimal of a yard, I divide by 3, and obtain .75 of a yard, the required decimal.

PROCESS.

$$\frac{12\ |\ 3.00\ in.}{\quad}$$
$$\frac{3\ |\ 2.25\ ft.}{.75\ yd.}$$

Hence, *2 ft. 3 in. = .75 yd.*

In this process, each quotient forms the decimal part of the next higher denomination.   In other respects, the process is the same as the general process of Reduction Ascending.

PROBLEMS.

Reduce to a denominate decimal of the next higher denomination

1. 3 pk. 5 qt. 1 pt. of grass seed.
2. 3 qt. 1¼ pt. of wine.
3. 7 doz. and 6 buttons.
4. 4 yd. 1 ft. 8 in.
5. 13 quires 6 sheets.
6. 203 ℔. 8 oz.
7. 15 h. 50 min. 24 sec.
8. 2 yd. 2 ft. 3 in.

CASE V. A denominate fraction to a compound number.

25. Ex. ⅗ of a day equals what compound number?

EXPLANATION.—To reduce ⅗ of a day to hours, I multiply by 24, and obtain 14⅖ hours.

To reduce the $\frac{2}{5}$ of an hour to minutes, I multiply by 60, and obtain 24 minutes.

Writing the hours and minutes of these results, in order, I have 14 hours 24 minutes, the required compound number.

PROCESS.

$$\frac{3}{5} \text{ da.} \times 24 = \frac{72}{5}\, h. = 14\frac{2}{5}\, h.$$
$$\frac{2}{5}\, h. \times 60 = \frac{120}{5}\, min. = 24\, min.$$

Hence, $\frac{3}{5}$ da. $= 14\, h.\, 24\, min.$

The processes in Cases V and VI are essentially the same as the general process of Reduction Descending.

PROBLEMS.

What compound number is equivalent to

1. $\frac{8}{15}$ of a gross?
2. $\frac{2}{3}$ of a square mile?
3. $\frac{11}{12}$ of an acre?
4. $1\frac{33}{64}$ bushels?
5. $\frac{1922}{2016}$ of a hogshead?
6. $\frac{3}{5}$ of a leap-year?

CASE VI. A compound number to a denominate fraction.

26. Ex. Reduce 14 h. 24 min. to the fraction of a day.

EXPLANATION.— To reduce 24 minutes to the fraction of an hour, I divide by 60; and I obtain $\frac{2}{5}$ of an hour, which I annex to the 14 hours, making $14\frac{2}{5}$ hours.

PROCESS.

$$24\, min. \div 60 = \frac{24}{60}\, h. = \frac{2}{5}\, h.$$
$$14\, h. + \frac{2}{5}\, h. = 14\frac{2}{5}\, h. = \frac{72}{5}\, h.$$
$$\frac{72}{5}\, h. \div 24 = \frac{3}{5}\, da.$$

Hence, $14\, h.\, 24\, min. = \frac{3}{5}$ da.

To reduce the $14\frac{2}{5}$ hours ($= \frac{72}{5}$ h.) to the fraction of a day, I divide by 24, and obtain $\frac{3}{5}$ of a day, the denominate fraction required.

The minutes in 14 hours 24 minutes may be made the numerator, and the minutes in 1 day the denominator of a fraction. Thus,

$$14\, h.\, 24\, min. = 864\, min.;$$
$$1\, da. = 24\, h. = 1{,}440\, min.;\ \text{and}$$
$$864\, min. = \frac{864}{1440}\, da. = \frac{3}{5}\, da.$$

PROBLEMS.

Reduce to denominate fractions the compound numbers

1. 2 qt. 1 pt. 3 gi.
2. 24 sq. ft. 18 sq. in.
3. 130 rd. 2 yd. 1 ft. 3 in.
4. 3 pk. 1 pt.
5. 24 cu. ft. 1,080 cu. in.
6. 8 h. 10 min. 21 sec.

§ **6.** PRICE, QUANTITY, AND COST.

27. In all transactions of purchase and sale, and of labor and wages, four elements are considered — viz., *price, the unit of price, quantity, and cost.*

28. *Price* is the sum paid or allowed for a unit, or for a fixed number of units of the commodity.

29. The *unit of price* is the number of units upon which the price is based.

> The unit of price may be 1 dozen, 1 hundred, 1 thousand, 1 ton, or 1 of any kind or denomination.

30. *Quantity* is the number of units or parts of a unit of the commodity.

31. *Cost* is the sum paid or allowed for the quantity.

CASE I. **Price and quantity given, to find cost.**

32. EXAMPLES.   Find the cost

1. Of $8\frac{1}{2}$ days' work, at \$2.25 per day.
2. Of 380 tomato plants, at \$1.75 per hundred.
3. Of 15,968 feet of lumber, at \$16.50 per thousand.
4. Of 8,385 pounds of iron castings, at \$40 per ton.

PROCESSES.

Ex. *1.* $8\frac{1}{2} \times \$2.25 = \$19.12\frac{1}{2}$.

Ex. *2.* $\begin{cases} \textit{380 plants} \div \textit{100} = \textit{3.80 hundred plants}; \text{ and} \\ \textit{3.8} \times \$\textit{1.75} = \$\textit{6.65}. \end{cases}$

Ex. *3.* $\begin{cases} \textit{15,968 ft.} \div \textit{1,000} = \textit{15.968 thousand ft.}; \text{ and} \\ \textit{15.968} \times \$\textit{16.50} = \$\textit{263.472}. \end{cases}$

Ex. *4.* $\begin{cases} \textit{8,385 lb.} \div \textit{2,000} = \textit{4.1925 T.}; \text{ and} \\ \textit{4.1925} \times \$\textit{40} = \$\textit{167.70}. \end{cases}$

EXPLANATIONS. The unit of price $\begin{cases} \text{in Ex. 1 is} & 1, \\ \text{in Ex. 2 is} & 100, \\ \text{in Ex. 3 is} & 1,000, \\ \text{in Ex. 4 is} & 2,000, \end{cases}$ and the number of units $\begin{cases} \text{is} & 8\frac{1}{2}. \\ \text{is} & 3.8. \\ \text{is} & 15.968. \\ \text{is} & 4.1925. \end{cases}$

I therefore find the cost, in each example, by multiplying the price by the quantity, *i. e.* by the number of units of price. Hence,

RULE.

Reduce the quantity to units of price, and multiply the price by this result.

PROBLEMS.

Find the cost

1. Of 429 barrels of flour, @ 7.06\frac{1}{4}$.

2. Of 91.88 A. of land, @ $112.50.

3. Of $\frac{7}{8}$ yd. of satin, @ $1.75.

4. Of 3,145 fence pickets, @ $2.25 per C.

5. Of 1,155 lb. of beef, @ $14.50 per C.

6. Of 15,690 ft. of lumber, @ $18.75 per M.

7. Of 85,432 bricks, @ $7.50 per M.

8. Of 2,784 pounds of hay, @ $13 per T.

9. Of 4,680 lb. of fertilizer, @ $27.50 per T.

CASE II. **Price and cost given, to find quantity.**

33. EXAMPLES.   Find the quantity that can be bought

1. Of tea for $30.73, at $.56 per pound.

2. Of beef for 44.27\frac{1}{2}$, at $11.50 per cwt.

3. Of bricks for $110.25, at $8.75 per thousand.

4. Of merchant iron for $125.46, at $85 per ton.

PROCESSES.

Ex. *1.* $\begin{cases} \textit{At \$1 a pound, \$30.73 will buy 30.73 pounds ; and} \\ \textit{30.73 pounds} \div \textit{.56} = \textit{54}\frac{7}{8} \textit{ pounds.} \end{cases}$

Ex. *2.* $\begin{cases} \textit{\$11.50} \div \textit{100} = \textit{\$.115, the price of 1 pound ;} \\ \textit{At \$1 a pound, \$44.27}\frac{1}{2} \textit{ will buy 44.27}\frac{1}{2} \textit{ pounds ; and} \\ \textit{44.27}\frac{1}{2} \textit{ pounds} \div \textit{.115} = \textit{385 pounds.} \end{cases}$

Ex. *3.* $\begin{cases} \textit{\$8.75} \div \textit{1,000} = \textit{\$.00875, the price of 1 brick ;} \\ \textit{At \$1 a brick, \$110.25 will buy 110.25 bricks ; and} \\ \textit{110.25 bricks} \div \textit{.00875} = \textit{12,600 bricks.} \end{cases}$

Ex. *4.* $\begin{cases} \textit{\$85} \div \textit{2,000} = \textit{\$.0425, the price of 1 pound ;} \\ \textit{At \$1 a pound, \$125.46 will buy 125.46 pounds ; and} \\ \textit{125.46 pounds} \div \textit{.0425} = \textit{2,952 pounds.} \end{cases}$

N

EXPLANATIONS.

The unit of price { in Ex. 1 is 1, in Ex. 2 is 100, in Ex. 3 is 1,000, in Ex. 4 is 1 T., } and the price of 1 is { $.56. $\frac{1}{100}$ of $11.50, or $.11$\frac{1}{2}$. $\frac{1}{1000}$ of $.8.75, or $.00875. $\frac{1}{2000}$ of $85, or $.0425. }

I therefore find the quantity, *i. e.* the number of units of price, by dividing the cost by the price of 1.   Hence,

RULE.

Find the price of 1, by dividing the price of a unit by the unit of price ; and then divide the cost by the price of 1.

PROBLEMS.

1. $3,029.81$\frac{1}{4}$
2. $10,336.50
3. 2\frac{13}{16}$
4. 68.78\frac{1}{4}$
5. $44.275
6. $640.74
7. 294.18\frac{3}{4}$
8. $18.096
9. $64.35

is the cost of how many

barrels of flour, at 7.06\frac{1}{4}$ per barrel ?
tons of iron, at $56.25 per ton ?
yards of ribbon, at $$\frac{5}{8}$ per yard ?
fence pickets, at $2.25 per hundred ?
pounds of beef, at $11.50 per cwt. ?
bricks, at $7.50 per thousand ?
feet of lumber, at $18.75 per thousand ?
pounds of hay, at $13 per ton ?
pounds of fertilizer, at $27.50 per ton ?

CASE III. Quantity and cost given, to find price.

34. EXAMPLES.   Find the price

1. Of 1 sewing-machine, at $2,372.50 for 65 machines.
2. Of transporting 1 cwt. of express freight from Chicago to New York, at $56.10 for 2,125 lb.
3. Of 1 thousand bricks, at 148.67\frac{1}{2}$ for 15,650 bricks.
4. Of a ton of hay, at $19.14 for 2,640 pounds.

PROCESSES.

Ex. *1.* $2,372.50 ÷ 65 = $36.50.

Ex. *2.* { *2,125 lb. ÷ 100 = 21.25 cwt. ; and* $56.10 ÷ 21.25 = $2.64. }

Ex. *3.* { *15,650 bricks ÷ 1,000 = 15.650 thousand bricks ; and* 148.67\frac{1}{2}$ ÷ 15.65 = $9.50. }

$$\text{Ex. 4.} \begin{cases} 2,640 \text{ lb.} \div 2,000 = 1.320 \text{ tons; and} \\ \$19.14 \div 1.32 = \$14.50. \end{cases}$$

EXPLANATIONS.

$$\text{The quantity or number of units} \begin{cases} \text{in Ex. 1 is } 65, \\ \text{in Ex. 2 is } 21.25, \\ \text{in Ex. 3 is } 15.050, \\ \text{in Ex. 4 is } 1.320, \end{cases} \text{and the cost of the number of units} \begin{cases} \text{is } \$2,372.50; \\ \text{is } \$56.10; \\ \text{is } \$148.67\tfrac{1}{2}; \\ \text{is } \$19.14; \end{cases}$$

I therefore find the price, in each example, by dividing the cost by the quantity, *i. e.* by the number of units of price. Hence,

RULE.

Reduce the quantity to units of price, and divide the price by this result.

PROBLEMS.

$$\begin{array}{lll}
1. \ \$3,029\tfrac{13}{16} \text{ for } 429 \text{ bar. of flour,} & & 1 \text{ barrel?} \\
2. \ \$10,336.50 \text{ for } 183.76 \text{ T. of iron,} & \text{is} & 1 \text{ ton?} \\
3. \ \$2.81\tfrac{1}{4} \text{ for } \tfrac{5}{8} \text{ bar. of kerosene,} & & 1 \text{ barrel?} \\
4. \ \$68.78\tfrac{1}{4} \text{ for } 3,057 \text{ fence pickets,} & \text{how} & 1 \text{ hundred?} \\
5. \ \$44.275 \text{ for } 385 \text{ lb. of beef,} & & 1 \text{ cwt.?} \\
6. \ \$640.74 \text{ for } 85,432 \text{ bricks,} & \text{much} & 1 \text{ thousand?} \\
7. \ \$294\tfrac{3}{16} \text{ for } 15,690 \text{ ft. of lumber,} & & 1 \text{ thousand?} \\
8. \ \$18.096 \text{ for } 2,784 \text{ lb. of hay,} & \text{for} & 1 \text{ ton?} \\
9. \ \$64.35 \text{ for } 4,680 \text{ lb. of fertilizer,} & & 1 \text{ ton?}
\end{array}$$

35. FORMULAS. $\begin{cases} \text{CASE I.} & Price \times quantity = cost. \\ \text{CASE II.} & Cost \div price = quantity. \\ \text{CASE III.} & Cost \div quantity = price. \end{cases}$

PROBLEMS.

1. 3 lb. 8 oz. of opium costs how much, @ $4.75 per lb.?

2. At $4.75 per lb., how much opium costs 16.62\tfrac{1}{2}$?

3. If 3$\tfrac{1}{2}$ lb. of opium costs 16\tfrac{5}{8}$, what is the price?

4. 755 broom handles cost how much, @ 1.12\tfrac{1}{2}$ per C?

5. At $4.50 per bar., how much kerosene costs 2.81\tfrac{3}{4}$?

6. 13,450 bricks cost how much, at $6.50 per M?

7. 5.62\tfrac{1}{2}$ buys how much wood, at $7.50 per cd.?

8. How much must I pay for 3,575 lb. of coal, at $6.50 per T.?

9. $61.68¼ for 27⁵⁄₁₂ gross of buttons, is how much per gross?

10. $237.82 for 12,826 barrel staves, is how much per C?

11. How much must a potter pay for 5,040 pounds of clay, at $16.50 per T.?

12. $250 pays for how much gas, @ $2.50 per M ft.?

13. $60.50 for 968 lb. of grapes, is how much per T.?

14. Find the cost of 59½ bu. of wheat, @ $.93¾ per bu.

15. $258 buys how much lumber, @ $24 per M?

16. How many tons of fertilizer can be bought for $111.56¼, at $28.33⅓ per ton?

17. A fruit dealer sold 47 bu. 1 pk. 2 qt. of chestnuts, at $3.25 a bushel. How much did he receive for them?

18. The water in a mill flume 1¾ rd. long, 10 ft. wide, and 6 ft. deep weighs 54 T. 281¼ lb. How much does 1 cu. ft. of water weigh?

19. I paid $8.10 for 35 lb. of ice three times per week from April 16 to Oct. 1. What was the price per C?

20. A hardware merchant sold 1,952 pounds of steel for $256.20. What was the price per ton?

21. A furniture maker paid $258.75 for ash lumber, at $45 per M. How much did he buy?

22. Find the cost of 12 pieces of French calico, averaging 36 yd. each, at $.16⅜ a yard.

23. A tanner bought a hide that weighed 97½ pounds, at 9¼c. a pound. How much did he pay for it?

24. Five loads of coal with the wagon weighed 3,219 lb., 3,074 lb., 3,621 lb., 3,342 lb., and 2,990 lb.; and the wagon weighed 964 lb. What was the value of the coal, at $5.75 per ton?

25. If one ton of ore yields 1,276.5 pounds of copper, how much ore will yield 857.8 pounds of copper?

§ 7. COMPOUND NUMBERS.

I. MONEY VALUES.

36. *Money* is the legal or recognized standard of the measure of value.

Money consists of coins, made of gold, silver, or other metal.

37. *A coin* is a piece of metal on which certain characters are stamped, by authority of the General Government, making it legally current as money.

United States coins are made of gold, silver, nickel, and bronze.

38. *Alloy* is a baser metal mixed with a finer.

    a. Pure gold or silver coins would be so soft as to perceptibly depreciate by wear. Hence, gold and silver coins are alloyed, to increase their hardness.

    b. Gold is alloyed with silver, and silver with copper.

    c. The United States gold and silver coins are .9 by weight pure metal, and .1 alloy. The alloy of gold coins consists of 9 parts, by weight, of silver and 1 part of copper ; and that of silver coins, .1 of pure copper.

    d. The bronze cent has .95 of copper and .05 of tin or zinc ; the 3-cent and 5-cent pieces, .75 of copper and .25 of nickel.

39. *Paper money* is a legal or recognized substitute for coin.

    a. *Treasury notes* are notes or bills issued by the General Government.

    b. *Bank-notes* or *bank-bills* are notes or bills issued by a banking company. (See **111,** page 316.)

40. *Currency* is the coin and paper money in circulation in trade and commerce.

Coin is commonly called *specie currency.* Treasury notes and bank-notes are commonly called *paper currency.*

41. United States Money.

Government Table.

10 mills	are 1 cent.
10 cents	" 1 dime.
10 dimes	" 1 dollar.
10 dollars	" 1 eagle.

Gold coins.—Double eagle, eagle, half eagle, 3-dollar piece, quarter eagle, dollar.
Silver coins.—Dollar, half dollar, quarter dollar, dime.
Nickel coin.—5-cent piece.
Bronze coin.—Cent.

Money value is commonly expressed in dollars and cents,—eagles being expressed as dollars, dimes as cents, and mills as fractions or decimals of a cent.

42. English Money is the money of Great Britain.

The denominations are the *pound* (£), the *shilling* (s.), the *penny* (d.), and the *farthing* (far. or qr.).

4 far.	are	1 d.
12 d.	"	1 s.
20 s.	"	1 £.

A *sovereign* is an English gold coin whose value is £1.

43. French Money is the money of France.

The denominations are the *franc* (fr.), the *decime* (dc.), the *centime* (ct.), and the *millime* (m.).

10 m.	are	1 ct.
10 ct.	"	1 dc.
10 dc.	"	1 fr.

The value of a franc is $.193.

44. Canada Money is the money of the Dominion of Canada.

The denominations are the *dollar* and the *cent*.

100 cents are 1 dollar.

20 cents are a shilling, and 5 shillings a dollar.

45. German Money is the money of the German Empire.

The denominations are the *pfennig* (penny), and the *mark*.

100 pfennige are 1 mark.

The value of a mark (Reichsmarken) is 23.85 cents.

II. MEASURES.

46. Surveyors' measures are the measures used by surveyors in measuring the boundaries, and in estimating the areas or square contents of lands.

The denominations are—(*1.*) For linear measures, the *mile*, the *chain* (ch.), and the *link* (l.); and (*2.*) For square measures, the *township*, the *square mile* or *section*, the *acre*, the *square chain*, *square rod* or *pole* (P.), and the *square link*.

47. *A Gunter's chain* is 4 rods or 66 feet long, and consists of 100 links, each 7.92 inches long. This chain is used by surveyors in measuring the boundaries of land.

Linear Measures.

100 l. are 1 ch.
80 ch. " 1 mi.

Square Measures.

625 sq. l. are 1 P. or sq. rd.
16 P.   " 1 sq. ch.
10 sq. ch. " 1 A.
640 A.   " 1 sq. mi., or sec.
36 sq. mi. " 1 Tp.

a. Since 100 links are 1 chain, 1 link is .01 of a chain, 35 links are .35 of a chain; and so on. Hence, links may be written either as hundredths of a chain, — thus, 15.44 ch.; or chains and links as a compound number; thus, 15 ch. 44 l.

b. Since a chain is 4 rods long, 25 links are 1 rod. The denomination *rod* is seldom used in linear chain measure.

c. Civil engineers on railroads and canals use an *engineers' chain*, which consists of 100 links each 1 foot long.

48. *Government lands* are commonly divided by parallels (east and west lines), and meridians (north and south lines), into townships 6 miles square.

In the same way each township is divided into 36 sections or square miles, each section into 4 quarter-sections of 160 acres each, and each quarter-section into 4 ¼-quarter-sections of 40 acres each.

a. For easy designation, convenient reference, and ready location on maps of government surveys, townships are numbered, in order, from a given parallel or base line, north; and ranges of townships from a given meridian, east or west.

b. *Tp. 25 N. of R. 6 W.* is the 25th township north of a principal base line, and in the 6th range of townships west of a principal meridian.

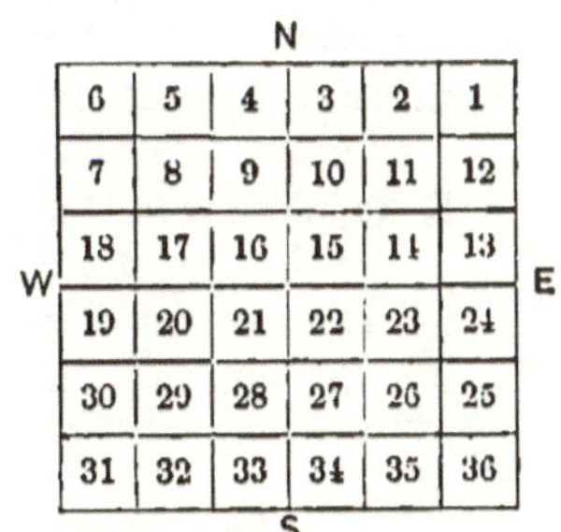

A TOWNSHIP. 6 miles square.

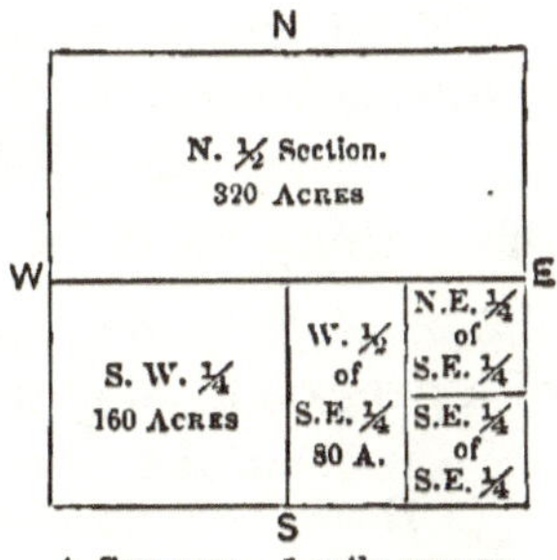

A SECTION. 1 mile square.

49. *Mariners* use the following denominations :

      6 ft.   are 1 **fathom**, in measuring depths at sea.
      120 fathoms   "   1 **cable's length**, for short distances.
      1.15 mi.   "   1 **knot**, or *nautical mile.*
      3.45 mi.   "   1 **league**, or 3 nautical miles.

50. In *geographical* and *astronomical calculations*

      1 geographic mi.   is 1.15 statute mi.
      3   "   "   are 1 league.   (l.)
      60   "   " or }   " 1 degree (deg.) of latitude, or
      69.16 statute   "   }   of longitude on the equator.

a. The knot is used in measuring the speed of vessels.

b. The nautical mile (or knot) and league are the same as the geographic mile and league.

c. The length of a degree of latitude is not quite uniform. 69.16 miles is the average length, and is the one adopted by the U. S. Coast Survey.

d. In measuring the height of horses, **4 inches are 1 hand**, the measure being taken directly over the shoulder.

e. In measuring the length   {   **6 points are 1 line.**
of clock pendulums,   { **12 lines are 1 inch.**

f. In measuring the {
length of the foot, {   **3 barleycorns or sizes, are 1 inch.**

g. The **sacred cubit** mentioned in the Bible is 21.888 inches.

h. The old road measures, 40 rd. are 1 *furlong* (**fur.**), and 8 fur. are 1 mi., are now but little used.

Circular and Angular Measures.

51. *A mathematical circle* is the area bounded by a circumference.   (See **254.**)

52. *A geographical circle* is the circumference of a mathematical circle.

53. *An angle of 1 degree* is 1 of the 360 equal angles that exactly fill the space about a common point in a plane.

54. *A geographical degree* is 1 of the 360 equal parts of a geographical circle.

      Angles are at a centre, and degrees are parts of a circumference. Hence, angles are not degrees.

55. *The measure of an angle* at the centre of a circle is that part of the circumference included between the sides of the angle.

> Since circles may be great or small, the degrees in their circumferences will be correspondingly great or small. An *angle* of 1 degree is constant; while the *measure* of the angle—*i.e.*, 1 degree in a circumference—varies with every change in the circumference of a circle.

56. Circular and angular measures are used

1. By *surveyors,* in determining the directions or bearings of land boundaries and other lines.

2. By *navigators,* in determining the position and course of vessels at sea.

3. By *geographers* and *astronomers,* in determining latitude and longitude; in determining the position and motion of the heavenly bodies; and in computing difference in time.

> The denominations of circular and angular measures are
>
> (*1.*) For surveyors and astronomers,—the *circumference*, the *quadrant* (quad.), the *degree* ($^\circ$), the *minute* ($'$), and the *second* ($''$); and
>
> (*2.*) For astronomers,—the *circle*, the *sign* (**S.**), the *degree*, the *minute*, and the *second*.

Surveyors and Navigators' Measures.			Astronomers' Measures.		
60$''$	are	1$'$.	60$''$	are	1$'$.
60$'$	"	1°.	60$'$	"	1°.
90°	"	1 quad.	30°	"	1 S.
4 quad.	"	1 circumference.	12 S.	"	1 Circle.

III. WEIGHTS.

57. *Avoirdupois weights.* Denominations in common use:

56 lb.	are 1 bu. of salt	} at the New York State Salt Works.
280 lb. (5 bu.)	" 1 bar. "	
100 lb.	" 1 cental of grain.	
100 lb.	" 1 cask of nails or raisins.	

58. Table of Avoirdupois Pounds in a Bushel,
As fixed by statutes in the States named.

	Cal.	Conn.	Del.	Ill.	Ind.	Iowa.	Ky.	La.	Mass.	Mich.	Minn.	Mo.	N.C.	N.J.	N.Y.	Ohio.	Or.	Penn.	Vt.	W.T.	Wis.
Barley	50			48	48	48	48	32	46	48	48	48	48	48	48	48	46	47	46	45	48
Beans				60	60	60	60					60			60						
Buckwheat	40	45		40	50	52	52		46	42	42	52	50	50	48		42	48	46	42	42
Clover seed				60	60	60	60			60	60	60		64	60	60	60			60	60
Indian corn	52	56	56	56	56	56	56	56	56	56	56	52	54	56	58	56	56	56	56	56	56
Oats	32	28		32	32	35	100 to 3 bu.	32	30	32	32	35	30	30	32	32	34	32	32	36	32
Potatoes		60		60	60	60	60					60		60	60		60		60	60	60
Rye	54	56		54	56	56	56	32	56	56	56	56		56	56	56	56	56	56	56	56
Timothy seed				45	45	45	45					45						44			46
Wheat	60	56	60	60	60	60	60	60	60	60	60	60	60	60	60	60	60	60	60	60	60

59. *Troy weights* are the weights used in weighing the precious metals and jewels, and in scientific experiments.

The denominations are the *pound*, the *ounce*, the *pennyweight* (**pwt.**), and the *grain* (**gr.**).

24 gr.	are	1 pwt.
20 pwt.	"	1 oz.
12 oz.	"	1 lb.

60. *Apothecaries' weights* and *measures* are weights and measures used by physicians in prescribing, and apothecaries in mixing, medicines.

The denominations are the *pound*, the *ounce* (**oz.** or ℥), the *dram* (**dr.** or ʒ), the *scruple* (**sc.** or ℈), and the *grain*.

Apothecaries' Weights.			Apothecaries' Fluid Measures.		
20 gr.	are	1 sc. or ℈	60 minims (or drops)	are	1 fluid drachm.
3 ℈	"	1 dr. or ʒ	8 fluid drachms	"	1 fluid ounce.
8 ʒ	"	1 oz. or ℥	16 fluid ounces	"	1 pint.
12 ℥	"	1 lb.	8 pints	"	1 gallon.

61. The *Government standard units* of the money, measures, and weights now in use, and from which the other denominations in the respective tables are determined, are given on the following page.

TABLES.	UNITS.	VALUES.
United States Money,	Dollar,	.900 silver, .100 alloy.
Lines, Surfaces, and Solids,	Yard,	3 feet, or 36 inches.
Liquid Measure,	Gallon,	231 cubic inches.
Dry Measure,	Bushel,	2,150.42 cubic inches.
Troy Weight,	Pound,	5,760 grains.
Avoirdupois Weight,	Pound,	7,000 Troy grains.

For ordinary purposes, 2150.4 cubic inches are called a bushel.

IV. COMPARATIVE VALUES.

62.

	DENOMINATIONS.	LIQUID MEASURE.	DRY MEASURE.
I. Of measures of capacity.	1 gal.,	231 cu. in.,	268.8 cu. in. (.5 pk.)
	1 qt.,	57.75 " "	67.2 " "
	1 pt.,	28.875 " "	33.6 " "

	DENOMINATIONS.	TROY WEIGHT.	AVOIRDUPOIS WEIGHT.
II. Of weights.	1 lb.,	5,760 gr.,	7,000 gr.
	1 oz.,	480 "	437.5 "

a. Multiplying the number of cubic inches in a liquid gallon by 7, and the number in a dry gallon by 6, we find that 7 liquid gallons contain 4.2 cubic inches more than 6 dry gallons. Hence, in ordinary computations, *it is sufficiently accurate to estimate* **7 liquid gal. = 6 dry gal.**

$$231 \times 7 = 1,617$$
$$268.8 \times 6 = 1,612.8$$

b. Multiplying the number of grains in a pound Troy by 175, and the number in a pound avoirdupois by 144, we have

$$5,760 \times 175 = 7,000 \times 144. \quad \text{Hence,}$$

175 pounds Troy = 144 pounds avoirdupois.

---

§ 8. LONGITUDE AND TIME.

63. The earth revolves east on its axis once in 24 hours, and the sun *appears* to pass west round the earth in the same time. That is, the sun *appears* to pass west over 15° in 1 hour, over 15′ in 1 minute, and over 15″ in 1 second. Hence,

The relative position to the sun, of any place on the earth, determines the time at that place.

A difference of 15° in longitude makes a difference of 1 h. in time.
    " 15′ " " " 1 min. "
    " 15″ " " " 1 sec. "

64. Longitude is reckoned east or west from a given meridian. The meridian selected for this purpose is called the *prime meridian.* The meridian generally used is that which passes through the Astronomical Observatory, Greenwich, England. Some nations also reckon longitude from the capital of their own country.

65. *Longitude, from Greenwich, of 14 important cities.*

Cities.	Longitudes.	Cities.	Longitudes.
Washington,	77° 0′ 15″ W.	Berlin,	13° 23′ 45″ E.
Philadelphia,	75° 10′ W.	Canton,	113° 14′ E.
New York,	74° 3′ W.	Cincinnati,	84° 39′ 21″ W.
Boston,	71° 3′ 30″ W.	Chicago,	87° 37′ 45″ W.
London,	5′ 38″ W.	New Orleans,	90° 2′ 30″ W.
Paris,	2° 20′ E.	St. Louis,	90° 15′ 15″ W.
Rome (Italy),	12° 27′ E.	San Francisco,	122° 26′ 45″ W.

CASE I. **Difference in time given, to find difference in longitude.**

66. Ex. The difference in time between Washington and London is 5 h. 7 min. 46 sec. What is the difference in longitude?

EXPLANATION.—Every second of difference in time makes 15″ of difference in longitude; every minute of difference in time, 15′ of difference in longitude; and every hour of difference in time, 15° of difference in longitude. Since either factor may be used as the multiplier, I multiply 5 h. 7 min. 46 sec. by 15, and obtain 76° 56′ 30″, the required difference in longitude.

PROCESS.

5 h. 7 min. 46 sec.
15
____
76° 56′ 30″

RULE.

Multiply the difference in time by 15.

The product will be the difference in longitude.

a. Mid-day, or any other given time, occurs *sooner* at any place east, and *later* at any place west of a given point. Hence,

b. Time-pieces are faster at any place east, and slower at any place west, of a given point, than they are at that point.

PROBLEMS.

Find the difference in longitude between two places, the difference in time being

1. 32 min. | *3.* 5 min. 20 sec. | *5.* 1 h. 8 min. 30 sec.
2. 54 sec. | *4.* 28 min. 45 sec. | *6.* 8 h. 12 min. 27 sec.

Find the longitude of a place whose time, compared with

Greenwich time, is | Washington time, is
7. 13 min. 20 sec. slow. | *10.* 2 h. fast.
8. 1 h. 10 min. fast. | *11.* 24 min. 52 sec. slow.
9. 6 h. 40 min. 12 sec. slow. | *12.* 9 h. 9 min. 9 sec. fast.

CASE II. **Difference in longitude given, to find difference in time.**

67. Ex. The difference in longitude between Washington and London is 76° 56′ 30″. What is the difference in time?

EXPLANATION.—Every 15° of difference in longitude makes 1 h. of difference in time; every 15′ of difference in longitude, 1 min. of difference in time; and every 15″ of difference in longitude, 1 sec. of difference in time. I therefore divide 76° 56′ 30″ by 15, and obtain 5 h. 7 min. 46 sec., the required difference in longitude.

PROCESS.

$$15)\overline{76°\ 56'\quad 30''}$$
$$5\ h.\ 7\ min.\ 46\ sec.$$

RULE.

Divide the difference in longitude by 15.
The quotient will be the difference in time.

PROBLEMS.

Find the difference in time between

1. Washington and Paris. | *4.* St. Louis and Canton.
2. Philadelphia and Rome. | *5.* Cincinnati and Berlin.
3. London and New Orleans. | *6.* Greenwich and Washington.
7–10. When it is noon at ⎰ ⎰New York,⎱ find the ⎰Boston.
11–14. 7 h. 30 min. A.M. at⎱ ⎰Chicago, ⎱ time at ⎱San Francisco.

§ **9.** METRIC SYSTEM OF MEASURES AND WEIGHTS.

68. A *meter* is a measure of length.

69. The *metric system* employs the meter as the uniform standard unit of all measures, — whether of length, area, volume, weight, or money value.

70. A *metric number* is a number by which units of successive denominations of measure, weight, or money value, are expressed in the decimal scale, or scale of 10.

Standard Units.

71. *The meter, the liter, and the gram are the three standard units of the metric system.*

   a. The *meter* is the unit of measures of length.
   It is 39.37+ inches long (or about 39⅜ inches).
   b. The *liter* is the unit of measures of volume.
   It is a cube whose edge is one tenth of a meter, or 3.937 inches.
   c. The *gram* is the unit of weight.
   It is the weight of a cube of distilled water whose edge is one hundredth of a meter, or .3937 of an inch.

72. Surfaces and volumes are simply the squares and cubes of the measures of length.

The *ar* is another name for the *square dekameter*, or 100 square meters of land; the *ster* is another name for the *cubic meter* of fire-wood; and the *tonneau* is another name for the weight of a *cubic meter* of water. Hence,

73. *Every possible dimension* (length, area, volume), *can be measured with the meter; every possible capacity with the liter; and every possible weight with the gram.*

Multiples and Divisors of the Standard Units.

74. The names of the multiples of the standard units are formed, by placing before the names of the standard units the Greek prefixes *deka, hekto, kilo.*

The names of the divisors of the standard units are formed by placing before the names of the standard units the Latin prefixes *deci, centi, milli.*

a. Deka signifies 10; hekto, 100; and kilo, 1,000.

b. Deci signifies .1; centi, .01; and milli, .001.

75. Spelling, Pronunciation, and Abbreviations of the Metric Units.

Multiple Prefixes.			Standard Units.			Divisor Prefixes.		
Spelling.	Pronunciation.	Abbreviation.	Spelling.	Pronunciation.	Abbreviation.	Spelling.	Pronunciation.	Abbreviation.
Deka	dĕka	D.	meter	meeter	m.	deci	dĕsĕ	d.
Hekto	hĕktō	H.	liter	leeter	l.	centi	sĕntĕ	c.
Kilo	kĭlō	K.	gram	grăm	g.	milli	mĭlĭ	m.
Myria	mĭrĭa	M.	ar	ar	a.			
			ster		st.			
			tonneau					

In writing metric numbers, the names of the places used correspond in meaning to the English names of the same places used in writing mixed decimal numbers. Thus,

76. All the multiples and divisors of metric numbers are in the scale of 10; they may be written as here shown.

These numbers may be read, giving name to each unit; thus, 7 Km. 6 Hm. 5 Dm. 4 m. 3 dm. 2 cm. 1 mm.; etc.

	thousands 0 Kilo	hundreds 0 Hekto	tens 0 Deka	ones or 0. ones or units	tenths 0 deci	hundredths 0 centi	thousandths 0 milli
	Km.	Hm.	Dm.	m.	dm.	cm.	mm.
Extension.—	7	6	5	4.	3	2	1 meters
	Kl.	Hl.	Dl.	l.	dl.	cl.	ml.
Volume.—	7	6	5	4.	3	2	1 liters
	Kg.	Hg.	Dg.	g.	dg.	cg.	mg.
Weight.—	7	6	5	4.	3	2	1 grams

In the same manner read

1. The numbers above, expressing volume.

2. The numbers above, expressing weight.

Any one of these numbers may be expressed in units of any one of its denominations, and read as ones and decimals of that denomination. For example,

The numbers expressing extension may be read in the denomination of the standard unit (the meter), thus: 7,654 and 321 thousandths meters.

Again,—this number may be expressed, either as millimeters, centimeters, decimeters, meters, dekameters, hektometers, or kilometers, and read accordingly.

7	6	5	4	3	2	$1^{mm.}$	
	7	6	5	4	3	$2^{cm.}$	.1
		7	6	5	4	$3^{dm.}$	.21
			7	6	5	$4^{m.}$	.321
				7	6	$5^{Dm.}$	.4321
					7	$6^{Hm.}$	.54321
						$7^{Km.}$	.654321

77. *In measuring and weighing,*

Measure all dimensions in meters, all capacities in liters, and all weights in grams, using decimals only.

78. *In computations, use*

1. Ar and *hectar* for area of land;

2. Square meter, square kilometer, square decimeter, and *square centimeter* for other areas;

3. Ster for solidity of wood;

4. Cubic meter, cubic decimeter, and *cubic centimeter,* for other volumes;

5. Tonneau for the weight of articles now estimated by the ton.

79. Metric Unit Equivalents.

A *meter* is $\frac{11}{10}$ of a yard, or a little more than 39.37 inches.

A *liter* is about .9 of a dry quart, or $1\frac{1}{18}$ liquid quarts.

A *gram* is about $\frac{1}{28}$ of an avoirdupois ounce.

A *kilogram* or *kilo* is about 2.2 pounds.

An *ar* is 3.95 square rods.

A *ster* is 35.32 cubic feet.

A *tonneau* is 2,204.6 pounds.

80. The successive units of any number expressing metric measure or weight are in the scale of 10. *Multiples* of any metric unit are expressed as integers, and *divisors* as decimals; and the metric number is written and read as other integers and decimals. Hence, *metric tables are unnecessary.*

81. Rule for Metric Notation.

Write the metric number the same as any other number in the decimal scale, with the addition of the symbol indicating the unit in which it is to be read.

82. Rule for Metric Numeration.

Read the number as a number in the decimal scale, giving to it the denomination indicated by its symbol. Or,

Read the units of each place separately, beginning at the left, and calling thousands kilo, *hundreds* hekto, *tens* deka, *tenths* deci, *hundredths* centi, *and thousandths* milli.

Exercises.

Read

1. $8^{Km.} 0^{Hm.} 5^{Dm.} 4^{m.} 3^{dm.} 5^{cm.} 2^{mm.}$
2. $5^{Kl.} 8^{Hl.} 3^{Dl.} 5^{l.} 2^{dl.} 4^{cl.} 8^{ml.}$
3. $7^{Kg.} 6^{Hg.} 1^{Dg.} 9^{g.} 4^{dg.} 7^{cg.} 3^{mg.}$
4. $9548^{m.}.263$
5. $95^{Hm.}.48263$
6. $954^{Dm.}.8263$
7. $954^{Dm.} 8^{m.}$
8. $1394^{l.}.528$
9. $13^{Hl.}.04528$
10. $130^{Dl.}.4528$
11. $130^{Dl.} 1^{l.}.528$
12. $5,278^{g.}.149$
13. $52^{Hg.}.78149$
14. $527^{Dg.}.8149$
15. $527^{Dg.} 8^{g.}.149$

Write

16. 8 kilometers 7 hektometers 3 dekameters 5 meters.

17. 5 meters 9 centimeters 4 dekameters 2 millimeters.

18. Twenty-eight thousand four hundred sixteen and five ten-thousandths centimeters.

19. Six liters six deciliters six centiliters six milliliters.

20. Three kiloliters four liters five and seven tenths deciliters.

21. Forty-one and five thousand one hundred sixty-five ten-thousandths kiloliters.

22. Thirty-seven and twenty-nine hundredths hektograms.

23. 3,869 and 218 thousandths kilograms.

24. Nine kilograms twenty-two grams three and forty-six hundredths decigrams.

83. *Metric numbers are added, subtracted, multiplied, and divided in the same manner as other decimal numbers. Hence, special rules for these processes are unnecessary.*

§ **10.** INTEREST.

I. Legal Interest.

84. ***Legal rate*** of interest is the rate allowed by law.

85. ***Usury*** is any rate of interest greater than the legal rate.

In most States, a party receiving usury is liable to a penalty.

86. Legal Rates of Interest.

States.	Rates %.	States.	Rates %.	States.	Rates %.
Alabama	8	Kentucky	6	N. C.	6 to 8
Arizona	10 to any	Louisiana	5 to 8	Ohio	6 to 8
Arkansas	6 to 10	Maine	6 to any	Oregon	8 to 10
California	7 to any	Maryland	6	Penn.	6
Colorado	10 to any	Mass.	6 to any	R. I.	6 to any
Conn.	6 to any	Michigan	7 to 10	S. C.	7
Dakota	7 to 12	Minnesota	7 to 10	Tennessee	6
Delaware	6	Mississippi	6 to 10	Texas	8 to 12
D. C.	6 to 10	Missouri	6 to 10	Utah	10 to any
Florida	8 to any	Montana	10 to any	Vermont	6
Georgia	7 to 8	Nebraska	7 to 10	Virginia	6
Idaho	10 to 18	Nevada	10 to any	Wash. T.	10 to any
Illinois	6 to 8	N. H.	6	W. Va.	6
Indiana	6 to 8	N. J.	6	Wisconsin	7 to 10
Iowa	6 to 10	New Mex.	6 to any	Wyoming	12 to any
Kansas	7 to 12	New York	6		

a. If no rate of interest is specified in written obligations involving interest, the legal rate is always understood.

b. The legal rate in any State in which two rates are given in this table, is the less of the two rates, unless a higher rate is specified. Any rate not exceeding the higher rate given is legal, if stipulated in writing.

II. Six Per Cent Method.

87. At 12% per annum, the rate per month is 1% ;
At 6% per annum ($\frac{1}{2}$ of 12%), the rate per month is $\frac{1}{2}$%.

RULE.

I. To find the per cent:—*Divide the time expressed in months by 2.*

II. To find the interest:—*Multiply the principal by the per cent.*

Or, since at 12% per annum the rate per month is 1%,—

Divide the principal by 2, and multiply the quotient by .01 of the time expressed in months.

PROBLEMS.

At 6% per annum, what is the per cent

1, 2. For 6 mo.? For 9 mo.? | *5.* For 1 yr. 6 mo.?
3. For 8 mo. 12 da.? | *6.* For 3 yr. 1 mo. 15 da.?
4. For 5 mo. 18 da.? | *7.* For 2 yr. 29 da.?

At 6% per annum, what is the interest

8–11. Of $250		4 mo. 9 da.?
12–15. Of $1,913.50	for	5 yr. 7½ mo.?
16–19. Of $629.37		4 yr. 20 da.?
20–23. Of $12,078		2 yr. 11 mo. 11 da.?

SHORT METHOD FOR DAYS OR FOR MONTHS AND DAYS.

At 6% per annum, the per cent

for 12 mo. (1 yr.)	is .06
" 60 da. ($\frac{1}{6}$ yr. or 2 mo.)	" .01
" 6 " ($\frac{1}{10}$ of 60 da.)	" .001
" 1 " ($\frac{1}{6}$ of 6 da.)	" .000$\frac{1}{6}$ or $\frac{1}{6000}$,

i. e., the per cent is $\frac{1}{6000}$ of the number of days. Hence,

88. RULE.

Divide the number of days by 6,000, and multiply the principal by this result.

Or, *Multiply the principal by a fraction whose numerator is the number of days, and whose denominator is 6,000.*

PROBLEMS.

At 6%, what is the interest of

1. $753 for 20 da.? | *5.* $10,000 for 3 da.?
2. $18,720 for 75 da.? | *6.* $500 for 18 da.?
3. $2,869.25 for 33 da.? | *7.* $21,315 for 93 da.?
4. $158.31¼ for 12 da.? | *8.* $50,000 for 1 da.?

Find the interest of	Find the interest of
9. $240 for 2 mo. 11 da.	*13.* $350.75 for 90 da.
10. $476 for 6 mo. 15 da.	*14.* $12,097 for 3 mo. 9 da.
11. $853.25 for 3 mo. 3 da.	*15.* $972 for 8 mo. 12 da.
12. $2,681.39 for 8 mo. 10 da.	*16.* $2,345.50 for 4 mo. 21 da.

III. The Six General Cases of Interest.

89. The per cent may be regarded as the product of the numbers expressing rate of interest and time (see **323,** *b.*) ; *i. e.,*

$$Per\ cent = rate\ of\ interest \times time,\ in\ years.$$

90. The terms used in interest correspond to the terms used in percentage, as shown below.

Terms used in interest.		Terms used in percentage.
Principal	*is*	*base ;*
Rate of interest	*is*	*per cent ;*
Interest	*is*	*percentage ;*
Amount (principal+interest)	*is*	*amount (base+percentage);*
Difference (principal−interest)	*is*	*difference (base−percentage).*

Considering the terms used in interest as interchangeable with those used in percentage—as given above,—

The six general cases of interest are readily deduced from the five general cases of percentage.

Case I.   Principal, rate of interest, and time given, to find interest.

91. In percentage, *base ×per cent=the percentage.* Hence,

Formula.—*Interest=principal ×per cent.*
This case has been fully considered on pages 257–264.

Case II.   Interest, rate of interest, and time given, to find principal.

92. In percentage, *the percentage÷per cent=base.* Hence,

Formula.—*Principal = interest÷per cent.*

Ex. $136.95 is the interest on what sum of money for 2 yr. 9 mo., at 6% ?

EXPLANATION.—$136.95, the interest, is the percentage; and .165, the per cent on $1 for 2 yr. 9 mo., is the per cent. I

PROCESS.

2 yr. 9 mo.=33 mo.=.165, per cent;
$136.95÷.165=$830, principal.

therefore divide $136.95, the interest or percentage, by .165, the per cent, and obtain $830, the base, which is the required principal.

PROBLEMS.

Find the principal, the interest of which

1. Is $50.75, at 5%, for 2 yr. 6 mo.

2. Is $1,748.50, at 8%, for 2 yr. 9 mo. 6 da.

3. At 6%, for 6 mo. 10 da., is $300.

4. At seven per cent for 365 days, is five cents a day.

5. For 2 yr. 4 mo. 12 da., at 6%, is $313.

6. At 4%, for 3 yr. 6 mo., is $5.11.

CASE III. **Principal, rate of interest, and time given, to find amount.**

93. In percentage, *base × (1+per cent)=amount.* Hence,

FORMULA.—*Amount=principal × (1+per cent).*

This case has been presented on pages 242, 243.

CASE IV. **Amount, rate of interest, and time given, to find principal.**

94. In percentage, *amount÷ (1+per cent)=base.* Hence,

FORMULA.—*Principal=amount÷ (1+per cent).*

Ex. What sum of money, at interest 2 yr. 9 mo., at 6%, will amount to $966.95 ?

EXPLANATION.—
$966.95, the amount of the required principal for 2 yr. 9 mo., at 6% per an-

PROCESS.

2 yr. 9 mo. = 33 mo. = .165, per cent ;
1 + .165 = 1.165, amt. of 1 ;
$966.95 ÷ 1.165 = $830, principal.

num, is the amount; and 1.165, the amount of 1 + the per cent on 1 for 2 yr. 9 mo., is the amount of 1 for the given time at the given rate. I therefore divide $966.95, the given amount, by 1.165 or by 1 plus the per cent, and obtain $830, the base, which is the required principal.

PROBLEMS.

What principal will amount

　　1. To $500.55 in 6 mo., at 7%?
　　2. To $356 in 1 yr. 4 mo., at 6%?
　　3. To $720.60 in 2 yr., at 8%?
　　4. To $135 in 10 yr., at 10%?
　　5. To $1,660.10 in 1 yr. 25 da., at 4%?
　　6. To $461.12 in 1 yr. 11 mo. 18 da., at 5%?

CASE V. Principal, interest, and time given, to find rate of interest.

95. In percentage,

The percentage ÷ *(base × per cent at 1%) = per cent.* Hence,

FORMULA.—*Rate of interest = interest ÷ (principal × per cent at 1%).*

Ex. At what rate of interest will $400 gain $60, in 2 yr. 6 mo.?

EXPLANATION.— $400, the principal, multiplied by .025, the per cent on $1 for 2 yr. 6 mo. at 1%, is

PROCESS.

$$2 \text{ yr. } 6 \text{ mo.} = 2\tfrac{1}{2} \text{ yr.} = .025, \text{ per cent at } 1\%;$$
$$\$400 \times .025 = \$10;$$
$$60 \times \tfrac{1}{10}\% = \tfrac{60}{10}\% = 6\%.$$

$10. Since $10 is the interest at 1% for the given time, $1 is the interest at $\tfrac{1}{10}$ of 1%, and $60 must be the interest at 60 times $\tfrac{1}{10}$ of 1%, or $\tfrac{60}{10}\%$, or 6%, which is the required rate of interest.

PROBLEMS.

Find the rate at which the interest

　　1. Of $36.50 for 4 yr. 5 mo. 26 da. is $7.373.
　　2. Of $278 for 3 yr. 5 mo. 12 da. is $47.95¼.
　　3. Of $311.50 for 1 yr. 4 mo. is $24.92.
　　4. Of $57.92 for 3 yr. 7 mo. 9 da. is $12.54.
　　5. Of $273.51 for 2 yr. 20 da. is $50.60.
　　6. Of $1,950 for 5 yr. 4 mo. is $364.

CASE **VI. Principal, interest, and rate of interest given, to find time.**

96. *Per cent = rate of interest × time;* and
Interest = principal × rate of interest × time.   Hence,

FORMULA.—*Time = interest ÷ (principal × rate of interest).*

Ex. In what time will $400 gain $60, at 6%?

EXPLANATION.—$400, the principal, multiplied by .06, the rate of interest, is $24, the interest on the principal for 1 year. If $1 were the interest for 1 year, $60 would be the interest for 60 years. But since $24 is the interest for 1 year, $60 is the interest for $\frac{1}{24}$ of 60 years, which is $\frac{60}{24}$ years, or 2½ years, or 2 yr. 6 mo., the required time.

PROCESS.

$$\$400 \times .06 = \$24;$$
$$\tfrac{60}{24} \; yr. = 2\tfrac{1}{2} \; yr. = 2 \; yr. \; 6 \; mo.$$

PROBLEMS.

In what time
1. Will $125 gain $13.29 interest, at 6%?
2. Will $150 gain $18.75, at 5%?
3. At 4½%, will $100 gain $100?
4. Will any sum double itself, at 1% a month?
5. At 10%, will $15,000 lose $750?
6. Will $340.25 gain $20.84, at 7%?

PROBLEMS IN THE SIX GENERAL CASES OF INTEREST.

1. The interest on a note at 9%, for 1 yr. 8 mo., is $42. For what sum was the note given?

2. May 5, I borrow $1,725 in Detroit, Mich., and pay it Nov. 15, with interest. How much do I pay?

3. A note for $600.50 and interest is dated, Cleveland, O., July 26, 1881. What amount is due Jan. 26, 1884?

4. What is the semi-annual interest of a mortgage for $4,375, on a house in Baltimore, Md.?

5. Sept. 3, 1884, a Kansas farmer pays $1,477.59, the amount of a mortgage on his farm, dated April 7, 1882. For what sum was the mortgage given?

6. What sum must be put at interest, at 6%, that a boy 15 yr. 4 mo. old may receive $2,010. when 21 years old?

7. In 4 years I am to receive $800. What sum should I receive now to cancel the claim, money being worth 5%?

8. A man in Pittsburgh, Pa., paid $134.40 for the interest on a mortgage of $420. How long had the mortgage run?

9. A young lady had $1,600 at interest, at 6%, until it amounted to $2,000. What was the time?

10. I paid $4.60 interest on a loan of $276, for 2 mo. 15 da. What rate of interest did I pay?

11. A lady whose expenses are $1 a day, has $9,125 in money. At what rate must she loan it, that the interest will pay her expenses?

12. A South Carolina planter paid $22.40 interest on a loan for 9 mo. 18 da. What was the loan?

13. I received $98.28 interest for 1 yr. 8 mo. 24 da. on a loan, at 7%. What was the sum loaned?

14. Oct. 31, 1882, a San Francisco lawyer collected a debt of $840, which had been due since May 29, 1880. What was the amount collected?

15. Philadelphia, Jan. 28, 1882, I paid $1,698.50, the amount of a note dated Sept. 18, 1878. For what sum was the note given?

16. April 4 of this year a Denver, Col., merchant paid a note dated June 27 of last year, for $3,650 and interest. What amount did he pay?

17. A Missouri lumberman paid $103.68 interest, at the highest legal rate, for a loan of $684. What was the time?

18. I bought a pair of horses for $450, and sold them at 20% advance, receiving in payment a note due in 1 yr. 3 mo. 15 da., at 6% interest. Eight months afterward I sold the note for $550. What rate of interest did I receive on the note? If the note was paid at maturity, what rate of interest did the buyer of the note receive on his investment?

IV. Exact Interest.

97. A year is either 365 or 366 days. A calendar month consists of 28, 29, 30, or 31 days; hence, a calendar month is never exactly $\frac{1}{12}$ of a year. But a day is either $\frac{1}{365}$ or $\frac{1}{366}$ of a year; and the exact interest for any number of days is always such a part of the interest for a year as the number of days is part of the year. Hence,

98. Rule.

I. *Compute the interest for one year by the general method.*

II. *Multiply the interest for one year by the time expressed in years and 365ths or 366ths of a year.*

99. Formula.—*Exact interest* $= \begin{cases} Prin. \times rate \times time\ in\ yr.\ and \\ 365ths\ or\ 366ths\ of\ a\ year. \end{cases}$

Problems.

Find the exact interest

Of	from	to	at the rate in
1. $84.25	March 1, 1885	Jan. 15, 1886,	Illinois.
2. $400	June 15	Aug. 24, 1885,	Indiana.
3. $3,225	Feb. 3, 1881	Sept. 2, 1882,	California.
4. $1,852.60	Oct. 10, 1885	Jan. 1, 1888,	Louisiana.
5. $7,325	Jan. 2, 1885	Nov. 30, 1887,	Virginia.
6. $32,782.52	July 20, 1882	Dec. 24, 1886,	Massachusetts.
7. $22,064.60	Jan. 8	May 15, 1884,	Michigan.
8. $8,673	April 10	May 1, 1883,	Pennsylvania.
9. $15,000 for 1 day of the year 1884,			New York.

10. $2,000 for 152 days of the year 1885, at 5%.

11. $6,500 from May 1, 1885 to Aug. 10 of the present year.

12. $9,355.25 from April 4 to July 7, 1884, at the rate in Colorado.

13. $867.40 for 63 days of a common year, at $4\frac{1}{2}\%$.

14. $91.65 for 93 days of a leap-year, at the rate in Texas.

15. $100,000 for three days of the year 1888, at 15%.

O

§ **11.** BUSINESS PAPER.

100. Business paper consists of written or printed documents, used as representatives of money value.

The principal classes of business paper are *notes, due-bills, orders, drafts,* and *receipts.*   (For forms, see pages 360–362.)

101. An *indorsement* of any business paper is a writing upon it, that

1. Assigns or transfers ownership; or
2. Gives security for the fulfilment of the obligation; or
3. Acknowledges a partial payment.

An indorsement is usually written on the back of the paper.

102. Negotiable paper is any business paper that may be transferred, with or without indorsement.

103. A promissory note is a paper that acknowledges a debt, and promises payment at a specified time, unconditionally.

1. The *maker* of a note is the person who signs it.

2. The *payee* is the person to whom the note is payable.

.3. The *indorser* is the party who writes his name upon the back of the note, as security for its payment.

4. *Days of grace* are three days allowed after the time named in the note has expired, before the note is legally due.

5. *Maturity* is the last day of grace.

  a. When the third day of grace falls on Sunday or on a legal holiday, the note matures on the second day of grace.

  b. The banks of Delaware, Maryland, Missouri, Pennsylvania, and Washington City charge interest for the day on which a note is discounted, and the day on which it matures,—making the interest period practically one day longer than in other States.

  c. In nearly all the States days of grace are allowed on all negotiable paper due at a future time.

6. The *face* of a note is the principal, or the sum named in the body of the note.

It does not include interest.

§ **12.** DISCOUNT.

104. *Discount* is a deduction from a selling price, or from an account, or from any obligation before it is due.

105. The *present worth* or *proceeds* of an obligation is its face minus the discount.

Discount is of three kinds, *commercial discount, bank discount,* and *true discount.*

I. Commercial Discount.

106. *Commercial discount* is a percentage deducted from the list price of goods, or from the gross amount of bills or other obligations, without regard to time.

a. *Per cent off* is another name for commercial discount.

b. The *proceeds* or *net value* of a bill is the gross amount minus the percentage.

107. Ex. Bought a bill of goods amounting to $487 at list prices, 15% off. What was the net value of the goods?

Process.

$$\$487 \times .15 = \$73.05, \text{ commercial discount; and}$$
$$\$487 - \$73.05 = \$413.95, \text{ net value;}$$

Or,

$$1 - .15 = .85, \text{ net rate; and } \$487 \times .85 = \$413.95, \text{ net value.}$$

108. In computations in commercial discount,

a. *Invoice price or amount of obligation = base;*

b. *Per cent off = per cent;*

c. *Commercial discount = percentage.*

109.
FORMULAS.
I. *Obligation × % off = commercial discount.*
II. *Obligation − commercial discount = proceeds.*
Or, III. *Obligation × net rate = proceeds or net value.*

Problems.

What is the commercial discount on a bill of goods

1. Invoiced at $300, sold on 3 mo., $2\frac{1}{2}\%$ off for cash?

2. Invoiced at $1,250, sold on 4 mo., 5% off for cash?

3. For \$862.50, sold on 90 da., $3\frac{1}{4}\%$ off for cash ?

4. For \$219.75, sold on 60 da., $2\frac{1}{8}\%$ off for cash ?

Find the { *5.* A book, the list price being \$2.50, 30% off.

cost of { *6.* A box of glass, list price \$8.90, 60% and 25% off.

7. 1 gross of fruit cans, at \$1.50 per doz., 40% and 5% off.

8. A case of boots (12 pairs), list price \$33, $16\frac{2}{3}\%$ and 3% off.

Find the commercial discount, and the cash proceeds, of invoices of goods of the following amounts:

9. Of \$852, sold on 60 days, 3% off for cash.

10. Of \$972.83, sold on 3 months, 4% off for cash.

11. Of \$1,500, sold on 30 days, commercial discount $1\frac{3}{8}\%$.

12. Of \$2,450, sold on 90 days, commercial discount 3%.

II. Bank Discount.

110. A *bank* is a chartered institution that receives and loans money, or issues bank-bills that circulate as money.

a. A *bank of issue* is one that issues notes or bank-bills.

b. A *bank of discount* is one that lends money, by discounting notes.

c. A *savings-bank* is one that receives money on deposit, paying interest on the sums deposited; and loans its deposits, by discounting notes with real-estate securities.

d. Some banks combine two of these kinds of business; and some, all of them.

111. *Bank-bills* or *bank-notes* are promissory notes issued by banks, and are payable on demand.

A *bankable note* is a promissory note payable at a bank.

112. *Bank discount* is interest paid in advance for the loan of money on a note.

113. The *term of discount* is the time from the date of the loan to the maturity of the note.

a. Bank discount is payable on the day of making the loan ; while legal interest is payable when the paper matures.   Hence,

b. *Bank discount exceeds legal interest, by interest on the legal interest for the term of discount.*

114. The ***proceeds*** of a bankable note are its face, minus the bank discount.

115. A ***protest*** is a written notice to the indorser of a note, informing him that the note has been presented to the maker, at maturity, for payment, and has not been paid; and that the holder looks to the indorser for payment of the note.

   a. *To hold an indorser responsible, a protest must be served on him on the last day of grace, unless he has written " protest waived " below his name.*

   b. Protests are usually made out and served by a ***notary public.***

116. Ex. Find the proceeds of a note for $2,500, due in 4 months, at 6%.

PROCESS.

$$4 \text{ mo. } 3 \text{ da. } = 4.1 \text{ mo.}$$
$$\$2,500 \times .06 = \$150, \text{ int. for 1 yr.}$$
$$\frac{\$150 \times 4.1}{12} = \$51.25, \text{ bank discount.}$$
$$\$2,500 - \$51.25 = \$2,448.75, \text{ proceeds.}$$

117. In computations in bank discount,

   a. *Face of note = principal, or base;*

   b. *Interest on face = bank discount, or percentage;*

   c. *Proceeds = face — bank discount, or difference.*

118. FORMULAS. $\begin{cases} \text{I. } \textit{Face} \times \textit{rate of interest} = \textit{bank discount;} \\ \text{II. } \textit{Face} - \textit{bank discount} = \textit{proceeds.} \end{cases}$

PROBLEMS.

What is the bank discount on a note

   1. For $250 due in 3 mo., at 10%?

   2. For $81.50 due in 6 mo., at 8%?

   3. For $1,640 due in 15 da., at 6%?

   4. For $2,375 due in 60 da., at 7%?

   5. For $495 due in 4 mo., at 5%?

Find the proceeds of bankable notes discounted as follows:

   6. $600 for 30 da., at 6%. | *8.* $3,500 for 4 mo., at 6%.

   7. $321 for 90 da., at 8%. | *9.* $418.50 for 10 da., at 10%.

Find the bank discount, and the proceeds, of notes as follows:

   10. $500 for 90 da., at 6%. | *12.* $10,000 for 4 mo., at 7%.

   11. $850.31 for 60 da., at 5%. | *13.* $1,250 for 2 mo., at 8%.

III. True Discount.

119. *True discount* is the amount of an obligation due at a future time, minus the present worth.

   a. *Equitable discount* is another name for true discount.

   b. The *equitable present worth* of an obligation due at a future time, is a principal, which, at a given rate of interest, will amount to the obligation.

120. In computations in true discount,

   a. *Sum to be discounted = the face, or the amount;*

   b. *Present worth = base, or principal;*

   c. *Amount — present worth = true discount, or percentage.*

The process of finding the present worth is therefore the same as Case IV, p. 309. Hence,

121. FORMULAS. $\begin{cases} I. \textit{Present worth} = \textit{amount} \div (1 + \textit{per cent}). \\ II. \textit{Discount} = \textit{amount} - \textit{present worth}. \end{cases}$

Ex. Find the true discount, at 6%, on $375.70 due in 8 mo.

EXPLANATION.—$375.70, the sum due in 8 mo., is the face; and 1.04, the amount of 1 plus the rate on 1 for 8 mo., is 1 + the per cent.

PROCESS.

$$8 \text{ mo.} = .04, \textit{per cent; and}$$
$$1 + .04 = 1.04, \textit{amt. of } 1;$$
$$\$375.70 \div 1.04 = \$361.25;$$
$$\$375.70 - \$361.25 = \$14.45.$$

I therefore divide $375.70, the sum to be discounted, by 1.04 or 1 plus the per cent, and obtain $361.25, the present worth. I then subtract $361.25, the present worth, from $375.70, the sum to be discounted, and obtain $14.45, the required true discount.

PROBLEMS.

1. What is the true discount on $100, due in 2 mo., at 6%?

2. On $854 due in 7 mo. 18 da., at 10%?

3. On $69.50 due in 1 yr. 6 mo., at 7%?

4. On $732.25 due in 4 mo. 23 da., at 6%?

What is the present worth $\begin{cases} \textit{5. Of } \$1,000 \text{ due in 2 yr., at } 5\%? \\ \textit{6. Of } \$3,500 \text{ due in 8 mo. 24 da., at } 6\%? \\ \textit{7. Of } \$1,275 \text{ due in 1 yr. 10 mo. 15 da., at } 10\%? \\ \textit{8. Of } \$91.42 \text{ due in 8 mo. 20 da., at } 6\%? \end{cases}$

Find the true discount on, and the present worth of, a note

9. For $925 due in 1 yr. 8 mo., discounted at 6%.

(See page 314, Article 103, c.)

10. For $2,992.54 due in 7 mo., discounted at $4\frac{1}{2}$%.

11. For $600 due in 4 yr., discounted at 5%.

12. For $560 due in 1 yr. 6 mo., discounted at 7%.

PROBLEMS IN DISCOUNT.

1. What is the net cash cost of a bill of goods amounting to $957.60, on 4 months time, 5% off for cash?

2. At 6% per annum, what is the discount for the present payment of a note for $1,375.70, due in 9 months?

3. What will be the proceeds of a note for $4,500, due in 6 months, discounted at a bank in San Francisco?

4. A broker buys a 6 months note, at 8% discount, and pays $2,250 for it. What is the face of the note?

5. Bought a bill of goods amounting to $1,890, on 8 months; and cashed it at a discount of 10% off for 30 days, and a further discount of 5% for cash. What was the net cash cost of the goods?

6. A Western dealer buys carriages in New Haven, Conn., amounting to $4,440, on 4 months, or 5% off for cash. How much will he make by borrowing the money at a New Haven bank, and cashing the bill?

7. For what sum must I draw my note, at 4 months, to borrow $2,685 at a bank in Baltimore?

8. An immigrant buys a Kansas farm for $950; terms $500 cash, balance in 2 years without interest. In 8 months he pays the balance, less 9% discount. How much does he pay?

9. Jan. 9 I took a note for $344 due in 9 months with interest. March 19 a bank in St. Paul, Minn., discounted the note for me. How much did I realize from the note?

10. What is the difference between discounting a bill of goods at 25% and 10% off, and discounting the same bill at 10% and 25% off?

§ **13.** COMPOUND INTEREST.

Interest is sometimes made payable annually, semi - annually, or quarterly, with the agreement between parties concerned that, if not paid when due, it is to be added to the principal, and the two are to form a new principal.

122. Compound interest is the interest on a principal formed by adding interest to a former principal.   Hence,

I. *The amount of the principal for the first interest term (i. e., for 1 yr., 6 mo., etc.) is the principal for the second interest term ; the amount of this principal for the second interest term is the principal for the third interest term ;* and so on.

II. *The final amount, minus the first principal, is the compound interest for the whole time.*

Ex. What is the compound interest of $372.50 for 2 years, at 6%.

EXPLANATION.—Since the amount of any interest term is the product of the principal multiplied by 1 plus the rate, I multiply the principal, $372.50, by 1.06, and obtain $394.85, the amount for 1 year. I multiply this amount by 1.06, as before, and obtain $418.54, the amount for 2 years. Then subtracting the principal, $372.50, from this amount, I have $46.04, the required interest.

PROCESS.

$372.50	*Prin.*
1.06	*1 + rate.*
$394.85	{ *Amt. for 1 yr., or Prin. for 2d yr.*
1.06	*1 + rate.*
$418.54	*Amt. for 2 yr.*
372.50	*Prin.*
$46.04	*Int.*

PROBLEMS.

At compound interest, what is the amount

1, 2. Of $624.45 for 3 years, at 6% ?   At 5% ?

3, 4. Of $25.75 for 4 yr. 2 mo., at 6% ?   At 4% ?

The required amount is the amount of the given sum for 4 years, plus the interest of this amount for 2 months.

5. Of $856.75 for 2 yr., at 4%, int. payable semi-annually ?

6. Of $364.50 for 2½ yr., at 6%, int. payable quarterly ?

What is the compound interest

   7, 8. Of \$781 for 5 years, at 7%?   At $3\frac{1}{2}$%?

   9. Of \$459.26 for $3\frac{1}{4}$ yr., at 4%, interest payable quarterly?

   10. Of \$437.50 for $1\frac{1}{2}$ yr., at 5%, interest due semi-annually?

   11. Of \$575 for 1 year, at 1% a month?

   12. What is the difference between the simple and the compound interest of \$4,275 for 6 years, at 4%?

SAVINGS-BANK ACCOUNTS.

123. Savings-banks add to each depositor's account, at the end of each interest term, the interest due on his deposits.

   a. With some savings-banks the interest term is 6 months; with some, 3 months; and with some, 1 month.

   b. Most savings-banks allow interest only on sums that have been on deposit a full interest term.

   c. The smallest balance on deposit at any one time during an interest term, is the sum on which interest is computed at the end of the term.

Ex. Interest at 4% per annum, payable semi-annually Jan. 1 and July 1, how much was due Jan. 1, 1883, on the following account?

Mechanics' Savings Institution in Acc't with Robt. Williams.

Dr. Cr.

1881					1881				
July	1	To Cash,	231	50	Nov.	10	By Check,	87	50
Sept.	15	" "	95	—					
Dec.	1	" "	50	—					
188					1882				
March	20	" Draft,	69	25	Jan.	5	" "	12	—
May	9	" Cash,	20	—	April	18	" "	44	—
July	1	" "	30	75	Aug.	25	" Draft,	110	75
Oct.	12	" Check,	24	—					
Nov.	27	" Cash,	7	50	1883				
					Jan.	1	" Check,	8	25

O 2

§ **14.** PARTIAL PAYMENTS.

I. National Method.

124. ***A partial payment*** is a payment of a part of an obligation that is due, or that is drawing interest.

125. U. S. Court Rule for Partial Payments.

I. *From the amount of the principal, computed to the time when the payment or the sum of the payments equals or exceeds the interest due, subtract the payment or the sum of the payments.*

II. *The remainder is a new principal, with which proceed as before.*

Ex. April 10, 1880, a note was given for $840, at 6% interest. Payments were made Jan. 19, 1881, of $185 ; and Nov. 3, 1881, of $30. What was due Jan. 5, 1882 ?

Explanation.—I first find the amount of the principal from the date of the note to Jan. 19, 1881, the time of the first payment, to be $879.06. Subtracting $185, the payment, from this amount, I obtain a remainder of $694.06 for a new principal. $30, the second payment, made Nov. 3, 1881, did

Process.

1881 yr.	1 mo.	19 da.		1882 yr.	1 mo.	5 da.
1880	4	10		1881	1	19
9 mo.	9 da.			11 mo.	16 da.	

$$9 \text{ mo. } 9 \text{ da.} = 9.3 \text{ mo.} = .0465, \text{ per cent.}$$
$$1 + .0465 = 1.0465, \text{ amt. of } 1.$$
$$\$840 \times 1.0465 = \$879.06, \text{ amt.}$$
$$\$879.06 - \$185 = \$694.06, \text{ new prin.}$$
$$11 \text{ mo. } 16 \text{ da.} = 11.5\tfrac{1}{3} \text{ mo.} = .057\tfrac{2}{3}, \text{ per cent.}$$
$$1 + .057\tfrac{2}{3} = 1.057\tfrac{2}{3}, \text{ amt. of } 1.$$
$$\$694.06 \times 1.057\tfrac{2}{3} = \$734.08, \text{ amt.}$$
$$\$734.08 - \$30 = \$704.08, \text{ bal. due.}$$

not exceed the interest due ; and I next find the amount of $694.06, from Jan. 19, 1881, to Jan. 5, 1882, which is $734.08. Subtracting from this amount $30, the payment made Nov. 3 1881, I have $704.08, the required amount due Jan. 5, 1882.

CONDENSED FORM OF WRITTEN WORK.

Dates.			Interest Periods.			Amts. of 1.	Principals.	Amounts.	Pay'ts.
1880 yr. 4 mo. 10 da.									
to '81	1	19	9 mo. 9 da.	=	9.3 mo.	1.0465	$840	$879.06	$185
' '82	1	5	11 16	=	11.5¼ mo.	1.057¼	694.06	734.08	30
							704.08		

PROBLEMS.

1. A store was sold in Indianapolis, Ind., for $4,750; payments, $2,100 cash, $1,200 in one year, and the balance in two years. How much was the last payment?

2. Memorandum:—Nov. 26, 1880, gave a note for $1,780, at 6%. June 25, 1881, paid $160; Nov. 1, 1881, paid $525. How much was due March 11, 1882?

3. On a note for $450, dated Louisville, Ky., April 15, 1881, $200 was paid Jan. 24, 1882. What amount was due Nov. 8, 1882?

4. A mortgage for $12,500, dated Detroit, Mich., Oct. 31, 1879, bears the following

Indorsements:—May 28, 1880, $900; Jan. 1, 1881, $650; July 14, 1881, $375; Nov. 29, 1881, $745; Aug. 11, 1882, $530.

What amount was due Jan. 22, 1883?

5. $765.   Springfield, Mass., *March 14, 1880.*

On demand, I promise to pay to Thomas Emerson, or order, Seven Hundred Sixty-five Dollars, with interest, for value received.

                              Nathaniel Parker.

Indorsements:—Oct. 31, 1881, $50; June 11, 1882, $285. Find the balance due, Sept. 25, 1882.

6. $2,500.   Washington, D.C., *Dec. 3, 1881.*

One year after date, we promise to pay to George D. Palmer, or order, Two Thousand Five Hundred Dollars, with interest, for value received.

                              Robinson, Clark & Co.

Indorsements:—July 2, 1882, $350; Nov. 8, 1882, $675. What was the balance due March 18, 1883?

126. When settlements are made within a year after interest commences, the computations of interest are often made by the

II. MERCANTILE RULE FOR PARTIAL PAYMENTS.

I. Compute the interest on the principal for the whole time.

II. Compute the interest on each payment, from its date to the time of settlement.

III. Subtract the amount of the payments from the amount of the principal.

In making computations by this rule, exact interest for days is commonly considered.

PROBLEMS.

1. If I borrow $1,250 for 1 yr., at 6%, and pay $625 in 155 da., how much do I owe at the end of the year?

2. On a mortgage for $3,125, dated July 5, 1880, a payment of $1,450 was made Dec. 31 of the same year. What amount was due Jan. 17, 1882, interest at 6%?

3. June 7, 1881, I borrowed $8,000, at $4\frac{1}{2}$%. Jan. 28, 1882, I paid $3,500; and Aug. 14, 1882, $2,750. How much was due Feb. 3, 1883?

III. ANNUAL INTEREST.

127. In some States, a written obligation containing the words "with interest annually," or "with annual interest," is a legal contract on the part of the maker of the obligation, to pay simple interest on the principal at the end of each year, whether the principal, or any part of it, is due or not. If the maker fails to pay the interest at the end of each year, the law allows to the holder, in the nature of damages, simple interest on the unpaid yearly interests, until they are paid; but it does not allow interest on these interests.

128. *Annual interest* is simple interest upon the principal, and upon each year's interest of the principal, due and unpaid.

129. Ex. 1. A note for $850, with interest annually, was taken up at the end of 5 years. How much interest had accrued?

Full Solution.

Interest due on principal at the end of each year, $850 × .06 = $51
1 yr.'s int. draws simple int. for 4 yr. + 3 yr. + 2 yr. + 1 yr. = 10 yr.
10 yr. at 6% = 10 × .06 = .60, per cent.
Simple int. on 1 yr.'s int. for 10 yr., $51 × .60 = $ 30.60
Interest on principal for 5 yr., $850 × .06 × 5 = 255

Total interest, $285.60

Ex. 2. What is the interest of $350 for 4 yr. 8 mo. 12 da., interest payable annually?

Full Solution.

Interest due on principal at the end of each year, $350 × .06 = $21
1 yr.'s int. draws simple int. for 3 yr. 8 mo. 12 da. + 2 yr. 8 mo.
12 da. + 1 yr. 8 mo. 12 da. + 8 mo. 12 da. = 8 yr. 9 mo. 18 da.
8 yr. 9 mo. 18 da. at 6% = 105.6 mo. = .528, per cent.
Simple int. on 1 yr.'s int. for 105.6 mo., $21 × .528 = $ 11.09
4 yr. 8 mo. 12 da. = 56.4 mo. = .282, per cent.
Interest on principal for 56.4 mo., $350 × .282 = 98.70

Total interest, $109.79

Hence, when interest is payable annually, the total interest of any sum of money for any given time is made up of

I. *The interest on the principal for the whole time;*

II. *The simple interest on one year's interest for the sum of the periods of time the several yearly interests remain unpaid.*

Problems.

At 6%, interest payable annually, find the interest of

1. $800 for 5 years.	*4.* $172 for 3 yr. 3 mo. 3 da.
2. $241 for 4 yr. 2 mo.	*5.* $387.50 for 5 yr. 4 mo. 15 da.
3. $124 for 6 yr. 8 mo.	*6.* $574.45 for 3 yr. 9 mo. 14 da.

7. $96.84 from Nov. 27, 1880, to July 10, 1884.

8. $1,000.46 from April 1, 1880, to July 10, 1885.

At 6%, interest payable annually, what is the amount

9. Of a note for $600, which has run 4 yr. 3 mo. 15 da. ?

10. Of a mortgage of $2,000, for 2 yr. 7 mo. 20 da. ?

11. Of $520 from Oct. 10, 1882, to the present day ?

IV. SPECIAL STATE LAWS FOR PARTIAL PAYMENTS.

130. VERMONT.

When notes, bills, or other obligations draw annual interest, and any part or the whole of this interest remains unpaid,—

I. Payments draw interest to the end of the yearly interest terms in which they are made.

II. The amount of any payment or payments made in any interest terms is applied

　　1st.—To cancel interest due on unpaid yearly interests ;

　　2d.—To cancel unpaid yearly interests ;

　　3d.—To cancel the principal.

　　The interest on the last unpaid balance must be computed to the date of settlement.

131. NEW HAMPSHIRE.

Payments not exceeding interest due at the end of the year, and made expressly on account of interest accruing but not yet due, do not draw interest.   At the end of the year they must be applied to the payment of the interest then accrued.

In all other respects the law is the same as in Vermont.

132. CONNECTICUT.

I. When a year's interest or more has accrued at the time of a payment, or when any payment is less than the interest due, and also in case of the last payment, the interest is computed by the U. S. Court Rule.

II. When less than a year's interest has accrued at the time of any payment, except the last, the amount of the payment from its date to the end of the full year is deducted from the amount of the principal for the full year ; the remainder is the new principal for the next interest term.

　　NOTE.—Pupils in any of these three States should be required to solve all the problems in partial payments (page 323) by the special law for their State.

§ **15**. BONDS.

133. A *bond* is a written obligation from one party, securing to another the payment of a given sum, at or before a specified time, with interest payable annually, semi-annually, or quarterly.

    a. Bonds are issued for the purpose of borrowing money.

    b. The principal bonds bought and sold by brokers are *government, state, city,* and *railroad bonds.*

United States securities or government bonds are designated as *registered* bonds and *coupon* bonds.

134. A *registered bond* is one that is recorded on the books of the Treasury Department at Washington, as the property of a certain person.

135. A *coupon* is an interest certificate attached to a bond.

136. A *coupon bond* is a bond to which coupons are attached.

    When the interest on a coupon bond is paid, a coupon is detached, by the holder, and given up as a receipt.

Bonds are usually named from the authority that issued them and the rate of interest they bear.

    Virginia 6's are bonds bearing 6% interest, issued by the State of Virginia.

Brokerage is $\frac{1}{8}$% to $\frac{1}{4}$% of the par value of stocks and bonds.

LIST OF THE PRINCIPAL U. S. BONDS OUTSTANDING JAN. 1, 1882.

Names of Bonds.	When Redeemable.	Rates of Interest.	Interest Payable.
Four-and-a-halfs of 1891	After Sept. 1, 1891.	$4\frac{1}{2}$%	Quarterly.
Fours of 1907	After July 1, 1907.	4%	Quarterly.
Three-and-a-halfs	At option of Gov't.	$3\frac{1}{2}$%	
U. S. Pacific RR. currency sixes	July 1, 1892, and July 2, 1894.	6%	Semi-annually.
Currency sixes	1895 to 1899	6%	Semi-annually

137. In compu- tations in bonds

a. *Par value or face of bond = base ;*
b. *Rate of premium or discount = per cent ;*
c. *Market value = amount or difference.*
Hence,

138. Formulas.

I. *Market value = face of bond* $\times \begin{cases} 1 + \textit{rate of premium, or} \\ 1 - \textit{rate of discount.} \end{cases}$

II. *Face of bond = mark t value* $\div \begin{cases} 1 + \textit{rate of premium, or} \\ 1 - \textit{rate of discount.} \end{cases}$

III. *Rate of premium = (market value − face) ÷ face.*

IV. *Rate of discount = (face − market value) ÷ face.*

Problems.

Find the market value of the following securities:

1. Of Panama RR. 500-dollar bonds, at 67, brokerage $\frac{1}{2}\%$.

2. Of Government $4\frac{1}{2}$'s of 1907, at $118\frac{1}{8}$, brokerage $\frac{1}{8}\%$. How many 100-dollar bonds can be bought

3. For $21,535, of Tenn. 5's, at 91, brokerage $\frac{1}{4}\%$?

4. For $3,944, of N. J. Central RR., at $115\frac{3}{4}$, brokerage $\frac{1}{4}\%$?

5. For $21,540, of Central Pacific RR., at $89\frac{5}{8}$, brokerage $\frac{1}{8}\%$?

6. For $7,048, of Mich. 7's, at 110, brokerage $\frac{1}{8}\%$?

Which is the better investment, and how much the better,—

7. Michigan 7's of '90, at 115; or Missouri 6's, at 112?

8. Georgia sevens, at 119; or Virginia sixes, at 116?

9. 5% bonds, at 102 ; or $3\frac{1}{2}\%$ bonds, at $87\frac{1}{8}$?

10. Government fours, at 102 ; or four-and-a-halfs, at 113?

11. How much will 3 1,000-dollar Government four-and-a-halfs cost, at $8\frac{1}{4}\%$ premium?

12. A capitalist invested $20,352 in New York City bonds, at 4% discount. What amount in bonds did he receive?

13. Currency 6's at 105, will pay what % on investment?

14. I invest $20,500 in Virginia sixes, at 111. The annual interest is what per cent on the investment?

§ **16.** EQUATION OF PAYMENTS.

139. *Equation of payments* is the process of finding the time for paying, in one sum, several debts due at different times, without loss to debtor or creditor.

a. The *term of credit* is the time that must elapse before a debt matures.

b. The *equated time* is the time for paying, in one sum, several debts due at different times.

140. Ex. Find the equated time for the payment of $300 due in 2 mo., $500 due in 4 mo., and $200 due in 6 mo.

Full Solution.

Int. of $300 for 2 mo. = int. of $1 for 300 × 2 mo., or 600 mo.
"   "   500 " 4 " = "   " 1 " 500 × 4 " "2,000 "
"   "   200 " 6 " = "   " 1 " 200 × 6 " "1,200 "
"   "$1,000 " ? " = "   " 1 " 1 thousandth of 3,800 "
3,800 mo. ÷ 1,000 = 3.8 mo. = 3 mo. 24 da., equated time. Hence,

Rule.

Multiply each term of credit by the number expressing the payment; and divide the sum of the products by the number expressing the sum of the payments.

The result will be in the same denomination of time as the given terms of credit.

Problems.

1. Find the equated time for the payment of $200 due in 3 mo., $240 due in 3½ mo., and $320 due in 5 mo.

2. I owe $425 due to-day, $150 due in 6 months, and $275 due in 9 months, and I wish to give one note due at the equated time. On what date must the note be made payable?

3. Jan. 1, a merchant owes the sums named in the margin, and he gives his note for the entire amount payable in one sum, at the equated time. When does the note mature?

$ 700	due Mar. 15.
250	" Apr. 1.
825	" Apr. 15.
1,000	" May 10.
1,425	" June 1.

§ **17**. EXCHANGE.

141. ***Exchănge*** is a transaction in which a party in one place pays money to a party in another place, by an order upon a third party, and without the transmission of money.

> **a.** ***Domestic*** or ***inland exchange*** relates to remittances made between places in the same country.

> **b.** ***Foreign exchange*** relates to remittances made between places in different countries.

142. A ***draft*** or ***bill of exchange*** is a written order for money, drawn in one place and payable in another.

> EXAMPLE.—A party in Cleveland, wishing to pay a creditor in New York, buys at a Cleveland bank a draft on a New York bank, payable to the order of the party in New York. The Cleveland party sends this draft to his creditor in New York, and the latter indorses it, presents it to the New York bank, and receives the face of the draft in money.

143. *A* ***sight draft*** is a draft payable at sight, *i. e.,* when presented.

144. *A* ***time draft*** is a draft payable at a future time named in it.

> **a.** Grace is allowed on time drafts, but not on sight drafts.
> **b.** Time drafts are subject to bank discount for the term of credit given.
> **c.** Any creditor may give a draft, or *draw* on a debtor.

NOTE.—See forms of drafts, page 362.

145. The parties to a transaction in exchange are the *drawer* or *maker*, the *buyer* or *remitter*, the *drawee*, and the *payee*.

1. The ***drawer*** or ***payer*** is the party who signs or issues the draft.

2. The ***buyer*** or ***remitter*** is the party who purchases the draft.

3. The ***drawee*** is the party on whom the draft is drawn.

4. The ***payee*** is the party to whose order the draft is made payable.

> The maker and remitter, or the remitter and payee, may be the same party; in either of which cases there will be but three parties to the transaction.

146. An *acceptance* is a written promise of the drawee to pay the draft at maturity.

> A drawee accepts a draft, by writing across its face *Accepted,* followed by his name. This acceptance makes him responsible for the payment of the draft at maturity.

147. The ***balance of trade*** between places or countries is the difference between the amounts due to and from each place or country by the other.

> EXAMPLE.—St. Louis owes New York $12,375,000, and New York owes St. Louis $10,500,000. The balance of trade between the two cities is $1,825,000 against St. Louis and in favor of New York. In this case, in St. Louis, exchange on New York is at a premium; and in New York, exchange on St. Louis is at a discount

Drafts are bought *at par, at a premium,* or *at a discount.*

148. *Rate of exchange* is the difference between the face of a draft and its cost.

> The rate of exchange is affected by the condition of the balance of trade between the two places concerned.

In computations in exchange

a. *Face of draft = base.*
b. *Rate of exchange = per cent.*
c. *Premium or discount = percentage.*

d. *Cost of draft =* $\begin{cases} Amount\ or \\ difference. \end{cases}$
e. *Face minus bank discount = proceeds of time draft.*

Hence, *any problem in exchange comes under one or more of the cases in percentage.*

149.
FORMULAS.

$$\text{I. } Face \times \begin{cases} 1 + rate\ of\ premium,\ or \\ 1 - rate\ of\ discount, \end{cases} = Cost.$$

$$\text{II. } Cost \div \begin{cases} 1 + rate\ of\ premium,\ or \\ 1 - rate\ of\ discount, \end{cases} = Face.$$

SUPPLEMENT.

Problems.

Find the cost of a sight draft

1. For $250, at $\frac{1}{2}$% premium.
2. For $456.50, at $2\frac{1}{2}$% premium.
3. For $1,325 at 15% premium.
4. For $631, at $2\frac{1}{2}$% discount.
5. For $389, at 15% discount.
6. For $2,750, at $1\frac{1}{2}$% discount.

Find the face of a sight draft which cost

7. $116.44, at $1\frac{1}{4}$% premium.
8. $1,000, at $\frac{1}{8}$% premium.
9. $835.62, at $\frac{1}{2}$% discount.
10. $3,521, at $2\frac{3}{8}$% discount.

On a time draft, compute both the discount and the rate of exchange, on the face of the draft.

Find the cost of a draft

11. For $500, at 60 da., premium at $\frac{1}{2}$%, interest 4%.
12. For $1,732, at 30 da., premium $\frac{5}{8}$%, interest 6%.
13. For $2,000, at 10 da., discount $\frac{1}{4}$%, interest 1% per mo.

14. How much will it cost me to make a remittance of $1,750 from Boston to Charleston, exchange on Charleston being at $98\frac{1}{2}$% (*i. e.*, at $1\frac{1}{2}$% discount)?

15. How much must a man in St. Louis pay for a sight draft on Boston for $532, exchange being $102\frac{1}{4}$?

16. A merchant in Burlington, Iowa, wishing to remit to a creditor in Philadelphia, buys a draft at $\frac{5}{8}$% premium, and pays $2,460 for it. What is the face of the draft?

17. A lawyer in Wheeling, W. Va., having $745.50 belonging to a client in Denver, purchases a sight draft with it on a Denver broker, at 103. What is the face of the draft?

18. What must I pay in Cincinnati for a draft on New York for $2,400, payable 60 days after sight, exchange on New York being $100\frac{5}{8}$?

19. I paid a San Francisco banker $6,117 for a draft on New York, payable 30 days after date, when exchange on New York was at 3% premium. What was the face of the draft?

20. A broker in Boston pays $1,352.62 for a draft payable at Columbus, Ohio, 30 days after sight, at $98\frac{1}{4}$. What is the face of the draft?

§ 18. RATIO AND PROPORTION.

I. RATIO.

150. *Ratio* is the relative value of two like numbers, expressed by the quotient of the first divided by the second.

The ratio of 12 to 4 is 3 $(12 \div 4 = 3)$; of $24 to $6 is 4.

Ratio is always expressed by an abstract number.

151. The *terms* of a ratio are the numbers whose values are compared.

a. The *antecedent* is the first term.

b. The *consequent* is the second term.

c. In expressing the ratio of 12 to 4, 12 and 4 are the *terms* of the ratio, 12 is the *antecedent*, and 4 is the *consequent*.

d. The terms of a ratio are called a **couplet.**

152. The *sign* of ratio is the colon (:), written between the terms. It is read "the ratio of."

12 : 4 is read "the ratio of 12 to 4."

Ratio may also be expressed in the form of a fraction, the antecedent being written for the numerator, and the consequent for the denominator. Thus, $12 : 4 = \frac{12}{4}$.

EXERCISES.

Read

1. $32 : 8 = 4.$
2. $\frac{32}{8} = 4.$
3. 56 men : 7 men $= 8.$
4. 7 men : 56 men $= \frac{1}{8}.$
5. 40 bu. : 16 bu. $= 2\frac{1}{2}.$
6. 16 bu. : 40 bu. $= \frac{2}{5}.$

Express, in both forms, the ratio

7. Of 12 to 4.
8. Of 49 to 7.
9. Of 5 to 30.
10. Of 9 to 72.
11. Of $.48 to $.06.
12. Of $9 to $15.
13. Of 28 yd. to 4 yd.
14. Of 5 lb. to $62\frac{1}{2}$ lb.
15. Of 1,756.25 mi. to 28.1 mi.

153. A *simple ratio* is a ratio that has but one antecedent and one consequent.

154. A *compound ratio* is the ratio of the products of the like terms of two or more simple ratios.

The simple ratio of 16 : 4 is $\frac{16}{4}$, or 4;

"   "   "   "   9 : 3 " $\frac{9}{3}$, or 3;

"compound"   " $\left\{ \begin{array}{c} 16 : 4 \\ 9 : 3 \end{array} \right\}$ is $\frac{16}{4} \times \frac{9}{3}$, or 4×3, or 12.

155. Rules for Finding Ratios.

I. To find a simple ratio :—*Divide the antecedent by the consequent.*

II. To find a compound ratio :—*Divide the product of the antecedents of all the simple ratios by the product of all the consequents.*

> *If the terms of a ratio are denominate numbers, reduce them to the same denomination.*

Problems.

Find the ratio

1. Of 45 to 15.	*4.* Of 12 h. to 16 h.	*7.* 3.5 mo. : 24.5 mo.
2. Of 14 to 112.	*5.* Of $1.25 to $6.25.	*8.* 35 da. : 4 da. 9 h.
3. Of 29 to 8.	*6.* Of $17\frac{1}{2}$ yd. to $2\frac{1}{2}$ yd.	*9.* 1 gal. 1 qt. : 10 gal.

Find the unknown number in each of the following expressions :

	Antecedent.	Consequent.	Ratio.		Antecedents.	Consequents.	Ratio.
10.	1,275	425	—		5 :	8	
11.	$300	$—	.75	*13.*	— :	3	=90
12.	— rd.	5 ft.	66		30 :	5	

Which is the greater, the ratio

14. Of 16 to 24, or the ratio of 28 to 84 ?

15. Of 4 ft. to 3 yd., or the ratio of 96 rd. to 1 mi. ?

16. The antecedents of a compound ratio are 12, 4, and 8 ; and the consequents are 36, 11, and 21. What is the compound ratio?

17. Compound the ratios 5 : 8, 72 : 3, 30 : 5.

18. The antecedents are $\frac{1}{21}$, $\frac{2}{3}$, and $\frac{3}{4}$; and the consequents are $\frac{2}{8}$, 6, and $\frac{21}{24}$. What is the compound ratio?

II. Simple Proportion.

156. **Proportion** is an equality of ratios.

157. **Simple proportion** is an equality of two simple ratios.

> Since the ratio of 15 to 3 equals the ratio of 10 to 2, these two ratios form the proportion, 15 : 3 :: 10 : 2.

158. The **sign** of proportion is the double colon (::), written between the ratios.   It is read "as" or "equals."

    a. The proportion $15:3::10:2$ is read "15 is to 3 as 10 is to 2," or "the ratio of 15 to 3 equals the ratio of 10 to 2."

    b. Proportion may also be expressed by the sign of equality. Thus, $15:3=10:2$.

159. Four numbers are required to express a simple proportion.

    a. The **extremes** of a proportion are the first and fourth terms.

    b. The **means** of a proportion are the second and third terms.

    Writing the proportion $12:4::15:5$ in the fractional form, and reducing the expressions to similar fractions—keeping the factors separate—we have

$$\frac{12}{4}::\frac{15}{5}=\frac{12\times5}{4\times5}::\frac{15\times4}{5\times4}$$

The factors 12 and 5 of the first numerator are the extremes of the given proportion; the factors 15 and 4 of the second numerator are the means; and the products of these two sets of factors are equal.   Hence,

160. Principle.—*The product of the extremes equals the product of the means.*

Applying General Problems XIV, XV, XVI, page 104, to this Principle, we have the following

161. Formulas.
$$\text{I.}\quad \frac{Extreme \times extreme}{either\ mean} = the\ other\ mean.$$
$$\text{II.}\quad \frac{Mean \times mean}{either\ extreme} = the\ other\ extreme.$$

The **solution of a proportion** is the process of finding one of its terms, when the other three are given.

Problems.

Find the unknown term in each of these 20 proportions:

1. $6:30::7:-$.	*3.* $6:8::-:12.$	*5.* $-:10::18:5.$
2. $1:3::4:-.$	*4.* $4:-::3:9.$	*6.* $9:-::3:5.$

7. $12 : 9 :: 16 : —$	14. $10\frac{1}{2} : 8\frac{3}{4} :: — : 7.$
8. $18 : 24 :: 24 : —$	15. $— : \frac{7}{12} :: \frac{9}{16} : \frac{3}{16}.$
9. $5 : 9 :: — : 8.$	16. $\$.16 : \$.48 :: —\,qt. : 3\ qt.$
10. $10 : — :: 21 : 14.$	17. $10\ lb. : —lb. :: 15 : 6.$
11. $— : 21 :: 35 : 15.$	18. $—oz. : 12\ oz. :: \$4 : \$9.$
12. $40 : — :: 8 : 5.3.$	19. $21 : — :: 9\ yd. : 3\ yd.$
13. $12.5 : 5 :: 27 : —$	20. $12\ mi. : 2\ mi. :: 19 : —$

162. From the preceding problems it will be seen that

The first term of a proportion is greater or less than the second, according as the third term is greater or less than the fourth.

163. In any problem in simple proportion three terms are given, and a fourth term is required.

   a. Two of the three given terms are like numbers; and the ratio of these two terms equals the ratio of the other known term and the required term.

   b. *To make a statement* in proportion, is to arrange the three given terms, so that two of them form one ratio; the remaining term and the required term, another ratio; and the ratios, a proportion.

Ex. If 16 acres of land produce 424 bushels of wheat, 27 acres will produce how many bushels?

EXPLANATION. — 16 acres and 27 acres form the first ratio, and 424 bushels and —— bushels form the second ratio. Since 16 acres are less than

PROCESS.

$$16\ A. : 27\ A. :: 424\ bu. : — bu.$$

$$\frac{27 \times \overset{53}{\cancel{424}}\ bu.}{\underset{2}{\cancel{16}}} = \frac{1431\ bu.}{2} = 715\tfrac{1}{2}\ bu.$$

27 acres, 424 bushels—produced from 16 acres—must be less than the number of bushels produced from 27 acres. I therefore write 424 bushels for the first term of the second ratio, or the third term of the proportion; and, since this term is less than the required term, I write 16 acres—the less of the two given like numbers—for the antecedent of the first ratio, and 27 acres for the consequent.

Solving the proportion, I have 715½ bushels, the required term.

If 424 bushels are made the consequent of the second ratio, 16 acres must be the consequent of the first ratio, and the required number of bushels will be the third term. Thus,

27 A.: 16 A. :: — bu. : 424 bu.

164. RULE FOR SIMPLE PROPORTION.

I. For the third term :— *Write the number that is of the same kind as the required term.*

II. For the first ratio :— *Write the other two numbers, the greater for the second term, when the required term is to be greater than the third term; and the less for the second term, when the required term is to be less than the third term.*

III. To find the fourth or required term :—

Multiply the second and third terms together, and divide the product by the first term.

a. *When necessary, reduce the terms of the first ratio to the same denomination, before solving the proportion.*

b. *Cancel all like factors from the given extreme and either mean.*

PROBLEMS.

Find the cost

1. Of 32 bu. of lime, at $14.25 for 57 bu

2. Of 9½ lb. of beef, at $1.78½ for 12¾ lb.

3. Of 11 yd. of broadcloth, when 6 yd. cost $30.75.

4. Of a barrel of flour, when 23 pounds cost $1.15.

5. Of 27 rm. 6 quires of paper, at $13.87½ for 11 rm. 2 quires.

6. Of 9⅜ cd. of wood, if 15.75 cd. cost $94.50.

7. Of 7 centals of wheat, @ $1.15 a bushel.

8. Of 3.25 tons of hay, when 2.9 tons cost $24.65.

9. Of 44½ gal. of milk, if 53 gal. 3 qt. cost $2.68.

10. If a carriage wheel makes 802 revolutions in running 3 mi. 60 rd. 12 ft., how many revolutions will it make in running 25 mi. 15 rd. 12 ft.?

11. If 475 yards of sheetings are made from 209 pounds of cotton, how many yards of sheetings can be made from 645 pounds of cotton?

12. If an ocean steamer runs 2,337 mi. in 10 da. 6 h., how many miles will she run in 5 da. 9 h. ?

13. The interest on a certain sum of money for 4 mo. 13 da. is $139.59. What is the interest on the same sum for 5 mo. 18 da. ?

14. How high is a church spire whose shadow is 119 ft. long, when a flag-staff 45 ft. high casts a shadow $56\frac{1}{4}$ ft. long ?

15. If there are 16 lb. of oxygen in 18 lb. of water, how much oxygen is there in 75 lb. of water ?

16. If $21\frac{1}{4}$ qt. of milk are required for $5\frac{2}{3}$ lb. of cheese, how many quarts will be required for 10.5 lb. ?

17. What is the cost of $\frac{3}{4}$ of an acre of land, at the rate of $187.50 for $\frac{5}{8}$ of an acre ?

18. The liabilities of a bankrupt merchant are $18,900, and his assets are $8,344. How much will a creditor receive on a debt of $2,250 ?

19. How much will $.87\frac{1}{2}$ of a barrel of apples cost, at $1 for $\frac{5}{8}$ of a barrel ?

20. If $5\frac{1}{2}$ cd. of limestone will produce 450.56 bu. of lime, how many cords of stone will be required to produce $1,663\frac{3}{4}$ bu. of lime ?

21. Bought 16 pieces of merino, each piece containing $42\frac{1}{2}$ yd., at the rate of $36.45 for 27 yd. What did it cost ?

22. I borrowed of a friend $675 for 8 months ; afterward I lent him $450. How long must he keep the loan, to balance the favor ?

23. If $8\frac{1}{2}$ tons of coal cost $46.75, what will 4 tons cost ?

24. At $$\frac{3}{8}$ for $\frac{3}{4}$ yd. of cloth, what is the value of $16\frac{1}{2}$ yd. ?

25. If a bird can fly $9\frac{3}{5}$ miles in $\frac{1}{6}$ of an hour, how far can it fly in $9\frac{4}{7}$ hours, at the same rate ?

26. If 8 men mow a meadow in 5 days, in how many days will 3 men mow it ?

27. If 300 sheep require 150 A. 156 sq. rd. of pasture, how many acres will 850 sheep require ?

28. If 156 pocket-knives cost $168, how much will 57 cost ?

III. Compound Proportion.

165. Compound Proportion is an equality of a compound and a simple ratio, or of two compound ratios.

$$\left.\begin{array}{c} 4:8 \\ 12:3 \end{array}\right\} :: 10:5, \text{ and } \left.\begin{array}{c} 4:8 \\ 12:3 \end{array}\right\} :: \left\{\begin{array}{c} 6:12 \\ 8:2 \end{array}\right. \text{ are compound proportions.}$$

166. A compound ratio is reduced to a simple one, by multiplying all the antecedents together for a new antecedent, and all the consequents together for a new consequent. (See ***155***.) Hence, the principle (***160***) applies equally to compound proportion.

PROBLEMS.

Find the unknown term in each of the following proportions :

$$1.\ \left.\begin{array}{c} 4:12 \\ 9:18 \end{array}\right\} :: 3:\text{—}$$

$$2.\ \left.\begin{array}{c} 12:3 \\ 3:4 \\ 4:5 \end{array}\right\} :: 5\tfrac{1}{4}:\text{—}$$

$$3.\ \left.\begin{array}{c} \$10:\$.06 \\ \$6:\$8 \end{array}\right\} :: 15 \text{ oz.}:\text{— oz.}$$

$$4.\ \left.\begin{array}{c} 40:\ 8 \\ 7:105 \end{array}\right\} :: \text{—}:6\tfrac{1}{4}.$$

$$5.\ \left.\begin{array}{c} \text{—}:21 \\ 48:1.6 \\ 1.5:.2 \end{array}\right\} :: 8\tfrac{3}{4}:2\tfrac{1}{10}.$$

$$6.\ \left.\begin{array}{c} 12:3 \\ 4:25 \end{array}\right\} :: \left\{\begin{array}{c} 28:\text{—} \\ 20:5. \end{array}\right.$$

167. Ex. If 6 weavers weave 81 yards of cassimere in 9 hours, how many yards will 10 weavers weave in 8 hours ?

EXPLANATION. — Since the required term is yards, I write 81 yards for the first term of the second ratio, or the third term of the proportion.

The required number of yards depends upon the number of weavers, and the number of hours, and the number of hours.

PROCESS.

$$\left.\begin{array}{c} 6 \text{ weavers} : 10 \text{ weavers} \\ 9 \text{ hours} : 8 \text{ hours} \end{array}\right\} :: 81 \text{ yd.}:\text{— yd.}$$

$$\frac{\overset{5}{\cancel{10}} \times 8 \times \overset{3}{\cancel{9}}\ \overset{9}{81}\ yd.}{\underset{2}{\cancel{6}} \times \cancel{9}} = 120 \text{ yd.}$$

and the number of hours. I therefore arrange the other given numbers in pairs, as the terms of the compound ratio. Thus, 6 weavers weave 81 yards, 10 weavers will weave more; hence, 6 weavers : 10 weavers; and in 9 hours they weave 81 yards, in 8 hours they will weave less; hence 9 hours : 8 hours.

Having made the statement, I solve the proportion, and obtain 120 yards, the required term.

168. Rule for Compound Proportion.

I. For the third term : — *Write the number that is of the same kind as the required term.*

II. For the compound ratio : — *Write each two of the given numbers that are of the same kind, as a couplet, always considering whether or not an answer depending upon these two terms alone would be greater or less than the third term, and if greater, write the greater of the two for the second term; but if less, write the less of the two for the second term.*

III. To find the fourth or required term :—

Multiply all the second and third terms together, and divide the product by the product of the first terms.

Adapt remarks *a*, *b*, after rule for simple proportion, *164*, to apply to compound proportion.

Note.—In solving problems, many teachers write the second and third terms on the right of a vertical line, and the first terms on the left—as here shown—in preference to writing them above and below a horizontal line.

$$
\begin{array}{c|ccc}
 & 81\,yd. & 9\,yd. & 3\,yd. \\
2\,6 & 10 & 5 & \\
9 & 8 & & \\
\hline
1 & 120\,yd. & &
\end{array}
$$

Problems.

1. If the floor of a room 13 ft. 6 in. by 18 ft. cost $12.16, what is the cost of the floor of a room 15 ft. 9 in. by 16 ft. 6 in. ?

2. If a cistern-pump factory, running 10 hours per day, makes 3,060 pumps in 27 days, how many pumps will the same factory make in 63 days, running 12½ hours per day ?

3. I paid $675 for a building lot 3⅝ rd. front by 11 rd. deep. Afterward I bought another lot 3½ rd. front by 13¾ rd. deep, at the same rate. How much did I pay for the second lot ?

4. A pile of gypsum stone, 1,225 ft. long, 12 ft. wide, and 4 ft. high, was drawn to a plaster mill by 10 teams in 21 days. At the same rate, how many days will it take 8 teams to draw a pile 1,607 ft. long, 16 ft. wide, and 5 ft. high ?

5. If $93.87 is the interest of $360 for 3 yr. 8 mo. 21 da., $13.02 is the interest of what principal for 1 yr. 6 mo. 18 da.?

6. In building a tight board fence 1 mi. long and 11 ft. high, around a fair ground, 480 8-inch boards were used. How many 10-inch boards will be required to build a fence 2,730 yd. long and 8 ft. high?

7. If 5 men make 150 pairs of boots in 6 days, how many pairs will 3 men make in 4 days?

8. An investment of $800 gains $70 in 15 months. At the same rate, how much will an investment of $356 gain in 8 months?

9. If 2,100 ft. of $1\frac{1}{4}$-inch flooring is required for the floors of a certain house, how much $1\frac{1}{2}$-inch flooring will be required for the floors of another house $2\frac{1}{4}$ times as long and $1\frac{1}{2}$ times as wide?

10. Four railroad passengers rode 36 mi., 60 mi., 72 mi., and 96 mi. respectively. They paid in proportion to the distances they rode, and the sum of their fares was $9.24. How much did each man pay?

11. The capacity of a bin 24 ft. long, 4 ft. 6' wide, and 4 ft. 8' deep is 405 bushels. What is the capacity of a bin $10\frac{1}{2}$ ft. long, 6 ft. wide, and 5 ft. deep?

12. If 3 men dig 453 bushels of potatoes in a week, how many bushels can 2 men dig in 5 days?

13. If 3 men can lay a sidewalk 240 ft. long and 6 ft. wide, in 15 days, in how many days can 5 men lay a walk 180 ft. long and 4 ft. wide?

14. A pile of 4-foot wood 244 feet long and 5 feet high, was sold for $152.50. What was the price per cord?

(8 ft. by 4 ft. by 4 ft. =1 cd.)

15. If in 16 days of 9 hours each, 9 bricklayers lay a wall 96 ft. long, 21 ft. high, and $1\frac{1}{4}$ ft. thick, in how many days of $11\frac{1}{4}$ hours each can 12 bricklayers lay a wall 126 ft. long, 28 ft. high, and $1\frac{1}{2}$ ft. thick?

§ **19.** POWERS AND ROOTS.

I. INVOLUTION.

169. A *power* is the product of equal factors.

  a. The *second power* or *square* is the product of two equal factors.

  b. The *third power* or *cube* is the product of three equal factors.

  c. The second power or square of 4 is 16 $(=4\times4)$;
  and the third power or cube of 4 is 64 $(=4\times4\times4)$.

170. *Involution* is the process of finding powers.

171. The *sign* of involution is an *index* or *exponent,* which is a small figure placed at the right of, and above, a number.

An exponent shows the required power of a number. Thus, 21^2 signifies the square of 21; 3.5^3 signifies the cube of 3.5.

172. Complete and learn the following table:

Numbers.	1	2	3	4	5	6	7	8	9
Squares.	—	—	—	—	—	—	—	—	—
Cubes.	—	—	—	—	—	—	—	—	—
Numbers.	.1	.2	.3	.4	.5	.6	.7	.8	.9
Squares.	—	—	—	—	—	—	—	—	—
Cubes.	—	—	—	—	—	—	—	—	—

PROBLEMS.

Find the following indicated powers:

1. 47^2	*4.* 901^3	*7.* $(\tfrac{3}{8})^2$	*10.* $.17^3$
2. 63^2	*5.* 218^2	*8.* $(\tfrac{5}{9})^3$	*11.* 20.16^2
3. 12^3	*6.* 139^3	*9.* $(15\tfrac{2}{3})^2$	*12.* $(1.03)^3$

II. EVOLUTION.

173. A *root* of a number is one of the equal factors that produce the number.

  a. The *square root* of a number is one of the two equal factors that produce the number.

  b. The *cube root* of a number is one of the three equal factors that produce the number.

  c. The square root of 64 is 8 $(64=8\times8)$;
  and the cube root of 64 is 4 $(64=4\times4\times4)$.

174. *Evolution* is the process of finding roots.

175. The *sign* of evolution is $\sqrt{}$; it is called the *radical sign.*

 a. $\sqrt{}$ placed before a number, indicates that the square root of the number is to be found.

 b. $\sqrt[3]{}$ placed before a number, indicates that the cube root of the number is to be found.

 c. $\sqrt{25}$ indicates that the square root of 25 is to be found ; and $\sqrt[3]{64}$ indicates that the cube root of 64 is to be found.

 d. A *perfect power* is a number whose exact root can be found.

 e. An *imperfect power* is a number whose exact root can not be found.

III. Extraction of the Square Root.

176. *Extraction of the square root* is the process of finding one of the two equal factors that produce a number.

 The least and the greatest integer that can be expressed by one figure are, respectively, 1 and 9; and by two figures 10 and 99.
 The least and the greatest decimal that can be expressed by one figure are, respectively, .1 and .9; and by two figures, .01 and .99.
 The squares of these numbers are

$$1^2 = 1 \qquad 10^2 = 100 \qquad .1^2 = .01 \qquad .01^2 = .0001$$
$$9^2 = 81 \qquad 99^2 = 9{,}801 \qquad .9^2 = .81 \qquad .99^2 = .9801$$

 Comparing these numbers with their squares, we see that

1. The square of an integer

expressed by $\left\{ \begin{array}{l} \text{one figure} \\ \text{two figures} \end{array} \right\}$ is expressed by $\left\{ \begin{array}{l} \text{one or two figures.} \\ \text{three or four figures.} \end{array} \right.$

2. The square of a decimal

expressed by $\left\{ \begin{array}{l} \text{one figure} \\ \text{two figures} \end{array} \right\}$ is expressed by $\left\{ \begin{array}{l} \text{two figures.} \\ \text{four figures.} \end{array} \right.$

and so on, of greater numbers.   Hence,

177. Principle I. *The square of any integer is expressed by twice as many figures as the integer, or one less than twice as many ; and the square of any decimal is expressed by twice as many decimal figures as the decimal.*

 From this principle it is evident that *the number of two-figure periods in a number equals the number of places in its square root.*

Squaring the integers 2, 20, and 25; and 9, 90, and 99; and the decimals .9, .25, and .99, we have

$$2^2 = 4 \qquad 9^2 = 81 \qquad .9^2 = .81$$
$$20^2 = 400 \qquad 90^2 = 8,100 \qquad .25^2 = .0625$$
$$25^2 = 625 \qquad 99^2 = 9,801 \qquad .99^2 = .9801$$

Separating the squares into two-figure periods, and comparing the numbers with their squares, we see that

1. The square of the left-hand digit is wholly in the left-hand period.   And

2. The square of the left-hand digit is the greatest square in the left-hand period.   Hence,

178. Principle II. *The square of the left-hand order of units of a number is wholly in the left-hand period of the power, and is the greatest square in that period.*

179. To determine the parts that make up the square of a number, we will square 56 by different processes.

$56 = 50 + 6$; and $56^2 = 56 \times 56$, or $50 + 6$ multiplied by $50 + 6$.

FIRST PROCESS.	SECOND PROCESS.	THIRD PROCESS.

$$
\begin{array}{rll}
56 = & 50 + 6 = & 50 + 6 \\
56 = & 50 + 6 = & 50 + 6 \\ \hline
336 = & 300 + 36 = & (50 \times 6) + 6^2 \\
280 = {}& 2,500 + 300 = 50^2 + & (50 \times 6) \\ \hline
3,136 = & 2,500 + 600 + 36 = 50^2 + 2 \times & (50 \times 6) + 6^2
\end{array}
$$

In the first process 56 is squared by the common method of multiplication.

In the second process the products of the units of the different orders are written separately.

In the third process the factors that make up the different parts of the product are kept separate, the multiplications and additions being indicated only.   This third process fully illustrates

180. Principle III. *The square of a number regarded as tens and ones equals the square of the tens, plus two times the product of the tens and ones, plus the square of the ones.*

The several steps, in their order, in extraction of the square root, are based on the three principles now given.

181. Ex. 1. Extract the square root of 3,136.

Explanation.— Separating the number into periods of two figures each, I find that the root will be expressed by two figures.

I write 25, the greatest square in the left-hand period, under the period; and 5, the square root of 25, for the tens of the root.

PROCESS.

$$31'36 \underline{|56}$$
$$25$$
$$2 \times 50 = 100 \overline{| \ 636}$$
$$2 \times 50 + 6 = 106 | \ 636$$

Subtracting 25 from 31, and to the remainder annexing the next period, I have 636. This number is made up of two times the product of the tens and the ones of the root, plus the square of the ones; *i. e.*, of $2 \times 50 \times$ ones $+$ ones^2.

Dividing 636 by 100 $(= 2 \times 50)$ regarded as a trial divisor, I obtain 6, which I write for the ones of the root; and since $100 = 2 \times 5$. tens, and $636 = 2 \times 5$ tens $\times$ the ones, $+$ the square of the ones, I also add 6 to 100, the trial divisor, making 106, the complete divisor. Multiplying this complete divisor by 6, the ones of the root, I have, *1st*,— 6×6, or the square of the ones; and *2d*,— 6×100, or two times the product of the tens and the ones. The product, 636, is the same as the dividend; and 56 is the square root required.

In extraction of the square root, only two periods of figures are considered in connection. Hence,

In obtaining any figure of the root except the first, the figure or figures of the root already found are regarded as tens, and the figure sought as ones; *i. e.*, each succeeding figure of the root is found in the same manner as the second figure of a root expressed by two figures. (See the solution of Ex. 2.)

Ex. 2. Extract the square root of 56,192.7025.

<table>
<tr><td colspan="2">Full Process.</td><td colspan="3">Common Process.</td></tr>
<tr><td></td><td>$5'61'92.70'25 \underline{| 237.05}$</td><td>$5'61'92.70'25$</td><td>$237.05$</td></tr>
<tr><td></td><td>4</td><td>4</td><td></td></tr>
<tr><td>$2 \times 20 = 40$</td><td>161</td><td>161</td><td>43</td></tr>
<tr><td>$2 \times 20 + 3 = 43$</td><td>129</td><td>129</td><td></td></tr>
<tr><td>$2 \times 230 = 460$</td><td>3292</td><td>3292</td><td>467</td></tr>
<tr><td>$2 \times 230 + 7 = 467$</td><td>3269</td><td>3269</td><td></td></tr>
<tr><td>$\begin{cases} 2 \times \ \ 2370 = \ \ 4740 \\ 2 \times 23700 = 47400 \end{cases}$</td><td>$237025$</td><td>$237025$</td><td>$47405$</td></tr>
<tr><td>$2 \times 23700 + 5 = 47405$</td><td>$237025$</td><td>$237025$</td><td></td></tr>
</table>

Ex. 3. Extract the square root of $\frac{289}{625}$.

Process. $\sqrt{\frac{289}{625}} = \frac{\sqrt{289}}{\sqrt{625}} = \frac{17}{25}$

182. RULE FOR EXTRACTION OF SQUARE ROOT.

I. To determine the number of figures in the root:— *Separate the number into periods of two figures each, beginning at ones in an integer, and at tenths in a decimal.*

II. To find the first figure of the root:—

1. *Find the root of the greatest square in the left-hand period, and write it for the first figure of the root.*

2. *Subtract this square from the first period; and to the remainder annex the next period for a dividend.*

III. To find the second figure of the root:—

1. *Double the root already found, considered as tens, for a trial divisor, by which divide the dividend; write the result for the second figure of the root, and also in the place of ones in the trial divisor, thus forming the complete divisor.*

2. *Multiply the complete divisor by the second figure of the root; subtract the product from the dividend; and to the remainder annex the next period for a dividend.*

IV. To find the succeeding figures of the root:— *Proceed with the second, and with each succeeding dividend, in the same manner as with the first.*

a. If any dividend is less than the divisor:— *Write a cipher in the root, and also on the right of the divisor; and annex the next period to the dividend, for a new dividend.*

b. If there is a remainder after all the periods have been used:— *Annex periods of decimal ciphers, and extend the work to any required degree of exactness.*

c. When the given number is an imperfect power:— *Write + after the root, to indicate that the root is not exact.*

d. If the right-hand decimal period contains but one figure:— *Annex a decimal cipher.*

e. To extract the square root of a mixed fractional number: —*First reduce it to a mixed decimal number, or to an improper fraction.*

PROBLEMS.

Extract the square root of | Find the value of

1. 2,916.
2. 582,169.
3. 29,735,209.
4. .0784.
5. .186624.
6. $\frac{729}{784}$.
7. $\sqrt{56.25}$.
8. $\sqrt{3,685.582681}$.
9. $\sqrt{.000289}$.
10. $\sqrt{\frac{324}{961}}$.
11. $\sqrt{1,423\frac{2147}{2401}}$.
12. $\sqrt{8}$. | 13. $\sqrt{78}$.

14. What is the length of one side of a square piece of land that contains 9,312.25 sq. ft. ?

15. The surface of the water in a square reservoir measures $12,488\frac{1}{16}$ sq. yd. How long is one side of the reservoir?

16. What are the dimensions of a box, the entire area of its 6 equal square sides being $522\frac{2}{3}$ sq. in.

17. A park is $\frac{4}{7}$ as wide as it is long, and its area is 82,256 sq. ft. What are its dimensions?

18. What is the length of one side of a square field whose area is $21\frac{1}{40}$ acres ?

19. An oblong field containing 12.1 acres, is 4 times as long as it is wide. What are its dimensions ?

IV. EXTRACTION OF CUBE ROOT.

183. *Extraction of the cube root* is the process of finding one of the three equal factors that produce a number.

The cubes of 1 and 9, 10 and 99, .1 and .9, .01 and .99, respectively, are

$$1^3 = 1 \qquad 10^3 = 1,000 \qquad .1^3 = .001 \qquad .01^3 = .000001$$
$$9^3 = 729 \qquad 99^3 = 970,299 \qquad .9^3 = .729 \qquad .99^3 = .970299$$

Comparing these numbers and their cubes, we see that

1. The cube of an integer

expressed { one figure } is expressed { one, two, or three figures, by { two figures } by { four, five, or six figures.

2. The cube of a decimal

expressed by { one figure } is expressed { three decimal figures, { two figures } by { six decimal figures.

And so on, of greater numbers. Hence,

184. Principle I. *The cube of any integer is expressed by three times as many figures as the integer, or one or two less than three times as many ; and the cube of any decimal is expressed by three times as many decimal figures as the decimal.*

From this principle it is evident that

The number of three-figure periods in a number equals the number of places in its cube root.

Cubing the integers 2, 20, and 25; 9, 90, and 99; and the decimals .9, .25, and .99, we have

$$2^3 = 8 \qquad 9^3 = 729 \qquad .9^3 = .729$$
$$20^3 = 8,000 \qquad 90^3 = 729,000 \qquad .25^3 = .015625$$
$$25^3 = 15,625 \qquad 99^3 = 970,299 \qquad .99^3 = .970299$$

Separating the cubes into three-figure periods, and comparing the numbers with their cubes, we see that

1. The cube of the left-hand digit is wholly in the left-hand period.   And

2. The cube of the left-hand digit is the greatest cube in the left-hand period.   Hence,

185. Principle II.   *The cube of the left-hand order of units of a number is wholly in the left-hand period of the power, and is the greatest cube in that period.*

186. To determine the parts that make up the cube of a number, we will cube 35 by different processes.

$35 = 30 + 5$; and $35^3 = 35 \times 35 \times 35$, or the product of $30 + 5$, $30 + 5$, and $30 + 5$.

First Process.	Second Process.	Third Process.
$35 =$	$30 + 5 =$	$30 + 5$
$35 =$	$30 + 5 =$	$30 + 5$
$175 =$	$150 + 25 =$	$(30 \times 5) + 5^2$
$105 =$	$900 + 150 =$	$30^2 + (30 \times 5)$
$1225 =$	$900 + 300 + 25 =$	$30^2 + 2 \times (30 \times 5) + 5^2$
$35 =$	$30 + 5 =$	$30 + 5$
$6125 =$	$4500 + 1500 + 125 =$	$(30^2 \times 5) + 2 \times (30 \times 5^2) + 5^3$
$3675 =$	$27000 + 9000 + 750 =$	$30^3 + 2 \times (30^2 \times 5) + (30 \times 5^2)$
$42875 =$	$27000 + 13500 + 2250 + 125 =$	$30^3 + 3 \times (30^2 \times 5) + 3 \times (30 \times 5^2) + 5^3$

The several parts of the cube, reading from the left, are

1st.	The cube of the tens,	27,000
2d.	Three times the square of the tens × the ones,	13,500
3d.	Three times the tens × the square of the ones,	2,250
4th.	The cube of the ones,	125

That is, $35^3 = 42,875$

187. PRINCIPLE III. *The cube of a number, regarded as tens and ones, is equal to the cube of the tens, plus three times the product of the square of the tens and the ones, plus three times the product of the tens and the square of the ones, plus the cube of the ones.*

188. The several steps, in their order, in extraction of the cube root, are based on the three principles now given.

189. Ex. 1. Extract the cube root of 42,875.

PROCESS.

$$42'875 \mid 35$$
$$27$$
$$3 \times 30^2 = 2,700 \mid 15875$$
$$3 \times 30 \times 5 = 450$$
$$5^2 = 25$$
$$3,175 \mid 15875$$

EXPLANATION.— Separating the number into periods of three figures each, I find that the root will be expressed by two figures.

I write 27, the greatest cube in the left-hand period, under the period; and 3, the cube root of 27, for the tens of the root.

Subtracting 27 from 42, and to the remainder annexing the next period, I have 15,875. This number is made up of three times the product of the square of the tens and the ones, plus three times the product of the tens and the square of the ones, plus the cube of the ones; *i. e.*, of $3 \times 30^2 \times$ ones, $+3 \times 30 \times$ ones^2, $+$ ones^3.

Considering the first figure of the root as tens, and multiplying its square by 3, I have 2,700 for a trial divisor. Dividing 15,875 by this trial divisor, I have 5 for the ones of the root.

Adding to the trial divisor 450 ($=3 \times 30 \times 5$) and also 25 ($= 5^2$), I have 3,175, the complete divisor.

Then, multiplying this complete divisor by 5, the ones of the root, I have 15,875, which is made up of, *1st,*—$5 \times 5 \times 5$, or ones^3; *2d,*—$3 \times 30 \times 5 \times 5$, or $3 \times$ tens $\times$ ones^2 ; and, *3d,*—$3 \times 30 \times 30 \times 5$, or $3 \times$ tens$^2 \times$ ones.

I have now used all of the given number, and 35 is the cube root required.

In extraction of the cube root, only two periods of figures are considered in connection. Hence,

Any figure of the root after the second, is found in the same manner as the second figure of a root expressed by two figures.

This is fully shown in the solution of Ex. 2.

Ex. 2. What is the cube root of 9,938,375?

FULL PROCESS.   COMMON PROCESS.

```
                                    9'938'375|215      9'938'375 | 215
                                    8                  8
Trial divisor, 3 × 20² = 1,200 |1938                   1,938     | 1,261
        3 × 20 × 1 =      60                           1,261
               1² =       1                            ──────
                       ─────                            677,375  | 135,475
Complete divisor,      1,261 |1261                      677,375
Trial divisor, 3 × 210² = 132,300 |677375
        3 × 210 × 5 =    3,150
               5² =        25
                      ───────
Complete divisor,     135,475 |677375
```

Ex. 3. Find the cube root of $105\tfrac{853}{1331}$.

PROCESS.

$$\sqrt[3]{105\tfrac{853}{1331}} = \sqrt[3]{\frac{140608}{1331}}$$

$$\frac{\sqrt[3]{140608}}{\sqrt[3]{1331}} = \frac{52}{11} = 4\tfrac{8}{11}.$$

190. RULE FOR EXTRACTION OF CUBE ROOT.

I. To determine the number of figures in the root:—

Separate the number into three-figure periods, beginning at ones in an integer, and at tenths in a decimal.

II. To find the first figure of the root:—

1. Find the root of the greatest cube in the left-hand period, and write it for the first figure of the root.

2. Subtract this cube from the first period, and to the remainder annex the next period for a dividend.

III. To find the second figure of the root:—

1. Square that part of the root found, considered as tens, and multiply the square by 3, for a trial divisor, by which divide the dividend; and write the result for the second figure of the root.

2. To the trial divisor add 3 times the product of the tens and ones of the root already found, and also the square of the ones, for a complete divisor.

3. Multiply the complete divisor by the second figure of the root; subtract the product from the dividend; and to the remainder annex the next period, for a second dividend.

IV. To find the succeeding figures of the root :—

Proceed with the second, and each succeeding dividend, in the same manner as with the first, until all the periods are used.

    a. If any dividend is less than the divisor : — *Write a cipher in the root ; annex two ciphers to the trial divisor, for a new divisor ; and the next period to the dividend, for a new dividend.*

    b. *Adapt remarks a, b, c, d, e, after rule for extraction of square root, Art.* **182**, *to apply to extraction of cube root.*

PROBLEMS.

Extract the cube root of   Find the value of

1. 148,877. | *4.* .658503. | *7.* $\sqrt[3]{178.453547}$. | *10.* $\sqrt[3]{\frac{216}{5832}}$.
2. 39,304. | *5.* .000512. | *8.* $\sqrt[3]{128.024064}$. | *11.* $\sqrt[3]{10\frac{1915}{4096}}$.
3. .006859. | *6.* 300.763. | *9.* $\sqrt[3]{119,095.488}$. | *12.* $\sqrt[3]{5\frac{84}{169}}$.

13. The capacity of a cubical cistern is 6 cu. yd. 19 cu. ft. 1,664 cu. in.   What is its size ?

14. Find one of the three equal factors of 118,805,247,296.

15. The contents of a wall are 216 cu. ft., its height is 2 times its thickness, and its length is 16 times its height. What are its dimensions ?

What is the inside measurement

16. Of a cubic box that will hold a bushel of wheat ?

17. Of a cubic can that will hold a gallon of oil ?

18. What is one dimension of a cubical bin that will hold the same number of bushels of wheat as a bin that is 12 ft. long, 7 ft. wide, and 4 ft. deep?

19. Find the inside measurement of a cubic box whose capacity equals that of a box 6 ft. 6 in. long, 5 ft. 5 in. wide. and 4 ft. 4 in. deep.

§ 20. MEASUREMENTS.

I. Applications of Square and Cube Root.

191. The most important applications of square root and cube root are, in finding the sides of right-angled triangles, and in computations of like parts of similar figures and similar volumes.

The principles upon which the applications of these processes are based are demonstrated in geometry.

To find the hypothenuse of a triangle.

192. The *hypothenuse* of a right-angled triangle is its longest side.

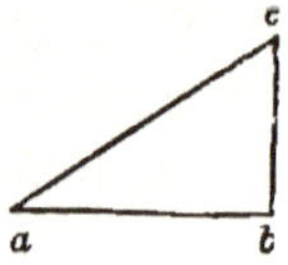

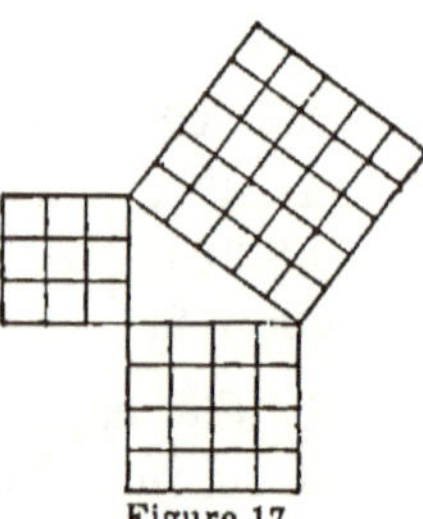

Figure 16.

193. The *base* and *perpendicular* of a right-angled triangle are the two sides that include the right angle.

    a. In the right-angled triangle $a\,b\,c$, the side $a\,c$ is the hypothenuse, the side $a\,b$ is the base, and the side $c\,b$ is the perpendicular.

    b. The two shorter sides are also called the *legs of the triangle.*

The area of the square described (or drawn) on the hypothenuse of a right-angled triangle, is equal to the sum of the areas of the squares described on the other two sides. Hence,

Figure 17.

194. *The hypothenuse of a right-angled triangle equals the square root of the sum of the squares of the other two sides.*

Problems.

1. My garden is a rectangle 116 ft. 2 in. long, and 87 ft. 9 in. wide. What is the distance between the diagonal corners?

2. Find the length of a hand rail to a straight flight of 19 stairs, each $10\frac{1}{2}$ in. wide and $7\frac{1}{4}$ in. high.

3. The four-sided roof of a house is 24 ft. by 30 ft. at the eaves, and the peak is 9 ft. higher than the eaves. What is the distance from either corner of the roof to the peak?

4. A ladder 39 ft. long reaches the top of a building 36 ft. high. How far from the building does its foot stand?

5. What is the distance from the top of a building 72 ft. high, to the opposite side of a street 82 ft. wide?

6. The distance between the diagonal corners of two intersecting streets of equal width, is 88 ft. How wide are the streets?

7. Find the side of a cube whose diagonal is 43.3 inches.

8. The rafters are 16.5 ft. long, and the gable is 26.4 ft. wide. How high above the eaves is the gable peak?

9. Three iron rods extend from the top of a derrick 30 ft. high, to the ground at the distances of 40 ft., 72 ft., and 133 ft. 4 in. from the foot of the derrick. Find the lengths of these iron rods.

10. What are the dimensions of the ends of the largest stick of square timber that can be cut from a log 22 inches in diameter?

II. Prisms, Cylinders, Pyramids, Cones, and Spheres.

195. A *polygon* is a plane figure whose sides are straight lines.

196. A *prism* is a solid whose bases are equal parallel polygons, and whose sides are parallelograms.

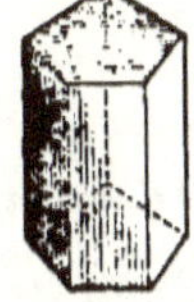 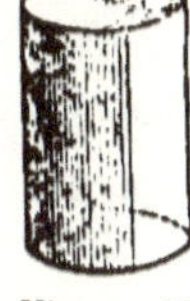

Figure 18.   Figure 19.

> The name of a prism is determined from the form of its bases or ends.

197. A *cylinder* is a solid of uniform diameter, whose bases are equal parallel circles.

> **a.** The *axis* of a prism or of a cylinder is a straight line that joins the centres of its bases.
>
> **b.** A *right prism* or a *right cylinder* is one whose axis is perpendicular to its bases.

198. A *pyramid* is a solid whose base is a polygon, and whose sides are triangles terminating in a point or vertex.

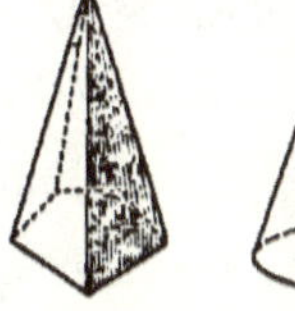 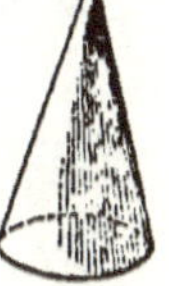

Figure 20.   Figure 21.

199. A *cone* is a solid, whose base is a circle, and whose top is terminated in a point or vertex.

a. The *axis of a pyramid or of a cone* is a straight line that joins the vertex with the centre of its base.

b. A *right pyramid* or a *right cone* is one whose axis is perpendicular to its base.

c. The *altitude of a pyramid or of a cone* is the perpendicular height of its vertex above its base.

d. The *slant height of a pyramid* is the distance from the vertex to the middle of one side of its base.

e. The *slant height of a cone* is the distance from its vertex to the circumference of its base.

CASE I. **To find the area of a prism, cylinder, pyramid, or cone.**

200. The entire surface of a prism consists of its bases and its sides.   And

The entire surface of a cylinder consists of its bases and its curved surface (which is equal to a parallelogram whose two dimensions are the length and circumference of the cylinder).

Ex. 1. What is the area of a prism 8 feet long and 14 inches square?

FULL SOLUTION.

$2 \times 14 \times 14$ sq. in. = 392 sq. in., area of the bases.

$4 \times 14 \times 96$ sq. in. = $\underline{5,376}$ sq. in., area of the four sides.

Total area, $5,768$ sq. in. = 4 sq. yd. 4 sq. ft. 8 sq. in.

Ex. 2. What is the area of a cylinder 8 feet long and 14 inches in diameter?

FULL SOLUTION.

$3\tfrac{1}{7} \times 14$ in. = 44 in., circumference.

$2 \times \tfrac{44}{2} \times \tfrac{44}{7}$ sq. in. = 308 sq. in., area of the bases.

44×96 sq. in. = $\underline{4,224}$ sq. in., area of curved surface.

Total area, $4,532$ sq. in. = 3 sq. yd. 4 sq. ft. 68 sq. in.

The number of units in the entire area of a prism or a cylinder is equal to the sum of the units in its bases, plus the units in its lateral surface.

201. The entire surface of a pyramid consists of its base and its lateral surfaces.   And

The entire surface of a cone consists of its base and its lateral surface (which is equal to a triangle whose base is the periphery of the base of the cone, and whose altitude is its slant height).

Ex. 1. The slant height of a pyramid is 16 inches, and the base is 7 inches square.   What is the area?

PROCESS.

$$7 \times 7 \text{ sq. in.} = 49 \text{ sq. in., } \textit{area of base.}$$

$$4 \times \frac{16 \times 7 \text{ sq. in.}}{2} = 224 \text{ sq. in., } \textit{area of the 4 sides.}$$

$$\textit{Entire area, } \overline{273 \text{ sq. in.}}$$

Ex. 2. The periphery of the base of a cone is 60 inches, and the slant height is 2 feet.   How many square inches are there on the surface of the cone?

PROCESS.

$$60 \text{ in.} \div 3\tfrac{1}{7} = \frac{210 \text{ in.}}{11}, \textit{diameter of base.}$$

$$\left(\tfrac{1}{2} \text{ of } \tfrac{210}{11} =\right) \tfrac{105}{11} \times \frac{60 \text{ sq. in.}}{2} = 286\tfrac{4}{11} \text{ sq. in., } \textit{area of base.}$$

$$\frac{24 \times 60 \text{ sq. in.}}{2} = \overline{720 \text{ sq. in., } \textit{area of curved surface.}}$$

$$\textit{Entire surface of cone, } 1,300\tfrac{4}{11} \text{ sq. in.}$$

The number of units in the entire surface of a pyramid or a cone is equal to the sum of the units in its base, plus the units in its lateral surface.

PROBLEMS.

Required,

1. The surface of a prism 1 ft. 9 in. long, and 8 in. square.

2. The area of a stick of timber 50 ft. long, and 7 by 10 in.

3. The curved surface of a granite column 18 inches in diameter and 20 feet high.

4. The outer surface of an open tank 8 feet in diameter and 6 feet deep.

5. The square yards on the surface of a conical spire 8 ft. 4' in diameter at the base, and 72 ft. 6' high.

Find the lateral surface

6. Of an octagonal (or eight-sided) spire 6 ft. on a side at the base, and 33 ft. slant height.

7. Of a hexagonal (or six-sided) prism whose faces are each 3 ft. by $9\frac{1}{8}'$.

8. Of a log 28 ft. long and 17' in diameter.

9. Of an octagonal spire, each side of the base measuring 5 ft., and the slant height 37 ft. 4 in.

Required, the entire area

10. Of a cone, the periphery being 40 inches, and the slant height 3 feet.

11. Of a cone, the diameter of the base being $11\frac{2}{8}$ inches, and the slant height 2 feet 6 inches.

12. Of a pyramid, the slant height being 27 inches, and the base 11 inches square.

Case II. **To find the volume of a prism, cylinder, pyramid, or cone.**

202. The volume in a portion of a prism or of a cylinder 1 foot long, equals the number of square units in either base; the volume of a portion of the same prism or cylinder 4, 5, or 6 feet long is 4, 5, or 6 times as much as the volume of a portion of the same prism or cylinder 1 foot long.

Ex. The area of the base of a hexagonal prism is 78 sq. ft., and its length is 19 ft. 6 in. What is its volume?

Process.

$$19\ ft.\ 6\ in. = 19.5\ ft.$$

$$19.5 \times 78\ cu.\ ft. = 1,521\ cu.\ ft.$$

I. *The number of units in the volume of a prism or a cylinder is equal to the product of the number of units in the base, multiplied by the number of units in the length.*

II. *The volume of a pyramid is one third as much as the volume of a prism that has the same base and altitude.* And

III. *The volume of a cone is one third as much as the volume of a cylinder that has the same base and altitude.*

Ex. 1. The area of the base of an octagonal pyramid is 35 sq. ft., and its altitude is 15 ft. 4 in. What is its volume?

Ex. 2. What are the cubic contents of a cone 6 ft. in diameter at the base, and 10 ft. 8 in. high?

PROCESS.

$$\frac{15\frac{1}{3} \times 35 \text{ cu. ft.}}{3} = 178\frac{8}{9} \text{ cu. ft., } \textit{volume of pyramid.}$$

PROCESS.

$$3\frac{1}{7} \times 6 \text{ ft.} = 18\frac{6}{7} \text{ ft., } \textit{circumference of base.}$$

$$\tfrac{2}{3} \times (\tfrac{1}{2} \text{ of } 18\frac{6}{7} \text{ sq. ft.}) = 28\frac{2}{7} \text{ sq. ft., } \textit{area of base.}$$

$$\frac{10\frac{2}{3} \times 28\frac{2}{7} \text{ cu. ft.}}{3} = 100\frac{4}{7} \text{ cu. ft., } \textit{volume of cone.}$$

PROBLEMS.

Required,

1. The volume of a cylindrical shaft of marble 2 ft. 3 in. in diameter, and 16 ft. 9 in. high.

2. The cubic contents of a stick of timber 24 ft. long, the bases being right-angled triangles, the two shorter sides of each of which are 18 in.

3. The capacity of a tube 8 ft. long and 4 in. in diameter.

4. The contents, in gallons, of a cistern 5 feet in diameter, and 6 ft. deep.

5. What are the cubical contents of a shaft 29 ft. long, and 9' in diameter?

6. What length of wire $\frac{1}{40}$ of an inch in diameter can be drawn from a cubic foot of brass?

7. How many tons of hay can be stored in a loft under a four-sided roof 30 ft. square and 10 ft. high to the peak?

In Case I, page 356,

8. Find the volume of the cone, problem 10.

9. Find the volume of the pyramid, problem 12.

10. In a stack of hay 19 ft. in diameter and 17 ft. high, with a conical top 17 ft. high, are how many tons?

11. A cistern $6\frac{1}{4}$ ft. in diameter, and 8 ft. deep, contains how many gallons? How many barrels?

12. A rectangular cistern 12 ft. long, 10 ft. wide, and 9 ft. deep will hold how many barrels of water?

Case III. To find the area, and the volume of a sphere.

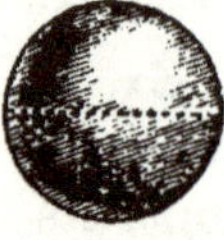

203. A *sphere* or a *globe* is a solid bounded by a curved surface, every part of which is equally distant from the point within, called its centre.

204. A *hemisphere* is one half of a sphere.   Figure 19.

205. I. *The area of a sphere is 4 times as much as the area of a circle of the same diameter.*

II. *The volume of a sphere is two thirds as much as the volume of a cylinder whose diameter and altitude are, each, equal to the diameter of the sphere.*

Ex. Find the area and the volume of a 13-inch globe.

FULL SOLUTION.

$3\frac{1}{7} \times 13$ in. $= 40\frac{6}{7}$ in., *circumference of 13-inch cylinder.*

$\frac{1}{2}$ of $13 = 6\frac{1}{2}$, and $\frac{1}{2}$ of $40\frac{6}{7} = 20\frac{3}{7}$.

$6\frac{1}{2} \times 20\frac{3}{7}$ sq. in. $= 132\frac{11}{14}$ sq. in., *area of base of cylinder.*

$4 \times 132\frac{11}{14}$ sq. in. $= 531\frac{1}{7}$ sq. in., *area of globe.*

$13 \times 132\frac{11}{14}$ cu. in. $= 1{,}726\frac{3}{14}$ cu. in., *volume of cylinder.*

$\frac{2}{3}$ of $1{,}726\frac{3}{14}$ cu. in. $= 1{,}150\frac{17}{21}$ cu. in., *volume of globe.*

PROBLEMS.

Required,

1. The area and the volume of a 15-inch school-globe.

2. The area of a 2-inch ivory ball.

3. The volume of a 10-inch foot-ball.

4. The area of a hemisphere 12 inches in diameter.

5. The volume of the earth, the diameter being 7,911 miles.

6. What is the area, and what is the volume, of the largest globe that can be turned from a block of mahogany which is a 10-inch cube?

III. Dimensions, Areas, and Volumes of Similar Surfaces and Similar Solids.

206. *Similar surfaces* and *similar solids* are such as are of the same form, without regard to size.

$$\text{The area of a square whose side is} \begin{cases} \text{2 inches, is 4 square inches.} \\ \text{5 inches, is 25 square inches.} \\ \text{8 inches, is 64 square inches.} \end{cases}$$

The areas of squares and other similar surfaces are to each other as the squares of their similar dimensions.

$$\text{The volume of a cube whose edge is} \begin{cases} \text{2 inches, is 8 cubic inches.} \\ \text{5 inches, is 125 cubic inches.} \\ \text{8 inches, is 512 cubic inches.} \end{cases}$$

The volumes of cubes and other similar solids are to each other as the cubes of their similar dimensions.

PROBLEMS.

1. A tract of Government land 160 rods square is a quarter-section. What is the length of one side of a square tract that contains 36,000 acres?

2. If a 6-inch cube of iron weighs 60.5 pounds, what is the weight of a 3-foot cube?

3. What is the circumference of a circle whose area is 3 times the area of a circle 20 inches in diameter?

4. The surface of a globe 1 foot in diameter is 3.1416 square feet. What is the surface of a globe 5 feet in diameter? Of a globe 6 inches in diameter?

5. Find the circumference of a globe whose volume is 64 times the volume of a globe 7 inches in diameter.

6. If the volume of a pyramid 20 ft. high is 4,600 cu. ft., what is the volume of a similar pyramid 100 ft. high?

7. The diameter of the base of a certain cone is 24 feet; and from the top part $\frac{1}{4}$ of its volume is cut off, by a plane parallel to its base. What is the diameter of the base of the part cut off?

A ball 6 inches in diameter weighs 32 pounds;

8. What is the weight of a ball 3 inches in diameter?

9. What is the diameter of a ball that weighs 500 pounds?

10. A certain watering-trough, 5 feet long, holds 12 pailfuls. What is the capacity of a similar trough 8 feet long?

§ **21.** FORMS OF BUSINESS PAPER.

NOTE.—Substitute other words for the words in Italics, as occasion may require.

I. PROMISSORY NOTES.

On Demand.

235\frac{84}{100}$ *Chicago, Sept. 15, 1882*

On demand I promise to pay to *Joseph Young*, or order, *Two Hundred Thirty-five and* $\frac{84}{100}$ Dollars, *with interest*, for value received.

Jas. T. Bryant.

Time, without Interest.

$60   *Detroit, Dec. 1, 1882.*

Six months after date, I promise to pay to *John Smith*, or order, at his office, *Sixty* Dollars, for value received.

Peter Jones.

Time, with Interest.

56\frac{37}{100}$ *Cleveland, Oct. 3, 1882.*

Ninety days after date, I promise to pay to *Wm. Brown*, or bearer, *Fifty-six and* $\frac{37}{100}$ Dollars, with interest, for value received.

David Greene.

Bankable Note.

$1,000   *Boston, June 21, 1882.*

Two months after date, I promise to pay to the order of *Edward Eliot*, at the *Fourth National* Bank, *One Thousand* Dollars, for value received.

Henry Hudson.

Joint Note.

$290   *St. Louis, Jan. 20, 1882.*

Sixty days after date, we promise to pay to *Henry W. Raymond*, or order, *Two Hundred Ninety* Dollars, for value received.

Davis & Williams.

Merchandise Note.

$750   *Milwaukee, Feb. 4, 1882.*

On the first day of August next, I promise to pay to *Ray & Mitchell*, or order, at *their mills in this City*, *Seven Hundred Fifty* Dollars, in *No. 1 wheat, at the market price when due*, for value received.

Edwd. Denton.

Judgment Note.

$400   *Pittsburgh, March 17, 1882.*

One year after date, I promise to pay to *Joseph Horne & Co., Four Hundred* Dollars, with interest, for value received.

And I do hereby authorize any attorney of any Court of Record in *Pennsylvania* or elsewhere, at any time after the above promissory note becomes due and remains unpaid, to confess judgment for the above sum, with release of errors.

Witness my hand and seal, the date above written.

Witness present,   *Abel N. Brown.* { L.S. }
  Chas. Clark.

II. Due-Bills.

Payable in Money.

$15   *Buffalo, July 1, 1882.*

Due *Sylvia J. Eastman Fifteen* Dollars, *one day* after date, for value received.

                                           Kate Stoneman.

Payable in Merchandise.

$96 $\frac{50}{100}$ *Portland, Nov. 29, 1882.*

Due *W. J. Hunt,* or bearer, *Ninety-six* Dollars and *Fifty Cents,* payable in *goods from our store.*

                                           Johnson, Luce & Co.

III. Orders.

Payable in Money.

                                           Hartford, May 17, 1882.

Mr. Peter Cooper,
  Please pay to *Henry H. Rice Ten* Dollars, on my account.

                                           Oliver Turner.

Payable in Merchandise.

                                           Burlington, March 18, 1882.

A. J. Mason & Co.,
  Please pay to *Andrew Adams,* or bearer, *Sixteen* Dollars and *Twenty-five* Cents ($16 $\frac{25}{100}$), *merchandise,* and charge to my account.

                                           B. F. Baker.

Bank Check.

$210 $\frac{50}{100}$ *Springfield, Sept. 1, 1882.*

THIRD NATIONAL BANK.

Pay to *E. A. Hubbard,* or order, *Two Hundred Ten* and $\frac{50}{100}$ Dollars.

                                           Wood & Harrison.

Q

IV. Drafts.

Sight Draft.

$493 $\frac{50}{100}$

Omaha, Neb., Aug. 14, 1882.

At sight, without grace, pay to the order of *Day & Martin, Four Hundred Ninety-three* and $\frac{50}{100}$ Dollars, value received, and charge to *our* acc't.

Porter & Bliss.

To *C. C. Gould,*
St. Paul, Minn.

Time Draft.

$900

Denver, Col., Feb. 10, 1882.

Ten days after date pay to *Edward Newton,* or order, *Nine Hundred* Dollars, for value received, and charge to acc't of

To *C. S. Griggs & Co.,*
Chicago, Ill.

G. W. Sumner.

Time Draft, collectible through a Bank.

$3,500

Philadelphia, Jan. 2, 1882.

Ten days after sight, pay to the order of *George H. Logan,* at the *Chemical Bank, Three Thousand Five Hundred* Dollars, and charge to acc't of

Thomas Hunter,
716 Filbert Street.

To *D. Appleton & Co.,*
New York City.

V. Receipts.

In Full of all Demands.

$97 $\frac{82}{100}$

Albany, June 27, 1882.

Received of *E. H. Ransom & Co., Ninety-seven* and $\frac{82}{100}$ Dollars, in full of all demands.

S. R. Gray.

By Agent or Clerk,—in Full of Accounts.

$500

Received, *Cincinnati, January 20, 1882,* of *Wm. T. Harris, Five Hundred* Dollars, in full of accounts to date.

David Pickering,
per *Henry Wood.*

For Note on Account.

$396 $\frac{62}{100}$

New York, May 4, 1882.

Received of *Anson Richmond* of *Troy,* his note at *three* months, dated 3d inst., for *Three Hundred Ninety-six* and $\frac{62}{100}$ Dollars, on account.

W. & B. Douglas,
87 John St.

§ 22. TAX, COMPOUND INTEREST, AND COIN TABLES.

I. Tax Table.

(Rate of valuation, 1½ mills on a dollar, or .15% of assured valuation.)

Prop.	Tax.	Prop.	Tax.	Prop.	Tax.	Prop.	Tax.
$1	$.0015	$10	$.015	$100	$ .15	$1,000	$1.50
2	.0030	20	.030	200	.30	2,000	3.00
3	.0045	30	.045	300	.45	3,000	4.50
4	.0060	40	.060	400	.60	4,000	6.00
5	.0075	50	.075	500	.75	5,000	7.50
6	.0090	60	.090	600	.90	6,000	9.00
7	.0105	70	.105	700	1.05	7,000	10.50
8	.0120	80	.120	800	1.20	8,000	12.00
9	.0135	90	.135	900	1.35	9,000	13.50

Ex. By the above table, find the tax of a person who is assessed on $5,642; and who pays for 3 polls, at $.62½ each.

PROCESS.

Tax on $5,000,		$7.50
" " 600,		.90
" " 40,		.06
" " 2,		.003
3 polls,		1.875
Total tax,		$10.34

II. Compound Interest Table.

Showing the amount of $1 at 2½, 3, 3½, 4, 5, 6, 7, and 8 per cent compound interest for any number of years from 1 to 20.

Years.	2½ per ct.	3 per cent.	3½ per ct.	4 per cent.	5 per cent.	6 per cent.	7 per cent.	8 per cent.
1	1.025000	1.030000	1.035000	1.040000	1.050000	1.060000	1.070000	1.080000
2	1.050625	1.060900	1.071225	1.081600	1.102500	1.123600	1.144900	1.166100
3	1.076891	1.092727	1.108718	1.124864	1.157625	1.191016	1.225043	1.259712
4	1.103813	1.125509	1.147523	1.169859	1.215506	1.262477	1.310796	1.360489
5	1.131408	1.159274	1.187686	1.216653	1.276282	1.338226	1.402552	1.469328
6	1.159693	1.194052	1.229255	1.265319	1.340096	1.418519	1.500730	1.586874
7	1.188686	1.229874	1.272279	1.315932	1.407100	1.503630	1.605782	1.713824
8	1.218403	1.266770	1.316809	1.368569	1.477455	1.593848	1.718186	1.850930
9	1.248863	1.304773	1.362897	1.423312	1.551328	1.689479	1.838459	1.999005
10	1.280085	1.343916	1.410599	1.480244	1.628885	1.790848	1.967151	2.158925
11	1.312087	1.384234	1.459970	1.539451	1.710339	1.898299	2.104852	2.331639
12	1.344889	1.425761	1.511069	1.601032	1.795856	2.012197	2.252192	2.518170
13	1.378511	1.468534	1.563956	1.665074	1.885649	2.132928	2.409845	2.719624
14	1.412974	1.512590	1.618695	1.731676	1.979932	2.260904	2.578534	2.937194
15	1.448298	1.557967	1.675349	1.800944	2.078928	2.396558	2.759032	3.172169
16	1.484506	1.604706	1.733986	1.872981	2.182875	2.540352	2.952164	3.425943
17	1.521618	1.652848	1.794676	1.947901	2.292018	2.692773	3.158815	3.700018
18	1.559659	1.702433	1.857489	2.025817	2.406619	2.854339	3.379932	3.996020
19	1.598650	1.753506	1.922501	2.106849	2.526950	3.025600	3.616528	4.315701
20	1.638616	1.806111	1.989789	2.191123	2.653298	3.207136	3.869685	4.660957

Use the compound interest table on page 363 as follows:

I. To find the amount of any given principal for years:—*Multiply the amount of $1 for the given number of years at the given rate %, by the number expressing the principal.*

II. To find the compound interest :—*Subtract the principal from the amount.*

When there are months and days in the given time :—*Find the simple interest on the amount for the months and days, and add it to the amount for the years. The sum will be the amount for the whole time.*

III. ESTIMATE OF VALUES OF FOREIGN COINS.

As proclaimed by the Secretary of the Treasury, January 2, 1882.

Country.	Monetary Unit.	Standard.	Value in U. S. Money.
Austria	Florin	Silver	$ .10,6
Belgium	Franc	Gold and silver	.19,3
Bolivia	Boliviano	Silver	.82,3
Brazil	Milreis of 1,000 reis	Gold	.54,6
British Possess. in N. A.	Dollar	Gold	1.00
Chili	Peso	Gold and silver	.91,2
Cuba	Peso	Gold and silver	.93,2
Denmark	Crown	Gold	.26,8
Ecuador	Peso	Silver	.82,3
Egypt	Piaster	Gold	.04,9
France	Franc	Gold and silver	.19,3
Great Britain	Pound sterling	Gold	4.86,6¼
Greece	Drachma	Gold and silver	.19,3
German Empire	Mark	Gold	.23,8
Hayti	Gourde	Gold and silver	.96,5
India	Rupee of 16 annas	Silver	.39
Italy	Lira	Gold and silver	.19,3
Japan	Yen	Silver	.88,7
Liberia	Dollar	Gold	1.00
Mexico	Dollar	Silver	.89,4
Netherlands	Florin	Gold and silver	.40,2
Norway	Crown	Gold	.26,8
Peru	Sol	Silver	.82,3
Portugal	Milreis of 1,000 reis	Gold	1.08
Russia	Rouble of 100 copecks	Silver	.65,8
Sandwich Islands	Dollar	Gold	1.00
Spain	Peseta of 100 centimes	Gold and silver	.19,3
Sweden	Crown	Gold	.26,8
Switzerland	Franc	Gold and silver	.19,3
Tripoli	Mahbub of 20 piasters	Silver	.74,3
Turkey	Piaster	Gold	.04,4
U. S. of Colombia	Peso	Silver	.82,3
Venezuela	Bolivar	Gold and silver	.19,3

ANSWERS TO WRITTEN PROBLEMS.

In most of the answers expressing United States money, when the mills are 5 or more, they are regarded as 1 cent; and when less than 5, they are rejected.

INTEGERS. ADDITION. Art. **39.** *A. 1*—19. *2*—19. *3*—26. *4*—15. *5*—14. *6*—19. *7*—26. *8*—25. *9*—23. *10*—19. *11*—20. *12*—19. *13*—21. *14*—18. *15*—21. *16*—19. *17*—32. *18*—25. *B. 1*—42. *2*—26. *3*—29. *4*—33. *5*—41. *6*—30. *7*—22. *8*—25. *9*—31. *10*—27. *11*—36. *12*—40. *13*—21. *14*—39. *15*—34. *16*—30. *17*—20. *18*—23. *19*—29. *20*—32. *21*—24. *22*—43. *23*—33. *C. 1*—102. *2*—76. *3*—94. *4*—103. *5*—92. *6*—113. *7*—74. *8*—88. *9*—86. *10*—118. *11*—89. *12*—68. *13*—64. *14*—72. *15*—82. *16*—80. *17*—67. *18*—78. *19*—60. *20*—79. *21*—66. *22*—75. *23*—77. *24*—73. *25*—81. *26*—84. *27*—65.

Art. **45.** *A. 1*—2,070. *2*—\$10,688. *3*—12,053. *4*—\$110.84. *5*—9,666. *6*—\$1,940,554. *7*—2,673,757. *8*—\$9,952.23. *9*—2,026,125. *B. 1*—\$166. *2*—\$89. *3*—\$105. *4*—\$133. *5*—\$77. *6*—\$90. *7*—\$131. *8*—\$82. *9*—\$113. *10*—1,731. *11*—1,521. *12*—1,830. *13*—1,748. *14*—899. *15*—946. *16*—2,325. *17*—1,416. *18*—1,244. *19*—\$170.35. *20*—\$102.09. *21*—\$181.83. *22*—\$249.02. *23*—\$301.89. *24*—\$60.83. *25*—\$258.99. *26*—\$138.04. *27*—\$138.66. *28*—\$119.99. *29*—\$242.79. *30*—\$167.54. *D. 1*—51,360. *2*—3,399,395. *3*—\$94,412.74. *4*—\$11,975.23. *5*—47,311,990. *6*—24,793,183,104. *7*—\$430,421.05. *F. 1*—3,366 lb. *2*—\$514.58. *3*—\$294.27. *4*—2,143 bu. *5*—644 lb. *6*—211 lb. *7*—\$26.38. *8*—957 cd. *9*—\$681. *10*—\$6,484. *11*—7,338 logs. *12*—\$420.

Art. **46.** *A. 1*—13,790. *2*—1,939. *3*—\$5,410. *4*—29,205. *5*—\$3.87. *6*—14,096. *7*—\$224. *8*—276 persons. *9*—282 barrels. *10*—134 rd. *11*—694 mi. *12*—\$2,405. *13*—1,989 bu. *C. 1*—\$17,995. *2*—\$27,918. *3*—36,816,218. *4*—\$8,156. *5*—\$80.10. *6*—\$5,842. *7*—\$20,855. *8*—\$444.92. *9*—\$2,810.44. *10*—270,011,432. *11*—48,637,000 sq. mi. *12*—3,784 cd. *13*—6,649 lb. *14*—\$28,216,103. *15*—\$743.42. *16*—\$1,660.44. *17*—\$7,144.44. *18*—\$1,110.90. *19*—3,198 bushels. *20*—\$1,836.79. *21*—69,515,137. *22*—939,626,817.

SUBTRACTION. Art. **59.** *A. 1*—432. *2*—411. *3*—436. *4*—374. *5*—367. *6*—63. *7*—223 pins. *8*—708 soldiers. *9*—2,485 shingles. *10*—15,992 pounds. *11*—\$14,441. *12*—\$3,804.98. *13*—\$37,126.44. *14*—\$5,626.75. *E. 1*—221,208. *2*—1,694,178. *3*—74,493,314. *4*—167,025,150. *5*—4,987. *6*—\$6,128. *7*—36,908. *8*—\$13.59. *9*—968,724. *10*—7,348,889. *11*—253,292,037. *12*—\$15,013.19. *13*—\$385.79. *G. 1*—28,607 T. *2*—282 baskets. *3*—\$777. *4*—\$1,464. *5*—5,351 children. *6*—\$9,376. *7*—\$814.76. *8*—\$6,080.81. *9*—\$1,880. *10*—\$2,272. *11*—14,513 bu. *12*—\$46,792. *13*—259 A. *14*—2,023 cd. *15*—19,419 ft. *16*—1,669 lb. *17*—24,484. *18*—2,160 square miles. *19*—3,247 lb.

Art. **60.** *A.* *1*—863. *2*—\$372,695. *3*—68,894,728. *4*—9,110,998,173
5—\$5,624.39. *6*—\$2,088.22. *B.* *1*—386. *2*—568. *3*—48,023. *4*—182.
5—47,637. *6*—47,455. *7*—938. *8*—1,990. *9*—10,200. *10*—1,052.
11—9,262. *12*—8,210. *13*—435. *14*—9,020. *15*—100,045. *16*—8,585.
17—99,610. *18*—91,025. *19*—\$953.25. *20*—\$4,758.25. *21*—\$98,466.25.
22—\$3,805. *23*—\$97,513. *24*—\$93,708. *25*—\$8.86. *26*—\$64.02.
27—\$180.58. *28*—\$55.16. *29*—\$171.72. *30*—\$116.56. *31*—1,998.
32—15,001,986. *33*—99,073. *34*—4,164. *D.* *1*—1,728. *2*—1,732.
3—48 yr. *4*—55 yr. *5*—211 yr. *6*—228 yr. *8*—\$5,320. *9*—\$10,761.
10—15,780 ft. *11*—8,285 rifles. *12*—116,664,982. *13*—12,863,002 bu.
14—\$16,156.

Review. *1*—\$1,155. *2*—7,018 persons. *3*—\$5,744. *4*—44,976,487.
5—\$449. *6*—\$3,056. *7*—\$10,031.19. *8*—175 hhd.; 176,235 lb.
9—181,169 T. *10*—1,492 copies.

Multiplication. Art. **73.** *A.* *1*—738. *2*—3,801. *3*—16,345.
4—76,992. *5*—75,728. *6*—\$3,928. *7*—\$32,562. *8*—\$28,228. *9*—\$544.70.
10—\$17,661.60. *11*—142,492 yd. *12*—771,024 ft. *13*—216,188 lb.
14—360,063 T. *B.* *1*—\$2,275. *2*—\$76,050. *3*—\$12.30. *4*—\$976.
5—840 lb. *6*—42,240 ft. *7*—\$51,072. *8*—221,160 gal. *9*—160,255 lb.
10—6,158,088. *11*—\$105; \$112.50. *12*—\$44.38.

Art. **77.** *1*—7,500. *2*—75,000. *3*—39,200. *4*—1,839,000. *5*—3,920,000.
6—28,930,000. *7*—478,000,000. *8*—58,054,000,000. *9*—45,360.
10—272,800. *11*—13,356,000. *12*—625,230,000. *13*—12,178,600,000.
14—450,430,000,000. *15*—7,620. *16*—996,000; 996,000,000. *17*—583,200;
583,200,000. *18*—194,850,000. *19*—146,400 bushels. *20*—29,400 lb.
21—294,000 gallons. *22*—42,800 lb. *23*—1,440 min. *24*—\$19,500.
25—\$2,500. *26*—\$8,800. *27*—\$87.50. *28*—\$350. *29*—\$4,860.
30—\$97.50. *31*—\$2,550.

Art. **80.** *A.* *1*—1,702. *2*—15,174. *3*—241,056. *4*—134,190.
5—1,222,904. *6*—6,139,776. *7*—48,727,272. *8*—3,845,355. *9*—149,598,976.
10—48,078,027. *11*—9,106. *12*—43,289; 155,318,240. *13*—11,702,718.
14—4,314,156 yd. *15*—2,368 lb. *16*—1,044 eggs. *17*—72,592 axes.
18—66,836 rm. *19*—67,482 lb. *B.* *1*—\$1,118,700. *2*—\$11,187.
3—\$35,560.20. *4*—\$52,406.25. *5*—\$10,252,602.23. *6*—\$6,000.
7—\$225,952. *8*—\$2,112. *9*—\$77,698.25. *10*—\$109,515. *11*—\$1,267.36.
12—\$7.56. *13*—\$8.68. *14*—\$236.16. *15*—\$70.08. *16*—\$6.21.
17—\$3,996.75.

Art. **82.** *1*—403,200. *2*—68,640. *3*—259,200. *4*—1,248,000,000.
5—308,160,000. *6*—3,360,000. *7*—7,822,118,707,200. *8*—2,623,023,200,000.
9—183,230,150,040. *10*—2,331,600 lb. *11*—42,000 words. *12*—\$20,400.
13—\$120,000. *14*—962,000 feet. *15*—174,000 lb. *16*—51,200 poles.
17—\$476. *18*—\$125. *19*—\$12,375. *20*—7,400 lb. *21*—43,240 lb.
22—124,800 sheets. *23*—\$850,000. *24*—\$325,000. *25*—3,895,500,000.

Art. **83.** *A.* *1*—6,158,088. *2*—326,442. *3*—793,032. *4*—70,376,400,000.
5—210,457,200. *6*—4,480,000. *7*—4,234,000. *8*—19,800,000.
9—116,550,000. *10*—266,486,552. *11*—756 passengers. *12*—1,344 A.
13—136,300 lb. *14*—8,400 barrels. *15*—34,823 T. *16*—\$232,650.

17—25,272 persons. 18—642,000 ft. *C.* 1—55,615; 490,609. 2—186,800; 1,500,000. 3—39,474; 3,508,800; 16,508,904. 4—70,641,120; 1,881,369,600. 5—59,373. 6—892,367,000. 7—27,618,720,000. 8—29,836,064,832. 9—14,946,816. 10—$100,608,000. 11—$56,068.74. 12—$111,457,304. 13—1,107,087,782,400. 14—$6,589,624,320. 15—258,720 lb. 16—56,940 times. 17—22,908 eggs. 18—631,800 mi. 19—21,600 sheets. 20—30,240 buttons. 21—$1,620. 22—81,765 bar. 23—$1,244.10.

Review. 1—900 sq. mi. 2—5,040 lb. 3—$322. 4—$64. 5—$984. 6—2,046 pickets. 7—$1,045.25. 8—$11,232. 9—289,085 pounds. 10—18,648 yd. 11—$200. 12—1,462 bu. 13—$58,500. 14—686 bu. 15—5,300 lb. 16—89 sets; 5,033 pieces. 17—$568.50 gain. 18—$15,146. 19—B, $1,350; C, $8,100; All, $10,125.

DIVISION. Art. **97.** 1—232. 2—212. 3—213. 4—411. 5—412. 6—206. 7—420 papers. 8—210 bricks. 9—506.

Art. **99.** 1—821 da. 2—401 da. 3—$4,688. 4—$6,525 received; $4,350 paid. 5—$1,208. 6—205 A. 7—$1,236. 8—251 lb. 9—$8,046. 11—948 bar. 12—339 da. 13—243 da. 14—37 mi. 15—$13. 16—$18. 17—184 bu. 18—8 cars. 19—$48,396. 20—105 days. 21—16 oz. 22—275 sacks. 23—$4. 24—$33. 25—5 farms, 18 A. remainder. 26—$1,005. 27—18 full cargoes. 28—212 bales, 48 lb. remainder. 29—$5.37. 30—120 pens. 31—18 mo. 32—23 sets. 33—$136.99. 34—16 cars. 35—$591\frac{953}{2376}$. 36—164 dozen pairs. 37—168 boxes. 38—24 bells. 39—40,508. 40—327.

Art. **102.** 1—6,475. 2—1,627. 3—$76\frac{275}{1000}$. 4—32,470. 5—7,250. 6—$3,296\frac{7810}{16000}$. 7—$4.30. 8—$.08. 9—$26.25. 10—$3.75. 11—$18.50. 12—$.56. 13—18 horses, $7 left. 14—375 bonds. 15—583 freight-cars.

Art. **104.** 1—15 steam-tugs. 2—192 thousand ft. 3—7 payments; last payment, $156,750. 4—$157\frac{53}{60}$ bu. 5—98 full reams. 6—48 organs. 7—43 chests. 8—24 hours. 9—$86\frac{695}{4500}$. 10—$153\frac{275}{2500}$. 11—$22\frac{299659}{365000}$. 12—$365,482\frac{32000}{700000}$. 13—$121\frac{1392}{24000}$. 14—$2,102\frac{39875}{41700}$. 15—$143\frac{10000}{75000}$. 16—105. 17—$25. 18—Quotient, 2,102; rem., 39,875. 19—376 horses.

Art. **105.** *A.* 1—831. 2—912,566. 3—$2,421\frac{26}{29}$. 4—8,769. 5—$372\frac{96}{100}$. 6—$399\frac{1100}{2500}$. 7—1,450. 8—$1,143\frac{685}{705}$. 9—$1,941\frac{420}{168}$. 11—$546\frac{2}{8}$; $409\frac{7}{8}$; $468\frac{3}{7}$. 12—4,122; 2,748; 2,061. 13—125; 327. 14—$1\frac{350}{700}$; $31\frac{665}{700}$; $71\frac{300}{700}$. 15—$1.01; $4.03; $19.70. 16—$6\frac{96}{150}$; $320\frac{9}{150}$; $436\frac{125}{150}$. 17—162. 18—$152.60. 19—288. 20—108. 21—$41\frac{1}{12}$. 22—$16\frac{6}{37}$. 23—$51\frac{11}{13}$. 24—$4.84. 25—4,400. 26—$961\frac{5300}{9000}$. 27—9,236. 28—3,273.
B. 1—4,059 sheep. 2—393 bar. 3—192 mi. 4—450 A. 5—3 dress patterns, 4 yd. rem. 6—48 machines. 7—44 da. 8—$2.25. 9—$.15. 10—500 oranges. 11—1,188 bar. 12—209 da. 13—$134. 14—70 bu. 15—4,124 bu. 16—23 full casks. 17—$17. 18—60 lb. 19—46 mi. 20—20 quires. 21—57 kettles, 164 lb. rem.

Art. **106.** 1—217. 2—510. 3—229. 4—353. 5—254. 6—518. 7—9 yr. 8—11 in. 9—31 miles. 10—135 gallons. 11—137 pupils. 12—245 yd. 13—$31. 14—$333.08.

Art. **107.** *1*—66,880. *2*—8,634,504. *3*—$675.91. *4*—260,618,400.
5—38,784. *6*—4,663,400. *7*—29,798. *8*—71. *9*—27,072. *10*—268.
11—248,400. *12*—666,639. *13*—$1,180. *14*—640. *15*—4,680,000.
16—7,000. *17*—2,297. *18*—36. *19*—15,225. *20*—1,158.

Review Problems in Integers. **A.** *1*—$83.33⅓; $19.23 5/13. *2*—4,855 bu.
3—$7,020. *4*—8,102 bar. *5*—$75,183. *6*—2,681 bales, 112 lb. rem.
7—96 mi. *8*—$244. *9*—1,405 yd. *10*—2,000 lb. *11*—3 yd. *12*—$4,427.
13—1,176 T. *14*—390 lb. *15*—14 payments; last payment, $975.
16—30 tubs. **B.** *1*—116 sheep. *2*—$4.80. *3*—22 cwt. *4*—$18.24.
5—$3; $4. *6*—640 A. *7*—109 head. *8*—$123. *9*—8 payments.
10—$7. *11*—$56. *12*—41 dress patterns. *13*—1,044 cd. *14*—Captain, $980; mate, $420; each sailor, $70. *15*—$36,150. *16*—Gained
$578. *17*—$4,348. *18*—$9,797.75. *19*—$669.25.

DECIMALS. ADDITION. Art. **124.** *1*—968.59254. *2*—13.88875 T.
3—3,324.35. *4*—$1,645.26. *5*—$294.27. *6*—$1.41. *7*—$2,413.425.
8—261.033 da. *9*—24 oz. *10*—2.839 T. *11*—40.05 A. *12*—25.125 bu.
13—14.725 bu. *14*—119,024.297458. *15*—$247.95. *16*—$310.255.
17—$14.33. *18*—737.1925 gal. *19*—2,460.40072.

SUBTRACTION. Art. **125.** *1*—125.92. *2*—77.166. *3*—1.02955.
4—373.875. *5*—19,517.76744. *6*—$62.85. *7*—$.017. *8*—$94.125.
9—$.935. *10*—$47.125. *11*—16.7 yd. *12*—281.4066 mi. *13*—1.66 in.
14—72.45 miles. *15*—10.75 gallons. *16*—68.13 rd. *17*—2.9375 lb.
18—85.3605. *19*—75.25 feet. *20*—371.25 grains. *21*—840.94946.
22—753.1875 lb. *23*—$.68¾. *24*—127.6875 barrels. *25*—$61.25.
26—$67.62. *27*—314.485 tons. *28*—$3.875. *29*—16.09375 bushels.
30—$2.40. *31*—431.89 T. *32*—34.55 gal. *33*—$13.22. *34*—55.266 A.
35—$272.20, gain on oats; $45.125, gain on corn; $317.325, loss on
wheat; neither gain nor loss on all.

MULTIPLICATION. Art. **126.** *1*—1,896.615. *2*—48,187.04. *3*—20.655.
4—17,526.25. *5*—348,572.16. *6*—$3,495.06. *7*—$73,337. *8*—$37,830.
9—$6,240. *10*—$1,275,493.45. *11*—1.1583. *12*—523,980.93. *13*—
$12,963.63. *14*—$19,342.25. *15*—4.013380638. *16*—82.5 ft. *17*—83 bu.
18—3,907.5 days (2 leap-years). *19*—1,791.875 lb. *20*—$1,045.25.
21—$12.76. *22*—$7.50. *23*—$573.50. *24*—$6,525.40. *25*—284.64426 T.
26—1.59494 T. *27*—785.925 lb. *28*—1,892.2725 gal.

Art. **127.** *1*—.0027328. *2*—.00588. *3*—.00002358. *4*—.00002793.
5—.00399432. *6*—.015 bushel. *7*—.09 mile. *8*—$.07. *9*—$.08.
10—.0279 gal. *11*—.000224.

Art. **128.** *1*—537.8. *2*—$23.10. *3*—687.94. *4*—59,604.3. *5*—$6.25.
6—$378,125. *7*—.62 mi. *8*—$42,697.50. *9*—$75. *10*—$712.50.

Art. **129.** *1*—8,642. *2*—$23,478. *3*—12.007655. *4*—$.80.
5—.00000496. *6*—16. *7*—151,136,355.78. *8*—$587,500. *9*—625.
10—49. *11*—.765 pound. *12*—1,568.75 yards. *13*—472.32 rods.
14—15,472.35 T. *15*—144.375 gallons. *16*—$8.57. *17*—$15,937.50.
18—$57.50. *19*—$102.375. *20*—$13.04. *21*—$100. *22*—$18.40
23—$8.10. *24*—$10.625.

Division. Art. **130.** *1*—.044. *2*—.023. *3*—.608. *4*—.07517. *5*—.036 T. *6*—.3125 bar. *7*—$2.25. *8*—$2.25. *9*—.625 bu.

Art. **131.** *1*—37. *2*—96. *3*—15 bar. *4*—23 sheets. *5*—19 overcoats. *6*—273 casks. *7*—17 loads. *8*—319 lb. *9*—.47 A.

Art. **132.** *1*—1,402.5. *2*—140.25. *3*—14.025. *4*—1.4025. *5*—.14025. *6*—.014025. *7*—1.4025. *8*—14.025. *9*—140.25. *11*—.421+. *12*—125.399+. *13*—$2.076+. *14*—$4.875+. *15*—9.24 oz. *16*—40.5 A. *17*—54.375 bu. *18*—$.337. *19*—$4,531.892+.

Art. **133.** *1*—130.03+. *2*—280. *3*—12 sacks. *4*—6.4 h. *5*—56 lb. *6*—14 bottles. *7*—.03125 gal.

Art. **134.** *1*—.023. *2*—.0625. *3*—.00625. *4*—.003125. *5*—.00546875. *6*—.037664+. *7*—.0053. *8*—$.04. *9*—.0095 oz. *10*—$.009.

Art. **135.** *1*—53.78. *2*—1.25. *3*—6.6227. *4*—$.0075. *5*—$.4375. *6*—2.06288. *7*—43.45 A. *8*—54.375 bu. *9*—9.375 mo. *10*—$41,319.30.

Art. **136.** *1*—.048. *2*—18,400. *3*—.078125. *4*—.00625. *5*—56.8 cd. *6*—40.5 times. *7*—422.4 lb. *8*—10.88 h. *9*—.512 h. *10*—65.625 bu. *11*—625.5 gallons. *12*—297.5 bushels. *13*—$5.375. *14*—280 lb. *15*—23 lounges. *16*—$1.875. *17*—.75 bu. *18*—43.5 yd. *19*—23 goblets, 3.5 oz. rem. *20*—407 T.; 1,105 lb. over. *21*—13 full car loads, 7 T. over. *22*—53 sheep, 1.5 bushels rem. *23*—7 lots, .075 A. rem. *24*—35 da., 3 lb. over.

Art. **139.** *2*—$6.03. *3*—$173.25. *4*—$244.50. *5*—$40.44.

Review. *1*—2.4. *2*—999.9. *3*—.00078125. *4*—$15.38+. *5*—14,525.28 T. *6*—$1,142.10. *7*—$18.25. *8*—$1.50. *9*—.125 bushel. *10*—.475 acre. *11*—$5,234.90. *12*—66 jars ; .25 pound left. *13*—58.625 bushels. *14*—$15,746.71. *15*—$18.375. *16*—$4.375. *17*—1,357.05 bushels. *18*—1.5946 T. *19*—.6875 of the vessel. *20*—Lost $712.875. *21*—$18.28+. *22*—$40.11. *23*—$92.50.

PROPERTIES OF NUMBERS. Factors and Divisors. Art. **144.** *1*—3, 3, 5, 7. *2*—2, 2, 109. *3*—3, 5, 37. *4*—863. *5*—3, 3, 3, 3, 3, 3. *6*—2, 3, 3, 53. *7*—2, 3, 11, 43. *8*—3, 3, 5, 7, 31.

Art. **145.** *1*—2, 2. *2*—2, 2, 2, 2, 2. *3*—2, 2, 2, 3. *4*—2, 2, 2, 5. *5*—3, 5. *6*—2, 2.

Art. **149.** *1*—32. *2*—240. *3*—28. *4*—51. *5*—351. *6*—15. *7*—72. *8*—28. *9*—14. *10*—405.

Art. **150.** *1*—14. *2*—4. *3*—28. *4*—18. *5*—9. *6*—6. *7*—5. *8*—450. *9*—20 rd. *10*—2 bu. in a bag ; 600 bags of wheat ; 432 bags of corn ; 392 bags of barley ; 893 bags of oats. *11*—40 yd.; 65 rooms. *12*—136 suits.

Multiples. Art. **153.** *1*—144. *2*—374. *3*—1,140. *4*—5,200. *5*—10,230. *6*—11,658.

Art. **156.** *1*—264. *2*—300. *3*—48. *4*—90. *5*—189. *6*—2,016. *7*—72. *8*—3,450. *9*—1,512. *10*—3,600. *11*—1,587,600. *12*—19,008.

Art. **158.** *1*—4,050. *2*—1,680. *3*—1,340. *4*—42,930. *5*—2,520. *6*—510. *7*—2,520. *8*—10,500. *9*—$5.40. *10*—960 bu. *11*—240 minutes; A, 20 miles; B, 15 miles; C, 12 miles. *12*—12,852 gal.

CANCELLATION. Art. **161.** *1*—3. *2*—5. *3*—4. *4*—8. *5*—9. *6*—85⅓. *7*—17. *8*—2. *9*—3½. *10*—5. *11*—7. *12*—4. *13*—9. *14*—20. *15*—1⅔. *16*—6 6/11. *17*—1. *18*—½. *19*—8 lb. *20*—22 cows. *21*—108 bu. *22*—96 mi. *23*—6 T. *24*—$74.67. *25*—40 da. *26*—30 da.

FRACTIONS. REDUCTIONS. Art. **177.** *1*—4/9. *2*—5/9. *3*—8/5. *4*—2/3. *5*—2/3. *6*—3/7. *7*—1/5. *8*—3/17. *9*—4/11. *10*—1 1/5. *11*—2 9/11. *12*—1 6/11. *13*—3/11. *14*—11/21. *15*—132/251. *16*—5/8 yard. *17*—2/3 da. *18*—$3/4; $4/5. *19*—7/8 lb. *20*—$1 8/5. *21.* 19/28 of a ton.

Art. **179.** *1*—156/464. *2*—140/160. *3*—45/600. *4*—33/275. *5*—450/600. *6*—132/297. *7*—133/255. *8*—480/1152. *9*—270/801. *10*—468/1184. *11*—444/1728. *12*—C. *13*—Crushed.

Art. **183.** *1*—6/42, 21/42, 28/42. *2*—33/88, 16/88. *3*—126/234, 221/234. *4*—60/120, 72/120, 40/120, 90/120. *5*—3465/4158, 2970/4158, 2310/4158, 1890/4158. *6*—6075/16200, 1944/16200, 1400/16200. *7*—960/2880, 360/2880, 576/2880, 240/2880, 1440/2880. *8*—46410/255255, 170170/255255, 39270/255255, 72030/255255, 102102/255255, 30030/255255. *9*—700/1120, 448/1120, 280/1120, 960/1120. *10.* 23,400. *11.* 6048/24192, 10080/24192, 6012/24192, 9072/24192, 21504/24192.

Art. **186.** *1*—28/48, 27/48. *2*—12/50, 35/50. *3*—10/24, 8/24, 16/24. *4*—6/36, 27/36, 16/36. *5*—28/40, 15/40, 16/40. *6*—10/12, 9/12, 11/12. *7*—840/1800, 1224/1800, 1000/1800, 825/1800. *8*—36/45, 38/45, 35/45, 33/45, 15/45. *9*—20/36, 9/36, 14/36, 30/36. *10*—1/7500.

Art. **188.** *1*—176. *2*—18. *3*—266. *4*—18 9/11. *5*—11 23/32. *6*—233 16/23. *7*—58 2/3. *8*—44. *9*—10 47/54. *10*—378. *11*—41 6/25. *12*—62½. *13*—4,402. *14*—276 4/5. *15*—180 5/7. *16*—151. *17*—168 3/4. *18*—85 22/27. *19*—625. *20*—433 53/133. *21*—19⅛ T. *22*—586⅔ bushels. *23*—$488½. *24*—$362¾. *25*—$945¾.

Art. **190.** *1*—162/6. *2*—97/4. *3*—291/8. *4*—382/53. *5*—1369/37. *6*—162/15. *7*—137/8. *8*—331/12. *9*—105/8. *10*—503/250. *11*—283/20. *12*—2257/30. *13*—1618/95. *14*—1027/81. *15*—4849/40. *16*—4353/50. *17*—781/145. *18*—1370/63. *19*—284/9. *20*—372/11. *21*—27873/237. *22*—221693/2567.

ADDITION. Art. **193.** *1*—89/130. *2*—1 29/60. *3*—1 43/140. *4*—7 11/20. *5*—0 22/63. *6*—1 7/12. *7*—26 107/150. *8*—1 20/30. *9*—8 107/300. *10*—246 41/60. *11*—43 5/72. *12*—18 58/315. *13*—4 1/144 yd. *14*—246 57/80 mi. *15*—$90 159/200.

Art. **194.** *1*—14 41/60 A. *2*—2 3/40 T. *3*—2 7/60. *4*—2 80/225. *5*—16 37/84. *6*—2 13/10. *7*—3 5/8. *8*—59 5/12. *9*—Entire salary. *10*—$2 9/50. *11*—5 99/128 cd. *12*—3 241/1152. *13*—1 137/300. *14*—27 457/610. *15*—109 11/20. *16*—140 99/160 miles. *17*—137 59/72 yd.

SUBTRACTION. Art. **196.** *1*—11/90. *2*—41/99. *3*—4/75. *4*—4/21. *5*—22/187. *6*—257/1380. *7*—1/340. *8*—9/160. *9*—179/714. *10*—1253/5280 miles. *11*—23¾. *12*—62 9/10. *13*—98 9/10. *14*—81 07/110. *15*—1/6. *16*—18 187/210. *17*—5 379/1155. *18*—65 9001/9000. *19*—297 889/2280.

Art. 197. 1—$\frac{12}{25}$. 2—$\frac{125}{408}$. 3—$\frac{161}{540}$. 4—$29\frac{1073}{5000}$. 5—$281\frac{9}{72}$. 6—$261\frac{189}{1190}$.
7—$\frac{9}{100}$ cd. 8—$\frac{33}{80}$ T. 9—$8\frac{49}{91}$. 10—$\frac{7247}{255}$. 11—$\frac{1700}{25283}$. 12—$\$4\frac{9}{20}$.
13—$15\frac{143}{100}$ mi. 14—$35\frac{13}{24}$ yd. 15—$\frac{7}{480}$. 16—$\frac{51}{160}$. 17—$14\frac{31}{40}$. 18—$6\frac{7}{101}$.
19—$7\frac{10}{104}$. 20—$1\frac{5}{16}$. 21—$\frac{7}{80}$. 22—$4\frac{13}{30}$. 23—$118\frac{31}{33}$. 24—$105\frac{31}{132}$.
25—$\frac{93}{200}$ A. 26—$1\frac{5}{56}$. 27—Increased by $\frac{1}{5}$. 28—$3\frac{25}{84}$. 29—$1\frac{19}{90}$; $\frac{7}{18}$; $1\frac{3}{5}$.

MULTIPLICATION. Art. 199. 1—$\frac{143}{252}$. 2—$\frac{90}{175}$. 3—$\frac{10}{13}$. 4—$\frac{575}{624}$.
5—$\frac{245}{2136}$. 6—$\frac{8}{25}$. 7—$\frac{580}{1206}$. 8—$\frac{22454}{67803}$. 9—$\frac{9}{22}$. 10—$\frac{10}{189}$. 11—$\frac{385}{1536}$.
12—$\frac{1}{2}$. 13—$\frac{2}{5}$. 14—$\frac{9}{14}$. 15—$\frac{9}{80}$. 16—$\frac{1}{50}$. 17—$1\frac{5}{7}$. 18—1. 19—$42\frac{2}{3}$.
20—11. 21—$348\frac{1}{3}$. 22—$\frac{16}{51}$ of a melon. 23—$\frac{1}{6}$ of the factory.
24—$\$1\frac{81}{128}$. 25—$7\frac{1}{6}$ A. 26—$80\frac{1}{3}$ rd.

Art. 200. 1—$2\frac{9}{35}$. 2—$11\frac{5}{17}$. 3—$7\frac{1}{2}$. 4—34. 5—370. 6—$8\frac{20}{66}$.
7—$238\frac{3}{4}$. 8—$46,405\frac{2}{7}$. 9—$42\frac{3}{16}$ bu. 10—$\$35\frac{3}{4}$. 11—$37\frac{1}{5}$ da. 12—$\$112\frac{8}{25}$.

Art. 201. 1—$4\frac{1}{2}$. 2—90. 3—$26\frac{2}{5}$. 4—$21\frac{17}{20}$. 5—$\$33\frac{3}{4}$. 6—$\$25.81\frac{1}{4}$.
7—$63,279\frac{1}{2}$. 8—$385,228\frac{12}{17}$. 9—$262\frac{1}{2}$ lb. 10—$805\frac{3}{4}$ lb. 11—$\$9.75$.
12—$\$16.55\frac{1}{2}$. 13—$\$386.74\frac{1}{2}$. 14—$\$4,216.40\frac{5}{8}$.

Art. 202. 1—$\$6\frac{3}{4}$. 2—$\$4\frac{1}{8}$. 3—$\$\frac{9}{16}$. 4—$\$6\frac{5}{12}$. 5—$\$8.33\frac{1}{3}$.
6—$\$7.38\frac{23}{32}$. 7—$\$56\frac{1}{4}$. 8—$\frac{1}{240}$. 9—$14\frac{6}{11}$ rd. 10—$\$3\frac{62}{80}$. 11—$\$7\frac{1}{2}$.
12—$36\frac{47}{120}$ mi. 13—$1\frac{3}{9}$. 14—$\$1\frac{33}{64}$. 15—$\frac{187}{480}$. 16—$\frac{2}{15}$. 17—$\$2.06\frac{1}{4}$.
18—$\$5.50$. 19—$\$1\frac{97}{320}$. 20—225 yd.

DIVISION. Art. 204. 1—$\frac{99}{112}$. 2—$1\frac{3}{35}$. 3—$\frac{55}{4480}$. 4—$\frac{1}{25}$. 5—$\frac{5}{24}$.
6—$14\frac{10}{21}$. 7—$8\frac{2}{5}$. 8—$1\frac{1}{3}$. 9—$12\frac{4}{35}$. 10—$1\frac{7}{33}$. 11—$1\frac{2}{3}$. 12—$\frac{5}{16}$. 13—$\frac{5}{8}$.
14—$\frac{24}{85}$. 15—$1\frac{2}{3}$. 16—$2\frac{87}{104}$. 17—$7\frac{22}{40}$. 18—$42\frac{6}{7}$. 19—63 sq. yd.
20—$\$\frac{9}{100}$. 21—$80\frac{1}{4}$ da.

Art. 205. 1—$\frac{9}{40}$. 2—$\frac{9}{55}$. 3—$\frac{3}{50}$. 4—$\frac{51}{1457}$. 5—$\frac{7}{20}$. 6—$\frac{2}{9}$. 7—$\frac{121}{144}$.
8—$44\frac{9}{68}$. 9—$17\frac{5}{12}$. 10—$208\frac{53}{60}$. 11—$100\frac{1}{28}$. 12—$210\frac{89}{270}$. 13—$\frac{1}{15}$ T.
14—$\frac{1}{10}$ T. 15—$\frac{35}{72}$ lb. 16—$\frac{5}{16}$ lb. 17—$\$1\frac{8}{15}$. 18—$159\frac{72}{88}$ lb.

Art. 206. 1—$15\frac{3}{7}$. 2—$40\frac{1}{2}$. 3—$210\frac{3}{8}$. 4—$73\frac{8}{10}$. 5—$1\frac{2}{7}$. 6—$37\frac{1}{3}$.
7—100. 8—$2\frac{6}{7}$. 9—$\$54\frac{2}{3}$. 10—$2\frac{2}{23}$ h. 11—$5\frac{17}{47}$ yd. 12—$59\frac{5}{17}$ doz.
13—24 pairs. 14—$35\frac{5}{17}$ yd. 15—32 blocks. 16—$20\frac{2}{3}$ bu. 17—$5\frac{5}{8}$ pages.
18—2,112 steps. 19—$\$22\frac{1}{2}$. 20—$\$\frac{200}{361}$.

Art. 207. 1—$\frac{11}{225}$. 2—$50\frac{3}{4}$. 3—$40\frac{1}{55}$. 4—28. 5—$\frac{135}{2092}$. 6—$7,991\frac{13}{17}$.
7—10. 8—$\frac{1}{15}$. 9—$\frac{5}{72}$ yd. 10—$3\frac{8}{35}$ A. 11—$27\frac{1}{2}$ quarts. 12—$\frac{11}{45}$ cd.
13—$\frac{15}{16}$ lb. 14—$\frac{11}{64}$ bu. 15—$\frac{3}{80}$ lb. 16—$7\frac{1}{2}$ da. 17—$\frac{12}{25}$ lb. 18—$5\frac{1}{3}$ da.
19—35 min. 20—$\$\frac{3}{50}$. 21—$15\frac{11}{28}$ da. 22—$\$\frac{1}{8}$. 23—$2\frac{143}{300}$ T. 24—$\frac{7}{25}$.
25—$\frac{4}{375}$. 26—$\frac{428}{459}$. 27—$13\frac{1}{3}$. 28—$2\frac{8}{21}$. 29—$\frac{2}{35}$. 30—$\frac{1}{8}$. 31—$\frac{900}{961}$.
32—$1\frac{1}{2}$.

Review. 1—$\frac{15}{85}$; $\frac{27}{153}$. 2—$282\frac{39}{47}$; $450\frac{69}{83}$; $182\frac{175}{234}$. 3—$\frac{180}{315}$, $\frac{252}{315}$, $\frac{140}{315}$.
4—$99\frac{37}{48}$. 5—$82\frac{1}{21}$. 6—$7,727\frac{1}{3}$. 7—$\frac{4}{195}$. 8—$\$3\frac{4}{15}$. 9—$8\frac{17}{25}$ pounds.
10—$123\frac{11}{12}$ acres. 11—$9\frac{1}{3}$. 12—$\$10,593\frac{1}{3}$. 13—$\$18\frac{9}{16}$. 14—1,360 lb.
15—$\$78$. 16—$\$16\frac{37}{48}$. 17—$\frac{4}{7}$; $\frac{7}{43}$; $\frac{5}{21}$; $\frac{9}{7}$; $\frac{9}{15}$. 18—Diminished $\frac{8}{55}$.
19—$\frac{3}{4}$. 20—$\frac{110360}{2493900}$. 21—$1\frac{7}{15}$; $\frac{2}{15}$; $\frac{8}{15}$. 22—$3\frac{8}{45}$; $1\frac{28}{45}$; $1\frac{13}{15}$.
23—$1\frac{9}{77}$; $\frac{9}{77}$; $\frac{24}{77}$. 24—$12\frac{25}{72}$; $2\frac{7}{72}$; $37\frac{1}{72}$. 25—$\frac{14}{15}$. 26—$\frac{2860}{165}$, $\frac{27}{165}$, $\frac{1080}{165}$

27—$70\frac{27}{32}$ yd.   28—$\frac{43}{48}$.   29—$21\frac{3}{7}$ acres to corn; $21\frac{3}{7}$ acres to potatoes; $7\frac{1}{7}$ acres to wheat.   30—$3\frac{1}{8}$ boots.   31—$16\frac{1}{5}$¢.   32—B; $14\frac{103}{120}$ mi.
33—27.40\frac{5}{13}$.   34—$3\frac{15}{16}$.   35—$\frac{52}{135}$.

COMPOUND NUMBERS. Reduction. Art. **220.** *1*—353,919 in.
2—985,140 sq. in.   *3*—$1,053\frac{1}{2}$ feet.   *4*—22,873 sq. ft.   *5*—8,831 qt.
6—234,128 cu. in.   *7*—1,539 in.   *8*—3,500,800 sq. rd.   *9*—2,800 A.
10—976 cu. ft.

Art. **222.**   *1*—77 ft. 1 in.   *2*—6 mi. 80 rd.   *3*—3 sq. mi. 30 A.
4—33 sq. yd.   *5*—72 rd. 2 yd.   *6*—540 bu. 3 qt.   *7*—191 gal. 3 qt. 1 pt.
8—5 sq. mi. 36 A.   *9*—3 cu. yd. 26 cu. ft. 624 cu. in.   *10*—8 sq. rd.
16 sq. yd. 4 sq. ft. 32 sq. in.   *11*—21 cd. 39 cu. ft. 1,000 cubic inches.
12—119 bu. 2 pk. 1 qt.   *13*—19 cd. 37 cu. ft.   *14*—215 gal. 3 qt. 1 pt.

Art. **223.**   *1*—6,408 tiles.   *2*—508 pt.   *3*—1,930 rd.   *4*—48,400 hills.
5—39 acres 146 square rods.   *6*—9 bu. 2 pk. 1 qt.   *7*—320 bottles.
8—507 pt. papers.   *9*—91 gal. 1 qt.   *10*—5 bu. 2 pk. 1 pt.

Addition.   Art. **226.**   *1*—208 gal. 3 qt.   *2*—39 A. 144 sq. rd.
3—55 cu. yd. 16 cu. ft. 1,007 cu. in.   *4*—14 yd. 6 in.   *5*—49 gal. 3 qt. 3 gi.
6—81 bu. 1 pk. 4 quarts.   *7*—21 cd. 96 cu. ft.   *8*—4 mi. 120 rd. 1 yd.
9—2,041 bu. 3 pk. 2 qt.   *10*—9 gal. 2 qt.   *11*—115 sq. yd. 5 sq. ft.

Subtraction.   Art. **228.**   *1*—2 miles 276 rods 2 feet 9 inches.
2—5 sq. rd. 29 sq. yd. 2 sq. ft. 36 sq. in.   *3*—5 yards 1 foot 5 inches.
4—4 bu. 2 pk. 3 qt.   *5*—50 cu. yd. 8 cu. ft. 762 cu. in.   *6*—87 cords.
7—1 mi. 174 rd. 3 yd. 2 ft. 6 in.   *8*—14 gal. 1 qt. 1 pt.

Multiplication.   Art. **230.**   *1*—853 bu. 6 qt.   *2*—1,098 mi. 3 rd.
3 yd. 2 ft. 6 in.   *3*—1 cu. yd. 1 cu. ft. 1,152 cu. in.   *4*—292 A. 80 sq.
rd. 14 sq. yd. 2 sq. ft. 32 sq. in.   *5*—230 gal. 1 pt.   *6*—848 mi. 226 rd.
3 yd.   *7*—24 cd. 24 cu. ft.   *8*—37 bu. 3 pk. 4 qt.   *9*—1 A. 60 sq. rd.
4 sq. yd. 4 sq. ft. 72 sq. in.   *10*—589 mi. 103 rd. 2 yd. 2 ft. 6 in.

Division.   Art. **232.**   *1*—1 mi. 259 rd. 2 yd. 2 ft. $10\frac{2}{3}$ in.   *2*—2 sq.
mi. 365 A. 119 sq. rd. 17 sq. yd. 2 sq. ft. $82\frac{2}{7}$ sq. in.   *3*—3 cu. yd. 3
cu. ft. 288 cu. in.   *4*—43 rd. 4 yd. 2 ft. $1\frac{3}{4}$ in.   *5*—21 A. 66 sq. rd. 136
sq. ft. $46\frac{4}{5}$ sq. in.   *6*—$1,340\frac{7}{25}$ cu. in.   *7*—6 kegs.   *8*—2.   *9*—2 rd. 2
yd. 2 ft.   *10*—12 cu. yd. 12 cu. ft.   *11*—65 bags.   *12*—60 sq. rd.

Art. **234.**   *1*—9,683 lb.   *2*—412 oz.   *3*—34 bar. 147 lb.   *4*—20 bar.
63 lb. 7 oz.   *5*—58 T. 10 cwt. 3 lb. 9 oz.   *6*—1,785 lb. 12 oz.   *7*—60 T.
472 lb. 8 oz.   *8*—281 lb. $3\frac{1}{4}$ oz.   *9*—47 lb. 2 oz.   *10*—41,716 packages.
11—26 T. 812 lb. 8 oz.   *12*—9 T. 8 cwt. 46 lb.   *13*—36 lb. 12 oz.
14—53 T. 875 lb.   *15*—1 T. 1,825 lb.   *16*—360 da.   *17*—33 lb. 14 oz.

Art. **235.**   *1*—1 wk. 3 da. 3 h. 14 min. 35 sec.   *2*—5 wk.   *3*—8,784 h.
4—31,556,929 sec.   *5*—1,047 da. 17 h. 54 min.   *6*—7 wk. 5 da. 3 h. 4
min. 51 sec.   *7*—12 da. 6 h. 40 min.   *8*—329 yr. 119 da. 22 h. 12 min.
9—267,120 min.   *10*—11 da. 13 h. 46 min. 40 sec.   *11*—6 yr. 20 da.
12—39 h. 20 min.   *13*—8 da. 1 h. 15 min.   *14*—4 da. 7 h. 30 min.

Art. **236.** *1*—Jan. 17, 1706.   *2*—67 yr. 9 mo. 22 da.   *3*—1 yr. 9 mo. 27 da.
4—4 mo. 24 da.   *6*—4 yr. 1 mo. 14 da.

Art. **237.** *1*—498 doz. *2*—3,739 sheets. *3*—2 grt. gro. 2 gro. 10 doz. 8. *4*—11 rm. 1 quire 15 sheets. *5*—25 rm. 13 quires 16 sheets. *6*—15 grt. gro. 1 gro. 4 doz. *7*—480 sheets. *8*—3,540 clothes-pins. *9*—$10\frac{1}{3}$ doz. pairs. *10*—5 gro.

Review. *1*—31 bu. 1 pk. 2 qt. 1 pt. *2*—2 gallons. *3*—250 days. *4*—10 gal. 1 pt. *5*—34 bu. 3 pk. 4 qt. *6*—15,000 lb. *7*—24 rd. 1 yd. 1 ft. *8*—1 A. 97 sq. rd. 213 sq. ft. 36 sq. in. *9*—\$245. *10*—2 cd. 96 cu. ft. *11*—59 bar. 75 lb. *12*—6 quires 12 sheets. *13*—285 bu. *14*—1,277 cu. yd. 21 cu. ft. *15*—81 mi. 120 rd. *16*—36 A. 137.25 sq. rd. *17*—12 da. *18*—204 T. 1,050 lb.

MEASUREMENTS. Rectangles, Triangles, and Trapezoids.
Art. **247.** *1*—324 sq. rd. *2*—30,100 sq. yd. *3*—2,175.5 sq. ft. *4*—303.052 sq. in. *5*—11 sq. ft. $40\frac{1}{2}$ sq. in. *6*—3,904.5 square rods. *7*—1,449.6 sq. yd. *8*—7 sq. ft. *9*—30,174 sq. ft. *10*—1,339.625 sq. mi. *11*—21 sq. rd. 27 sq. yd. 4 sq. ft. 72 sq. in. *12*—6,400 sq. ft. *13*—800 A.

Art. **248.** *1*—36 rods. *2*—22 rods. *3*—$49\frac{19}{44}$ rods. *4*—$30\frac{5}{21}$ rods. *5*—1,192 ft. *6*—$822\frac{22}{26}$ ft. *7*—162.4125 ft. *8*—$112\frac{1}{116}$ ft. (=112.0086+ft.). *9*—$304\frac{144}{161}$ rd. *10*—176.65+rd. *11*—565.7458+rd. *12*—327.8898+rd. *13*—$8\frac{1}{3}$ feet. *14*—$2\frac{262}{333}$ yards. *15*—$8\frac{1}{2}$ ft. *16*—$8\frac{47}{111}$ ft. *17*—$9\frac{29}{30}$ ft. *18*—$12\frac{1}{2}$ ft. *19*—16 ft. *20*—27 ft.

Art. **250.** *1*—1,134 sq. in. *2*—4,608 sq. ft. *3*—$224\frac{5}{16}$ sq. ft. *4*—$1,185\frac{7}{8}$ sq. ft. *5*—3,948 sq. rd. *6*—$14\frac{5}{8}$ in. *7*—4 ft. 11 in. *8*—42 ft. *9*—24 ft. *10*—$56\frac{8}{111}$ rd.

Art. **251.** *1*—270 sq. in. *2*—575 square feet. *3*—35,805 sq. yd. *4*—148 sq. ft. 88 sq. in. *5*—$123\frac{1}{4}$ sq. ft. *6*—509.90625 sq. ft.

Art. **252.** *1*—$240\frac{1}{2}$ sq. in. *2*—775 sq. yd. *3*—$30.164\frac{1}{16}$ sq. mi. *4*—$100\frac{20}{33}$ sq. rd. *5*—$46\frac{1}{4}$ sq. yd. *6*—$91\frac{2}{3}$ sq. ft.

Art. **253.** *1*—203 A. 145 sq. rd. *2*—$81\frac{23}{27}$ yd. *3*—18 ft. 9 in. by 40 ft. *4*—$253\frac{1}{3}$ sq. yd. *5*—351 feet. *6*—49 sq. ft. 94 sq. in. *7*—41.4 feet. *8*—\$5,862.50. *9*—$18\frac{33}{55}$ rd. *10*—2,495 ft.

The Circle. Art. **255.** *1*—$25\frac{1}{7}$ ft. *2*—8 ft. $4\frac{4}{7}$ in. *3*—53 ft. $5\frac{1}{7}$ in. *4*—3 ft. $4\frac{6}{7}$ in. *5*—9 ft. $6\frac{5}{22}$ in. *6*—5 ft. 3 in. *7*—170 yd. 4.9+in. *8*—$5\frac{1}{4}$ in.

Art. **256.** *1*—$10,028\frac{3}{4}$ sq. ft. *2*—$201\frac{1}{7}$ sq. in. *3*—$707\frac{1}{7}$ sq. in. *4*—$41,367\frac{5}{8}$+sq. rd. *5*—8,148.732+sq. rd. *6*—79,577.464+ sq. yd.

Art. **257.** *1*—16.9964+mi. *2*—170.45+sq. ft. *3*—$254\frac{1}{7}$ sq. ft. *4*—688.265+sq. rd. *5*—$201\frac{1}{7}$ sq. in.

Rectangular Solids. Art. **260.** *1*—1,155 cu. ft. *2*—3,052.5 cu. ft. *3*—861 cu. ft. *4*—2,002 cu. ft. *5*—3,944.2 cu. ft. *6*—5,184 cu. in. *7*—1,000.32 cu. in. *8*—1,377 cubic inches. *9*—1,252.8 cubic inches. *10*—64.21325 cubic inches. *11*—232,000 cu. yd. *12*—87,000 cu. yd. *13*—339,648 cu. yd. *14*—360,000 cu. yd. *15*—197,640 cu. yd.

Art. **261.** *1*—64 inches. *2*—$45\frac{5}{7}$ in. *3*—$44\frac{4}{25}$ in. *4*—86.4 in. *5*—$42\frac{114}{203}$ in. *6*—125 ft. *7*—$187\frac{1}{2}$ ft. *8*—78.43137+ft. *9*—$112\frac{1}{2}$ ft.

10—$103\frac{15}{17}$ feet.   11—$5\frac{1}{3}$ inches.   12—18 ft. $3\frac{3}{7}$ in.   13—4 ft. $8\frac{3}{5}$ in.
14—$2\frac{3}{11}$ in.   15—$92\frac{4}{7}$ ft.   16—$3\frac{1}{3}$ ft.

Art. **262.** 1—84 loads. 2—$9\frac{27}{32}$ cd. 3—1,728 cubes. 4—$137\frac{12}{13}$ cu. yd. 5—36 ft.

BUSINESS MEASUREMENTS. Art. **265.** 1—21,489.3 cubic inches.
2—1 gal. 1.236+ qt. 3—$1,289\frac{1}{10}$ bu. 4—2,240 sq. ft.; 22.40 squares.
5—33 squares; $6,187\frac{1}{2}$ square feet. 6—3,456 slates. 7—$67\frac{1}{2}$ bunches.
8—$76.80. 9—23.6 bunches. 10—$677\frac{7}{9}$ square yards. 11—$233\frac{1}{3}$.
12—$466\frac{2}{3}$ cubic yards. 13—$5,898.75. 14—50 panes. 15—$12\frac{1}{4}$ boxes.
16—$9.54. 17—$67.55. 18—$431\frac{11}{27}$ cubic yards. 19—$444\frac{4}{9}$ loads.
20—$13,481\frac{13}{27}$ cu. yd. 21—27 ft. 22—72 hhd. 23—256.4749 + bar.
24—$67\frac{1}{12}$ square feet. 25—14,580 bricks. 26—$113\frac{3}{4}$ cubic feet.
27—$219\frac{1}{3}$ perches; $28\frac{35}{128}$ cd. 28—$16.18\frac{3}{4}$. 29—45 feet; 540 feet.
30—1,800 bricks. 31—$559.10. 32—$3,226\frac{2}{3}$ cu. yd. 33—$17.82.
34—$38\frac{1}{4}$ perches. 35—160 sq. ft. 36—96 sq. ft. 37—$24\frac{11}{30}$ cu. ft.
38—400 sq. ft. 39—180 sq. ft. 40—112 ft. 41—$30.37\frac{1}{2}$. 42—501.6 bu.
43—1,024 bu. 44—28 bu. 45—6,528 bu. 46—502.2 bu. 47—$66\frac{2}{3}$ T.
48—$1\frac{57}{88}$ T. 49—$2\frac{52}{55}$ T.

Review. 1—1,512 square rods. 2—$918\frac{3}{4}$ sq. rd. 3—2,714.4 sq. rd.
4—1,649.375 sq. rd. 5—$35\frac{3}{5}$ sq. yd. 6—$31\frac{3}{8}$ sq. yd. 7—$42\frac{3}{16}$ sq. yd.
8—$37\frac{1}{2}$ sq. yd. 9—209.035 sq. yd. 10—82.80+ sq. yd. 11—247.35 sq. yd.
12—97.9861+ sq. yd. 13—$31\frac{1}{4}$ cu. ft. 14—$51\frac{9}{16}$ cu. ft. 15—$51\frac{9}{16}$ cu. ft.
16—$51\frac{9}{16}$ cu. ft. 17—$140\frac{27}{250}$ cu. ft. 18—$290\frac{5}{18}$ cu. ft. 19—$171\frac{7}{8}$ cu. ft.
20—$255\frac{5}{54}$ cu. ft. 21—$214\frac{23}{36}$ cu. ft. 22—$111\frac{27}{38}$ cu. ft. 23—265 sq. in.
24—13.3647 + A. 25—36 sq. in. 26—2,150 persons. 27—$49.87\frac{1}{2}$.
28—$26.30. 29—16 ft. 30—$8\frac{7}{8}$ yards. 31—9 in. 32—10 ft. 8 in.
33—600 rd. 34—18 ft. 35—6 ft. 4 in. 36—2,046 pickets. 37—288 sq. ft.
38—24 A. 108 sq. rd. 39—24 ft. 40—13 sq. yd. 41—4 sq. ft. 24 sq. in.
42—160 rd. 43—$32\frac{3}{11}$ sq. rd. 44—$67.20. 45—310 sq. rd. 46—468 cu. ft.
47—4 cu. ft. 108 cu. in. 48—$12\frac{1}{3}$ hours. 49—2 ft. 6 in. 50—$8\frac{8}{9}$ feet.
51—$89\frac{13}{15}$ bu. 52—$163\frac{7}{11}$ sheets. 53—$32.50. 54—$.21. 55—$23.94.
56—$427\frac{247}{539}$ bar. 57—$6\frac{59}{60}$ in. 58—134,744 bricks. 59—$\frac{1}{6}$ of the wall.
60—$140.16. 61—$76.82. 62—$2.54. 63—$55\frac{11}{18}$ T. 64—3,360 ft.
65—$1.36\frac{1}{2}$. 66—$18.62. 67—$56\frac{1}{3}$ bushels; $45\frac{1}{15}$ bushels. 68—$81.04.
69—$12.80. 70—$466.36. 71—$48\frac{23}{125}$ cd. 72—$33\frac{11}{40}$ T. 73—576 bu.
75—10 ft. $3\frac{1}{5}$ in. 76—$20\frac{1}{2}$ in. by $30\frac{1}{4}$ in. by $42\frac{1}{8}$ in.

PERCENTAGE. THE FIVE GENERAL CASES. Art. **276.**
1—38 sheep. 2—110 pupils. 3—3.3 gal. 4—14,400 A. 5—$1,234\frac{3}{8}$ bu.
6—7,350 men. 7—$2,062\frac{1}{2}$ Lehigh; 2,875 Lackawanna; $1,312\frac{1}{2}$ Pittston.
8—$789\frac{7}{9}$ bu.

Art. **278.** 1—6%. 2—$\frac{1}{2}$%. 3—$6\frac{2}{3}$%. 4—1500%. 5—20%. 6—35%.
7—8%. 8—18%. 9—$7\frac{17}{19}$%. 10—$6\frac{1}{4}$%.

Art. **280.** 1—1,300 tons. 2—92 miles. 3—$2,777\frac{1}{2}$. 4—$1,900.
5—2,000 sacks. 6—$11\frac{1}{4}$¢. 7—125 pupils. 8—125 sq. rd. 9—$.25\frac{5}{24}.
10—$3\frac{1}{3}$ lb.

Art. **282.** 1—$8.40. 2—$492. 3—$82\frac{1}{2}$¢. 4—$328.50. 5—$266\frac{2}{3}$

Art. **284.** *1*—$450. *2*—$337.50. *3*—$1,875. *4*—$1,680. *5*—$1,750.
6—$90. *7*—$42\frac{38}{41}$ yd.

Special Applications. Art. **287.** *1*—$.25. *2*—$.58. *3*—$.09.
4—$340. *5*—$23.43$\frac{3}{4}$. *6*—6$\frac{1}{4}$¢. *7*—65¢. *8*—80¢. *9*—274.4 lb.
10—$.663. *11*—$2.08. *12*—$3.25. *13*—$2. *14*—85¢. *15*—8$\frac{1}{3}$%.
16—16$\frac{2}{3}$%. *17*—11$\frac{71}{164}$%. *18*—33$\frac{1}{3}$%. *19*—25%. *20*—17$\frac{11}{17}$%. *21*—20%.
22—$97.83. *23*—$208.33$\frac{1}{3}$. *24*—$.64$\frac{3}{7}$.

Art. **290.** *1*—$20.75. *2*—$209.06$\frac{1}{4}$. *3*—$45.50. *4*—$59.25.
5—75.37\frac{1}{2}$. *6*—$19.40$\frac{5}{8}$. *7*—12$\frac{1}{2}$%. *8*—2$\frac{995}{2315}$%. *9*—Investment,
$1,323.81; Com., $66.19. *10*—Investment, $12,000; Com., $400.
11—$2,565.85. *12*—$5,490.20. *13*—20,000 lb. *14*—$278. *15*—$6,004.
16—$2,475.

Art. **294.** *1*—$90. *2*—$39.29$\frac{3}{4}$. *3*—$29.25. *4*—$9.37$\frac{1}{2}$. *5*—84.37\frac{1}{2}$.
6—$45. *7*—$731.25. *8*—$\frac{1}{4}$%. *9*—1$\frac{1}{2}$%. *10*—$\frac{1}{2}$%. *11*—2%. *12*—$1,266.66$\frac{2}{3}$.
13—$4,500. *14*—$1,950.

Art. **295.** *1*—37.37\frac{1}{2}$. *2*—$3.728. *3*—1$\frac{53}{185}$%. *4*—$\frac{3}{8}$%. *5*—$\frac{3}{4}$%.
6—A, $4.92; B, $5.91; C, $8.86; D, $2.95; E, $16.73. *7*—$1,425.23.
8—$9,350. *9*—2%; $66, $9, $24, $45, $15, $36, $12, $18.

Art. **303.** *1*—140.62\frac{1}{2}$. *2*—$218.04. *3*—$963.83. *4*—$2,169.07.

Art. **311.** *1*—107\frac{3}{x}$ per share. *2*—$84 per share. *3*—$35.87$\frac{1}{2}$.
4—107.18\frac{3}{4}$. *5*—$8,625. *6*—87 shares. *7*—25 shares. *8*—6$\frac{14}{47}$%.
9—6$\frac{1}{4}$%. *10*—$3,393.75. *11*—$1,741.87$\frac{1}{2}$. *12*—15 shares.

Art. **318.** *1*—Reed, $1,008.82; Clark, $1,441.18. *2*—A, $6.25;
B, $8.75; C, $7.50. *3*—Hanover, $4,950; Globe, $3,960; Ætna,
$3,300; Franklin, $2,970. *4*—Bates, $354.86; Davis, $473.14.
5—Capital: G's, $20,000; H's, $30,000; K's, $25,000. Dividends:
G's, $4,960; H's, $7,440; K's, $6,200. *6*—E, 672 bales; F, 400 bales;
G, 552 bales; H, 296 bales. *7*—W., $11,700; J., $26,325; B., $32,175.
8—A, 70 bu.; B, 87$\frac{1}{2}$ bu. *9*—A, 24$\frac{12}{17}$ shares; B, 47$\frac{1}{17}$ shares; C,
28$\frac{4}{17}$ shares. *10*—Hilton, $23.58; Roberts, $26.42. *11*—A, $2,982$\frac{1}{12}$;
B, $2,455$\frac{5}{8}$; C, $2,280$\frac{5}{12}$; D, 701\frac{2}{3}$. *12*—A, $647.92; B, $161.98; C,
$323.96; D, $809.90.

Interest. Art. **325.** *1*—$28.02. *2*—$16.05; $337.05. *3*—$58.62$\frac{1}{2}$.
4—$147.06. *5*—$182.47. *6*—$4,312.50. *7*—$2,655. *8*—$78.41.

Art. **327.** *1*—$14.28. *2*—$3.13. *3*—$54.53. *4*—$272.09.
5—$301.61. *6*—$3,523.35. *7*—$2,759.32. *8*—$294. *9*—$60.55.

Art. **329.** *1*—$71.82. *2*—$45.84. *3*—$303.94. *4*—$44.76.
5—$3.64. *6*—$35.27.

Art. **331.** *1*—$193.75. *2*—$106.56. *3*—$63.61. *4*—$36.92.
5—$119.26. *6*—$135.63. *7*—$74.59. *8*—$44.53. *9*—$25.84.
10—$83.48. *11*—$87.19. *12*—$47.95. *13*—$28.63. *14*—$16.61.
15—$53.67. *16*—$290.63. *17*—$159.84. *18*—$95.42. *19*—$55.38.
20—$178.90. *21*—$116.25. *22*—$63.94. *23*—$38.17. *24*—$22.15.
25—$71.56. *26*—$146.50. *27*—$80.58. *28*—$48.10. *29*—$27.92.

30—$90.18.   31—$102.55.   32—$56.40.   33—$33.67.   34—$19.54.
35—$63.18.   36—$65.93.   37—$36.26.   38—$21.65.   39—$12.56.
40—$40.58.   41—$219.75.   42—$120.86.   43—$72.15.   44—$41.87.
45—$185.27. • 46—$87.90.   47—$48.35.   48—$28.86.   49—$16.75.
50—$54.11. 51—$3,730.57. 52—$2,051.81. 53—$1,224.87. 54—$710.88.
55—$2,296.37.   56—$2,611.40.   57—$1,436.27.   58—$857.41.
59—$497.62. 60—$1,607.46. 61—$1,678.75. 62—$923.31. 63—$551.19.
64—$319.90.   65—$1033.37.   66—$5,595.85.   67—$3,077.72.
68—$1,837.30.   69—$1,066.32.   70—$3,444.56.   71—$2,238.34.
72—$1,231.09.   73—$734.92.   74—$426.53.   75—$1,377.82.
76—$6,004.54.   77—$3,302.50.   78—$1,971.49.   79—$1,144.20.
80—$3,696.18.   81—$4,203.18.   82—$2,311.75.   83—$1,380.04.
84—$800.94.   85—$2,587.29.   86—$2,702.04.   87—$1,486.12.
88—$887.17.   89—$514.89.   90—$1,663.26.   91—$9,006.81.
92—$4,953.75.   93—$2,957.24.   94—$1,716.30.   95—$5,544.19.
96—$3,602.72.   97—$1,981.50.   98—$1,182.89.   99—$686.52.
100—$2,217.68.   101—$2,365.94.   102—$1,301.26.   103—$776.82.
104—$450.84.   105—$1,456.36.   106—$1,656.15.   107—$910.88.
108—$543.77.   109—$315.59.   110—$1,019.46.   111—$1,064.67.
112—$585.57.   113—$349.57.   114—$202.88.   115—$655.36.
116—$3,548.90.   117—$1,951.90.   118—$1,165.22.   119—$676.26.
120—$2,184.55.   121—$1,419.56.   122—$780.76.   123—$466.09.
124—$270.51. 125—$873.82. 126—$85.08. 127—$95.06. 128—$88.17.
129—$85.97. 130—$99.27. 131—$90.09. 132—$85.46. 133—$96.87.
134—$88.99. 135—$327.07. 136—$365.42. 137—$338.94. 138—$330.46.
139—$381.60. 140—$346.29. 141—$328.52. 142—$372.36. 143—$342.09.
144—$2.12. 145—$2.37. 146—$2.20. 147—$2.14. 148—$2.47.
149—$2.24. 150—$2.13. 151—$2.41. 152—$2.22. 153—$654.
154—$204. 155—$22. 156—$131.25. 157—$145.60. 158—$1,957.04.
159—$219.15. 160—$5.94. 162—$39.20. 164—$1,090. 165—$810.55.
166—$1,388.17. 167—$1,164.17. 168—$2,970.18. 169—$669.30.

Review. 1—21,525 votes. 2—1st, 36%; 2d, 34%; 3d, 30%. 3—36 mi.
4—$.33¾. 5—Loss, $2. 6—12½%. 7—$.90. 8—$6,310. 9—$118.75,
fees; $831.25, remitted. 10—$44,314.29. 11—$254.94. 12—$120.75.
13—2¼%.   14—$2,287.50.   15—$590.   16—$6.83.   17—$99.96.
18—$436.82.   19—$2,175.   20—$1,200.   21—$2.13½.   22—12%.
23—2¢ apiece; 30¢ a dozen.   24—$9,800; $6,500; $10,250; $7,150.
25—922.722 + bushels.   26—$2,650.   27—$2,185. • 28—$5,941.25.
29—$841.42.   31—$\frac{9}{46}$ of the ship.   32—200 bushels.   33—14¾%.
34—$6,958.40.   35—11¼%.   36—$1,004.25.   37—$675.   38—230%.
39—10%.   40—$282.49.   41—50%.   42—It is $92.60 per annum
cheaper for him to buy the farm.   43—$72.24.   44—$1.45$\frac{5}{11}$.

SUPPLEMENT.

METHODS OF PROOF. *Art.* **5.** *1*—354,455. *2*—5,084.4751. *3*—3$\frac{37}{40}$. *4*—$18,330.63. *5*—227,933. *6*—75.7917. *7*—2$\frac{600}{2000}$. *8*—3,121,788. *9*—167.18081. *10*—$4,426.98$\frac{3}{4}$. *11*—1$\frac{5563}{71555}$. *12*—68. *13*—69$\frac{5}{12}$. *14*—5.242+. *15*—6.42+. *16*—36.4. *17*—4$\frac{24}{35}$.

SHORT METHODS. *Art.* **12.** *1*—308,520. *2*—4,557,168. *3*—202,875,372. *4*—18,438. *5*—86,922. *6*—1,282.68. *7*—2,800.28. *8*—.00030848.

Art. **16.** *1*—1,940. *2*—43,875. *3*—245,500. *4*—455. *5*—5,037.5. *6*—119. *7*—40.62\frac{1}{2}$. *8*—$6,250. *9*—$660. *10*—$1.80. *11*—$468.75. *12*—$423.

Art. **17.** *1*—742,104. *2*—6,835,158. *3*—169,693,029. *4*—8,020,619,793. *5*—227,640,772,359. *6*—2,694,251,157,219.

Art. **18.** *1*—725. *2*—66. *3*—3,737$\frac{3}{4}$. *4*—5,005$\frac{5}{9}$. *5*—10.24. *6*—80.5. *7*—34$\frac{7}{16}$.

Art. **19.** *1*—1,712. *2*—26$\frac{9}{10}$. *3*—198. *4*—7.14. *5*—$38.28. *6*—177.4. *7*—$2.27. *8*—$.1127. *9*—$65. *10*—3.4 yd. *11*—65 lb. 15 oz. *12*—578.46 bar.

CONVERSE REDUCTIONS. *Art.* **21.** *1*—$\frac{3}{8}$. *2*—$\frac{73}{80}$. *3*—$\frac{17}{20}$. *4*—$\frac{13}{80}$. *5*—$\frac{2}{3125}$. *6*—$\frac{11}{160}$. *7*—18$\frac{3}{4}$. *8*—$\frac{1}{6250}$ mi. *9*—$\frac{11}{400}$ wk. *10*—$$\frac{1}{6}$.

Art. **22.** *1*—.35. *2*—.40625. *3*—.2727+. *4*—.00004. *5*—18.75; 7.075. *6*—.555+ da. *7*—19.3636+ yd.

Art. **23.** *1*—19 hours 12 minutes. *2*—1 foot 10$\frac{1}{2}$ inches. *3*—70 rd. *4*—21 bu. 3 pk. 4 qt. *5*—2 qt. 1 pt. 1$\frac{1}{3}$ gi. *6*—2.5344 square inches. *7*—273 da. 18 h. *8*—13 cwt. 1 qr. 9$\frac{1}{3}$ lb.

Art. **24.** *1*—.921875 bu. *2*—.90625 gal. *3*—.625 gro. *4*—.8282+rd. *5*—.6625 ream. *6*—.10175 T. *7*—.66 da. *8*—.5 rd.

Art. **25.** *1*—6 doz. 4$\frac{4}{5}$. *2*—426 A. 106 sq. rd. 20 sq. yd. 1 sq. ft. 72 sq. in. *3*—146 sq. rd. 20 sq. yd. 1 sq. ft. 72 sq. in. *4*—1 bu. 2 pk. 1 pt. *5*—60 gal. 2 gi. *6*—219 da. 14 h. 24 min.

Art. **26.** *1*—$\frac{23}{32}$ gal. *2*—$\frac{198}{2178}$ sq. rd. *3*—$\frac{8600}{21120}$ mile. *4*—$\frac{49}{64}$ bu. *5*—$\frac{197}{210}$ cu. yd. *6*—$\frac{3269}{9000}$ da.

PRICE, QUANTITY, AND COST. *Art.* **32.** *1*—$3,029.81$\frac{1}{4}$. *2*—$10,336.50. *3*—1.53\frac{1}{4}$. *4*—$70.76$\frac{1}{4}$. *5*—167.47\frac{1}{2}$. *6*—$294.18$\frac{1}{4}$. *7*—$640.74. *8*—$18.096. *9*—$64.35.

Art. **33.** *1*—429 bar. *2*—183.76 T. *3*—4$\frac{1}{2}$ yd. *4*—3,057 pickets. *5*—385 lb. *6*—85,432 bricks. *7*—15,690 ft. *8*—2,784 lb. *9*—4,680 lb.

Art. **34.** *1*—7.06\frac{1}{4}$. *2*—$56.25. *3*—$4.50. *4*—$2.25. *5*—$11.50. *6*—$7.50. *7*—$18.75. *8*—$13. *9*—$27.50.

Art. 35. 4—$8.49¾. 5—26 gallons 1+quarts. 6—$87.425. 7—¾ cd.
8—$11.61⅞. 9—$2.25. 10—$1.85. 11—$41.58. 12—100 M feet.
13—$125. 14—$55.78¼. 15—10¾ M ft. 16—3 T. 1,875 lb. 17—$153.77.
18—62½ lb. 19—$.32¼. 20—$262.50. 21—5,750 feet. 22—$72.
23—$9.02. 24—$32.85. 25—13 cwt. 1 qr. 21 679/2553 lb.

LONGITUDE AND TIME. *Art. 66.* 1—8°. 2—13' 30". 3—1° 20'.
4—7° 11' 15". 5—17° 7' 30". 6—123° 6' 45". 7—3° 20' W. 8—17° 30' E.
9—100° 3' W. 10—30° E. 11—6° 13' W. 12—137° 17' 15" E.

Art. 67. 1—5 hours 17 minutes 21 seconds. 2—5 h. 50 min. 28 sec.
3—5 h. 59 min. 47 7/13 sec. 4—10 h. 26 min. 3 sec. 5—6 h. 32 min. 12⅔ sec.
6—5 h. 8 min. 1 sec. 7—11 min. 58 sec. P.M. 8—8 h. 46 min. 25 sec. A.M.
9—1 hour 6 min. 17 sec. P.M. 10—9 hours 40 min. 44 sec. A.M.
11—7 hours 41 min. 58 sec. A.M. 12—4 hours 16 min. 25 sec. A.M.
13—8 h. 36 min. 17 sec. A.M. 14—5 h. 10 min. 44 sec. A.M.

INTEREST. *Art. 87.* 1—3%. 2—4½%. 3—4⅕%. 4—2⅕%. 5—9%.
6—18¾%. 7—12 29/60%. 8—$5.37½. 9—$84.37½. 10—$60.83. 11—$44.21.
12—$41.14. 13—$645.81. 14—$465.62. 15—$338.37. 16—$13.53.
17—$212.41. 18—$153.15. 19—$111.29. 20—$259.68. 21—$4,076.33.
22—$2,938.98. 23—$2,135.79.

Art. 88. 1—$2.51. 2—$234. 3—$15.78. 4—$.32. 5—$5. 6—$1.50.
7—$330.38. 8—$8.33. 9—$2.84. 10—$15.47. 11—$13.23. 12—$111.72.
13—$5.26. 14—$199.60. 15—$40.82. 16—$55.12.

Art. 92. 1—$406. 2—$7,899.85. 3—$9,473.68. 4—$260.71.
5—$2,204.23. 6—$36.50.

Art. 94. 1—$483.62. 2—$329.63. 3—$621.21. 4—$67.50.
5—$1,592. 6—$419.84.

Art. 95. 1—4½%. 2—5%. 3—6%. 4—6%. 5—9%. 6—3½%.

Art. 96. 1—1 yr. 9 mo. 8 da. 2—2 yr. 6 mo. 3—22 yr. 2 mo.
20 da. 4—8 yr. 4 mo. 5—6 mo. 6—10 mo. 15 da.

PROBLEMS IN THE SIX GENERAL CASES OF INTEREST. 1—$280.
2—$1,788.73. 3—$690.57½. 4—$131.25. 5—$1,204.64. 6—$1,500.
7—$666.67. 8—5 yr. 4 mo. 9—4 yr. 2 mo. 10—8%. 11—4%. 12—$400.
13—$810. 14—$982.43. 15—$1,413.45. 16—$3,930.85. 17—1 yr. 6
mo. 6 da. 18—I rec'd 2 7/8%; Buyer of note rec'd 9 13/16%.

EXACT INTEREST. *Art. 99.* 1—$4.43. 2—$4.60. 3—$356.25.
4—$206.32. 5—$1,278.76. 6—$8,713.86. 7—$540.16. 8—$29.94.
9—$2.46. 10—$41.64. 12—$240.27. 13—$6.74. 14—$1.86. 15—$122.95.

DISCOUNT. *Art. 109.* 1—$7.50. 2—$62.50. 3—$28.03. 4—$4.67.
5—$1.75. 6—$2.67. 7—$10.26. 8—$26.68. 9—$25.56; $826.44.
10—$38.91; $933.92. 11—$20.62½; $1,479.37½. 12—$73.50; $2,376.50.

Art. 118. 1—$6.46. 2—$3.31. 3—$4.92. 4—$29.09. 5—$8.46.
6—$506.70. 7—$311.37. 8—$3,428.25. 9—$416.09. 10—$7.75; $492.25.
11—$7.44; $842.87. 12—$239.17; $9,760.83. 13—$17.50; $1,232.50.

Art. 121. *1*—$.99. *2*—$50.87. *3*—$6.60. *4*—$17.05. *5*—$909.09. *6*—$3,352.49. *7*—$1,073.68. *8*—$87.62. *9*—$84.47; $840.53. *10*—$77.61; $2,914.93. *11*—$100.17; $499.83. *12*—$53.48; $506.52.

PROBLEMS IN DISCOUNT. *1*—$909.72. *2*—$59.87. *3*—$4,339.88. *4*—$2,345.38. *5*—$1,615.95. *6*—$133.72. *7*—$2,741.19. *8*—$401.79. *10*—No difference.

COMPOUND INTEREST. *Art. 122.* *1*—$743.73. *2*—$722.88. *3*—$32.83. *4*—$30.32. *5*—$927.37. *6*—$422.01. *7*—$314.39. *8*—$146.58. *9*—$63.41. *10*—$33.64. *11*—$72.92. *12*—$108.24.

Art. 123. *1*—$280.81.

PARTIAL PAYMENTS. *Art. 125.* *1*—$1,705.54. *2*—$1,218.15. *3*—$283.75. *4*—$11,998.12. *5*—$542.13. *6*—$1,643.92.

Art. 126. *1*—$678.42. *2*—$1,872.13. *3*—$2,128.96.

Art. 129. *1*—$268.80. *2*—$66.03. *3*—$58.08. *4*—$35.96. *5*—$141.53. *6*—$141.69. *7*—$22.72. *8*—$357.61. *9*—$769.98. *10*—$2,333.07.

BONDS. *Art. 138.* *1*—$337.50. *2*—$118.25. *3*—236 bonds. *4*—34 bonds. *5*—240 bonds. *6*—64 bonds. *7*—Mich. 7's, $\frac{235}{322}$%. *8*—Geo. 7's, $\frac{350}{493}$%. *9*—5's, $\frac{1850}{2001}$%. *10*—4½'s, $\frac{350}{5765}$%. *11*—$3,247.50. *12*—$21,200. *13*—5$\frac{5}{7}$%. *14*—5$\frac{15}{37}$%.

EQUATION OF PAYMENTS. *Art. 140.* *1*—4 mo. *2*—3 mo. 29 da. after to-day. *3*—May 1/4.

EXCHANGE. *Art. 149.* *1*—$251.25. *2*—$467.91. *3*—$1,523.75. *4*—$615.23. *5*—$330.65. *6*—$2,708.75. *7*—$115. *8*—$998.75. *9*—$839.82. *10*—$3,606.66. *11*—$499. *12*—$1,724.64. *13*—$1,986.33. *14*—$1,723.75. *15*—$543.97. *16*—$2,444.72. *17*—$723.79. *18*—$2,389.80. *19*—$5,970.72. *20*—$1,380.93.

RATIO AND PROPORTION. *Art. 155.* *1*—3. *2*—$\frac{1}{8}$. *3*—3$\frac{5}{8}$. *4*—$\frac{3}{4}$. *5*—$\frac{1}{5}$. *6*—7. *7*—$\frac{1}{7}$. *8*—8. *9*—$\frac{1}{8}$. *10*—3. *11*—$400. *12*—20 rd. *13*—72. *14*—16 to 24. *15*—4 ft. to 3 yd. *16*—$\frac{32}{693}$. *17*—90. *18*—$\frac{8}{441}$.

Art. 161. *1*—35. *2*—12. *3*—9. *4*—12. *5*—36. *6*—15. *7*—12. *8*—32. *9*—4$\frac{1}{9}$. *10*—6$\frac{2}{3}$. *11*—49. *12*—26.5. *13*—10.8. *14*—8$\frac{3}{5}$. *15*—1$\frac{3}{4}$. *16*—1 qt. *17*—4 lb. *18*—5$\frac{1}{3}$ oz. *19*—7. *20*—3$\frac{1}{6}$.

Art. 164. *1*—$8. *2*—$1.33. *3*—$56.37½. *4*—$9.80. *5*—$34.12½. *6*—$56.25. *7*—$13.42. *8*—$27.62½. *9*—$2.22. *10*—6,298$\frac{1}{14}$ revolutions. *11*—1,465$\frac{10}{11}$ yd. *12*—1,225½ mi. *13*—$176.32. *14*—95.2 ft. *15*—66$\frac{2}{3}$ lb. *16*—39$\frac{3}{4}$ qt. *17*—$130.71. *18*—$993$\frac{1}{3}$. *19*—$1.40. *20*—20.309 + cd. *21*—$918. *22*—1 year. *23*—$22. *24*—$18.56¼. *25*—559$\frac{19}{38}$ miles. *26*—13$\frac{1}{3}$ da. *27*—427 A. 122 sq. rd. *28*—$61.38.

Art. 166. *1*—18. *2*—22½. *3*—$\frac{3}{25}$ oz. *4*—2$\frac{1}{12}$. *5*—$\frac{7}{18}$. *6*—175.

Art. 168. *1*—$13. *2*—8,925 pumps. *3*—$787.15. *4*—57$\frac{11}{24}$ days. *5*—$120. *6*—434 boards. *7*—60 pairs. *8*—$16.61. *9*—8,505 feet.

10—$1.26 ; $2.10; $2.52 ; $3.36.   11—253⅛ bushels.   12—251⅔ bu.
13—4½ da.   14—$4.   15—20 4/25 da.

POWERS AND ROOTS.   *Art. 182.*   1—54.   2—763.   3—5,453.
4—.28.   5—.432.   6—$\frac{27}{28}$.   7—7.5.   8—60.709.   9—.017.   10—1⅗.
11—37 36/49.   12—2.8284+.   13—8.83176+.   14—96.5 ft.   15—111.75 yd.
16—9⅓ in.   17—96 ft.; 336 ft.   18—58 rd.   19—22 rd. by 88 rd.

Art. 190.   1—53.   2—34.   3—.19.   4—.87.   5—.08.   6—6.7.
7—5.63.   8—5.04.   9—40.2.   10—⅓.   11—2 3/16.   12—1.76485+.
13—5 ft. 8 in. cube.   14—4,910.   15—48 ft. long, 1 ft. 6' wide, and
3 ft. high.   16—12.9+in. cube.   17—6.135+in. cube.   18—6 ft. 11.42'+.
19—64.12+in. cube.

MEASUREMENTS.   *Art. 194.*   1—145 ft. 7+in.   2—20 ft. 2.48+in.
3—21.213+feet.   4—15 feet.   5—109.123+feet.   6—62 ft. 2.7+in.
7—25 in. nearly.   8—9.9 feet.   9—50 feet; 78 feet; 136 ft. 8 in.
10—15.55+in. square.

Art. 201.   1—5⅝ sq. ft.   2—142 sq. ft. 92 sq. in.   3—94 sq. ft. 41½ sq. in.
4—201 square feet 20¼ sq. in.   5—105 sq. yd. 5 sq. ft. 139+ sq. in.
6—88 square yards.   7—13 sq. ft. 99 sq. in.   8—124¾ square feet.
9—82 sq. yd. 8⅔ sq. ft.   10—5 sq. ft. 127 3/16 sq. in.   11—4 sq. ft. 63.54 sq. in.
12—4 sq. ft. 139 sq. in.

Art. 202.   1—66 cubic feet 1,081 13/16 cubic inches.   2—27 cu. ft.
3—1,206 6/9 cubic inches.   4—881.632+gal.   5—12 cu. ft. 1,411⅘ cu. in.
6 — 55 mi. 945 5/11 yd.   7 — 5 5/6 T.   8 — 1,503.09 1/11+cu. in.
9—1,066.13+cu. in.   10—23 tons 1,624 pounds.   11—1,836.734+gal. ;
58 bar. 9.734+gal.   12—256 bar. 14.96+gal.

Art. 205.   1—4 sq. ft. 131½ sq. in.; 1 cu. ft. 89¾ cu. in.   2—12¼ sq. in.
3—523.8+cu. in.   4—2 sq. ft. 51¾ sq. in.   5—259,234,508,342 41/64 cu. mi.
6—314⅔ sq. in.; 523 17/21 cu. in.

Art. 206.   1—7½ miles.   2—13,068 pounds.   3—108.87+inches.
4—78.54 sq. ft.; 113.0976 sq. in.   5—88 inches.   6—575,000 cu. ft.
7—15.119+ft.   8—4 lb.   9—15 in.   10—49.152 pailfuls.